THE MAGE'S DILEMMA

DAPHNE ASHLING PURPUS

ISBN: 0692354727
ISBN 13: 9780692354728
Library of Congress Control Number: 2014959952
Purpus Publishing, Vashon, WA

DEDICATION

This novel is dedicated to my family: Pamela, Eric, Kelly, Josie, Jan, and Stephanie.

Other Books in This Series

Dragon Riders
The Egg That Wouldn't Hatch
Dragon Magic
The Dragon Who Chooses Twice
The Girl, the Gryphon, and the Dragon

CONTENTS

ACKNOWLEDGMENTS

So many people have helped, inspired, and supported me. Once again I'd like to thank the folks at National Novel Writing Month (NaNoWriMo) for all their encouragement and pep talks. This year I participated in Camp NaNoWriMo as well as the regular NaNoWriMo, which resulted in three novels. *The Mage's Dilemma* was written during November 2014.

Next I'd like to thank the members of my Wednesday bridge class, who have been unfailing in their support of my efforts. I also would like to thank my students—both past and present—at Student Link, Vashon's alternative high school, who continue to inspire me with their drive, determination, maturity, and insight in the face of major adversities.

In addition I would like to give thanks to some special people, in no particular order: Cynthia Zheutlin, for her gentle wisdom and insight; Nan Hammett, for her friendship and collegial support; Nell Coffman and everyone at Fair Isle Animal Clinic, for keeping my family happy and healthy; Lydia Schoch, for her empathy and encouragement; Peter Scott, for his interest and encouragement; Anja Moritz, for her wisdom, kind support, and wonderful lunches; Karen Hain, for her kindness and for keeping my body moving; and Blythe Bartlett, for her support and her eager reading of my novels.

MAP OF THE
FOUR NATIONS

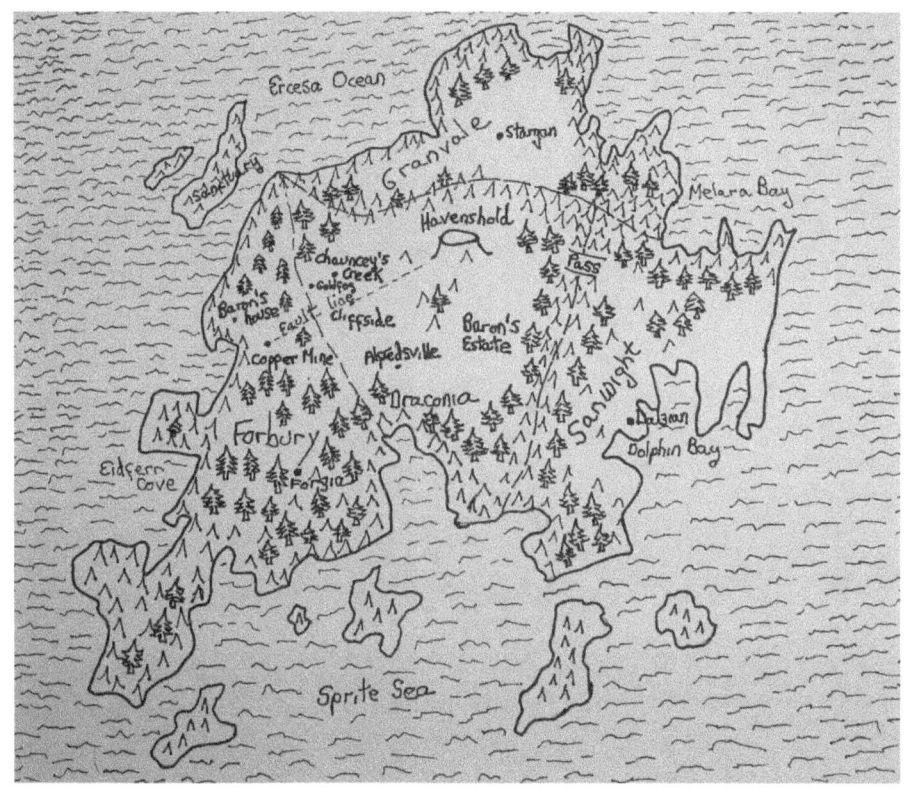

LIST OF CHARACTERS

Chloe: a young woman who's the mage for the entire world. She also runs Pathfinder Academy. Her story is told in the book *Dragon Magic*.

Calliope: the telepathic library cat

Rya: a fifteen-year-old girl who recently has arrived in Havenshold to be an apprentice to her uncle, Clyde, a carpenter. Her story is told in the book *The Girl, the Gryphon, and the Dragon*.

Clyde: Rya's uncle, Aster's father, Harmony's son. He's an enormously talented carpenter but the only one in his family without magical abilities.

Aster: Clyde's daughter. She's bonded with a yellow dragon, Jasmine, and they also have a small female white dog, Sasha, in their bond. The three of them are traveling ambassadors for all of Draconia. The story of their bonding is told in *The Dragon Who Chooses Twice*.

Jasmine: a yellow female dragon bonded with Aster and Sasha

Sasha: a female white telepathic dog, bonded with Aster and Jasmine

Gregory: a volcanologist, the son of the baron. He is married to Emily.

Artemis: a female fox who recently has arrived in Havenshold and is bonded to Rya

Bertha: a brown bear who is the seer for the world

King Alfred: the founder of Draconia and the first leader of the dragons and riders who arrived in the world 540 years ago

William: a dragon rider, bonded with the male brown dragon Thunder. He is an expert in telepathic communications and is married to Jake, Emily's second-oldest brother.

Jake: a dragon rider, bonded to a female brown dragon named Harmony. He is Emily's second oldest brother and is married to William.

Emily: the current leader of the dragons and riders as well as the town of Havenshold. She is bonded to the female purple dragon Esmeralda and comes from a large family.

Esmeralda: a female purple dragon, who, with her bonded partner, Emily, leads the dragons and riders. She is Matilda's youngest offspring.

Libby: the name the library uses when she takes on human form

Todd: a retired dragon rider, married to Amy, bonded with the male green dragon Jupiter. With Amy they have six children: Hans, Jake, Emily, Robert, Michael, and Hannah. They also have fostered a number of young people, including Lucy and Chloe.

Jupiter: a male green dragon bonded to Todd

Amy: a retired dragon rider bonded to the female green dragon Fern. She's Todd's wife and the mother of Hans, Jake, Emily, Robert, Michael, and Hannah, as well as a foster mother to many young people, including Lucy and Chloe.

Fern: a female green dragon bonded to Amy

Clotilda: the queen of all of Draconia. She's bonded to a female purple dragon, Matilda.

Matilda: a female purple dragon bonded with Clotilda. Together they rule Draconia.

Lucy: a dragon rider bonded with Harriet, a female blue dragon. She's married to Gretchen. Her journey to become a dragon rider is detailed in *The Egg That Wouldn't Hatch*.

Harriet: a small female blue dragon who made history in *The Egg That Wouldn't Hatch*

Gretchen: a dragon rider bonded with a female red dragon, Ruby, and married to Lucy

Sage: a female telepathic cat who lives with Lucy and Gretchen. She's Calliope's mother.

Hans: Emily's oldest brother, a dragon rider bonded with Fire Dancer, a female orange dragon. Together they serve as the queen's ambassadors to the other three nations. Before that, they were the leaders of the dragons and riders, posts Emily and Esmeralda now hold.

Fire Dancer: a female orange dragon bonded with Hans. She's the mother of Firebird.

Arryn: a sixteen-year-old girl who works for Lena. She ran away from home when she was fourteen.

Lena: an older woman who has lived a troubled life. She owns a shop that sells consignment pottery.

Rupert: a dragon rider bonded with Whipper, a male purple dragon. He's Emily's second-in-command. He's married to Emily's sister, Hannah.

Whipper: a male purple dragon bonded to Rupert. He's Esmeralda's first offspring.

Ron: a Havenshold vegetable vendor

Robert: one of Emily's younger brothers. He isn't a dragon rider but rather an architect who works in Alfredsville.

Michael: Emily's other younger brother, also not a dragon rider. He's a traveling botanist, surveying all the flora in Draconia.

Hannah: Emily's sister and the youngest of Amy and Todd's children. She is a dragon rider, bonded to Firebird, and is married to Rupert.

Firebird: a female orange dragon, bonded with Hannah, and the offspring of Fire Dancer

Nurse Beatrice: the chief nurse at Havenshold Hospital

Dr. Brian: Havenshold's doctor

Jaluhz: Draconia's volcano. Havenshold is built on her side.

Damian: a new arrival in Havenshold who works for Lena

Frank: Damian's friend, who also works for Lena

Mary: a Havenshold merchant who owns the yarn and sweater shop

Lance: Gregory's younger brother, the baron's second son, who manages the baron's large estate in Havenshold

Harmony: a woman with strong telepathic and magical skills. She's Clyde's mother and Aster and Rya's grandmother. She also has a daughter, Mildred, who's an artistic recluse as well as Rya's birth mother.

Baron Geldsmith: Known simply as "the baron," he's the richest man in the world. He owns a large estate in Havenshold, managed by his younger son, Lance, and a large mining operation in Forbury. He bonded later in life with a gryphon named Oswald. The story of his early attempt to capture the throne of Havenshold is told in *Dragon Riders*.

Oswald: a gryphon born with only one wing, which had to be amputated for the sake of his balance. He's bonded with the baron.

Georgette: an apprentice nurse at Havenshold Hospital

Martha: a Havenshold resident who runs the Havenshold boardinghouse

Miss Bronson: Arryn's former teacher from the village where Arryn grew up

Steve: Arryn's brother-in-law

Camille: Arryn's older sister

Miss Crimson: the teacher for Havenshold School

Zeke: a Havenshold resident

Norman: a Havenshold resident who is mentally challenged. He's Zeke's brother.

Marigold: the woman who's in charge of the makeshift community that has sprung up along the fault line at what used to be Cliffside

Nancy: Gretchen's mother. She relocated to Chauncey's Creek after Cliffside was destroyed in an earthquake. She now runs a café in Chauncey's Creek.

Dr. Penelope: a veterinarian and also a transplant to Chauncey's Creek from Cliffside

Arnold: Mayor of Chauncey's Creek

Hazel Winsong: Chloe's mother, a seamstress, and the organizer of the support group for Chloe's energy net

Zelda Winsong: a dress designer who is Chloe's sister

Henry Winsong: Chloe's father

— 1 —

GETTING READY

Chloe sat at her desk, twiddling her midlength dark red hair with her right hand and doodling on a piece of paper with her left. She wore her favorite purple slacks and a bright pink sweater, both of which were very comfortable, just the way she liked her clothes to be. She was finding it hard to get started this morning. No doubt that was in part because it was the quiet time of the year, between the winter solstice and the new year. Most folks in Havenshold took this time off to relax and celebrate, and Chloe certainly wasn't averse to that plan. But as the head of Pathfinder Academy, she needed to prepare for the start of the next school year on January 2. Normally—if such a concept existed for the world's only mage—she would have completed all her preparations before the solstice. But this year she'd been in Goldfog, helping Rya deal with the repercussions of last autumn's mudslide, the deceit and treachery behind that incident, and finally the lovely winter solstice celebrations in Goldfog, during which Rya graduated from her required schooling. Chloe's skills as both a magician and an educator had been needed, which meant that she was now behind in her preparations. This was her second year as the head of Pathfinder, so at least she knew what she needed to do.

Just then Calliope, a white cat with brown and tan spots, hopped up on Chloe's desk. *What are you doing?* Calliope asked.

Chloe laughed. "Not what I'm supposed to be doing. I was thinking about Goldfog and Rya."

Well, you didn't take me along on that trip, but I guess you needed me to run the library while you were off doing your mage thing, answered Calliope as she plopped herself onto the stack of papers in front of Chloe.

Chloe petted her as she said, "I really missed you. I'm glad I'm back. We have a new group of students coming with the start of the school year, and I know they'll need your guidance as well."

Right, said Calliope with a definite hint of sarcasm. *Most people can't hear me. Only a few are telepathic. Well,* she said then paused before going on. *Those who are dragon riders can, and some of the others, like Gregory, can as well. But he's married to a rider, and not just any rider, but the head of all the riders, so I guess that's why. But who knows if any of these new students will even notice me.*

Chloe laughed at that. "You wouldn't let them *not* notice you, whether or not they could understand you. After all you are the library cat."

You've got that right! And Sasha had better remember that. She's only a dog, even if she does have a rider and a dragon looking after her. Aster is nice, and Jasmine...well, for a dragon, she's pretty neat. I love her yellow scales—not as soft as my fur, of course, but sparkly. So they're all right, and Sasha and I have a good time. But now you're talking about there being a fox in Havenshold, and we've never had a fox here in town. I don't know about having her come into the library. Cats and foxes don't really get on.

Chloe heard the underlying worry in Calliope's thoughts. She scratched the cat behind the ears and said, "Artemis is a lovely young red fox, sweet and kind, and don't forget—she's not only bonded to Rya, but both Rya and Artemis are now orphans, so they need us. Artemis's mother was killed in the Goldfog landslide, if you recall, and Rya's parents were murdered."

I know, said Calliope. *That's really horrible, and they're new to Havenshold and all. I guess it'll be OK for a fox to visit the library but only as long as she remembers who's boss here.*

Chloe ruffled Calliope's fur. "I'm sure you'll make that very clear indeed. Now I really do need to get some work done, and my tea is getting cold."

OK, I get the hint. I'll curl up on your couch and take a nap.

Once Calliope was settled on the couch across from the desk, Chloe looked through the folders she'd set up for each of the new students, as well as those for the continuing students. Pathfinder Academy was designed to help those who had finished their required schooling but who didn't know what they wanted to do next. Students came from all over Draconia, not just from Havenshold. If there had been a dragon-egg hatching, some of the students would be those who hadn't been chosen by a dragon, but this past solstice hadn't been a hatching year. So the new students were all recent graduates who hadn't found an apprenticeship or a career path.

Chloe loved being able to help young people find their purpose in life. She remembered very well what it had been like eight years ago when she was fifteen-year-old candidate who hadn't been chosen as a rider. That was a very dark time in her life, until she'd met Bertha, the one and only seer for this world, who just happened to be a bear, and learned that she was a mage, a magician capable of saving the world and helping people, at least now that she was fully qualified. However, of all her roles and jobs, Chloe loved being head of Pathfinder Academy the most and was really glad that last year Gregory had asked her to succeed him.

She shook her head and looked again at the folders. *I'm not getting much done*, she thought. *I can't seem to stay focused on this task.* She stood up and walked over to the corner of her office to her teapot and made herself a fresh cup of strong black tea before trying once again to organize her thoughts around the new students. After all there were only eight of them and just six continuing, so it wasn't that tricky.

Just as Chloe opened the first folder and grabbed her pen, she heard a knock at the door, along with a hiss from Calliope. She looked up and saw Rya and Aster, along with Sasha and Artemis, standing outside her glass door. Chloe stood and walked around her desk as she motioned for them to come in.

"What brings you four here?" she asked, as she gave hugs all around.

Aster said, "We wanted to give Rya and Artemis the tour of Havenshold, which certainly wouldn't be complete without a visit to the library." Looking over at the couch, she said, "Hi, Calliope. We also wanted you to meet Artemis. Is that OK?"

Calliope, who'd already stood up warily, jumped over to Chloe's desk before telling her, *I'm the library cat, and what I say goes. Just ask Sasha. She'll tell you.*

Artemis bowed deeply holding up one of her front paws, which was white-tipped on her lovely orange fur, before responding. "I know. Sasha already has told me about all your activities and how you keep everyone and everything in order here. I'm honored to meet you."

What! You can talk out loud the way dragons can? And you're telepathic too. How's that possible? You're a fox. I thought only dragons could do that...well, and Bertha of course, but she's a seer.

Artemis bowed again and spoke telepathically this time, knowing everyone in the room would hear her that way also. *I really don't know. So much has happened since the landslide, and I know Rya and I are a very different bonded pair. There's never been a fox-human bonded pair...that we know of anyway. Just the dragon-human magical pairs here in Draconia and then the gryphon-human pairs in Forbury, the unicorn-human pairs in Granvale, and the dolphin-human pairs in Sanwight. No one knows why I'm the way I am, but that doesn't change the fact that I'm very happy to meet you, and I know you're the famous library cat. I hope we can be friends.*

Calliope stared hard at Artemis, admiring her beautiful orange fur and realizing that she was about the same size as Artemis. Then she looked over at Sasha and said, *Is all that true? Is she to be trusted?*

Definitely, answered Sasha. *Aster, Jasmine, and I spent the entire fall with Rya and Artemis, and they're both wonderful.*

OK, fur ball, if you say so, answered Calliope. Then she turned and looked at Artemis, staring right into her eyes. *Sasha says you're OK. So welcome to the library and just remember who's boss here.*

Thank you, said Artemis, bowing yet again.

Chloe laughed. "Well, I'm sure glad that's all settled. Now, Rya, how are you settling in? I'm sure Havenshold must seem very strange to you. And please take a seat, both of you."

As Rya and Aster settled themselves on Chloe's couch, Chloe handed them each a mug of tea, thinking how much alike the two girls were. That wasn't surprising, since they were cousins. Both had short brown hair which tended to have cowlicks from the way each of them twirled it. Both had brown eyes and tanned skin from being outside a lot. Aster, a year older and an established dragon rider, carried herself with more confidence. Rya, at fifteen, was still rather scrawny, and she seemed nervous in her new environment.

Calliope looked at Sasha and Artemis and said, *Want to go play? I can show you the whole library if you want.*

Artemis looked up at Rya and asked, "Is that OK?"

Rya ruffled Artemis's shiny orange fur. "Sure. You go play and get to know Calliope better."

Calliope, Sasha, and Artemis raced out the door into the main part of the library.

Chloe sat down behind her desk. "So, Rya," she said, "have you started your apprenticeship with Clyde yet?"

Rya took a sip from her mug. "No, not yet. Uncle Clyde thought it would be good for me just to get used to my new home until after the new year. Aster's let me have her old bedroom, and it's so nice."

Aster laughed. "Well," she said, "I'm not home all that often, and after all, Jasmine and I do have our lovely cave in the rider complex. I'm glad you can keep my dad company. I know it's been hard for him, living alone the last couple years since Jasmine and I bonded."

Smiling, Rya said, "It's so funny to have a new family. I thought I'd lost everything in the landslide when my parents were killed. And then I learned I was a foundling and then that my mother had me adopted and that I have a birth family, with a grandmother and a cousin and an uncle and even a mother. I just keep pinching myself to see if I'm awake and if this is all real."

Chloe chuckled. "Yes, your world has certainly changed since that fateful day when you saved your teacher and classmates from the terrible mudslide."

"Yeah," Rya said, nodding. "And then there's the whole magic thing. I never knew I was telepathic before, and I guess that's because I'm only telepathic with my blood family. I'm not like you and Aster, being able to talk telepathically with anyone."

Aster gave Rya a friendly punch in the shoulder. "Maybe so, but you're the only one who's empathic with the natural world. You knew that mudslide was coming. No one else did. And you know what the weather's going to be. Not just a guess, but for real. No one else can do that."

"I guess," said Rya. "I just take that for granted, as it's always been a part of me, even if my abilities are now growing." She stopped for a minute, putting her mug down then looking at Chloe. "I...uh..." She hesitated then went on. "I've never been this close to the volcano. I mean, I know all of you in Havenshold are used to living right around the volcano, and I know the dragons love the hot springs. Aster and Jasmine have let me have a soak too, and that was super. But...uh..."

"What's bothering you?" Chloe asked, looking at Rya with concern in her eyes.

"Well, as I said, I've never been this close to her. After all, Goldfog is nearly as far away from her as possible in Draconia, so I might be wrong. But she doesn't seem happy."

"What?" exclaimed Aster.

"Just what do you mean?" asked Chloe in a puzzled voice.

"I don't know really," said Rya, staring down at the floor, "and maybe I'm just getting used to her, but she seems sad. I can't put my finger on it. It's just a feeling."

"Your feelings are well worth listening to," said Chloe, grabbing a piece of paper so she could make notes. "You keep calling the volcano 'her.' Why's that?"

"Because that's what she calls herself. I don't know. She just is a her, definitely female, and she's very sad. I haven't found out why. And I don't know if she's always like this and I just didn't feel her before because I was too far away."

"But you don't think so, do you?" said Chloe.

Rya twisted her hands and looked down at her lap. "No, I don't. I think something has changed, and she's now sad and also worried. I'm trying to reach out to her, but she doesn't really know me yet. I just thought I should tell you what I'm sensing about her."

Chloe thought for a minute then said, "I'm glad you came to me. Obviously we all know how dangerous it can be living on the side of a volcano. You mentioned some of the benefits, which certainly are extensive. When King Alfred and his company arrived in Draconia, the other three nations already were established. But no one had wanted the land around the volcano. The dragons and their riders were very happy to take it, and over the five hundred forty years since their arrival, the dragons and their riders have tamed the land and made a good home for us all—riders and nonriders alike. Draconia has grown and prospered, and thanks to Gregory and others, we've found ways to use the energy the volcano produces, not only for Draconia but also our entire planet, which relieves the pressure within the volcano and also gives us something we can trade for things we can't get in Draconia. After all, Granvale has much better farming land, and so forth. But all this depends on a happy volcano."

Aster spoke up. "We should talk with Gregory. He's our volcanologist, so maybe he knows something. I didn't see him in his office when we came into the library."

"I'm the only one working here over the holiday break," said Chloe. "Gregory's home with Emily, and William isn't here either. He and Jake went camping. Anyway, you're right, Aster, we do need to contact Gregory. Are you sensing an urgency about this, Rya?"

"I don't think so," she said then sighed. "I've never communicated with a volcano, so I'm not sure, but I don't think she's angry or even really worried. Just sad, very sad."

"OK, then," said Chloe. "You two continue touring Havenshold, and I'll get in touch with Gregory. I know he'll want to hear about this right away. If I find out anything, I'll tell you, and please, Rya, if you sense anything else, come to me right away, no matter when. Or give a telepathic shout to Aster and have her contact me. This is too important to us all."

Rya nodded and said, "I promise."

"Now where have Sasha and Artemis gotten to?" said Aster as she and Rya stood. "We need to get out of here so you can do your work, Chloe, and so you get some downtime too. My dad's cooking up a storm, and you'd be most welcome for dinner, if you'd like."

Chloe grinned as she also stood up. "Oh, that would be lovely! That gives me the incentive to work hard on these folders. And I'll try contacting Gregory as well. See you tonight, and thanks!"

Rya and Aster each gave Chloe a hug, and then they all went into the main room of the library, where they found Artemis and Sasha with Calliope. As they left, Calliope said, *You two are always welcome here, Artemis. I'm glad I got to meet you. You're really nice, even if you are a fox.*

"Thanks, Calliope, and you're really nice for a cat as well!"

The four of them left, and Chloe picked up Calliope for a hug. "So having a fox in the library isn't so bad after all."

Hmph, said Calliope. *I guess not. Once we let the dog in, the place was going downhill anyway. But Artemis is friendly and both she and Sasha know who's boss, so yes, it is nice, and I had fun playing with them.*

"Well, enough play and visit time. I need to get some serious work done."

As the two of them returned to Chloe's office, Chloe to work and Calliope to nap, Chloe wondered just how a volcano could be sad.

– 2 –

GREGORY'S ADVICE

After Rya, Aster, Artemis, and Sasha left, Chloe worked on her student files until lunchtime. Then she decided to take a walk to see if Gregory and Emily were home. The day was cold, but it was sunny, and she thought a brisk walk would help her sort her thoughts.

"Keep an eye on things while I'm gone, Calliope," she said, as she grabbed her coat and hat.

Always, said Calliope, opening an eye briefly before going back to sleep.

Chloe chuckled then grabbed her notes from her earlier conversation with Rya and headed out of her office and through the main part of the library. She never ceased to marvel at this building. King Alfred and his riders had built it five hundred years ago, but it never failed to change to meet the current needs. Chloe knew why, and she'd even participated in some of the changes, making her own apartment in the back of the building and making offices for Gregory and William. She also knew the library was actually alive, a wonderful presence that had chosen to call herself Libby and who took on human form in an apartment next to hers in the rear of the building, but very few people knew that.

As Chloe stepped out of the library, she murmured, "See you later, Libby" and waved. Once she was through the doors, they locked with a click. Chloe walked down the front stairs and into the main courtyard for the dragon riders' complex, located in the center of Havenshold. She waved at a few riders she passed as she left the rider complex and headed toward the home Gregory and Emily had built.

As leader of the dragon riders, Emily had a cave where she and her purple dragon, Esmeralda, had lived before she and Gregory had married. But then they decided to build a home near that of Emily's parents, Todd and Amy, both retired dragon riders.

Chloe enjoyed the walk. It was a lovely crisp winter day, and it felt good to stretch her legs. She passed the small cottage where her father, Henry, lived, and thought again how much happier he was now after his divorce. He had been able to open up his own workshop behind the cottage, building the most fantastic wooden toys, which were in high demand. At the moment he was delivering a large shipment in Alfredsville.

The road went passed a series of houses of varying size. Many retired dragon riders lived just outside town, settling here when they decided to raise families. There were also couples like Emily and Gregory who just preferred living outside the rider complex. Most of the houses were standard one or two story, with square or rectangular shapes. However, there was always the exception, and she smiled as she walked past one home that looked as if it were part of a maze, with wings taking off in a variety of directions. This was the home of Amy and Todd, Emily's parents, and their green dragons, Fern and Jupiter. Chloe remembered when she first saw the house that Amy had warned her about getting lost. The house was very large as Amy and Todd had six children, now all grown, as well as several foster children, including Chloe herself.

Several houses farther along the road she came to Emily and Gregory's. She was pleased to see Gregory outside, raking the last of the fall leaves. She waved. "Hi, Gregory. Working hard, I see."

He looked up, pushing his light brown hair out of his face, and laughed. "Always something to do around a home. What with all the hoopla over the events in Goldfog, I fell behind in my fall chores. I'm just glad that we don't have any snow at the moment. But I'll be caught up once I mulch this last batch. You're lucky with your apartment."

"I know," said Chloe. "Very lucky. I was wondering if you have a few minutes. Something's come up that I'd like your opinion on."

"Sure," said Gregory. "Let me just get these last few leaves into the compost pile. Emily's inside, if you want to head on in."

"Thanks." Chloe walked around to the back kitchen door. She knocked and heard a cheery "Come in."

Emily was at the table, cutting bread and cheese for sandwiches. She looked up as Chloe walked in. "Sorry to just barge in," Chloe said, "but something came up this morning that I found a bit worrying, so I wanted to pick Gregory's brain. Hope that's OK."

"Of course," said Emily. "The world doesn't stop just because we're taking a couple of weeks off. Let me take your coat, and have a seat. Have you had lunch yet?"

Chloe shook her head. "Not yet, but don't let me interrupt yours."

Emily laughed with a twinkle in her brown eyes. "I know you're not one for cooking. I have some soup on the stove, and I'm making sandwiches. Why not have lunch with us, and we can discuss whatever is troubling you?"

Just then Gregory walked into the kitchen and went to the sink to wash his hands. "Sounds like an offer that can't be beat," he said.

"You two know me too well," said Chloe. "I'd be very happy to have lunch with you. Can I do anything?"

"Just sit yourself down at the table, and we'll have everything ready in a jiffy," said Emily.

Chloe watched as Gregory and Emily moved in concert—obviously very used to this routine—and before she knew it, a large bowl of steaming split pea soup and a cheese sandwich were at her place. Once everyone was seated, and after they'd gotten a chance to take a few bites, Gregory said, "So what's troubling you?"

"Hm," began Chloe. "Well, do you know Rya or at least something about Rya?"

Emily laughed. "Yes, he does. I share everything with him, so I told him all about the events in Goldfog last fall."

"I understand," said Gregory, "that this young woman is quite remarkable in many ways."

"Yes," said Chloe, "that's certainly true. She's very bright and managed to graduate from Goldfog School despite being dyslexic. And that was after her parents were murdered, and she was shot herself, and a lot of other things. She's gone through a great deal, and we were very fortunate to have your father and Oswald at her side, along with Aster and Jasmine."

Gregory laughed hard enough to swallow wrong, and once he stopped coughing, he said, "Yes, my father the baron and his trusty gryphon, Oswald, have told me all about their part in this as well. They couldn't be prouder of Rya if she were their own child. I know they're planning a visit as soon as they think she's settled into her new life as a carpenter's apprentice."

Chloe nodded, took another spoonful of Emily's delicious soup, and went on. "We all think Rya's pretty remarkable, but right now I want to discuss her empathic abilities, her empathy with the natural world."

"You mean her ability to predict mudslides? It really was amazing that she was able to save those nineteen students and her teacher by getting them under the tables before the slide hit. Most of Goldfog wasn't so fortunate," said Gregory.

"Ah, so you're aware of her abilities," said Chloe. "Well, that's why I'm here. Rya and Aster stopped by my office this morning, ostensibly as part of the tour of Havenshold that Aster was giving her cousin, but really, I think, it was because Rya is worried. She tried to downplay it all, and she said she'd never lived on a volcano, so she wasn't sure about the urgency of her feelings. She feels the volcano is sad and something is going to happen."

"Sad?" Gregory raised an eyebrow, his green eyes twinkling. "How can a volcano be sad?"

"How can a library build offices?" said Emily with a grin. "This is Havenshold. And in fact our entire world, all four nations, is filled with magic. And we know the planet is sentient, working at saving itself and all life on it, based on our new knowledge about how King Alfred and his company got here. So given all that, I'm sure we could have a sad volcano," she concluded as she stood up and began clearing the dishes from the table.

"Ah," said Chloe, "so Gregory knows about the time travel then. I wasn't sure."

"Yes," said Emily. "Gregory can keep a secret, so yes, he's one of the few who knows what Aster discovered last winter. But how does that fit in here?"

"I'm glad you know, Gregory, because that makes it much easier for me to share my very muddled thoughts. Thanks to Aster's research, and the memories of both Matilda and Esmeralda, Bertha, Libby, and I learned that in the alternate reality that King Alfred came from, the volcano already had erupted—and erupted badly—devastating all the lands that are now Draconia. By the time the eruption occurred, the world was so corrupt that it had destroyed all magic, including the gryphons and unicorns. The dolphins headed out to sea and safety."

Gregory joined Emily at the sink and began drying the dishes that Emily had washed. "I think I remember that the memories which Matilda and Esmeralda shared with Queen Clotilda, you, and Emily, were really horrendous. And they only shared a small portion of the collective purple dragon memories. I don't think I want to know much more about that time."

"Yes, I agree. We've learned our sentient planet tried a number of different options to fix herself, so to speak," continued Chloe, sipping from her mug of tea. "First she brought dragons into this world—I suspect thinking that dragons would be harder to defeat. She gave the dragons a need for human bonds so that we have what we have today, the magically bonded pairs that are supposed to protect the planet. However, when the hatred of dragons and their riders escalated to the point where they were being hunted to extinction, the planet sent the dragons and their riders back in time."

"That's right," said Emily, as she filled a plate with oatmeal cookies and brought them over to the table. "I'd never thought about it before, but when King Alfred and his company arrived here in our world, there were no dragons, and no one had seen dragons before."

"Yes," said Chloe, holding a cookie in her left hand. "Aster and I have been putting those pieces together. Aster really is a first-class historian, even if she's only sixteen."

Emily laughed. "Well, that's a year older than Rya. But do go on."

"Yes, please," said Gregory as he sat down again and reached for a cookie. "I sure hadn't figured this part out."

"Well, when King Alfred arrived," Chloe explained, "he was welcomed by the other monarchs, and there were no problems because the world already had the three nations with their bonded pairs. Magic was still alive and well. The planet had moved the dragons and their riders far enough back in time to get them away from the corruption and destruction. According to the fragments of King Alfred's notes that are in the library, the dragons and their riders had moved before in times of persecution, but they thought they had moved in space, to a new planet, rather than in time on the same planet."

"Got it," said Gregory, "but what does all this have to do with the volcano being sad?"

"I'm not sure," said Chloe, "but in the alternate world that King Alfred came from, the volcano already had erupted. In fact that eruption was in the distant past."

"And we don't know just how far back in time the planet moved King Alfred. But obviously Draconia is still here," Emily said. "It's not the best land, for sure, as it's rocky and has no farming, but it hasn't been devastated by an eruption in the memory of our current world."

"Exactly," said Chloe. "What if the planet moved King Alfred back to the time well before the eruption that took place in his alternate world? After all, she moved dragons and their riders back in time before, and Aster and I suspect that each time she moved them farther away from the desolate world that the planet had become, trying desperately to save herself."

"And our world has changed," said Emily, pushing a lock of her brown hair back behind her ear. "The purple dragons keep the memories of their race, and both Esmeralda and Matilda know the truth of the time travel. They confirmed it when Esmeralda and I took you and Aster to the palace to meet with Queen Clotilda and Matilda."

"That's right," said Chloe. "They also let us know that when the dragons and riders were sent back in time the last time, the mandate to save the planet and use magic for good was strengthened. This sentient planet is determined to survive."

"That's good," said Gregory, reaching for the last cookie on the plate. "And thanks to the last few graduating classes of dragons and their riders—beginning really with your class, Emily—we've learned a lot more about magic and its importance."

"Right," said Emily. "So what does that mean now, Chloe?"

"First I think we need to take Rya's feelings seriously. That's why I'm here really. I wanted to find out if you, Gregory, have sensed anything different about the volcano lately, anything that seems amiss."

"No," said Gregory, as he stood up and began pacing around the kitchen. "I've tracked the tremors, but they're just about where they always are. Living on a volcano does mean we experience tremors and occasional earthquakes, but I haven't seen any changes."

"Rya admitted," said Chloe, taking another sip of tea, "that she might not be sensing anything new. She's never been to Havenshold, and Goldfog is far enough away from the volcano that she might not have sensed her from there. Oh, yes, by the way, not only is the planet female, but according to Rya, the volcano is as well."

"Got it," said Gregory with a smile, bringing more hot tea to the table. "May I make a suggestion?"

"Certainly," said Chloe, accepting more tea from Gregory.

"I haven't met Rya, but all the reports I've heard about her make me think we'd better listen to what she has to say. I also think Lucy should step up her communications with the moles in her earthquake-prevention network."

Emily laughed. "I know she communicates with moles, and I know it really helps, and she and her partner, Gretchen, have done a fabulous job of mapping the fault zones and steam vents, but I still see the scared young girl, who'd just been rescued from her abusive father, missing her right hand and lower arm, sitting on the bench in my parents' backyard, not sure what being fostered by them meant, and telling my dad he couldn't dig his heated sandpit for all our family's dragons any closer to the bench because the moles wouldn't like it."

Gregory laughed at this memory as well. "Your dad can get carried away, and he was determined to use the volcano's steam vents under their property to make a sandpit big enough not only for his Jupiter and your mom's Fern but also for all your family's dragons. Given the number of them, it's no wonder that he wanted it big."

"Yes, and then Lucy got chosen as a rider in the ceremony never to be forgotten," said Emily.

"The first time in history that a dragon egg refused to hatch until the rider she'd chosen, who wasn't even a candidate, came onto the hatching grounds," said Gregory.

"I'm so glad Hans was leading the riders then," said Emily, refilling her own tea mug. "The uproar over Harriet's unorthodox hatching was intense. Thank heavens also for your dad, Gregory."

"Yeah, he kept saying that if a gryphon born with only one wing, which then had to be amputated, could bond with a fifty-one-year-old man, why couldn't a dragon—a perfect, beautiful, blue dragon—bond with a one-armed rider? My dad really has come a long way," mused Gregory, smiling.

"Yes, he has," said Chloe. "I can't believe he ever started a war to gain the throne of Draconia. And he and Oswald are obviously meant to be together. They do so much good everywhere now."

"But back to your suggestion, Gregory," said Emily, taking them back to the present.

"Yes, you're right. We need to meet with Lucy and Gretchen as well as Rya and Aster," said Gregory, standing and taking the remaining dishes to the sink.

Emily nodded. "Esmeralda and I will be there too. I don't know if Esmeralda's memories will help, but I know she'll want to try. Too bad Bertha is hibernating. She's got the secret vault with all the information from King Alfred's time in the back of her cave up in the mountains outside Havenshold, a vault that only she, as the ursine seer can open or access, and now she's asleep."

Chloe grinned and said, "I believe Libby received some of that information."

Emily's brown eyes lit up. "Yes, the magical library. I felt so honored the first time I met her. I knew you had something going on over there. Do you think we should have our meeting as a breakfast meeting with her? Her breakfasts rival your dad's, Gregory."

"I've never met Libby," said Gregory, "but I'd be honored if she would allow that. What do you think, Chloe?"

Chloe was silent for a moment, and her eyes seemed unfocused. Gregory and Emily just waited. Then Chloe said, "Yes, she says she'd love to have us all for breakfast tomorrow if that works for everyone."

Gregory looked at Emily. "Sure nice to have a mage in our midst. She can communicate with anyone." Emily laughed and nodded. Then Gregory summed things up. "So we want Lucy and Gretchen, which also means Harriet and Ruby. Hey, how big is Libby's apartment anyway? There'll be a lot of dragons there at the rate we're going."

Chloe laughed. "Just leave that to Libby and me. The room will be as large as it needs to be. In fact I think we might hold the meeting in the central room of the library so you and Gretchen will have access to all your maps."

"Great," said Gregory. "So we'll have Lucy and Harriet, Gretchen and Ruby, and Aster and Jasmine."

"And Sasha," interrupted Emily, "and I'm sure Lucy and Harriet will bring Sage, as Sage never passes on a chance to see her daughter."

"Yes, and Calliope would be hurt if her mom didn't come," said Chloe, "but thankfully the cats don't need much space. Keep counting, Gregory."

"Right then...so far I've got three riders, three dragons, a dog, and a cat. Continuing, we need Rya, and I understand she's bonded to a fox named Artemis," he said, holding up his fingers to emphasize the count, and looking at Chloe, who nodded and smiled. "Going on then, there'll be Emily, Esmeralda, and me, as well as you, Chloe, with Calliope of course. Wow! Good thing most folks are on break or we'd have a real crowd."

Chloe chuckled. "We do have a lot of terrific talent here. I'm feeling much more positive about all this. I'm sure with all of us working together we can come up with a plan to find out why the volcano is sad. Again, Rya said she didn't feel any urgency. She said the volcano may have been sad for a long time. But we do want to try to see why. An eruption of the scale that was reported from King Alfred's alternate world would be devastating."

Emily and Gregory nodded. "But now we have a mage," Emily said, smiling. "If you can divert an asteroid to keep the planet safe, I'm sure you can handle a volcano."

"Gee, thanks," said Chloe with a sigh. "Just remember how much help I had for that job."

Gregory put an arm around Emily's shoulders. "And you'll have all that help again," he told Chloe. "We're behind you all the way."

Chloe stood up. "Thanks so much, and thanks also for the lunch. I'll head back and ask the others if the meeting time works for them. I'm glad Lucy and Gretchen have stayed in the rider complex and haven't taken off somewhere for their vacation."

"Unless we hear otherwise, we'll be at the library for breakfast tomorrow," said Emily.

Chloe walked back to the library thinking how lucky she was to have so many stalwart friends.

— 3 —

OATMEAL AND EGGS

The next morning Chloe got up earlier than usual. Once she was dressed, she walked over to the spot on her living room wall where a magical door allowed her to connect with Libby's apartment. Libby was sitting in her overstuffed chair, knitting as usual. She looked like Chloe's idea of the ideal grandmother: a bit plump, with white hair that occasionally stuck out, a twinkle in her green eyes, and a welcoming smile. She was wearing a plaid skirt with a green sweater this morning, and large pink fluffy slippers.

"Good morning, Chloe. So we're having another early-morning meeting. If I didn't know better, I'd say these folks just like my breakfasts."

Chloe laughed. "You know it's you they come to see. I don't think any of them really believe that you're actually the library. After all, until Gregory started Pathfinder Academy, this building was nothing more than a beautiful architectural structure that was rarely used. People were too busy settling the land to take time for books."

"I know, and I became pretty darned sleepy after King Alfred died. I'm so happy to have a purpose again and to have people coming in to use me. William's telepathy studies always bring an interesting mix of folks. And Gregory works so hard that it's fun to surprise him with the occasional cup of tea or sandwich."

Chloe grinned. "You're so sneaky, magically putting things out for everyone. I'll never forget how long it took me to realize that you were responsible for the mug of black tea that was inevitably at my favorite chair in the back of the library when I first was a student here."

Libby's laugh was warm and full. "It gives me so much pleasure now, and it's fun as well. So what do you have planned for this morning?"

"I thought we should meet in the main area of the library, as there'll be so many of us. You've met nearly everyone. This will be Gregory's first time to meet you, but since he has his office here, you already know him. So that just leaves Rya and Artemis, but I know you'll enjoy them as well.," said Chloe.

"You've shared so much of their history with me that I feel as if I know them already. Rya is so young to have had so much dumped on her, but I was really impressed when she donated her very sizable inheritance of the Shelhammer land to Goldfog to be used for the benefit of all the villagers. That land is nearly unique in Draconia for its flatness and soil. What a gift to the village."

"Yes, Rya is amazing in a lot of ways, and I know she's going to make a fabulous carpenter or woodworker, especially with her uncle Clyde as her guide. I'm glad she decided on that apprenticeship. Clyde, Aster, Jasmine, and Sasha will watch over her and support her. After all, she's still only fifteen, and her life has been turned upside down."

Libby nodded. "So the main room. Shall we set things up the way we do for school orientations, with a long buffet table at the back?"

Chloe nodded as well and took another sip from the mug of tea that had appeared on the table next to her. "Yes, I thought that would work best. If you'll take care of the food—"

Libby interrupted with a snort. "Sure will. Don't want to leave that to you, although you do conjure up a reasonable stew. Still, cooking isn't your area of expertise."

"I probably would have starved by now if I weren't a mage," Chloe said with a grin. "I know magic isn't supposed to be used for everyday things that people can do on their own, but—"

Libby smiled. "But," she said, finishing Chloe's thought, "you can't manage cooking on your own! And that's a good use of your magic. I'll never forget hearing about how you nearly burned down Amy and Todd's home when you forgot that your oatmeal was still cooking on the stove and the pan burned dry and the bottom fell out."

"I know, and it's just lucky that Amy came home and found it when she did. I just don't seem to concentrate on cooking," Chloe chuckled. "Being a mage has its perks for sure. I mean I don't teleport myself when I can walk or fly on a dragon. I only conjure things when needed, well, mostly. Doing dishes is easier if I just whisk them away. I certainly don't use telepathy or draw on the powers of others without their permission."

Libby looked at Chloe and said, "You are much more apt not to use your powers, even when it is perfectly appropriate, because you still don't feel as if you deserve them. Trust me, if you ever were misusing your magic, Bertha or I would certainly let you know. Besides, the world is much safer if you don't cook," she concluded with a warm and loving chuckle.

"Thanks, Libby. Anyway, if you'll make breakfast, I'll set up the seats and pillows. Shall we head on out?"

Libby nodded, changing her slippers for a pair of boots, and soon both women were in the main room of the library. Libby's apartment had another magical door that appeared at the rear of the library, a door that then disappeared once they entered the library's stacks. They walked into the main area, with its lofty ceiling, numerous cozy chairs in reading nooks, a glass wall in front of several offices along one side, and another office just inside the main doors, also with glass walls. In addition a spiral staircase in the back led up to the observatory, complete with a telescope. This observatory had been heavily used when Chloe saved the planet from an asteroid. The entire space gave off a feeling of light and openness. The single office was William's and deliberately had been placed just inside the front doors so those participating in his telepathy studies wouldn't feel overwhelmed and at the same time wouldn't disrupt the rest of the library. On the other side, there was a lab where Chloe taught some science classes, then Gregory's office, and then Chloe's. Libby and Chloe had designed the layout, and Chloe had created most of it as part of her mage training. By the time the others arrived, the room was set for the comfort of all the expected guests.

Just as Chloe and Libby were taking one last look around the room, the front doors clicked open, and Emily, Gregory, and Esmeralda came in. Gregory shook hands with Libby and said how glad he was to meet her. They were quickly followed by Lucy, Gretchen, Harriet, Ruby, and Sage, who immediately headed toward Chloe's office to find Calliope, just as Calliope walked out of the office.

Mom, said Calliope as she raced over to the lovely brown tabby. After sniffing and tumbling over each other, they soon hopped into one of the overstuffed chairs, nestled together, and promptly fell asleep.

The last to arrive were Aster, Jasmine, Sasha, Rya, and Artemis, and Chloe welcomed them then introduced Rya and Artemis to Libby.

"Hi," said Rya, as she shook Libby's hand. "Is it true that you're the library and that you're over five hundred years old?"

Libby chuckled as she put an arm around Rya's shoulder. "You'll learn soon enough that you never want to ask a woman her age. Now how do you like Havenshold, and what do you think of me?"

Rya wasn't sure how to answer that. She stammered, "Uh... uh," as the rest of the group laughed.

"Now don't put her on the spot, Libby," said Emily. "You know we all think you're incredible, both as a building and as a person. The library radiates harmony and peace, and we're most fortunate that King Alfred's riders built you." She bowed deeply to Libby, who blushed a bright pink.

Chloe said, "Well, now that we're all here, grab your plates. There's plenty of Libby's excellent food on the buffet tables in the back. Once you've filled your plates, find a comfy spot, and we'll get this meeting underway."

Sage, Calliope, and Sasha elected to find a spot out of the way in one of the reading nooks, where they could eat their fill and enjoy each other's company. Libby always made them a special kibble which all three loved. They knew if anything exciting happened, they'd be called, but meetings were usually boring in their opinion. They invited Artemis to join them, but she declined, saying she'd better keep Rya company, as she could feel Rya was really nervous.

Libby had set up a lovely breakfast buffet. She'd provided staples such as oatmeal and scrambled eggs, but also added a grilled tofu, spinach, and mushroom dish—a particular favorite of the dragons, along with various coffee cakes and rolls. There were even pancakes with heated syrup for the pancake lovers in the group. Everyone found more than enough to fill their plates.

Once everyone was settled, with Artemis sharing a chair with Rya, Chloe called the meeting to order. "We all know why we're meeting, and now that everyone has gotten a chance to meet you, Rya, could you explain to everyone what you've found out about the volcano?"

Rya put her fork on her plate, which she then placed on the table next to her. She twisted her hands nervously and looked around the room. Artemis snuggled closer, and Rya stroked her silky fur. Finally she said, "Well, uh, I'm not sure. I guess you all know that I'm able to tell what's going on in the natural world, like with the weather and so on."

There were nods and smiles around the room. Rya continued, "And I've only been in Havenshold for a few days. I've lived all my life in Goldfog, which is a long ways away, practically in Forbury."

This remark caused many chuckles. Rya gave a small smile that brought out her dimples and said, "So I'm a lot closer to the volcano than before. I don't know if what I'm sensing is new or not. But she's sad," she finally blurted out.

"Sad," said Lucy in a puzzled tone. She and Gretchen had finished eating and were sitting on one of the couches. Gretchen's arm was draped over Lucy's shoulders, making Lucy's missing right arm nearly unnoticeable.

"Yes," Rya said. "That's the only way I can describe it. She feels sad. And I get the feeling that something is going to happen but that it isn't imminent. That's all." She looked down at Artemis and kept petting her.

"Thanks, Rya," said Chloe. "Now, Gregory, any thoughts?"

"Well, as I told you yesterday," he began, sitting down again with another full plate of food, "I haven't noticed any changes in the seismic patterns. I did go over all my charts last night just to be sure I hadn't missed anything, but I saw no changes. Lucy, anything from the moles?"

There were many smiles at this statement, but at the same time, everyone knew of the great work Lucy and Gretchen had done, mapping the inside of the volcano—its fissures, faults, vents, and so forth. Lucy could communicate telepathically with the moles, and Gretchen was a fabulous cartographer, so together they made a formidable team as well as a very cute couple.

"I checked in with the closest moles early this morning," Lucy answered, "and they say that overall things seem the same. But one of my moles said something strange. She said her children reported the sound of digging, but they didn't think anything about it. They just wanted to be sure another mole wasn't approaching their territory. Moles generally live alone, and they're very territorial. When they didn't see any sign of another mole, they dismissed it completely."

"Digging," said Emily, as she stood to take her plate back to the buffet table. "We don't have any digging going on."

"Well, I'll check further and see if I can get a location," said Lucy.

Libby looked up from her knitting saying, "I gather that some of you already have thought about a possible connection to King Alfred and the world he came from, our alternate reality that we hope never will come to pass."

Chloe, Emily, and Gregory nodded. "Some of you may not be aware of our true history," Libby went on. "We've kept the actual facts pretty hush-hush, so I'm asking all of you to keep what I'm about to tell you a secret. If you don't think you can do that, then I'll ask you to leave. This is for the safety of our planet."

Once everyone agreed, Libby went on. "Esmeralda, you can certainly correct me if I get anything wrong."

Esmeralda looked up, the sun from the skylight making her iridescent purple scales sparkle, and gave a chuckle that was very musical and rich in tone before saying, "I'm a lot younger than you."

Libby looked at her and smiled but then, not to be outdone, said, "Maybe, but your memories are a lot older than even me."

Esmeralda nodded. "Very true."

Libby, with her knitting needles clacking, continued, "I'll keep this brief and only highlight the relevant parts, so those of you who haven't heard the story, please bear with me. If you need more information, you can check with those who have heard it. The main point is that our planet has had an alternate history, and King Alfred and his company traveled back in time, not space. In that alternate history, the volcano had erupted, destroying the land that is now Draconia. That eruption occurred long before King Alfred's time, even before there were any dragons on this planet. And it happened after all gryphons and unicorns had been destroyed. The planet was being desecrated, and the volcanic eruption actually was just a small part of that destruction. Humans contributed to the pollution and slaughter of our wonderful planet, a planet that's as sentient as I am."

It took a moment before everyone chuckled as they remembered that Libby was actually a building. Libby nodded and went on, "The issue we're facing is what caused the volcano's eruption and whether it's inevitable."

Chloe said, "I sure wish Bertha were here and not hibernating. We could use our ursine seer about now."

Libby laughed. "You know Bertha," she said. "She'll be here when needed, but I'm glad you brought that up. Before Bertha and her cubs...I guess you call them cubs, even though they're pretty much fully grown, went into hibernation, she felt uneasy. She didn't really have anything specific to tell me, but she did give me a book just in case we needed to know more about the history from the alternate world. That bear is looking out for us even as she sleeps."

"A book," said Emily. "How's that going to help us?"

"It's a history book King Alfred brought with him from his old world," said Libby.

"A history book?" exclaimed Aster, jumping up from the couch where she was sitting next to Rya. "May I see it?"

"As our only historian, you'd better do more than just see it," Libby said with a smile. "The volume King Alfred chose was a natural history book that discusses the planet's evolution. I don't know how he knew we'd need that, and of course hopefully a regular history book wouldn't be needed, as we're doing our best to make sure that history is never repeated."

"And the purple dragons hold that history in their memories so we can ensure it never happens again," said Esmeralda, uncurling her tail and stretching.

"Exactly," said Libby. "But we don't have a record of what happened before the planet brought the dragons into existence. The gryphons and unicorns wouldn't have it either since they were exterminated by then."

"I wonder how King Alfred knew to bring that book with him? After all, as far as he ever knew, he and his company were being transported magically to another planet," said Emily, frowning in concentration.

Libby smiled, looking a bit smug. "I suspect the planet made that happen. Anyway, however it got here, we do have it. Here you go." She handed a large, heavy book to Aster.

Aster returned to her spot on the couch, holding the book with care and reverence. She turned the pages excitedly. "Wow, this is amazing. I'll start studying it immediately."

Libby nodded. "Bertha never has been able to calculate how far back in time King Alfred traveled, but we all think it must have been a very long time. Now we know that the planet brought them back before they were created, before the volcano had erupted, before the gryphons and unicorns had been destroyed, back to a time when the planet was still healthy and functioning."

Chloe ran her fingers through her hair and stood so she could pace a bit. Finally, she said, "But that was over five hundred years ago. Is there any way to figure out when the volcano erupted before? Could we be approaching that time in our current timeline?"

"That's an excellent question," said Libby. "I'm hoping Aster might be able to figure that out."

"But that can't be our only approach," said Gregory, who also decided to stand, returning his plate to the table and refilling his tea mug.

"For sure," Chloe said. "We need to investigate all possibilities."

"The dragon riders should support Lucy's investigation of possible digging," Emily suggested, as she pulled out a notepad and began jotting down ideas. "Mining isn't allowed in Havenshold and its environs for obvious reasons. We have enough earthquakes and tremors without digging or blasting in an already unstable area. We need to be sure someone isn't causing the volcano any problems."

"I agree," Gregory chimed in, "and Lucy, Gretchen, and I will help with the mole information and our maps."

Chloe noticed Rya and Artemis sitting quietly and looking a bit overwhelmed by all the discussions. She walked over to a chair next to Rya and sat down. "Rya," she said, "do you think you'll be able to communicate more with the volcano? Is there any chance you might be able to establish—I don't know—some kind of rapport with her? You've already sensed that she's female and sentient."

"I don't know," said Rya. "I didn't even know about all this telepathy stuff until a couple months ago. I just don't know," she concluded, twisting Artemis's fur between two of her fingers.

"Ouch," said Artemis, as her fur got tangled.

"Sorry," said Rya as she smoothed Artemis's fur.

"Thanks, but remember," said Artemis with a surprisingly gentle voice, "you and I didn't even meet until the mudslide. We've learned so much since then. Think how far we've come. And now you have me. I'm sure we can do something. Give it a try at least."

Rya smiled, bent down, and kissed the top of Artemis's head then looked up at the group. "Artemis is right. We'll do our best. And we'll also keep telling the volcano how much we rely on her, how special she is, and how much we value her. That's got to help, don't you think?"

Libby held up her knitting to check the progress on the rainbow scarf she was making as she said, "It'll count for a lot, young Rya. You just love our volcano with all your heart. You're the one she's opened up to. This is such a new form of telepathy that you're our trailblazer, just as Lucy was with the moles and other animals."

"Hey," said Emily, "that means William is going to go wild when he and my brother Jake get back next week from their camping trip. Prepare yourself, Rya. William's going to bombard you with questions."

Everyone laughed at that except Rya, who looked worried. Noticing her wrinkled forehead, Chloe patted her on the arm and said, "Don't worry. You'll like William. He's a bit of a geek, but he's extremely smart, and no one has learned more about telepathy than he has. He'll just want to hear from you what it's like to be able to sense the weather or know that a volcano is sad."

Rya nodded slowly then said, "But what about my apprenticeship? I'm training with Uncle Clyde right after New Year's. I made a commitment, and I want to learn to work with wood the way he does."

Aster reached over Artemis so she could give Rya a hug. "Don't worry," she said. "My dad will understand that you have to care for the volcano also, and there's no time limit on your apprenticeship. So my dad, William, and you will work out a schedule that works for everyone. You'll see."

Rya smiled then said, "I just want to do what's right. I really like it here in Havenshold. I miss my mom and dad a lot, but I'm really lucky to have discovered a whole new family I never knew existed. I'll do my best for sure."

"Rya," Emily said as she placed her notepad in her lap and looked directly at Rya, "we already love you. All you need to do is be yourself. There's a new world here waiting to greet you, waiting for you to explore it, and Clyde, Aster, Jasmine, Sasha and everyone will help you and Artemis feel that this is your new home."

"Thanks," said Rya, her dimples showing again, "and yes, it sure is a different world. I've never been in the same room with four dragons before."

Esmeralda answered, "You'll get used to it. Here in the rider complex there are lots of dragons and riders."

"If you're going to 'love up' our volcano," Jasmine added, sitting up and stretching carefully so that she didn't bump the other dragons, "then hang out with dragons. We all love that volcano."

Harriet, her blue scales shining in the sunlight that streamed through the east windows, said, "Ruby and I would be honored to show you around. You could even fly with us, if you want."

"And I'm always up for someone to oil my gorgeous red scales," said Ruby, as Gretchen thumped her lovingly on the back.

"Right," said Rya, her voice warming with enthusiasm. "Cool. And thanks. I'll be sure to take you up on that."

"Well, do we all have enough to be getting on with?" asked Libby as she put her knitting into her bag and stood.

Chloe said, "I think so, and I'm sure we all have places to go, so I hereby adjourn our lovely breakfast meeting." She waved her arms, and the buffet vanished.

Sage, Calliope, and Sasha rejoined the group as Sage said, *Well, if the food's gone, so am I.*

Everyone stood, thanked Libby and Chloe, and left. Once they were all gone, Chloe picked up Calliope and turned to Libby. "So do you think we can tame a volcano?"

"Let me ask you something. Do you think the volcano should be tamed? Do you think we have a right to change nature?"

"That's a tough question," said Chloe.

"Just something to ponder," said Libby. "Well, I've been human long enough. Have a lovely day."

Chloe laughed as Libby disappeared.

— 4 —

SANCTUARY

By early evening Chloe was definitely ready to call it a day and head with Calliope to their apartment at the rear of the library. She didn't usually feel compelled to check the front doors as the library closed since Libby took care of all that automatically, but today for some reason she did. When she got to the entrance, she saw a shape huddled just outside. *What's going on?* she wondered, as she opened one of the big glass doors. Stepping outside she saw that it was a person wrapped in a very old coat.

Chloe went over and touched the person on the shoulder and stepped back as a teenage girl flinched and turned toward her. A look of complete terror flashed in the girl's eyes as she said, "I need sanctuary."

Without a moment's hesitation, Chloe went to her and helped her stand. "Please come inside," said Chloe. "You're freezing. You'll be safe here, I promise. Now let's get you warm."

Chloe guided the girl into the library and led her to the couch in her office. Calliope sized up the situation and immediately joined the girl on the couch, saying, *She's frozen. How long was she out there? And why?*

I don't know, Chloe replied. *Let's get her warm then hear her story.*

Chloe found a thick wool blanket and wrapped it around the girl as she asked, "What's your name? I don't think we've met."

"A-Arryn," she stammered as her teeth chattered.

"Pleased to meet you, Arryn. I'm Chloe, and this here is Calliope. I'm going to warm you by heating this blanket. Is that OK?"

Chloe was always gentle and careful in her use of magic, as she knew some people were scared of it. When Arryn nodded, Chloe, with a gesture of her hand, heated the blanket so that its warmth would seep into Arryn. After a few minutes, Arryn's teeth stopped chattering. Gradually she relaxed and snuggled into the couch, petting Calliope.

Once Chloe was sure Arryn was warm enough, she asked, "Are you hungry? We haven't had dinner yet, and we'd be happy to share with you."

Arryn didn't notice, but a pot of delicious vegetable stew materialized in Chloe's snack area, along with three bowls, two spoons, and a loaf of bread. When Arryn nodded shyly, Chloe filled the bowls, handing a bowl and spoon to Arryn and a smaller bowl to Calliope, and then she took her own bowl and spoon and placed them on her desk. She cut some bread for her and Arryn before settling into her desk chair.

Arryn nearly inhaled the soup and bread, and Chloe quickly gave her refills on both. Chloe noticed that she was very thin and tall, unnaturally pale with scraggly long brown hair and sad-looking brown eyes. *Why am I thinking of the volcano?* thought Chloe. *Is sadness going to be the mode around here now?*

Once Arryn had her fill, Chloe removed the dishes then said, "Can you tell me why you were huddled outside the library and why you need sanctuary?"

Arryn sat for a moment, pulling the blanket more tightly around her shoulders before hugging Calliope. Finally she said, "I didn't know where else to go. And I couldn't take staying at the shop with her yelling at me anymore."

Chloe nodded and gently asked, "What shop?"

"The pottery shop just outside the dragon riders' complex in the village square," said Arryn.

Chloe said, "I've never been in that particular shop, but I have seen it. So you work there?"

"Not exactly," said Arryn.

Calliope said, *This isn't going anywhere very fast, is it?*

No, answered Chloe. *She's been traumatized and is afraid on so many levels. I feel the fear radiating off her. We need to be patient to gain her trust.*

Chloe stood up, went over toward Arryn, and sat in a chair next to the couch, thinking it would seem less threatening than sitting behind her desk. "Why don't you tell me your story, Arryn? I can't help you unless I know what you need."

"You won't throw me out, will you?" asked Arryn, her voice shaking from fear now instead of cold.

"No, I won't. I've promised you'll be safe here, and I don't break my promises."

"You're sure?" said Arryn, pushing Calliope away as she started to stand. "No matter what?"

Chloe put a hand on Arryn's arm and looked directly into Arryn's eyes. "No matter what."

Arryn took a deep breath, relaxed on the couch as Calliope jumped back into her lap, then said, "I'm an orphan and a runaway."

"I ran away from home when I was about your age. It's unfortunate, but it happens. How old are you, Arryn?"

"Sixteen."

"Then you'll have finished school, and you're entitled to be on your own if you want," said Chloe.

"But she wouldn't let me finish school," cried Arryn, twisting her hands on top of Calliope. "She made me work in the shop and sleep in the back room. I was her slave. She didn't let me have friends or even leave the shop."

"How did you come to be at the shop?" asked Chloe, in a calm matter-of-fact voice.

"When I ran away, I came to Havenshold. She saw me in the marketplace the first day I was here. She seemed nice, and she offered me a job and a place to stay. But once I was there, she changed. Some days she was OK, but then she'd yell for no reason...just the way my dad did before he died."

Chloe patted Arryn's shoulder. "Why don't you start at the beginning, before you ran away? Let's see if we can get the story in order, and then I'll be able to help you."

Arryn nodded, thought for a minute, stroked Calliope's fur, then began. "We lived out in the country in a small village called Duncansville. Camille, my older sister, was married and had a place next door to Mom and Dad's. Dad was...I don't know... someone we were really careful around. He could be a lot of fun, but then something would trigger him, and he'd start yelling, shouting names at me or even Mom, saying how stupid I was, or how clumsy, or whatever. Then once his rant was over, he'd be back to being nice, and he couldn't understand why I was afraid of him."

Chloe nodded, and reached for her tea mug. "I've met a few people like that. I call them loose cannons."

Arryn giggled at that. "Hey, that's good." Then she looked worried again. "Well, he sure was, and so home was a scary place. I could never figure out, no matter how hard I tried, how to please him. Then when I was eleven—oh, I'll never forget the day. I spilled a pitcher of milk as I was setting the breakfast table, and he slapped me. He didn't always do that. And then he launched his rant about how we couldn't afford to waste anything and what a clumsy idiot I was and was I too stupid even to set the table and on and on, until suddenly his eyes glazed over, and he crashed to the floor, knocking over the entire breakfast table. He was dead. The doctor said it was a heart attack."

"Oh, that's awful," said Chloe, moving over to sit next to Arryn on the couch. "I'm so very sorry."

"Yeah, I killed my dad," said Arryn.

"No, you didn't," said Chloe immediately. "He killed himself."

"That's not what my mom said. She said if I'd been better, cleverer, smarter, like Camille, then he wouldn't have yelled, which brought on the heart attack."

"I'm sorry, but that's just not true. And didn't you say he yelled at your mom also?"

"Sometimes but not often, and usually he only yelled at her for bringing me into the world," said Arryn, staring down at her lap and twisting her hands.

"Well, they were both wrong, but please continue with your story."

"My mother never really recovered from my father's death. She became more and more depressed. I tried to help—really I did," said Arryn, looking up at Chloe as Calliope licked her hand.

"I'm sure you did, sweetie, but you were only a child. What about your sister?"

"Yeah, Camille tried, but she'd just had a baby, her second in two years, so she was overwhelmed just trying to take care of her kids, and her husband never really got along with my parents. My mom got worse and worse, and finally she faded away—she died of depression, the doctor said—when I was fourteen."

"So that's when you were orphaned. But surely your sister offered you a home?"

Arryn slowly nodded before saying, "Yeah, she did, but then I overheard Steve, her husband, saying he didn't want a brat in his house, and he had all he could do to feed his own family. Camille said I was family, and they started arguing. I didn't want to be a burden to anyone, and my sister didn't have it easy at all, so I just packed my few clothes in a sack and left in the night, walking toward the volcano. I knew the dragon riders were supposed to be good and kind—I'd learned that in school—so I figured that was a good place to head. But it hasn't turned out that way."

"Well, it will," said Chloe firmly. "The dragon riders are good and kind and help anyone in need. Now tell me more about this shop. And who is this woman?"

"Her name is Lena, and she runs the pottery shop. She gets pots from various artists, buying them cheap then selling them for a lot more. She's old and very heavy and does what my dad did—what did you call it? A loose cannon? It's not just me that she gets mad at. She yells at the artists sometimes, saying that deliveries are late or that they're asking for too much money. They get upset because she doesn't pay her bills on time, but I guess they don't have any other choice for selling their pots."

Chloe stood up, walked back to her desk, and sat down. She pulled out a notebook and a pen and said, "So what do you do for her?"

"I keep the shelves in order. She's a real slob. She can't organize anything, and if I didn't keep picking up after her and filing her paperwork, rearranging the shelves to show off the pots to the best advantage and so on, well, I don't think she'd do nearly as much business. But of course she never says thanks."

"Where do you live? What does Lena pay you?" asked Chloe, as she jotted down some notes.

"She doesn't pay me. She says I'm not worth anything and I should just be grateful for room and board. And she doesn't have any security for the shop, so she makes me sleep on the floor in the storage room. I've asked for a cot, but she says it would just clutter up the place. What a joke. The place is already cluttered. She brings me her leftovers from her dinner the night before, and that's supposed to count for my three meals."

"You've been there for two years? Did you ever think about leaving before this?"

"Every moment of every day, but Lena made me sign some sort of paper when she first took me in, and she says that if I try to leave she'll get the law after me. She says I'm hers until she says otherwise."

Calliope hissed and then resumed licking Arryn's arm.

"That's just plain wrong and evil," said Chloe, looking up from her notes. "Did anyone else sign the paper when you did?"

Arryn shook her head, staring down at Calliope in her lap. "No, it was just me. She didn't sign anything, and no one else was there. But I've heard about apprenticeships, and I figured it was something like that."

"Actually, thankfully, they're nothing like that. But what changed? Why did you come here?"

Arryn looked up at Chloe with a small smile on her face. "Two girls about my age came into the shop yesterday. It sounded like one of them was new to Havenshold and the other was showing her around. I'd put a gorgeous rainbow pot in the front of the shop, and they came in to look at it. I heard them talking, and I guess they'd just been here because the new girl kept saying how wonderful you are and how much better she felt after talking with you. They seemed to think you're in charge or have power or something. I'd heard about asking for sanctuary in my history class when I still lived at home, and I've just had all I can take. So when Lena left for home late this afternoon,

I ran away. I figured I'd have to spend the whole night waiting for the library to open, so I'm really glad you found me sooner."

"So am I," said Chloe, shaking her head. "Well, tomorrow we will sort everything out, but I don't want you to worry about a thing. Lena has broken a number of laws, and whatever else happens, you won't be going back to her."

"Truly," said Arryn, petting Calliope some more, "those girls were right. You are wonderful."

"You just haven't seen the real Havenshold yet. Now it's getting late. How about for tonight you come with me to my apartment? It's only a one-bedroom, so you'll have to sleep on my couch, but it's pretty comfy, and I have lots of blankets." Chloe stood and walked over to the couch.

"It sounds perfect," said Arryn, standing up as she held onto Calliope.

"In the morning we'll go talk with Emily. She's the head of the dragon riders and all of Havenshold, and I know she's going to want to know about Lena."

"But what am I going to do? I can't go back to my sister," said Arryn, panic rising in her voice.

Chloe put an arm around Arryn's shoulders and said, "We'll let your sister know where you are and that you're safe and being cared for. Then we'll find you a proper place to stay. I'm also the head of Pathfinder Academy, which takes in students who've completed their required education but don't know what they want to do yet. You haven't completed the required education—"

"Lena wouldn't let me go to school," Arryn interrupted defensively, pulling away from Chloe.

"I know," said Chloe, patting Arryn on the shoulder. "I'm suspecting she didn't want anyone to know you were in Havenshold. We can get your records from your old school. I figured you wouldn't want to go back to a regular school since you're a year or two older than the oldest students, so I'm thinking we should just complete your required education here at Pathfinder Academy, which also will give you a chance to decide what you want to do after that. Now follow me, and I'll show you where my apartment is."

The two of them walked to the rear of the library, Arryn carrying Calliope. There was a door at the back of the stacks that had a window in it with pretty purple curtains, as well as a bell next to the door. Chloe unlocked the door and led Arryn into her apartment.

"Are you still hungry?" asked Chloe.

Arryn shrugged.

"I'll take that as a yes. Let me fix you another bowl of vegetable stew, which you can eat while I make up a bed for you on the couch."

"Thanks," said Arryn, looking around the room and noticing all the wall hangings and pillows. "You have some really nice things," she said. "I really like all the weavings showing scenes with dragons. Everything is so colorful. I love the pale pink walls. My home was all done in white which turned dingy after awhile."

"Thank you. I do like color, especially in the winter. I have a friend who's a weaver, and my mother and sister are seamstresses, so I received a lot of these things as housewarming presents when I set up this apartment over a year ago."

Once Arryn had devoured another bowl of stew, Chloe gave her a pair of pajamas, which just floated on her. Chloe was tall and thin herself, but no where near as painfully thin as Arryn. However the pajamas were comfy and Arryn seemed pleased. Then Chloe got her settled in the living room before she and Calliope retired to her bedroom. As Chloe got ready for bed, she told Calliope, "That young lady has been through way too much. I don't think she'll run away now. I think I've convinced her I'm trustworthy. But how about if you keep an eye on her just in case?"

Calliope swiped a paw across her face and said, *My thoughts exactly. Leave your door open a crack, and I'll be on watch.*

"Thanks, Calliope. We'll meet with Emily first thing tomorrow. This Lena sounds like a monster. Of course we've only heard Arryn's side of the story, and we don't know anything about her abilities, but just looking at how thin she is and how threadbare her clothes are, it's pretty obvious that she hasn't been treated at all kindly."

And there's also no getting around the fact that she should have been in school for at least one of the two years she's been in Havenshold.

"So true. Well, I'm tired, and the day started early enough with our breakfast meeting. Thanks for watching out for her. Good night, sweet Calliope, and thanks for letting Arryn pet you and carry you. I know you don't necessarily want that a lot of the time, but you sure understood she needed you."

Mom taught me well, answered Calliope.

Chloe smiled, pulled up her covers, and fell asleep almost before her head touched her pillow.

— 5 —

CONFRONTATION

Arryn was still sleeping when Chloe got up the next morning. Calliope was nestled on top of her, and the two of them looked very cozy. Chloe showered, dressed, and started the coffee before she finally woke Arryn.

"Good morning," said Chloe, as Arryn rubbed the sleep out of her eyes. "Would you like to shower before breakfast? I've found some clothes that might do for the moment. We can always get you something else later."

Calliope jumped off Arryn and onto the counter in Chloe's small kitchen. Arryn sat up and said, "I don't want you to go to any trouble. You've done so much for me already."

"None of that," said Chloe, kindly but firmly. "Here in Havenshold—and in fact I hope most places in this world—we look out for each other. Lena is the exception. You need warm clothes. Personally"—she went on to shift the mood to something lighter—"I have no interest in clothes or styles or fashions. I just wear bright colored slacks with deep pockets and sweaters at this time of year, anything that is comfortable. This is a source of much dismay to my grandmother, who still does perfect beadwork on various garments, as well as my mother, and certainly my younger sister, who's a fantastic fashion designer.

Now you get showered and dressed while I make us some breakfast, and then I'll tell you about all the fuss I made when I found out I had to have proper impressive mage robes for formal occasions. Now scoot." Chloe ruffled Arryn's brown hair playfully.

"OK," said Arryn. "If you're sure. Lena only let me shower on Sundays. She said she didn't want me wasting water."

As Arryn headed to the bathroom, Chloe watched, shaking her head in shock.

Once Arryn was dressed, the two of them sat down to eat, after Chloe put a bowl of kibble out for Calliope. "So I promised to tell you about the mage robes," said Chloe.

Gulping down her oatmeal, Arryn looked up in interest. "What are mage robes?"

"Well, apparently people thought that since I'm the only mage not only for Draconia but also our entire world—all four nations—I had an image to maintain. My mom and grandmother always have been big on images. But it wasn't just them. Emily and even Queen Clotilda insisted I dress for the part."

"Wow," said Arryn, munching on some toast.

"Yeah, it was a big deal. And I admit I can be stubborn. I like comfortable clothes. I don't do skirts and dresses and fancy stuff. I dress—well, as you've seen me—in comfortable slacks and shirts, things that are practical, easy to move in, and so forth. In fact you're wearing one of my outfits that I resized for you."

"You've been sewing already?" said Arryn.

"No," Chloe said with a laugh. "I used my magic. I can't sew any more than I can cook,-

"You're a great cook," interrupted Arryn.

"Well, I haven't actually cooked anything. I use my magic to make food, but I'm glad that you like it."

"Wow," said Arryn, putting her spoon down.

"So, as I was saying, you needed something to wear right away, so I used my magic. Anyway, back to my first mage robes. My sister was apprenticed to one of the best designers in Havenshold, and she helped negotiate something that my mother and the others would find suitable but that I could move in. I got purple velvet robes, with my mother and grandmother's impressive beadwork but with a length just below my knees so I wouldn't trip going up and down stairs."

This remark got an actual giggle from Arryn, which pleased Chloe. *There's a young girl still inside her*, she thought as she went on. "Yes, and I got pockets, something that horrified my mother, but they're concealed, and really, with the fullness of the robes, even my mother couldn't find them. So it all worked out. But you can see why I'm not the one to discuss clothes with."

Arryn smiled. "I've never had new clothes, so I don't know anything about fashion. But I like what you made for me, however you did it. No one has done that for me...well, not since I was little. My mom used to make my clothes, as she'd done for my sister before she learned to make her own. But then after my dad died, well, my mom just never coped after that."

"You don't have to wear the latest fashions, and you don't have to have a lot. But you do need clean, serviceable clothes, and at this time of year, you need warm ones. We'll get you some sweaters and a good coat later this morning after we talk with Emily."

Arryn stood and took her dishes to the sink. She picked up Chloe's as well then began to do the dishes. As she worked she said, "When will we meet with Emily?"

"I've already set up an appointment for this morning. We can head over to her office once we're ready."

As they walked from Chloe's apartment back into the library, they heard someone banging on the front doors and shouting loudly.

49

"That's Lena," said Arryn, turning pale and obviously struck with terror.

"Listen, you go back into the apartment and promise you'll stay there. Calliope will keep you company. Don't come out, but don't run away either. Promise?"

Arryn nodded, still shaking. Chloe reopened the apartment door, calling out, "Calliope, you look after Arryn for me, OK?"

Sure thing, answered Calliope.

Once the apartment door was firmly shut and locked, Chloe headed out to the front doors, saying, "Coming," while sending her thoughts to Libby to protect Arryn.

The second Chloe opened the library doors, the woman Arryn had identified as Lena barged in, shouting, "Where is she? You have no right to her. She's a thief, and I know she's here."

Chloe looked at the woman, noticing that she was very heavy, although not very tall, with long brown hair heavily streaked with grey which she'd attempted to put up, but which was falling down in a number of places. Her clothes were rumpled and dirty, and there was an unpleasant smell emanating from Lena that was overpowering. Chloe took a step back and said, "Good morning. I'm Chloe. I don't believe we've met."

"I know who you are," snapped Lena. "Don't think because you're some high-and-mighty mage that you can take what's mine. I know my rights."

"I wouldn't dream of taking anything of yours," said Chloe. "And again who are you?"

"I'm Lena. Everyone knows that. I own the pottery shop in the marketplace. That's beside the point. You have my girl. Give her back. She's a runaway, and she's stolen a very valuable pot. I will have her, and I'll have her now."

"Why do you think she's here?" Chloe asked calmly, as she noticed Lena was breathing heavily from the exertion of walking up the front library stairs. "And would you like to sit down?"

"No, I don't want to sit. I don't want anything from the likes of you. I want my property."

"I haven't seen your pot," answered Chloe.

"I meant the girl," snarled Lena. "She's mine. I took her in off the street and gave her a home. I've done everything for that ungrateful wretch, and this is how she pays me back. Well, she won't get away with it. I know what's right. I may not have your fancy learning, but I know right from wrong. Now give me the girl."

"Again why do you think she's here?" asked Chloe, as she played for time.

"I asked around when she wasn't at the shop this morning, and someone said they saw her camped out on your steps. She has to be here. She doesn't have anywhere else to go."

"Is she your apprentice?" said Chloe, trying to ascertain what the situation was from Lena's perspective. "Why do you say she's yours?"

"She signed a paper saying that she'd work for me if I gave her room and board. I've done that, so she's mine unless I say different. I know my rights."

"I think we'd better take this matter to Emily and Esmeralda. They're the final authority in Havenshold for all residents."

"Now listen here. I don't want to get messed up with dragons. I just want my property. You give me that girl right now. Don't you do any magic either."

"I wouldn't dream of it. But you know, Arryn has rights also. I'm afraid I can't hand her over when she has requested sanctuary. You're welcome to meet us—"

"Sanctuary." Lena's face turned deep red. "Oh, so she is here! That brat's got no rights to anything. She's mine. I've given her everything. She owes me, and now my best pot is gone. She took it. Everyone loved it—I even had a buyer lined up to pay a good price. It had a perfect rainbow on it. Now turn her over so

I can beat the truth out of her," said Lena, waving her fists and waddling closer to Chloe.

Chloe noticed that Lena's breathing was getting even more ragged and that her large stomach was hanging down over her very large legs. *This woman's going to drop dead if she doesn't calm down*, Chloe thought.

Sending all the calming energy toward Lena that she could, Chloe moved toward the doors, opening the one closest to her, and saying, "I'm sure you're right, and all we need to do is regularize this with Emily and Esmeralda. They're expecting us now. So if you'll just head to the dragon riders' headquarters, I promise Arryn and I will meet you there. Now, please, let's get this settled properly. You want that, don't you?"

"I had it all settled," said Lena. "It'll take me a few minutes to find that paper, and then I'll be there and you'll see. No mage or dragon is keeping me from what I'm owed."

"We'll see you there then, as soon as you can find your agreement with Arryn," said Chloe as Lena finally left the library.

Chloe hurried back to her apartment. "Arryn, oh, Arryn," she said, giving her a big hug. "That woman is horrible. Quickly now—we want to get to Emily's office before Lena does. She has to go to her shop to find the paper you signed."

Arryn was still shaking. "She can't take me, can she?"

"Definitely not!" answered Chloe firmly. "But we have to do this properly. Let's go. Here, this coat will be big on you. I'm not as thin as you are, but it will have to do for now. Calliope, hold down the fort. We'll be back as soon as this is decided."

Chloe took Arryn through what was technically her front door, although she rarely used it, preferring the library entrance. Her front door was at the back of the library, which enabled Chloe to take a back route to Emily and Esmeralda's office at the dragon riders' headquarters. It was only a short walk, and soon the two of them were seated with Emily and Esmeralda.

Once Chloe quickly explained everything that Arryn had shared with her, as well as her encounter with Lena, she said, "Lena is on her way. She had to go back to the pottery shop for the paper Arryn signed."

"That may take her a while," Arryn said, "because I filed it in the cabinet, in a file with my name on it, but she never files anything."

Emily nodded. "And just to be very clear, you didn't take the pot she's accusing you of stealing, correct?'

"I didn't take anything, just the clothes I was wearing," said Arryn.

Emily stood and went to her office door. "Rupert, would you please come in here for a moment?" She returned to her desk as Rupert, a tall, slim young man with blond hair and deep blue eyes, entered. She introduced him to Arryn, telling her, "Rupert is my main assistant, my second-in-command, so if for any reason you need help and you can't find Chloe or me, you can trust Rupert to help. And Rupert, I have a mission for you."

"Anything," he said, looking very eager.

"In a few minutes, a very angry woman named Lena will be coming in to see me," said Emily.

"The pottery lady?" asked Rupert.

"Yes, I'm afraid so. Anyway, once you show her in, could you then hightail it to Lena's shop and look for a pot with a rainbow on it? Arryn, can you give us more of a description?"

"Uh, yeah, it's about three feet tall, but thin, and it has a gorgeous rainbow swirling around it," said Arryn. "Last I saw it, it was in her front window."

"Right, and if I find it," Rupert said, turning back to Emily, "what do I do?"

"If you find it, bring it back and also see if anyone in the marketplace has seen the pot in the window lately. It's a long shot, but we might get lucky."

"Got it. As soon as Lena comes, I'll head out. Anything else?"

Emily shook her head. "No, that's plenty. Thanks."

As Rupert left the office, Emily turned to Chloe and Arryn. "I know this has been a terrible experience for you, Arryn. Chloe, do you know anything about Lena?"

Chloe shrugged. "Not really. I've never even noticed her shop, but then I'm not much of a shopper."

Emily laughed. "That's the understatement of the year. Anyway, I'm in no way excusing anything she's done, and Arryn, you won't be with her anymore, just so you know. The discussion will get heated once she arrives. But I think, in fairness to Lena, you should know something about her.

"Lena came from an abusive family, probably even worse than yours, Arryn. When her mother became ill with a heart condition, Lena was blamed for her illness. And when her mother died, Lena was left on her own. She wasn't able to finish school, and in fact I think she dropped out with less schooling than you've already had. She's scraped and struggled her entire life. We've tried to help her because, as you'll be learning, the dragon riders protect and help anyone who needs it. She could have free meals, for instance, in the rider cafeteria. We tried to get her medical help as well, as she has some real health issues that are only getting worse. In the last few years, I've tried countless times to help her, to get her to see a counselor, lots of things. But she absolutely refuses, and since her husband died, she's been getting worse. She's actually a very scared person who feels extremely vulnerable. But her defense mechanism is anger. She's lashed out at me many times, and when I've called her on it, she always denies that she's angry and says I'd know it if she really got angry.

"She honestly believes that, I think, and doesn't realize how others perceive her. This makes it even harder to help her, and of course her view of the world is that everyone is out to get her. Her anger makes that reality come true. Hers is a very sad tale, and I'm sorry to say, I don't think now, at her age, that she'll change."

"Thank you for telling us all that," Chloe said, as she nodded to Arryn. "As you say, it doesn't make what she's done right, but it's more understandable, and I have a great deal of compassion for her. And Arryn, your life will change as you allow the world in. You have a chance now to become someone very different from Lena. Your beginnings may have similarities, but that's where it'll end. You'll see."

Arryn nodded slowly then said, "I can kinda understand what you've said, Emily. I've had a hard time understanding why Lena lives the way she does. She may not have much, but she could keep what she has clean and cared for. And her business is such a mess that I know she's losing money, but she never listens to me. I've found bills that she's never sent out, for instance. I don't know anything about running a business, but anyone could see she isn't doing it right."

"You have the picture," Emily said, as she jotted down some notes.. "And every once in a while, when it looks as if she's going to have to close the shop, folks come to her aid, but it's like throwing away resources because she just lets it all dwindle away or she spends it on something extravagant instead of saving it to pay bills. Anyway, I wanted you to understand. I honestly think that Lena has a good heart deep down inside, and I even suspect it was that good heart that prompted her to take you in. But her sense of her own unworthiness—the fact that she doesn't think she's entitled to anything—has made her bitter and grasping."

Just then they all heard shouting in the hallway, and then Rupert opened the door. Before he had a chance to announce her, Lena stormed into the office, shouting, "That girl is mine," and she slapped a paper onto Emily's desk. "You give her to me now. I've had enough of this."

Lena was panting from her exertions, so Emily quickly said, "Good morning, Lena. Would you like to take a seat while I look at this?"

For a moment Chloe thought she wouldn't sit down, but then Lena tramped over to the couch and all but fell into it, before saying, "You'll see. It's all in order, and that wretch signed it and everything."

Emily read the short note then looked up. "You're right, Lena. Arryn did sign this."

"See, told you so," Lena said, glaring at Chloe. "You should have handed her over when I came to the library."

Emily said, "Actually, no, Lena, she shouldn't have. This document has no validity. I mean, it—"

"I know what 'validity' means. I ain't stupid, even if I don't have all your book learning."

"Of course. But there are a number of problems with this arrangement," said Emily.

"The only problem is that she ran away. She's mine."

"No, she's not," said Emily firmly. "This isn't an apprenticeship agreement. All it says is that Arryn will work for you until you say otherwise, and in return you'll feed and house her."

"Yeah, well that's right and I did," said Lena as she tried to get up from the couch but then just sank further into it. "She's the one who broke that agreement, and she stole a valuable pot, and now she has to pay. I need her."

"We'll get to the pot in a moment. However, with any agreement of this kind, you also must provide education and training. You didn't allow—"

Lena waved her right hand in the air and cut her off. "I trained her just fine. I've taught her everything she needs to know. She doesn't need any schooling. I didn't finish school, and I'm just fine."

"However," said Emily, "our laws require young people to stay in school until they either graduate or turn sixteen. You had Arryn sign this when she was only fourteen, and since she was a minor, her signature isn't binding."

"She knew what she was signing. I made her read it," said Lena.

"I'm sure she did. She's told us as much. Nevertheless you broke the law, Lena."

"Laws. They're just made to keep rich folks rich and poor folks poor."

"And then there's the matter of room and board," continued Emily, glancing down at her notes. "How did you provide those?"

"I gave her a blanket so she could sleep in the storage room at the shop. That way she could be a guard as well. And I brought her my leftovers from home, plenty of food. What's wrong with that?"

"Have you taken a good look at her, Lena? She's painfully thin. And she has only tattered clothes and no coat at all."

"My clothes aren't any better," said Lena defensively, tugging at her torn sleeve, "and what does she need a coat for? She wasn't supposed to leave the shop."

"Lena, you're just making this worse for yourself. What you're describing is child slavery. Arryn has no friends, no bed, no decent food or clothes. I'm sorry, but that isn't by any stretch of the imagination proper room and board."

"She has as much as I did at her age," said Lena. "She doesn't need anything more."

"I don't doubt that you had a horrible childhood, Lena, and you and I have talked many times about how your life could change for the better. But you always refuse any offers of help."

"I don't take charity! I've always taken care of myself!" shouted Lena.

Emily took a deep breath. "Yes, I guess you have, Lena, but it's no life for anyone, and Arryn won't be going back with you."

At that statement, Lena struggled out of the couch, and before anyone could stop her, she lunged for Arryn. "We'll see about that. She still has to pay for that pot."

Lena was stronger than she looked. She grabbed Arryn and tried to rip her from her chair. Just then Esmeralda lifted her head and growled, startling Lena into dropping Arryn's arm.

"You get that dragon away from me!" Lena shouted, backing up and nearly falling into the couch. "I don't care if you have a dragon and a mage, I'm taking this girl."

Just then there was a knock on the door, and Rupert entered, carrying a gorgeous rainbow pot. The moment Lena saw the pot, she stepped away from Arryn and said, "So you found it. I told you she stole it."

Rupert put the pot on Emily's desk as Emily asked, "So, Rupert, where did you find this? And by the way, Lena, I sent Rupert to your shop the minute you came into this office."

"You had no right to do that!" Lena hollered.

"Yes, we did. We were investigating the crime you reported. Now, Rupert, where did you find this?"

"It was hidden under a blanket in the back of the storage room," Rupert answered.

"See, that's where she put it. That's where she sleeps, and that's her blanket," said Lena, grinning at this information.

"Then I did as you asked and checked to see if any of the other shop owners had noticed anything. Several of them confirmed that the pot was in the front window this morning," said Rupert.

"That's a lie," yelled Lena. "They all hate me."

Emily held up a hand to silence Lena and said, "Continue, Rupert."

"I lucked out, as Ron—you know, the vegetable vendor," said Rupert, and Emily nodded. "Well, he moves his cart every few hours, and he was outside Lena's shop this morning. He saw Lena trying to lift it off the display, and he went over to offer her help. All she did was yell at him that she was doing just fine, so he walked away. Several minutes later he saw that the pot was gone."

Emily shook her head as Lena fell back onto the couch. "Lena, there are penalties for false accusations. It looks as if you tried to frame Arryn, which only compounds your crimes. You haven't cared for her. You've kept her prisoner, and you've violated the laws about education. You could be fined severely for that, even lose your shop. But Arryn doesn't want that. She just wants to leave. So here's what's going to happen. Rupert is going to escort you back to your shop, and he'll bring your pot as well. You'll promise not to bother Arryn ever again, and as long as you keep your promise, we'll drop the other charges."

"I'm not promising anything. Do whatever you like," said Lena, as Rupert helped her stand. Once she was on her feet, she shook off his hand. Rupert turned to pick up the pot, and again Lena made a dash for Arryn. This time Esmeralda stood and, with her massive body, blocked Lena, moving so that she had to head for the door. As Lena left the office, she screamed, "Don't think you've heard the end of this, girl! You're mine, and I'll have you or else no one will."

Rupert followed after her, shutting the door as they left. Arryn buried her head in her hands and sobbed. Chloe put an arm around her, and Emily walked over to her as well. Esmeralda put her front right paw in Arryn's lap, which really startled Arryn, and then Esmeralda said, "That woman won't be bothering you ever again, no matter what she threatens. We're going to make sure of that."

Arryn looked at the others and dried her eyes with the handkerchief Emily offered. She looked at Esmeralda's gorgeous iridescent purple scales and even stroked one before she said, "Thank you, everyone."

Emily returned to her desk, and Esmeralda curled back up, this time right at Arryn's feet. Then Emily said, "So now we start your life again, properly this time. You certainly haven't had a very good welcome from Havenshold. First you have a sister. Would you want to return to her?"

"No," said Arryn wistfully. "Camille has her own troubles. She doesn't need me, although I know she loves me."

Emily nodded. "I'll make sure she's told where you are and knows you're being taken care of."

Chloe said, "Arryn and I talked a bit yesterday, and we formulated the start of a plan. She'd like to attend Pathfinder Academy to finish her schooling."

"That's a great idea," said Emily. "You're just a bit old for Havenshold School, so I don't think you'd be comfortable there, and you're old enough now to be on your own, so you have the right to choose. And since, as I understand it, you don't really know which path you want to take, Pathfinder is the perfect place for you. Chloe, you can supplement her studies with whatever she needs to finish the required education."

"That was my thought as well," said Chloe, "so I'm sending for her school records."

"Arryn, I'll have the messenger I send to your sister pick up your school records at the same time. Do you have anything you'd like the messenger to tell her?"

Arryn thought for a moment. "Just that I love her, and once I get settled, I'll write."

"Sounds good," said Emily, making some notes before continuing. "And then there's the matter of where you'll live."

"Can't I just stay with you, Chloe? I'm fine with the couch."

Emily and Chloe chuckled gently, and then Chloe said, "I'd love to have you, Arryn, but we'll see a lot of each other during your classes. You need more than that. You deserve a proper bed in a proper home."

"And I think I've got just the right spot," said Emily. "My mom was saying just the other day how empty their house feels now, and maybe they should move to a smaller place."

"Would Anne and Todd foster Arryn? That would be so perfect," said Chloe, and then turning to Arryn she went on, "I fostered with them, and they're the most wonderful people. I lived there for six years until I finally moved into my own apartment."

Emily laughed. "Yes, my parents have had a number of fosters. I guess raising six children wasn't enough for them."

"Six!" exclaimed Arryn.

"Yep, 'fraid so. I have a younger sister and four brothers, two older and two younger. My parents love young people. Chloe, why don't you take Arryn shopping and have lunch, which will give me time to ask my folks?"

"You know how much I love shopping, don't you?" said Chloe with sarcasm in her voice.

"You don't have to," said Arryn. "I'm fine."

Chloe laughed. "No, Emily's right. It'll be a fun way to show you to the real Havenshold, and with any luck, I can find someone with more fashion sense to help me out."

Chloe and Arryn stood. Emily came over and gave Arryn a hug as she said, "Try not to worry. We're going to make things right for you. Now drive Chloe nuts by asking to go into every shop in the marketplace."

Arryn frowned then realized Emily was joking, so she smiled and said, "Right."

As Emily saw them out of the building, she told Chloe, "I'll check with Mom and Dad, but I know they'll be thrilled. Talk with you this afternoon. And why don't you see if Aster and Rya are free? I'm sure Arryn would enjoy meeting them, and I bet they'd be happy to help you two pick out clothes."

Chloe smiled and said, "Thanks, Emily. That's a great idea." Then she turned to Arryn and said, "How about finding clothes and friends."

Arryn smiled and nodded.

— 6 —
A NEW START

As soon as Chloe and Arryn started walking to the marketplace, Chloe mentally contacted Aster. *Hi, Aster. Any chance you and Rya would like to meet me and a new student in the marketplace? She needs clothes, and I also think she could use some friends her own age.*

Sure, Chloe, replied Aster, and her laughter could be heard even in her telepathic voice. *You aren't that much older than us, you know. Twenty-two is hardly ancient. But if you need two teenagers, we'll be happy to oblige. I think you really just want someone with more fashion sense,* she teased.

You're right. Can you meet us at Anita's Second Chance Shop? That would be a great place to start.

See you in a few minutes.

Chloe then turned to Arryn and noticed she was just staring around in a daze. They were walking across the rider complex towards the arch that led to the marketplace and riders and dragons were bustling in and out of the complex. Arryn seemed fascinated by all the activity in the complex but also apprehensive, as she noticed various townspeople bringing in supplies or heading over to the hospital wing. Her brown eyes darted this way and that, as if she were afraid that Lena might still be hanging around.

"It's going to be fine, Arryn," Chloe said gently, patting Arryn's arm. "And guess what?" she went on in an upbeat tone as she guided her toward the entrance to the marketplace. "Remember you said you'd overheard two girls talking about me when they were admiring the pot? Well, that was Aster and Rya, and I just contacted Aster, and she said they'd be happy to meet us at Anita's Second Chance Shop."

"They would?" said Arryn tentatively.

"Yes, and Aster is sixteen, just like you. She's been a dragon rider for a year, and she and Jasmine—that's her dragon, a gorgeous yellow dragon—are roving ambassadors for Queen Clotilda. But they're here for the holidays, helping Rya, who's fifteen, settle into Havenshold. I'll let Rya tell you her own story, but she's had a really rough time, especially this past fall, and she just found out that she'd been adopted but that her birth family is related to Aster's. They're cousins, and Rya is going to be an apprentice with her uncle Clyde, Aster's father, to learn all about woodworking and carpentry."

"Wow! They've done so much," said Arryn, her brown eyes opened wide in amazement.

"Rya's just where you should be, and where you will be once you begin at Pathfinder. The only difference is that she had a lot of help last fall, so she's graduated, and she already picked her path. But you're both just starting out in a new place."

As they walked through the archway that separated the rider complex from the main town of Havenshold, Arryn stopped. "I don't want to go past Lena's shop," she said firmly.

"We won't," Chloe told her. "Lena's is on Third Street, on the far edge of the marketplace. We're going to go down First Street, just off to the left here. Have you ever been to Anita's?" She wanted Arryn to think about something other than Lena.

Arryn shook her head. "No. What is it?"

"Well, a long time ago someone smart figured out that kids grow really fast and are always in need of new clothes, but the old ones sometimes are still perfectly good. So a swap shop was set up for parents to bring in outgrown clothes and trade them for larger sizes. Then new parents can get the smallest ones readily and easily.

"Then the whole concept just took off. People realized they get tired of certain outfits, or the clothes don't fit right anymore or they just feel like a change, so over time the resale shop has grown to the point where it now carries nearly everything. They even have some very reasonably priced basics, such as underwear, that are new. And now it's become a popular thing to say that you got an outfit at Anita's. It shows an awareness for recycling perfectly good clothes without harming the planet."

"That sounds great," said Arryn. Then she looked down at her feet and muttered, "But I don't have anything to trade."

"No worries there either. Emily expects me to send any bills from today to her, and they'll be taken care of by a fund that the riders manage. Remember how Emily said Lena could have had a lot of help if she'd just been willing? This is how. Havenshold takes care of its own, and in fact the dragons and riders help folks in need in a variety of ways all around Draconia. That's why Queen Clotilda has roving ambassadors like Aster and Jasmine...oh, yes, and Sasha, Aster's dog, who would be most upset if she thought we forgot that they're a trio."

Arryn smiled and said, "I'd love to meet them."

"And you will. We'll start today with Aster and Rya."

Just then as Chloe and Arryn turned onto First Street, two young women came up and hugged Chloe. "Hi, there," said Aster.

Chloe quickly introduced them to Arryn.

"Great to meet you," Rya said. "Hey, didn't we see you in the pottery shop?"

Arryn nodded and twisted her hands as Chloe quickly stepped in to save Arryn any embarrassment. "Yes, Rya, she was there, but it was a very bad situation, and now Arryn is going to be a student at Pathfinder Academy."

"That's great about Pathfinder, and sorry for your bad deal," said Rya.

Aster chimed in, "I'm a Pathfinder graduate. It's the best. Now you need new clothes, I gather. Well," she said in a confidential voice, as she put an arm around Arryn's shoulders, "it's lucky Rya and I are here to help."

Arryn smiled a bit hesitatingly, but nonetheless she smiled.

The four of them walked past a florist shop and a bakery before reaching Anita's Second Chance Shop. Arryn was amazed at by the bright colors. It seemed as if each shop was painted in a different color and that made the entire marketplace seem very cheery and inviting. The windows each had different displays, and Arryn just stared at the front window of Anita's, which showed all sorts of winter clothes for all sizes. There were outer garments, as well as slacks, sweaters, shirts, even shoes.

"Shall we go in and see what they have?" said Chloe.

Aster took charge as they entered the shop. She grabbed Rya with one hand and Arryn with the other and said, "Come on. I know just where we want to look first."

The three girls took off as Chloe watched in wonder and gratitude. *Was I ever that carefree?* she wondered. She followed them, nodding at people she knew and making her way back to an obviously teen section. She watched as Aster and Rya pulled clothes off the racks, handing them to a stunned Arryn, and saying, "You have to try this." Soon Arryn was laden with an armload of clothes. Aster then guided them to the dressing rooms. As she did, she looked back at Chloe, saying, "I'll send her out to show you anything we think looks good."

Chloe chuckled. "Thanks." She was glad to find a chair near the dressing rooms, as she figured the girls would be a while. Soon she heard lots of giggling, and she was happy to discover that some of that laughing came from Arryn. This outing was obviously just what the girl needed.

Arryn emerged from the dressing room a number of times, each time in a different outfit, and each time looking embarrassed and a bit worried. But as Chloe complimented her on them, Arryn seemed to gain some confidence. Finally, once everything had been tried on and either accepted or rejected, Aster came out alone and said in a hushed tone, "She needs underwear. I'm going to go grab some packages, OK? Sad to say, she's so malnourished that she really hasn't much breast development, but I'm going to get some bras for her confidence. They do come in pretty darned small sizes."

"Thanks, Aster," said Chloe. "You're doing a terrific job. And I like what you've found for her. You got things that are a bit roomy, but not noticeably so, and you've found things that are flattering and also disguise her wraith-like thinness."

"Once she gets some proper nourishment, she'll fill out just fine," said Aster with the easy confidence of the young.

Aster was back in a few minutes, and Chloe noticed she'd also snagged some pj's and a robe. As she headed back into the dressing room, Chloe thought, *Aster may be the same age as Arryn, but she's gained so much maturity because of what she's been through. I'm really glad Emily suggested having her come along. I'm sure all this is easier for Arryn with new friends helping.*

At last the trio emerged, and Arryn was wearing one of her new outfits, a pair of turquoise slacks and a pink knit shirt. She looked radiant as she smiled shyly.

Aster and Rya were carrying the rest of the clothes, and they made their way up to the checkout stand. Chloe handed the cashier an authorization slip from Emily so the bill would be sent to her. Aster joked, "Isn't Emily going to be surprised?"

"Oh, dear," said Arryn, blushing. "This is too much, isn't it?"

"No," said Chloe quickly. "Aster's just kidding. Emily knows exactly what you need, and this is just right."

"I've never had so many clothes before," said Arryn. "I really don't need so many."

"Yes, you do," said Aster, and Rya nodded.

Rya looked over at Arryn and said, "I know how you feel. Aster did the same thing for me a few days ago, and I've now got more clothes than I've ever had. But you know what? It feels nice to have a few choices about what I wear. And realistically our wardrobes are still much smaller than what many teens have. So please don't worry. You deserve this!"

Still looking a bit unsure, Arryn turned to Chloe. "Is she right?"

"She's definitely right! And a new look also will help you realize just how much your life is changing. Besides, if we didn't do this, your foster mom, whether that's Emily's mother or someone else, certainly would have. Trust us. This is perfect."

"Now put on your new coat, and let's head for lunch," said Aster. "I'm starving!"

"You're always starving," teased Chloe, as she signed the receipt for the clothes. "Now where do you all want to go for lunch?"

"The cafeteria," said Aster without a moment's hesitation. "That way Rya and Arryn can see more dragon riders, and the menu is the best in town."

"Sounds good," said Chloe.

Aster and Rya insisted on carrying all the parcels so Arryn could just look around. They walked the rest of the way through the marketplace, being careful not to go past Lena's shop. Aster and Rya, who'd already had the tour, pointed out all their favorite spots, a craft shop, a music store, and another bakery. As they passed the ice cream parlor, Aster said, "Maybe we could come back here for a sundae after our lunch."

"We'll see," said Chloe.

They walked back through the archway into the rider complex and turned toward the largest building, which housed the dining hall, medical facilities, and assorted offices. Meals in the dining hall were served buffet style, so Aster and Rya found a safe spot for all their packages, and the four of them lined up to pick out their meals. It was the lunch hour so lots of riders were stopping in, and Aster was fantastic at making casual introductions. Rya wasn't quite as much in awe as Arryn, probably, Chloe thought, because Aster had brought her before. But Arryn couldn't stop staring at everyone. Finally she said, "I had no idea there were so many people in Havenshold."

"Well, since you weren't allowed to leave Lena's shop," Chloe said, "and since most people probably aren't buying pots every day, you weren't likely to see many. Havenshold is the largest town in Draconia, and the capital, Alfredsville, is the next most populous."

Once they were seated with their lunches, the conversation slowed. Chloe was glad to see that Arryn filled her tray not only with lots of food but also with a good, healthy variety. She'd picked a green salad, a bowl of pasta with tomato sauce, and several rolls. And none of them had chosen from the dessert section, so Chloe knew a trip to the ice cream parlor was definitely on their agenda.

As they were finishing up, Aster asked, "So Arryn, what did you do in Lena's shop? Did you get to make pots?"

"No," said Arryn. She took a deep breath before going on. "Lena doesn't make pots. She takes them on consignment from various artists. She isn't very nice, and she tries to cheat the artists, but I think she's not very bright either, so she's not successful. I tried to organize things for her, and I set up the displays."

"Well, you have a great eye for displays. I haven't stopped in often, but I've noticed that you shift the pots around so that different ones are featured. And Rya and I just had to come in to see that rainbow pot. I'd love to know who made that. I've never seen anything like it."

Noticing that Arryn seemed to be handling the questions without too much panic, Chloe decided to ask some of her own. Something about Lena was still bothering her. "Arryn, does Lena do anything except sell other artists' pots? That doesn't seem like enough to keep her in business."

Arryn twisted her hands, which seemed to be a habit of hers when she was nervous or anxious. Chloe was sorry she'd asked, but then Arryn said, "Well, it would be enough if she did it fairly and if she were organized. But you're right—she's neither. And people try to help her with various fund raisers when things get especially bad. But lately I've overheard her talking to a couple guys I don't know, and I think she's got something else going on."

"Hmm," said Chloe, "that's the feeling I was getting from her. I know you've done a lot for Lena, but I just kept thinking she wanted you for something else also."

"Yeah," said Arryn. "She didn't say anything in particular. But she kept hinting that she was glad I'm so small. That she was going to make use of that. The way she said it, I got scared." She turned to Aster. "That's why, when you and Rya came into the shop yesterday, and I overheard you talking about Chloe, well, I decided I was getting out of there right away. I didn't want to find out what Lena had in mind or why she was glad I'm so thin. It couldn't have been anything good."

"Hey, that's right," said Aster, turning to Rya. "We went there right after yesterday's meeting, so I remember we were talking about how good you were, Chloe, at making Rya feel comfortable in a room with a bunch of strangers, many of whom were dragons."

"I think I was meant to overhear that," said Arryn. "Anyway, I wasn't being nosy, but what you said gave me the courage to try. Before then, for the last two years, I honestly had no idea anyone would care. I couldn't figure out where to go. So thanks," she finished, turning a bit red with embarrassment.

"I'm glad we helped," said Rya, smiling.

"And yes, I think it was meant to be," agreed Aster.

Chloe noticed that everyone was finished, and she thought Arryn could use more distracting, so she stood and said, "Shall we bus our trays and head for the ice cream parlor?"

"For sure," said Aster.

After putting on their coats and grabbing all the parcels, the foursome headed out through the archway again on their way to the ice cream parlor. As they passed Sweaters and Yarns, Aster said, "Hey, look at those sweaters! Aren't they fabulous? Rainbow yarn in different patterns. And look. They have three of them. What do you think? Should we check them out?"

Chloe looked at the trio and said, "Obviously."

They entered the shop, and Mary, the owner, came over to show them the sweaters. "I just made these," she said. "I've been trying out different patterns, and I found someone who can dye yarn in swirls. What do you think?"

Aster spoke for them all. "They're totally awesome. Do you have three that would fit us? I think we'd all like the rainbow color." She turned to look at Rya and Arryn, who nodded. "But we'd also like them to be different patterns." Again the other two nodded.

"I can certainly do that," said Mary, and before they knew it, the girls were each wearing a new sweater. They put the tops they'd been wearing in one of the bags, and this time Aster said, "Guys, this is my treat. We'll not only be able to remember the day we all became friends, but we'll also remember that we have a lot in common even though we're very different and from different places. OK?"

Rya said, "Thanks, Aster, but you didn't have to do this."

"Yes, I did," said Aster firmly. "Now to the ice cream parlor."

They'd just sat down at a table in the ice cream parlor when the bell over the door jingled. Chloe looked up and smiled. "Over here, Amy," she said to the tall woman with nearly white short hair and sparkling brown eyes, definitely marking her as Emily's mother.

Amy came over to the table and pulled out a chair. She then said, "You must be Arryn. I'm Amy, Emily's mom."

"And this is Rya, my cousin," added Aster.

"Pleased to meet you as well, Rya," said Amy. "Welcome to Havenshold. And from the look of all the parcels over there in the corner, I'd say you've all have been on a shopping spree. Good for you."

Just then the waitress brought over the four chocolate sundaes they'd ordered. "Wow, those look so good that I think I'm going to have to have one too," Amy said.

The waitress nodded and left to get another sundae. Amy turned to Arryn. "I've talked with Emily, and she said you're looking for a home."

"Well, I don't have a place to live right now. I slept on Chloe's couch last night, which was great," said Arryn, not noticing that Amy looked over her head to Chloe, "but everyone says I should have a real bed."

"And they're right," Amy said quickly. "I also understand you'll be attending Pathfinder Academy. Do you know that

Emily's husband, Gregory, started it and that now Chloe runs it, and she was also one of our fosters? So that makes it seem fated that you, as a new student, should foster with Todd and me."

"Well, if you're sure," said Arryn, her forehead wrinkled with uncertainty.

"I'm very sure," said Amy. "And you know what? You'll be doing us a favor if you agree."

Just then the waitress brought over Amy's sundae, and Arryn, looking a bit puzzled, waited until the waitress left before saying, "Doing you a favor? How can that be?"

"I'll tell you," said Amy, and then she took a bite of her sundae before continuing. "First we had Hans and then Jake and then Emily and then Robert, followed by Michael, and finally Hannah. But of course they grew up. And four of them—Hans, Jake, Emily, and Hannah—became dragon riders, which means they left home when they were chosen as riders at an egg hatching when they were twelve. You can imagine that the house, which once had six lively kids, seemed pretty empty. So Todd and I decided to offer our home to those who needed a place and became foster parents to orphans. We had Lucy, but not for long, because she quickly was chosen as a dragon rider. We were luckier with Chloe. She wasn't chosen."

"What?" exclaimed Arryn. "Why not? She's great!"

"Thank you, Arryn," said Chloe, "But it turned out that my path was to become a mage instead of a rider."

"And that was our good fortune on many levels," Amy went on. "Among other things, it meant we were able to foster Chloe for six years while she trained. Naturally, in the way things should be, once she saved us all from the asteroid, she decided it was time for her to get her own apartment. That was two years ago, when she also took over running Pathfinder

Academy, and we're very proud of her. But guess what? Our home is once again pretty empty."

"Oh," said Arryn, as Amy finished her sundae.

"Yes," Amy said. "In fact Todd and I were just thinking about maybe moving into a smaller place, but we love our home. It was built in a very unorthodox way. Every time I got pregnant, he pounded a hole in a wall and added another room. He always said if I could grow a baby he could grow a room.

"And then I mentioned all the dragon riders in our family. Todd and I are retired riders paired with Fern and Jupiter, gorgeous greens. Then we have four more dragons, who are paired with our children. Add to that two more for Lucy and her partner Gretchen, because let me tell you, once you're one of our fosters, you're family for life, and Hannah just married Rupert, so there's yet another dragon.

"Our current home has a lovely, big, heated sandpit that Todd built so that when the kids come to visit, there's a warm spot for all the dragons. It would be hard to find a place that would accommodate us as well as what we have. So you see, if you'll let us foster you, until you finish your schooling or apprenticeship or whatever you choose, you'd be doing us a big favor."

Aster looked over at Arryn and said, "Really, how can you turn down an appeal like that?"

Arryn smiled and looked back at Amy. "If you're sure, well, I guess I can't pass up such a wonderful offer. Thank you so much."

"Excellent," said Amy as she stood up. "And I take it all those parcels are yours? By the way, I like the sweaters you three are sporting. Same yet different. Very nice."

Chloe grinned. "Would you like me to teleport Arryn's packages to your home? Will she have Emily's old room, as Lucy and then I did?"

"Yes to all of that," said Amy with a laugh. "Emily thought, in light of what Arryn's been through, that it would be good if we did everything by the book, so I need to take Arryn back to Emily's office to sign official fostering papers. And then who knows what we might want to do? Right, Arryn?"

Looking a bit overwhelmed, Arryn just nodded.

Amy went on, "So it would be nice if we didn't have to worry about packages. And if a foster mom can't call in a favor from the mage, well, who can?"

Aster and Rya gave Arryn hugs. Aster said, "It's been terrific meeting you, and thanks for letting us help you with your clothes. We'll have you over for dinner really soon so you can meet Dad, Jasmine, and Sasha."

"Thanks," said Arryn, and then her mouth dropped open as the pile of parcels vanished.

The rest of them laughed as Rya said, "It can be a bit disconcerting to be around a mage, but it's all good. I'm sure we'll do lots of things together. Us newcomers have to stick together!"

Arryn could only nod as Chloe said, "Thanks, Amy. I'm sure Emily filled you in on everything."

Amy nodded then spoke privately to Chloe. *Don't worry. We'll watch her carefully. Lena won't get her hands on Arryn again. Todd's already talking about walking her to and from school once the holiday break is over.*

I knew we could count on you two, and she couldn't be in better hands. Thanks so much.

"Are you ready, Arryn?" asked Amy. "Let's go beard that daughter of mine in her den. And who knows? Maybe we'll see my youngest son-in-law as well. Say," said Amy, as she and Arryn headed out of the ice cream parlor, "have you ever ridden a dragon?"

Chloe, Aster, and Rya laughed as they followed them out. Aster said, "Arryn's not going to know what hit her."

Chloe chuckled. "You've got that right. I remember what it was like when I first arrived at Amy and Todd's. There's no better place for Arryn to be."

– 7 –

KIDNAPPING

After Chloe returned to her office, she turned to her records and checked on the housing for the new students who didn't live in Havenshold. Pathfinder Academy was growing in reputation, and this year—even though it wasn't a hatching year, so there were no candidates who hadn't been chosen—she had a lot of new students, a record of eight in fact. Well, counting Arryn, it was nine. Most of them were from small villages outside Havenshold. She did have two students who had just graduated from Havenshold School, and they'd continue to live with their parents when they weren't in school. But that left six students to find housing for, and those six would be arriving in Havenshold for the New Year's celebrations in a week, so she needed to figure out their housing arrangements. Thankfully none of the new students were orphans, so they just needed lodging and an agreement to be supervised by their hosts.

Chloe was busy with her lists, matching names of students with names of prospective hosts, trying to pair similar interests and so forth, when Emily interrupted her train of thought.

Chloe! Help!

What's wrong?

Someone bashed my mom over the head, and Arryn's miss-ing, answered Emily, her distress radiating through her tele-pathic communication.

Where are you?

Right outside the main arches.

Be right there.

On the word *there,* Chloe materialized next to Emily and Esmeralda at the arches. Despite her concerns, Emily shook her head and said, "No one makes an entrance quite like you, Chloe."

"Thanks," said Chloe with a shrug. "Now what happened and how's Amy?"

"I don't have all the details. Apparently she was attacked as she and Arryn were coming to see me. As soon as my mom went down, Fern let out a bellow that could be heard for miles, and she was here nearly as quickly as you were, but by then Arryn already was gone." Emily took a deep breath and started pacing back and forth in front of Esmeralda.

"Fern lifted my mom and took her to the hospital and now refuses to leave her side. The doctor checked her out and said it looks like she only has a broken arm and a nasty bump on her head from where she was knocked unconscious, but they want to keep her overnight just to be sure. Nurse Beatrice isn't happy having a dragon in her ward, but she's been nursing dragon rid-ers long enough to take it in stride. My dad, Jupiter, and Hannah are in there now, but I bet Beatrice will manage to chase them out. Thank heavens Hannah's dragon Firebird didn't storm in as well." Emily waved her hands in a helpless gesture, and then said in a quavering voice, "How could this happen?"

Chloe put an arm around Emily's shoulders and said, "We'll figure this out." Then while she looked over the scene of the attack, others began to arrive. As Emily predicted, a miserable Todd and Jupiter arrived along with Hannah and Firebird. They quickly were joined by Rupert, and his purple dragon, Whipper. Rupert put an arm around his wife and said, "I'm so sorry. But I'm sure she'll be fine."

Hannah nodded and looked over at her sister. "Mom's sleeping now, and you know Nurse Beatrice—she chased us all out. It was funny, though, when she tried to suggest that Fern should also leave. Fern just glared at her as only a dragon can, and Beatrice, not daunted in the least, shrugged and said, "Have it your own way."

"But she wouldn't let us stay," said Jupiter miserably.

Todd stroked Jupiter's neck as Jupiter curled up next to him and said, "We're connected to them. We'll know if anything changes. But you're right. I wanted to stay as well."

Just then Gregory came running over to the group and put his arm around Emily's shoulders. "I just heard. I'm so sorry. Is there anything I can do to help?"

"Thanks, hon," Emily said. "We're trying to figure out what to do. Mom's safe, and she'll be fine. We all know her well enough to realize that even a broken arm won't slow her much. So let's concentrate on finding whoever attacked her and rescuing Arryn. I know most of you haven't yet met Arryn, but Chloe, Rupert, and I have, and we've also heard Lena's threats, so that seems to be the place to start."

"When I escorted her out of your office, Emily, and back to her shop," said Rupert, "she did nothing but rant and rave about 'that ungrateful girl,' and how she was going to get her back. I didn't take it too seriously because Lena can barely walk; she's so heavy and her legs are so swollen. I didn't think she could really do anything except spew venomous, hateful words."

Emily said, "That's what I thought as well, so don't blame yourself."

"If anyone should be taking the blame," began Chloe, frowning and slipping a loose strand of hair behind her ear, "it's me.

I felt right from the beginning that there was more to Lena and her story than we knew. This morning, while we were shopping, I got a chance to talk a bit more with Arryn, and she said Lena told her she had planned to use Arryn for another job. She said Arryn was perfect for it because she's so small. That, and hearing about me, proved to be the catalyst that gave Arryn the courage to run away."

"Did Arryn know what this job was?" asked Emily, looking at Chloe.

"I don't think so," said Chloe, "but I thought I'd get another chance to talk with her, so I didn't push her. She's been through so much. Maybe if I had, this wouldn't have happened."

"I doubt that, and 'what ifs' won't get her back anyway," said Emily, her voice sounding more in command than it had since the attack.

Todd spoke up. "How old is Arryn?"

"She's sixteen," said Emily, "but she's horrible malnourished, and so she's extremely, unhealthily thin. She could squeeze into places most of us couldn't."

"Well, she's our foster," said Todd. "I don't care about any paperwork that may not yet have been signed. She's ours, and Amy has taken to her. Amy already has let us know that. Right, Jupiter?"

"Right. She's been sending us messages constantly since she walked into the ice cream shop," agreed Jupiter, his green scales glistening in the afternoon sun as he turned his eighteen foot long body toward Todd.

"So Arryn's now family," concluded Todd, "and even if she weren't, we need to do all we can to find her."

"You're exactly right, Dad," said Emily. "And we should start with Lena's shop. She already knows me, Rupert, and Chloe, so I'd like to ask you, Hannah, to check out Lena's shop."

"No!" yelled Todd, Gregory, and Rupert in unison.

Hannah grinned. "Listen, guys, get off your male protective dragons and stop shouting. Not that I don't appreciate your concern. Dad, I'm an adult, a dragon rider, and this is part of my job. Gregory, you're an awesome brother-in-law, and I appreciate your concern, but again this is what I do. And Rupert, dear, you know I can do this and that I'm the right person for the job. I can just go into the shop as any other shopper. I'll ooh and ah over some pots, and Lena won't suspect a thing."

"And remember, Hannah," said Emily, "This is just reconnaissance. You aren't doing a rescue mission. You're just getting the lay of the land."

"Right," said Hannah with resignation in her voice. "One day I'll get to have the fun."

Firebird, a gorgeous orange dragon who was just a bit smaller than Jupiter, said, "You mean *we* will! You can't do a rescue without me, so no heroics."

"Yeah, I get it. I'll be back as soon as I look around the shop," promised Hannah as she headed out into the marketplace.

"Meanwhile what else can we be doing?" asked Emily. "Where could they have gone in such a short time? Fern was here almost instantly after Mom was attacked, and while I know she was distracted by Mom's pain, she still would have noticed anyone struggling with a girl, but she said she didn't see them at all. Arryn wouldn't have gone willingly. I'm sure of that."

"Arryn might have been knocked unconscious also," said Todd.

"True, but then we'd have the culprits trying to run with someone slung over a shoulder—again not something Fern would have missed seeing. So where did they go?"

As the group was looking around for the quickest way out of sight, Hannah returned looking very glum. "The shop is closed, and the sign says, GONE OUT OF BUSINESS."

"What? Are you sure?" asked Emily.

"Very sure," answered Hannah. "I saw Ron with his vegetables near the shop, and he said that earlier, right after Rupert brought Lena and her pot—which, by the way, is in the window and gorgeous—anyway, right after Lena got back to her shop, she shut the door and put up the CLOSED sign. Then Ron heard shouting. He said it sounded like Lena and a couple of guys."

"But there were no guys there when I left her," said Rupert, with a puzzled expression on his face. "Did Ron see them go inside?"

"No," said Hannah, shaking her head. "I asked him, and he said he didn't see anyone enter except you and Lena. But she was yelling, and angry voices were yelling back. Then he saw her slap another sign on the door, and the shop went quiet. After a while his curiosity got the better of him, and he went over to the door. That's when he saw the GONE OUT OF BUSINESS sign. Since then he's seen nothing."

"We need to get into that shop," said Emily decisively. "There has to be another entrance."

Hannah added, "On my way back I also asked a number of merchants along the street if they'd seen the attack or if they'd seen anyone carrying a young girl, but nobody had."

"That was an excellent idea, though," said Emily, smiling at her sister. "Thanks for covering that angle."

Chloe nodded and said, "I wish I could sense Arryn. I've been trying, but she doesn't have any telepathic abilities, and I just don't know her well enough. I just can't feel her at all."

"Don't feel badly, Chloe," Esmeralda said. "I tried to pick up a scent to track them, and I failed at that. There are just too many scents. But I think they must have run away from the marketplace toward the outer unused caves. That would get them out of sight pretty quickly, and Fern would have been coming in from the other side, so that might explain their quick disappearance."

"Thanks, Esmeralda," said Chloe. "What do you think, Emily? Should some of us check out the shop while others comb the caves?"

"My thoughts exactly," answered Emily, looking around at the group. "Why don't you and Hannah go to the shop? The rest of us, and our dragons, will comb the surrounding."

Hannah smiled and nodded. "It'll be nice to work with you, Chloe. Firebird, you'll have to stay here because the street the shop is on is way too narrow for you, but we'll call if we find anything."

Now it was Firebird's turn to grumble. "Fine. I sit here while everyone else is out looking."

"Well, you want to be close in case Chloe and I need you, don't you, silly?" Hannah said, as she rubbed Firebird's bright-orange scales.

Firebird nodded glumly as they all took off to their appointed tasks. Hannah and Chloe chatted while they walked to the shop. After Chloe told her what she knew of Arryn's history, Hannah said, "I can sure see why my mom and dad want to take her under their wing. We've got to find her."

"For sure," said Chloe, as they arrived at the pottery shop. Chloe tried the door, and it was locked, but then that was no obstacle for a mage. Once the door was unlocked, they entered and began to search.

"Rupert didn't see another entrance when he was here earlier," said Chloe, "so it must be hidden."

"What's behind this street?" asked Hannah.

"Nothing," answered Chloe. "I think it backs right up to the mountain."

They searched the storage room first. The room was about four foot by six foot and there were dusty shelves along each of the walls filled with boxes stacked haphazardly. They noticed rat droppings off in one corner. The floor was concrete, cracked with age, and there were a few old fabric scraps spread on it to serve as rugs. Against the back wall there was one shelf which was noticeably cleaner, and on it there was a thin blanket, carefully folded, two books, and a small obviously well loved stuffed bear. Hannah picked up the bear and the books as she looked around the small room and said with real horror in her voice, "You mean Arryn lived here for two years? That's definitely cruel torture."

"I know," said Chloe, her voice mixed with anger and sadness.

The two women banged on walls, pulled up the few floor coverings, and moved boxes, but there definitely wasn't an exit from the storage room. They moved back into the shop and did the same drill there, starting with the back wall, which was lined with more shelves also jammed with boxes and boxes of receipts and bills. Suddenly Chloe exclaimed, "Look! This part of the shelving moves. See how there are scuff marks on the floor? It must swing out."

"Let's see," said Hannah, putting the books and bear on a nearby counter. They pulled on one side to find that the shelves swung easily away from the wall, revealing a passageway straight into the mountain.

"This has to be where they went," said Chloe. "Now listen, Hannah. We're going to follow the passageway, but you have to stay right next to me at all times. I need to be able to touch you in case of trouble so I can teleport us both out. Are you clear about that? Rupert would kill me if anything happened to you."

Nodding, Hannah added, "And if he didn't, the rest of my family would. You know, I may be thirty-four, but I'm still the youngest sibling, and I guess I'll never lose that title. They all think they need to watch over me. It's sweet, but it also can be annoying. Anyway, I'll stay right with you. I've always wondered what teleporting would feel like."

"Great. Let's go," said Chloe, and the two women stepped into the passageway. It was wide enough for them to move side by side, which made sense because it had to accommodate Lena's large frame. When they were far enough away from the door that the passageway was dark, Chloe produced a small flashlight.

"Neat trick," said Hannah in an effort to ease the tension.

"Comes in handy," agreed Chloe, smiling.

They walked deeper into the passageway, and suddenly it opened out into a giant cavernous cave with a number of passages branching off it. There was an orange-red glow coming from the cavern and the walls seemed to shine. They noticed an occasional sparkle that might have been a gem, but mostly the walls were glassy black obsidian. The passages took off in a number of directions, some leading downward, but most of them leading in unknown directions. There was heat rising from below and the entire scene took their breath away.

"Wow," said Chloe in a whisper.

"Who did this?" asked Hannah, also in a whisper.

"I'm guessing, but I suspect Lena and company dug the passageway we just came down, but this cavern is a natural part of the volcano," said Chloe.

"What do we do now?" asked Hannah, her voice trembling slightly from fear.

"We turn around and head back out. We need to find Gregory and his maps, Lucy and her moles, and a lot of other folks to help with this. If we aren't careful, we could disrupt the volcano. If we startle Lena and her thugs, they might just kill Arryn. We need help."

Hannah said, with her relief evident in her voice, "I agree."

They turned around and carefully, so as not to dislodge any loose debris, headed back to the shop. Once inside, they slid the shelving back into place, grabbed the two books and the stuffed bear, before they locked the shop up and headed back to the rider complex. As they walked, Chloe called to Emily, *I don't know what you're finding, but we've found a lot, and we need Gregory and in fact everyone who was at the breakfast meeting.*

Did you find Arryn?

No, but I think I'm beginning to understand what's going on. Should we meet at Gregory's office?

Yes, answered Emily. *He and I will come right away, and you can ask Lucy, Gretchen, Rya, and Aster. I want all the dragons to continue to patrol the entire mountainside. If nothing else, it should keep Lena wondering. Let Hannah know she and Firebird can join the other dragons now.*

Right. See you soon.

"Emily and Gregory are going to meet me at the library," Chloe told Hannah, "and we'll have Lucy, Gretchen, Rya, and Aster as well. Emily says all the dragons are going to keep patrolling, and you and Firebird can join Rupert and the others in that."

"Excellent," said Hannah.

"And please, if you see anything at all, don't tackle it, but get in touch with Emily for further orders. We want to keep Lena guessing, but we don't want to do anything that might endanger Arryn."

"I'll be sure everyone knows that. And good luck figuring out that cavern. If possible, I'd love to explore it at a later time. It's really beautiful. I've never seen anything like it!"

"I agree it's beautiful, but I don't know how safe it would be. Remember, this is a live volcano we're talking about."

"Well, she's a real beauty," said Hannah as they reached Firebird.

Hannah vaulted onto Firebird, and Chloe watched as they circled once above her then headed out to join the others. She kept her eyes on the orange spot until it was hidden by the mountain. She then walked back to the library, and as she did, she contacted the others who had attended the meeting and asked them to meet her as soon as they could. Fortunately no one was very busy, and once they heard about the attack against Amy and Arryn's kidnapping, they were willing to do whatever it took. They all promised to be at the library within the hour.

— 8 —

A PLAN OF ACTION

Once everyone had arrived, they met in Gregory's office so they could use his large hanging maps. Gregory put up the one that showed the area near Lena's shop, and then Chloe began.

"Hannah and I found a new passageway that leads from the back of Lena's shop into a very large cavern. The cavern itself appeared to have multiple passageways."

Gregory thought for a moment then pointed to a spot on the map. "I think it must be here, don't you, Gretchen?"

Gretchen stood and went over to the map. "Hmm," she began. "A large cavern, you say."

"Yes," said Chloe. "I'm not good with sizes, but I'm sure several dragons could fit inside it. Of course they wouldn't be able to fit in the passageways."

Lucy chuckled. "Maybe we should add another unit of measurement to our system: the dragon. Of course that would be difficult since the difference between Harriet, who's petite and Jasmine, who's quite large, is a lot."

"Well, it gives us an idea anyway," said Gregory with a chuckle. "So I think this has to be the spot for the cavern." He pointed to the map again.

"But where did they go after that? And how did the thugs who have Arryn get to the same place as Lena?" asked Emily, as she took a drink from her tea mug. "There's no way they could have run through the marketplace carrying Arryn and not have someone see them. Hannah checked just to be sure and verified that no one saw them."

"The kidnappers must have used another entrance," Gregory said. "They obviously know this area extremely well. What can they be up to?"

"I don't know," said Chloe, "but they have Arryn, who must be terrified. She was just beginning to trust us, and now this."

"We'll find her," said Aster. "We have to. We can worry about what they're up to after that."

Chloe noticed that Rya, who was sitting between her and Emily, was staring down at her hands, twisting them, but not saying anything. "Rya, are you OK?"

"Not really," she muttered, as she brushed her dark-brown hair away from her face. "I keep thinking of when Artemis and I were buried in that cave, when Dirk tried to kill us."

Artemis jumped up into her lap, and Rya hugged her before going on. "We weren't there long, thanks to you, Aster—as well as Jasmine, Oswald, and the baron—but it was horrible, and Artemis was hurt, and I didn't know if either of us would live. I'll never forget that terror. What must Arryn be feeling? She's been gone for a couple hours now."

"I know," said Chloe in a soft and gentle voice, patting Rya's arm. "And we'll find her. There's a difference here, however, which you need to remember. Lena wants Arryn to do something. I don't know what. That's the part of the puzzle we don't know. But the fact that she wants Arryn to do something means they aren't trying to kill her. They need her alive. Dirk needed you dead. That's a huge difference."

Rya nodded, still clinging to Artemis. "And the other thing that's wrong is the volcano. She's very distressed right now."

Gregory looked carefully at Rya as both he and Gretchen sat back down at the table. Then he said very gently, "Can you tell us anything more?"

Rya shook her head, and said, her voice starting to rise in panic, "That's just it. I feel so helpless. I can't get anything more from the volcano."

Emily reached over and placed a hand on Rya's shoulder. "Please, we know you're doing your best, and certainly it's a lot more than any of us can do. Just keep telling us what you're sensing. That's all we ask."

"But what if it isn't enough?" asked Rya her eyes shining with the start of tears.

Lucy looked across the table at Rya and smiled as she said, "It's a big piece of our puzzle, Rya, but remember, you have us as well. We do have other tools." She turned to Gregory, who was sitting between Emily and Gretchen. "I know a mole who lives in that area. She'll be sleeping now. I've learned that moles sleep in four-hour shifts and are most active late at night and early in the morning. My best bet is to try to contact her late tonight. I can see if she knows of any humans near her. I may have to wait for her to investigate, but I hopefully should have some information by early morning."

"Can't we do anything now?" asked Rya.

"If it were summer and still light, yes," said Gregory, "but unfortunately if we go in where Hannah and Chloe were, Lena and her group could exit the way the kidnappers came in, a spot that we have yet to find, and we might never see them. There are just too many places where there might be exits and in the dark, even with torches, the kidnappers could get past us. As hard as it is, I think we need to wait for light and then we'll position the dragons so they are watching on the mountainside."

Emily agreed. "This is going to be a hard night for all of us, but especially for Arryn. If we plan this well, with any luck we'll have her out of there in the morning."

Chloe noticed that no one said anything about what Lena and the kidnappers might do to Arryn if their capture were imminent, but she was sure they were all thinking it. However, she couldn't think of an alternative. Night wasn't their friend right now, and they did need to find out what Lucy's mole had to say.

"Let's meet at Lena's shop at first light then," said Chloe, as she gathered the empty tea mugs and made them disappear. "Lucy, hopefully you'll have more information for us then. Unfortunately the dragons won't fit in the passageway."

"But I will," interrupted Artemis, "and I'm a great tracker. I used to go out with my mother and look for lost sheep. Rya's dad never knew, but we helped keep his herd together."

Rya ruffled Artemis's silky fur then finally looked up at the others said, "She really is. If she hadn't found us a safe place to hide from Dirk, neither of us would be here now."

Emily smiled. "We're lucky to have you, and thank you for your offer of help, Artemis."

Chloe went on, "And I think we should have all of us, plus maybe a few more riders, Emily, if that's possible."

"I'm sure Rupert and Hannah want to be there. That'll give us nine plus Artemis. I'm going to try to keep my dad out of it, but that might not be possible. With him we'd have ten people altogether."

"Excellent," said Chloe, as she stood. "Well, let's call this meeting over, and please, everyone, keep sending strengthening, healing thoughts to Arryn. As Rya said, she must be feeling terrified, lost, and maybe even betrayed. After all, Emily, Esmeralda, and I promised her that she wouldn't be harmed by Lena, and obviously we didn't succeed in keeping that promise.

We need to surround her with loving thoughts until we can rescue her."

They all nodded as they stood. As they were preparing to leave, Chloe said, "Rya, would you and Artemis like to join me for dinner?"

Rya looked startled by the invitation and glanced over at Aster, who said, "That's fine, Rya. And I want to talk to my dad about shoring up volcanic passages. I don't know if he knows anything about that, but he's our carpenter. Can't hurt to ask, and I know he'd want to help."

Gregory heard this and looking up from his paperwork said, "I should have thought of that. Please, Aster, ask Clyde if he'd like to join in on the hunt. His knowledge could prove very helpful, especially if we end up in passages that were made by humans instead of the volcano. I wish my dad were here with all his knowledge of mining, but he and Oswald aren't arriving from Forbury until tomorrow afternoon."

Once the others had left, Chloe took Rya and Artemis to her apartment. Then, to Rya's surprise, Chloe knocked on a door that was hidden behind a wall hanging. Hearing "Come in," Chloe opened the door and ushered Rya and Artemis into another apartment, a small cozy room with overstuffed pink furniture. Rya heard "Good evening" and noticed Libby, wearing a pink sweater and red knit pants, sitting in one of the chairs, knitting and smiling.

"Hi," said Rya, her brown eyes alight with wonder. "So this is where you live."

Libby chuckled, pushing her spectacles up her broad nose. "In a manner of speaking, yes. When I choose to take human form, I find this room very comfortable. But please, have a seat. You too, Artemis, and welcome."

Chloe sat in her usual chair, and Rya and Artemis took the couch, with Artemis curling up in Rya's lap. Then Calliope appeared, licking her paws, and plopped down in Chloe's lap.

"I thought you could use some time—and maybe some help—in sorting all this out," Chloe told Rya. "Since the mudslide this past fall, you've been through a lot, and during the meeting I suspected it was getting to you, especially with Arryn's kidnapping and the situation with the volcano."

A tear slid down Rya's cheek as she said, "I miss my mom and dad so much—especially my mom right now."

"I know, dear," said Libby, shifting her knitting bag so that the yarn would pull more easily. "You've been very brave. Your world has been turned upside down not once but several times in the last few months. Change takes time to process, and you haven't had that time yet."

"Sometimes I feel guilty for being happy to have found out about my birth family," Rya said. "I now have a wonderful grandmother, Harmony—oh, I wish she were here too—and Clyde is a great uncle and mentor. It's incredible to have a friend my own age, so having a cousin like Aster is fantastic. And my birth mom, Mildred...well, she talks to me telepathically every week or so, and I know she really does love me. I admire her a lot. She's not only a very talented artist, but she also obviously knows herself. She knew she wouldn't make a good, nurturing mother so she found me the best parents ever, her childhood friends, George and Mary. She does look after me, and always has, but it isn't the same as having someone right here, is it?"

"No, it isn't," said Chloe, shaking her head.

"And then there's all this magic stuff," Rya continued, as she twisted her hands through Artemis's fur. "I never knew about magic before, never thought I had it. I didn't realize that my knowing about weather and stuff was magic, never knew I was telepathic, even if my abilities are limited to Artemis and my blood kin, but now, in Havenshold, I'm seeing it every day. People do it so naturally, but I'm not used to it."

Chloe nodded. "And now you're sitting in an apartment with the library in human form and a mage."

Rya gave half smile. "I like you both...I really do. And I'm really glad to know you, and I think you're neat, Libby. But it's all so different. And now I'm the only one who says the volcano is sad and that she's a she. What if I'm wrong? Maybe I just don't know volcanoes. Maybe everything's fine, and I'm making everyone worry for nothing. Oh, I just don't know about anything anymore," she finished, with a shake of her head.

"Listen here," said Libby, waving a knitting needle at Rya. "You know a lot, young lady. Don't start doubting yourself. If it hadn't been for you, Miss Crimson and all your fellow students would have died. You have a gift, and yes, you're still learning, but then so am I, and you know how old I am. Now, first off, you need dinner," she concluded, and with another wave of her knitting needle, three bowls of a vegetable pot pie with a golden brown crust as well as a bowl of cat kibble appeared, one for each of them, as well as napkins and spoons. "Now try that out. I'm a much better cook than Chloe."

Chloe laughed. "She's right about that. Dig in."

As the four of them ate, Libby went on. "I wish Bertha weren't hibernating. She muttered something about the volcano the last time we spoke, but she wasn't specific. Dealing with a seer, at least our seer, is a real art, as you might imagine."

Rya stopped her spoon halfway to her mouth. "Uh, no...I mean, I'm not sure. What's a seer exactly?"

Libby laughed—a laugh that was kind and warm and just felt good. Then she said, "Well, that's a good question. Bertha is our world's only seer, and she's a bear. Bears are very special guardians in our world, but that's a story for another day. Bertha's quite old but not as old as me. It was her grandmother who met King Alfred, if I'm remembering correctly. Bertha is the one who first realized that Chloe is a mage, and she also predicted the so-called War of the Asteroid, and—"

"That's another thing," said Rya, interrupting then saying, "Sorry."

"No, go ahead. What's another thing?" said Libby.

"Well, Aster's told me about most of this stuff so I'd know about the people I've been meeting, and she said that you, Chloe, found out six years before the actual arrival of the asteroid that there would be a disaster from space and that you had six years to learn to be a mage and prepare and all that."

Chloe nodded. "Yes, when Bertha and I first met, she told me the asteroid would hit in about six years. You never really can get a seer to commit to a timeline. And then, as things got closer, she kept revising the timeline."

Rya shook her head and said, "Yeah, timeline. I had about five minutes'—maybe not even that—notice before the mudslide. I don't work on timelines. Well, sometimes I know what the weather's going to be for a week or so, but generally if it's a disaster, I only know a few minutes before."

"And that was enough," said Libby gently.

"But with this volcano, I don't know if something's going to happen or when, because I've never worked like that," said Rya, as she put her empty bowl on a nearby table then noticed a plate of chocolate chip cookies. Looking over at Libby she motioned to the cookies and when Libby nodded, she grabbed several she sat back down and said, "so I would love to know that I had six years or three months or something."

Libby smiled, which made her eyes twinkle. "I agree, and that's why I said I was sorry that Bertha's hibernating. I'd really like to try to make her give us more information."

"And so would I," said Chloe. "Bertha is the best. Yes, she can be annoying and aggravating at times, but she's also amazing in what she knows. She'd be able to help. I know she would."

Suddenly they all heard a crash as one of the tables fell over, and then a large bear grumbled, "You've rearranged again, Libby. And what do you mean by calling me annoying and aggravating?"

"Bertha!" yelled Chloe as she stood up. Calliope quickly jumped out of the way as Chloe ran over to hug a massive brown bear, seven feet long, four feet high at her shoulders, and weighing at least five hundred pounds.

"Now why are you folks waking up a sleeping bear?" said Bertha grumpily. "And is there any more pot pie? If you're going to wake me, you'd better feed me."

Libby smiled. "Welcome. Good to see you too." A very large bowl of the vegetable pot pie materialized in front of Bertha, who had sat down on the floor by the couch. "And may I introduce Rya and Artemis?"

After Bertha slurped an enormous amount of pot pie, she looked over at the couch and said, "Pleased to meet you, I'm sure. But why am I here again? Why couldn't you just let me sleep? I was dreaming about a hive full of honey and I was just about to snare it."

Chloe laughed. "Oh, Bertha, you're fantastic, and it's so good to see you. We hadn't actually decided we needed to bother you. You came before we could get that far."

"Well, I sort of was listening," said Bertha, in a warm deep gentle voice.

"If you eavesdrop you might hear things you don't like," said Libby with a chuckle.

"Yeah, well that's true. But I've heard about Rya. Her ability to see things coming is sort of what I do. It's not really a seer ability, but it's related so to speak, so I really wanted to meet her."

Then Bertha turned to Rya and said, "So what's it like?"

Rya wrinkled her forehead and said in a puzzled tone, "What's what like?"

"Knowing about the weather and mudslides and all that," said Bertha, waving a paw dangerously close to Libby's knick-knacks, which seemed to jump out of the way.

Rya shook her head. "I can't really describe it."

"Try. Humor this old bear."

"Well, I just know what the weather's going to be. It doesn't feel like anything. I just know."

"What about the mudslide?" Bertha prodded.

"I just had a premonition that mud was coming toward the school. It was mostly a feeling...a feeling of harm, I guess. It's hard to put into words."

Bertha nodded. "Yes, it is hard to put into words, isn't it? So, now, as I understand from what I overheard," she continued, glaring a bit at Libby before turning back to Rya, "you're now worried about our volcano. Why?"

Chloe started to say, "Bertha..." but Bertha held up a paw and shook her head at her.

Rya thought hard before replying, "As I've told the others, I'm not sure. I've never been this close to a volcano before. So I could be totally wrong."

"Stop right there, young lady," said Bertha. "You can't go doubting yourself. That's being disrespectful of your gift. Let me tell you this: you may not always be right. You may think something is one way then find out it's a bit different. But you're never to doubt your gift. I'm sure you've heard about how I met Chloe as well as my predictions about the asteroid."

When Rya nodded, Bertha went on, "Well, all I knew when I first met Chloe was that she was going to stop an attack on the planet and that somehow that attack was coming from space. I didn't have specifics. And I didn't know just when. I could tell—and this will come with experience—that it would be a number of years, so I said six or more. I had to say something. All I knew was that it wouldn't be the next day but that Chloe would have to train hard and fast to be ready."

"You old phony," said Libby fondly.

"Not really," said Bertha, shaking her head. "I want Rya to know that sometimes we don't have all the information right away. Now the mudslide was caused by some jerk setting off dynamite in a water-soaked cliff. That was an immediate event. But the asteroid took years to travel to us. So the details were a lot less specific. I see the big picture. I don't predict weather or mudslides or even earthquakes, all of which would be helpful. My abilities are geared toward planetary disasters. That's one way we're different in our abilities, Rya. I've also been trained, and you haven't, and we'll need to talk about that at some point."

Libby cut in. "But before you went to hibernate, you did mutter something about the volcano."

Bertha nodded. "Yes. That's a planetary disaster in the making. And I think you, Rya, are here for a reason. I didn't know the volcano was sad or indeed that it was a she. You have a very special empathic relationship with this planet, the likes of which I've never seen."

"But I don't know what it means," said Rya, her voice nearly a wail, "or what will happen."

"At the moment neither do I," Bertha said between mouthfuls of pot pie. "I do know there isn't an immediate danger, which is why I felt perfectly comfortable taking my winter nap."

"OK," said Chloe, "we understand that. You'd never leave us unprotected. But I'm concerned about Rya. She's been through a lot, and she doesn't know how to use her powers or what she should be doing. And when we add Arryn's kidnapping to that, it just puts things over the top."

Bertha put a paw on Rya's knee, and as she did, Artemis gave a low growl. Bertha chuckled and said, "Now don't you take on so, Miss Artemis. I'm a vegetarian, and I don't eat foxes, and even if I did, I wouldn't eat bonded animals. Furthermore I wouldn't harm this charming young lady under any circumstances."

Artemis muttered, "Sorry."

"No need to be sorry. You and Rya have one of the strongest bonds I've ever felt, and I've never known of true bonds between humans and anyone else except dragons, gryphons, unicorns, and dolphins. You two are unique in many ways, and I treasure that.

"Now back to the matter at hand, as I really do need to return to my nap or I might get *really* grumpy. Rya, you need to keep in contact with the volcano. I'll give you something to think about. What exactly are you and the others worried about?"

"Well, that the volcano will erupt and kill us all," replied Rya as if that were the most obvious thing in the world.

"Exactly," said Bertha with a self-satisfied grin. Seeing the puzzled looks on Rya and Chloe's faces, she went on. "You're seeing it from your perspective, which is perfectly natural. But what about looking at if from hers? Do you think she wants to kill people? Volcanoes, by their very nature, are meant to erupt. When this happened in the alternate reality, I suspect the volcano might have seen the eruption as a good thing, wiping out humans who were hell-bent on destroying this magnificent planet. But what about now? Thanks to the time travel of King Alfred and company—and the greater awareness given by the planet to the magical creatures, especially the dragons—our path seems to be a lot healthier."

"So the volcano wouldn't want to hurt us," said Rya with a sudden glimpse of understanding.

"Precisely," said Bertha, now looking positively smug, sitting upright with her front paws in her lap. "So I suggest you start loving up this volcano, so to speak. See if you can get closer to her and learn more about her. Try to see things from her side.

What I can tell you, before I cut out of here, is that nothing is going to happen until probably fall at the earliest. And what's going to happen is still a big question mark. Chloe, you're also going to be instrumental in this. If you can move an asteroid, you can plug up a volcano. But should you?

"Now I'll just leave those unanswered questions in the air. After all, you need something to think on while I sleep. And Rya, if Clyde agrees, and you can get some time off this summer, I'd love to have you come up to my meadow. You and Artemis can play with my kids, Berla and Boris, and you and I can study together. Any questions before I return to my nap?"

"Thank you so much, you old grumpy bear," said Libby. "Nice to know you always have an ear out."

"Who's calling whom old?" said Bertha, and with another wave of her paw, she was gone, back to her cave in the mountains about an hour north of Havenshold.

Rya stared at the empty spot before finally saying, "Wow, she's something."

Chloe and Libby laughed and nodded.

Artemis said, "I think I like her."

Calliope decided it was time to put her two cents into the conversation. *Chloe and I have spent a lot of time up in her meadow, and I would agree. And Boris and Berla are fun. I hope you two get to spend some time there.*

"Calliope's right, Rya," Chloe said, "and I'm sure Clyde will give you some time this summer. Even apprentices get vacations. But let's get back to the matter at hand. How are you feeling about things now?"

Rya smiled and relaxed into the couch, gently rubbing Artemis's fur. "I'm doing a lot better. I still wish my mom were here. Mildred said I shouldn't call her 'Mom' because she didn't raise me, so I mean my adopted mom."

Chloe nodded. "Yes, that makes perfect sense."

Then, as Libby offered more tea, Chloe was quiet. She sent out a telepathic call to Aster's grandmother,. *Harmony, can you hear me?*

Loud and clear. What's up?

I really think Rya needs you. Any chance you could pop in for a bit? I could teleport you.

Funny you should mention that, Harmony said. *I'm with the baron and Oswald right now. The baron has a couple of his men looking after my island so I could come to Havenshold for a visit. Don't tell anyone, as I want it to be a surprise, but the three of us will be there tomorrow afternoon or early evening.*

Oh, that's good news. I'll keep your secret. See you soon.

Chloe rejoined the conversation with Libby and Rya. Libby winked at Chloe to say she knew what was in the wind, as Rya was saying, "So you're really a building. But you look so real."

"And a building isn't real?" said Libby with a smile.

"Well, yes," Rya said a bit nervously, "but..."

Chloe said, "We'd better save this philosophical discussion for another day. It's getting late, and we have an early start tomorrow."

"Oh," said Rya, as her forehead crinkled with worry, "for a bit I nearly forgot poor Arryn."

"Well, you needed a break, and worrying won't help her or you," Chloe said with a smile. "So you and Artemis get back to your uncle's and get a good night's sleep. Tomorrow will be here soon enough."

Chloe, Calliope, Rya, and Artemis all stood. "Thanks, Libby," Rya said. "You're the best."

"You're most welcome," said Libby. "Happy to help."

Chloe showed Rya and Artemis through the front doors of the library so they would find their way home by the route they were used to, and then she and Calliope took Chloe's own advice and headed to bed as well. Once Chloe and Calliope had settled in the bed, Chloe said, "I wonder where Arryn is now."

— 9 —

DAWN RAID

While Chloe and the others were trying to figure out what had happened, Arryn was trapped in a passageway with Lena, Damian, and Frank. How could things have gone so wrong after such a lovely afternoon? Was Amy alive? Damian had hit her so hard that he knocked her unconscious. It had been a couple hours since she'd been kidnapped, and she saw no way to escape. Once again Lena had her.

"Now get in there," said Lena, pointing to a very narrow opening in the cavern. "We can see something shiny in there so you're going to get it for us. You're the only one small enough to crawl in there."

She gave Arryn a shove toward the opening. Arryn bent down and started to crawl and then slither and wriggle her way into the opening. She couldn't see anything once she was inside, as her body blocked the little light that there was. "I can't see anything," she called back to the others.

Damian grabbed her by the legs and yanked her out. Then he shoved a light into her hands and said, "There. Now no more excuses."

Arryn held onto the light, a glow stick like the miners used, and crawled back into the opening. She saw something up ahead, but it seemed a very long way away. Slowly she wriggled her way down the passage. As she went, she brushed something furry, and a mole scooted out of her way. "I'm sorry. I didn't mean to disturb you," Arryn said quietly, not knowing whether the mole could understand her.

Finally Arryn saw the end of the passage, and there was something there, a bright-green stone that sparkled in her weak light. She grabbed it and held it tightly; it was about the size of a small stone. Then she wiggled backward to get herself out. The second she was moving toward the exit, Lena called, "Did you get it?"

"Yes," said Arryn.

As soon as she was within Damian's reach, he again yanked her out by the legs, scraping her up and down her body, tearing and snagging her new rainbow sweater. *Why is this happening?* she thought. *Will Aster and Rya forget about me?*

Once she was out, she handed the stone to Lena. "Yes," said Lena, doing as much of a dance as she could, given her size and the confined space. Her large belly swung from side to side as she jiggled around. "Yes, I knew there was something more than the copper we've been finding."

She turned to Damian and Frank. "This emerald is my retirement. You boys can have all the rest of the gems and copper we've dug out."

Damian laughed, and the laugh wasn't pleasant. He was a tall, heavy man with nearly black hair and brown eyes. He had a scar running down the side of his right cheek, and he looked threateningly at both Arryn and Lena. Then he hit Lena in the face and snatched the stone and jammed it into his pocket. "That's what you think, old woman. We have other plans."

Lena cried out in pain and stumbled backward. Then she yelled at Damian, "What do you mean? I've housed you and made sure the authorities didn't find you. You two work for me. Now give me that."

Damian snarled, "Frank and I never worked for you, you fool. We used you. We needed access to the cavern, and your shop was perfectly positioned. We'd heard about that passageway from friends of ours. You're a fool. Now move out of the way."

"No!" screamed Lena, as she lunged toward Damian. "That stone is mine!"

Frank, who was nearly as tall as Damian and very muscular, grabbed Lena and held her with her arms behind her back as Damian pulled out a knife and slashed her across the right side of her face, narrowly missing her eye. Then Frank shoved her toward the edge of the ledge they were on. Lena toppled over the edge, falling twenty-five feet or so and barely catching herself on a much smaller ledge. Arryn looked over and saw that one of Lena's legs was bent at a very unnatural angle. She was only secured to the ledge by the hood of her old ragged sweatshirt, which was caught on a rock outcropping.

"Hang on, Lena," said Arryn. "I'll find a way to help you."

"No you won't," said Damian, picking up a large rock and hitting Arryn over the head. Arryn crumpled in a heap, but just as she was passing out, she thought she felt the earth shake and heard a large crash. *So this is how it ends,* she thought as she slipped into unconsciousness.

At dawn Chloe and the others met as planned at what once was Lena's shop. But when they arrived, they found a deep, rubble-filled depression. "What happened?" Emily said.

"I don't know," said Chloe. "Obviously a cave-in of some sort, but why?"

Aster bent over and looked into the pit and said, "I can see shards of that gorgeous rainbow pot. Everything's destroyed. How are we going to find Arryn?"

Rya fell to the ground, sobbing, nearly crushing Artemis in her arms. Chloe rushed to her side. "She said she had to do it," Rya said through her tears. "She said she had to do it."

Chloe gently put an arm around her. "Who, Rya?"

"Jaluhz," sobbed Rya.

"Jaluhz?" asked Chloe, handing Rya a handkerchief. The others gathered around to listen.

Rya dried her eyes and looked around at the group. "Jaluhz is the volcano. And she's very distressed. There was so much anger and hatred inside her that she shuddered, trying to dispel it. That's what caused the collapse."

"What do you mean by 'hatred inside her'?" asked Chloe in a puzzled voice.

Shaking her head as if to clear it, Rya said, "I'm not sure. Jaluhz doesn't really talk, but she sends something like images, and I'm starting to be able to see them. She showed me images of men inside her, fighting, and then she shook. I'm sorry. I don't know anything more."

"Don't apologize," said Emily, looking at Rya with real respect. "You gave us something to go on. Is there any way to find out if there are people alive inside Jaluhz?"

Rya closed her eyes and took several deep breaths as she loosened her grip on Artemis, but then she shook her head. "Jaluhz is too upset, too sad. She just keeps giving me images of helplessness and a need to protect herself and the planet. It's not easy to understand."

"Then we need to try something else," said Emily. "Lucy, what have you found out from your moles?"

"This collapse happened late yesterday afternoon, probably while we were meeting at the library. I found one mole who had seen someone—I suspect Arryn, because she startled him, and he scurried away, but she said she was sorry for bothering him. That was before the collapse, though."

"We need the dragons," said Emily. "And we believe there is—or was—another entrance somewhere on the mountainside."

Esmeralda landed beside the group. "After yesterday's tremors," she said, "the other dragons and I didn't notice any changes in the mountain, but during the night, an area of the mountain outside of town started to sink. It's possible there was a tunnel below, and unlike this collapse, the tunnel's collapse wasn't immediate. But I suspect the sinkhole in the mountain is where the tunnel was."

Gregory pulled out his map and studied it. "Yes, there was a tunnel here, where you're describing, although it wasn't a main tunnel. Hmm, yes, that could be their entrance."

"Chloe," said Emily, "how long was the passageway you and Hannah found? How long was it before you saw the cavern?"

Chloe thought for a few moments then said, "I don't know exactly. Maybe fifty feet or so. Definitely longer than Esmeralda here...maybe as long as three or four of you, Esmeralda."

"We really do need to add 'dragon' to our length measurements," said Gregory.

"I'm more than fifteen feet long," said Esmeralda, "so that would make for a long passageway, and we have all the debris from the shop here as well."

"We have to do something," cried Rya. "Jaluhz is in pain, and we have to find Arryn."

Chloe put an arm around Rya and said, "We will, Rya. We're just figuring out the best *something*."

"Let's treat this the way we did the mine collapse in Forbury," Lucy suggested. "Remember how Sage and I were able to locate the buried miners to find those who were still alive? We can do that again. Harriet is bringing Sage now."

"Yes," said Emily with the first enthusiasm anyone had shown so far. "Why didn't I remember that? Do you think you'll be able to tell if anyone's down there? They may be a long way down."

Lucy smiled as she said, "We won't know unless we try."

Just then Harriet arrived with Sage on her back. The sight was quite amusing, a gorgeous brown tabby sitting on top of a lovely blue dragon, both looking very regal. Sage jumped down and marched over to Lucy. *So we're on another rescue,* Sage said, speaking her thoughts so that everyone could hear her.

"Yes," answered Lucy. "We think there were at least four people in the volcano when the tunnels collapsed."

Lucy and Sage wandered carefully around the pit then worked their way behind the remaining shops, next to where Lena's had been. Finally Lucy said, "We can't find anything here. Could we go to the other sinkhole?"

"Yes, of course," said Emily, as she and Gregory got onto Esmeralda. Aster had called out to Jasmine, who arrived along with Ruby, and soon they were all just outside the village on the mountainside.

"Good," said Lucy, as she and Sage climbed down from Harriet. "This is just as you described, Esmeralda, a gradual caving in. I think that'll make it easier for us, and certainly we can cover a larger area without shops in our way."

Lucy and Sage got to work, and everyone else stayed very quiet. Chloe was impressed by the way Lucy and Sage proceeded methodically across the sinkhole, each of them covering the ground so that nothing was missed. After what seemed like an interminable time, Sage finally sat down and called out to all, *I hear the very faintest sound of breathing...and an even fainter sound of sobbing.*

Lucy moved carefully over to Sage, sank to the ground, and said, "Sage's senses are much stronger than mine, but I agree. I think there might be two people down here. We haven't found anything else."

"Right then," said Emily. "We need the dragons to dig here. Esmeralda, can you set that in motion and make sure everyone knows to dig as carefully as possible so as not to cause a further collapse?"

Esmeralda sent out a loud call to the other dragons then said, "Yes, we've learned from the gryphons. They help out with more mine collapses than we do and have been very helpful with instructions."

"I wish my dad and Oswald were here," said Gregory, "but since Oswald doesn't fly, it takes them longer to get places."

"Let's see how it goes," said Chloe. "I'll contact Oswald and the baron telepathically to see where they are and whether they have any suggestions. If necessary I can try to teleport them here, but honestly Oswald has grown into a very large gryphon, even without wings."

"Ask Oswald if he can speak directly to me," Esmeralda told Chloe, "and then I can send images of what we're finding, and he can advise us. That's nearly as good as having him here."

"Right," said Chloe, and everyone got to work.

The digging went slowly but efficiently. The dragons were able to move a lot of dirt away from the spot Sage and Lucy had found. Sage and Lucy kept checking and refining the location. Esmeralda reported any suggestions she received from Oswald. Gregory and Clyde found some lumber to try to reinforce spots in the ground as the dragons dug.

Chloe sat by Rya and Artemis and said, "Try to do what Bertha suggested last night. Surround Jaluhz with love. Let her know we're trying to remove the hatred and anger so it won't disturb her. Keep talking to her, even if you don't think she can talk back. And send her images of what we're doing to let her know we aren't invading her but are trying to repair what others have done."

Rya nodded. "I'll try. You know, she really is magnificent. And I do love her. She seems very special. I mean she's a volcano, powerful and regal even, so why should she care about us at all. But she does. She cares about everything on the planet and that seems pretty amazing."

"I'm beginning to pick up what Rya is seeing," Artemis added. "I'll send my love to Jaluhz as well."

Chloe smiled, a warm smile that included her eyes. "Excellent. You two make quite a team. Just keep letting her know how much you love her and how special she is."

The hours went by, and the digging continued. It wasn't until late afternoon, nearly a full day after the collapse, that Lucy let them know they were really close. "There are definitely two people alive down there," she reported. "One of them is unconscious. The other is in a great deal of pain."

Suddenly Harriet said, "I've found a body. It's a man."

"And there's another body next to him," said Ruby.

Carefully Gregory, Emily, Gretchen, and Aster uncovered the two men, one of whom was clutching a large emerald. Both had been crushed to death in the collapse. As they moved the bodies aside and covered them with a tarp, Gregory said, "So that's what they were after. What a waste."

Emily pried the emerald out of the grip of the one man and then looked carefully at the bodies and said, "I think I've seen these guys on Forbury's criminal watch list."

"Well, I'd say they were found, and the sentence was carried out," said Gretchen in a grim voice.

The digging resumed, and before long they found an opening, a large pocket that hadn't collapsed. Aster exclaimed, "I see a rainbow sweater! That has to be Arryn."

Chloe walked over to the hole. "Yes, I see where you're looking, Aster. I think I should teleport her out. Do we have blankets?"

Emily nodded and brought over a large pile of blankets. Chloe concentrated and began by shifting some of the rubble before she lifted a barely conscious Arryn, keeping her body as flat as possible to prevent any further injuries. Dr. Brian and Nurse Beatrice had been called earlier and were standing nearby, ready to assess Arryn's condition.

While Dr. Brian, a gray-haired man, on the short side, with a medium build and brown eyes, was checking on Arryn, Chloe and Emily climbed into the empty space. Once they were down there, they saw a further open space below the ledge they were standing on. They could see Lena on a small ledge, on just holding on. "Lena," called Emily. "Can you hear me?"

"I'm dying," sobbed Lena. "I've lost everything."

"We're here to help you now. Just hang on," said Emily.

Lena squirmed as she looked up at them, and there was a ripping sound followed by a scream. Chloe acted without even thinking, snatching Lena magically and all but flinging her as she teleported her out of the hole. It wasn't gentle, but it was effective.

Dr. Brian rushed over to where Lena had landed. "Nurse," he called out, "we need bandages. She's lost a lot of blood, and she's still bleeding quite heavily." He looked down at Lena's right leg and added, "And her right leg is badly broken."

Chloe and Emily crawled out of the hole and went over to Lena, who mercifully had passed out from the pain. "Dr. Brian," said Chloe, "I'm sorry I wasn't more careful, but I just reacted."

Emily said, "Good reactions. She was headed into a pit of lava."

Dr. Brian looked up at Chloe. "There's no doubt Emily is right. You saved her life, and you didn't cause any further injuries. It looks like both her knife wound and leg injury are nearly a day old. Could I ask you to *gently* teleport her to my surgery center? Now that there isn't the threat of imminent death..." He smiled at her then to let her know he was kidding.

"Of course," said Chloe.

"Esmeralda can take you and Nurse Beatrice if you'd like," offered Emily.

"Or I can teleport you both," offered Chloe.

"If you're sure," said Dr. Brian after looking at Nurse Beatrice.

"Certainly," said Chloe. "I'll send you two first, then Lena. And what about Arryn? How is she?"

Dr. Brian said, "I don't like the look of the bump on her head. She's not completely conscious and I suspect a concussion."

"Well then I'll teleport Arryn right after I move Lena," said Chloe.

"Excellent," said Dr. Brian, gathering up his bag.

Once all that had been accomplished, Chloe went over to Rya and Artemis. "Can you find out what Jaluhz would like us to do with this hole? We've removed all the hatred, I think."

Rya and Artemis were very quiet. Finally Rya said, "Jaluhz is definitely calmer, and she's sending us images of a filled-in hole. I don't think she cares what it looks like on our side. She just seems to need some security and privacy."

"OK," said Chloe before she turned to Emily. "Can you have the dragons fill this hole back in and pack it down securely so no more misguided treasure hunters can ever get into that cavern?"

"My thoughts exactly," said Emily. "Mining isn't allowed on this mountain, and now we have an excellent example of why it's prohibited. I'll assign several riders and their dragons to secure the area. I'm guessing then that you and I will want to go to the hospital."

Chloe nodded as Aster, Rya, and Artemis said, "We're going too."

"I'd figured on that," Chloe said. "Aster, will Jasmine and Sasha come or stay?"

Jasmine came over and answered her question. "Nurse Beatrice isn't big on dragons being in her hospital, and she already has Fern there. So we'll stay here and help with the repair. The more of us who work at it, the faster it'll go."

Lucy agreed and then said, "Gregory, Gretchen, and I will check the maps and our information from the moles to make sure there aren't other easy access points. But please keep us posted, especially about Arryn."

"Will do," said Chloe as she, Aster, Rya, and Artemis left.

As they walked to the hospital wing in the rider complex, Aster said, "Arryn looked so fragile. And did you see that her sweater was all torn?"

Rya nodded. "Do you think that shop might have another one? Could we get her one just like it?"

Chloe said, "I'm sure we can. Mary, the shop owner, seemed touched by you girls. If she doesn't already have one like Arryn's, I bet she'll knit one up in no time."

They walked through the hospital's main doors and found Amy and Todd in the waiting room.

Amy came over and hugged Chloe. "Thank you so much for finding Arryn."

"How are you?" asked Chloe, noticing the neon-pink plaster cast on Amy's right arm, inside a bright-pink sling.

"Oh, this," said Amy, waving her injured arm then wincing. "It's nothing. I was released this afternoon, but when we heard about Arryn, well, we stayed."

"You're supposed to be resting," Todd said. "You also have a minor concussion, remember. Will you please at least sit down?"

"Yes, mother hen," said Amy with obvious affection, and the entire group chuckled.

"Have you heard anything about Arryn's condition?" asked Aster.

"No, nothing," said Todd. "We didn't even see her. I guessed you teleported her right into the surgery," he finished, looking at Chloe.

"Yes, both her and Lena," said Chloe.

"That dreadful woman," muttered Todd.

"She certainly has a lot to answer for," said Chloe. "But she's also a victim, and she's lived as a victim her entire life. I hope now Emily will be able to reach her."

Nurse Beatrice, a silver-haired woman of average height, with a sturdy build and a no-nonsense look about her, came through the surgery doors. "I have to get back," she said, "but I wanted you to know that Arryn will be fine. She has a very nasty bump on her head and a minor concussion, but she's woken up, and we've moved her to the ward. She'll have to stay here for at least a day or two, but she'll be fine."

Amy hugged Todd and Rya, and Aster cheered as Chloe said, "Is there any chance we could see her, just for a minute or so?"

"As long as you keep it short, I think that would do her a world of good. But no excitement."

"And what about Lena?" asked Chloe.

"She's seriously injured. The slice across her face nicked a vein in her neck and caused her to lose a lot of blood. Thankfully it was a very small nick, and Dr. Brian was able to repair it. I have to get back now, because her right leg is very badly broken. And with her poor health to begin with, well, we'll just have to see. But we're doing all we can."

"Thank you," said Chloe.

As Nurse Beatrice headed back into surgery, Amy told the group, "Follow me. I know the way all too well after yesterday."

They all walked quietly over to the room where Arryn lay in bed. Artemis gently climbed onto the foot of the bed as the others surrounded Arryn.

"Arryn," said Amy softly, as she brushed some hair back from Arryn's face, being very careful to avoid the shaved spot with the stitches on the top of her head.

Arryn opened her eyes and looked around at all of them then back at Amy. "You're OK," she said. "I was so worried. I thought they'd killed you."

Amy smiled as she sat in the chair Todd had placed next to the head of Arryn's bed. "No, I'm fine. Just a broken wing, and look how pretty Dr. Brian made my cast."

"I'm so sorry," Arryn said. "If it hadn't been for me..."

"Now just stop right there," said Amy in a gentle but firm tone. "None of this was your fault. And we've all been so worried about you. You're the one who really suffered in all this. What you went through must have been horrible."

Arryn started to cry, and then Aster said, "Don't think about it now. You're not supposed to get upset. If you do, Nurse Beatrice will throw us out. Trust me, you don't want to get on her wrong side."

"She's been very nice to me," said Arryn.

"Nurse Beatrice is absolutely the best," Todd said with a grin, "and we all know it. But we know better than to get between her and one of her patients."

Arryn smiled as her eyes began to close.

"We'll let you get some rest," said Amy. "But we'll be back, keeping an eye on you until you can come home with us, hopefully in a day or two."

"You still want me?" said Arryn tentatively.

"You know what I said about getting between Nurse Beatrice and her patients?" Todd said. "Well, that's nothing compared to what would happen if someone got between us and one of our family, and remember, you're family now! You're stuck with us, like it or not."

Arryn gave a small smile then said, "I like that a lot."

Nurse Beatrice came bustling in. "That's enough for now. You can come back later—in small groups, mind you—and for short visits. Arryn needs her rest."

"We'll be back," said Rya, and the others chorused similar good-byes.

As they headed back out of the hospital, Rya said, "Aster, let's go see about that sweater."

"Definitely," said Aster, and she, Rya, and Artemis took off at a run.

Chloe turned to Amy and Todd, saying, "Thank you for what you're doing for Arryn. She's going to need a lot of help to get through this. Things were bad enough for her before the kidnapping. But I know you two are just the right folks to help her."

Todd put an arm around his wife's good shoulder and said, "We'll certainly try. And we did all right with *you*, didn't we?"

"The best," said Chloe, with a grin on her face and a twinkle in her eyes.

"We need to get you home now, dear," said Todd. "You have to rest if you're going to be ready when Arryn needs you."

"I know," said Amy. "But we are coming back this evening, right?"

"Of course," said Todd, as they waved good-bye to Chloe.

— 10 —
CONSEQUENCES

Chloe, Aster, Rya, and Artemis arranged to meet outside the hospital right after they all had early dinners so they could visit Arryn. Chloe noticed that Rya was carrying a bag with a brightly wrapped present as they arrived.

"Hi, there," said Chloe. "Were you successful?"

"Yes," said Rya waving the box. "Mary had another sweater that's just about the same. It's not absolutely identical, but she said she'd be happy to make another one if Arryn wanted."

"I'm sure this'll be lovely," said Chloe, as she opened the door to the hospital wing.

At the front desk, Nurse Beatrice looked up as they came in. "Here to see Arryn? You'll be pleased to know she's looking and feeling a lot better, and Dr. Brian is pleased with her progress."

"That's great," said Aster.

"Yes, and now will you introduce me to your cousin? Things were a bit hectic this afternoon."

"Oh, yes," said Aster. "Sorry. Nurse Beatrice, this is Rya and Artemis. They're now living in Havenshold. Rya is apprenticed to my dad."

"I'd heard that," said Nurse Beatrice, stepping out from behind her desk. "You couldn't have a better teacher than Clyde."

Rya nodded. "I know, and I'm so grateful. Pleased to meet you," she said as they shook hands.

Nurse Beatrice turned to Artemis. "I don't believe I've ever met a fox before. I understand you're quite an exceptional fox at that."

Artemis bowed then held out her front right paw as she said, "I've heard you're the exceptional one. Pleased to meet you, and thank you for taking care of Arryn."

Nurse Beatrice looked a little taken aback by Artemis but quickly recovered. She bent to shake Artemis's paw and said, "Well, you certainly have elegant manners. And you're a lot smaller than a dragon. Thank heavens. I love dragons—don't get me wrong. But they can take up a lot of space in a hospital ward."

"Very true," said Artemis.

"Well, I imagine you all didn't come here to gab with me, so you know the way. Head on in. Amy and Todd are there already. I sure hope Dr. Brian releases Arryn soon because Amy sure isn't getting much rest running back and forth to see her."

"Thanks," said Chloe, and the four of them went through the door to the ward.

Artemis raced ahead and jumped onto Arryn's bed as the others followed her. Chloe said, "You're looking much, much better, Arryn. Your color is back and your eyes are clear."

"Yes, isn't she?" agreed Amy.

"Dr. Brian says that if she has a good night, she might get to come home tomorrow," Todd added. "He said it would be better for both Arryn and Amy, and after all, Amy has nursed a lot of kids through a lot of scrapes, so she'll know what to watch for."

"That's terrific," Chloe said with a smile.

"You're wearing the pj's we bought at Anita's yesterday," said Rya.

"Gads, I can't believe it was only yesterday that we went shopping," said Aster. "So much has happened since then."

"Hey, where did you get that cute bear?" said Rya looking at the giant pink bear Arryn was cuddling.

"Amy and Todd," said Arryn. "I named her Carnation. Isn't she adorable? Do you like her purple bow?"

Aster grinned. "Yes, the purple bow really sets off her pink fur. She looks really soft too."

"She is," said Arryn, squeezing Carnation to show just how cuddly she was. "I've never had anything like her."

Amy looked at Arryn and said, "Well, it's high time you did."

Todd stood then helping Amy up as he said, "We'll be leaving now, Arryn, but we'll be back first thing in the morning so we can talk with Dr. Brian."

Amy bent over and kissed the top of Arryn's head, and Todd patted her shoulder as they left.

Arryn looked at her visitors and said, "Everyone's been so nice. Emily and Esmeralda were in here before Todd and Amy came."

"We were all very worried," said Chloe, as she sat down in the chair Amy had vacated.

"Hey, Arryn," said Rya, pulling a box out of the bag she was carrying. "Look what we got you." She handed the brightly wrapped box to Arryn.

"What? You guys didn't have to get me anything."

"Open it," said Rya excitedly.

"OK," Arryn said, and carefully removed the bow and placed it on the bedside table. She slit the paper open under the tape, trying hard not to rip it. Rya started to squirm, but Aster put a hand on her shoulder and shook her head as she whispered, "Let her open it the way she wants."

Arryn folded the paper and put it next to the bow before lifting the lid off the box. When she saw the sweater inside, she burst into tears, grabbing it out of the box and hugging it tightly.

"We couldn't help notice," said Aster, "that yours got kinda demolished in the tunnels."

"Yeah, so we went back to the shop," said Rya eagerly, "and Mary, the lady who helped us, was so sorry to hear what happened to you that she gave us this at no charge. It's not exactly the same, but it's pretty close."

"It's perfect!" Arryn exclaimed. "One of the hardest parts of the entire terror was when Damian tore my beautiful new sweater, the one that linked the three of us. I really thought I'd lost everything then."

Chloe handed Arryn a handkerchief. "You haven't lost a thing," she said. "Events just sidetracked you for a bit. I'm really glad Aster and Rya were able to get you a new sweater, but even without that, you'd better get used to the fact that you're a part of us now."

"You know what else?" said Rya, bubbling with enthusiasm. "Mary said, if you wanted, when you're feeling better, that she'd love to see you. She said she'd teach all of us to knit, if we wanted."

"Knit?" said Aster. "Don't think that's for me."

"Yeah, me too. I'm more into wood," said Rya, "but still it was really nice of her to offer."

"My mom knitted," said Arryn wistfully. "She was going to teach me."

"Well, then," said Chloe, "maybe that's something you might want to pursue once you're healthy again. Now I think we'd better go before Nurse Beatrice throws us out. I'm sure you need your rest."

Artemis, who had quietly but determinately been moving closer and closer to the head of the bed, now licked Arryn's arm and said, "I'm so glad you are OK."

Arryn hugged her and said, "Thanks, Artemis."

Chloe, Rya, and Aster all gave Arryn hugs, as Artemis jumped off the bed

As they left, Rya said, "We'll be back. Never fear!"

Just as they reached the ward door, it opened from the other side, and the baron, Oswald, and Harmony walked in.

"Grandma!" shouted Aster and Rya as they raced to hug Harmony, a grey-haired, tall, slim woman with brown eyes, looking like an older version of her granddaughters.

Chloe shook the baron's hand and ruffled Oswald's fur as she said, "You made good time."

"We just arrived in Havenshold," said the baron, a tall, muscular silver-haired man with kind brown eyes and a tanned complexion.

"I insisted that we see Arryn immediately," said Oswald.

Chloe beamed as she said, "Well, you really helped Esmeralda and the rest of us find her, so let me introduce you to her."

Arryn's mouth hung open in amazement as she stared at Oswald. She'd never seen a gryphon before. She noticed first that he was missing the wings of most gryphons, and he was about the size and look of a large lion, with lovely tawny fur, except that he had the beak and claws of an eagle.

Oswald led the way and said, as he reached the bed, "Hello. I'm Oswald. You must be Arryn. The last time I saw you, through Esmeralda's eyes, you were looking pretty banged up. I'm so glad to see you looking full of color again."

"Thanks," said Arryn. "You know, I've never met a gryphon before."

The baron introduced himself to Arryn as he shook hands with her. Then he said, "And you'll never meet another gryphon like this fellow. He's the best. Can't believe he wanted to bond with me."

"Of course I did," said Oswald, nudging him affectionately.

Harmony came over to meet Arryn as well, with Aster beside her and Rya holding her hand as if she'd never let go of it. "Pleased to meet you, Arryn. I'm Harmony, Aster and Rya's grandmother. I'm so sorry about what you went through, but I'm so happy you were rescued."

"Thank you," said Arryn.

Nurse Beatrice bounded in to say, "Visiting hours are over. This young lady needs her rest."

Chloe said, "OK, OK. We're just leaving."

"Grandma, you're staying with us, aren't you?" said Rya, still holding Harmony's hand.

"Yes, dear, for the rest of the holidays."

"We were on our way to take Harmony to Clyde's when Oswald insisted on stopping here," the baron said. "Then we're going to my ranch to stay with Lance."

Chloe turned to Arryn. "Lance is the baron's younger son, Gregory's brother," Chloe explained. "He manages the baron's estate in Draconia."

"Oh," said Arryn. "I'm sure meeting a lot of people all of a sudden. But you're all very nice," she added hastily.

Harmony offered her a gentle smile. "But even nice things can be too much, I know. You rest, and we'll catch up with you over the next few days."

They all headed out of the ward as Nurse Beatrice settled Arryn for the night.

Amy and Todd returned to the hospital before breakfast. They wanted to be sure to catch Dr. Brian on his rounds.

"I really hope she can come home today. She needs some tender loving care," said Amy, as they entered the hospital.

"I agree, hon," said Todd.

Nurse Beatrice didn't look at all surprised to see them. "Dr. Brian is with Lena now and will be around to check on Arryn shortly," she said.

"How's she doing, Beatrice?" asked Amy.

"That's one spunky kid. After all she's been through, she's a survivor for sure. She had a good night. I had to wake her now and again because of the concussion, but she went right back to sleep, and I didn't see any problems. Well, except for the fact that..." Then, seeing the worried expressions on Amy and Todd's faces, Nurse Beatrice went right on. "...except she won't let go of her bear."

Amy let out a big sigh of relief, and Todd smiled as he said, "I'd forgotten your strange sense of humor."

"Go right on in and keep her company," said Nurse Beatrice.

Amy and Todd walked into the ward, very pleased to notice the giant smile on Arryn's face the moment she saw them. And, as Nurse Beatrice had said, she had her arms wrapped around Carnation.

"Will I get to leave the hospital today?" asked Arryn.

Todd lifted the bag he was carrying and said, "We sure hope so. Amy picked out some of your new clothes for you to change into."

Arryn looked down at her bear and said, "I really liked the clothes I had on yesterday, but they got ruined."

Amy put her good arm around Arryn. "Clothes can be replaced. You can't, so never forget that. And just think how much fun you and I can have shopping."

Dr. Brian walked into the ward. "Good morning. And yes, Amy's right. You're a very lucky young lady. That rock, judging by the size of your lump and the length of the split it made in your scalp—well, you're lucky to be alive. You have a very good, thick skull," he said with a smile. "Now let me take a look at you."

Dr. Brian listened to Arryn's heart, checked her stitches, felt the bump on her head, and read Nurse Beatrice's notes. He examined her pupils, and finally he had her stand and walk across the room and back.

At last he seemed satisfied. "You may go home now, as long as you promise to be good."

"Yeah," said Arryn, nearly bouncing with excitement.

Dr. Brian looked at Arryn and Amy, his brown eyes twinkling as he smiled. "I suspect, if you're both in the same place, it'll be easier for Todd to make sure you both rest. Don't forget, Amy, you also have a minor concussion. Neither of you should be running around for several days."

"Aye, aye, Doc," said Amy with a mock salute.

"Seriously, take it easy, both of you, for the next couple of days, and then ease back into your regular activities. Arryn, I understand you're starting at Pathfinder Academy next week after the New Year's celebrations. You want to be fit and ready for that."

Arryn nodded, still hanging onto Carnation.

"Don't worry," said Todd, smiling. "I have two dragons on my side. Fern and Jupiter will sit on them if they aren't good."

"Right then," said Dr. Brian. "Provided neither of you has any complications, I need to see Arryn again in two weeks to remove her stitches, and Amy, you need to come back in six weeks, when I hope we'll be able to remove your cast. Meanwhile you can ditch the sling as pain allows, but please don't be in a hurry about it."

"Hey, Arryn, do you think we'll start any new fashion trends—me with my pink cast and sling and you with the shaved spot on your head?"

"Not likely," said Arryn with a smile, as she began to feel comfortable with Amy's kidding.

"We'll find you a cute hat or two, if you like, that you can wear until your hair grows out. And once it grows a bit, who knows? You might want to have a different haircut."

"I haven't had my hair cut for years," said Arryn, running a hand through her stringy brown hair, which fell below her shoulders.

"Maybe we'll need a day at the spa," Amy said, grinning.

"May I interrupt all these plans?" said Dr. Brian. "Are you both clear on your instructions?"

"Yes," said Amy, looking at Arryn, who nodded.

"And I'm very clear on them as well," said Todd.

"Then I'll leave you to get dressed. Nurse Beatrice will be in shortly with the written instructions and your discharge papers," said Dr. Brian. "Please take care."

"Dr. Brian," called Arryn.

When he turned around, she said, "Thank you so much."

"My pleasure," he told her. "Just don't make a habit of getting mugged or kidnapped, either of you."

"Believe me, they won't," said Todd, who stood to leave while Arryn got dressed.

Once Nurse Beatrice had been in and read them all their instructions yet again, she gave Arryn a hug and said they could all leave. Amy and Todd slipped on their coats, with Todd helping Amy with her cast and sling, and then Todd handed another coat to Arryn as Amy said, "This might not be the best fit, but it was all I could find. It's an old one of Hannah's, but it should work until we can replace your other coat."

"Thanks, Amy," said Arryn, as she slipped into the bright blue coat, which was a bit short and also a bit big around, but as Amy said, it would keep her warm, and that was what it was supposed to do.

When they got outside the hospital, Arryn was startled to see two large green dragons. Todd said, "Meet Jupiter," as he pointed to the larger of the two, "and Fern. We thought it would be less strenuous to fly home. The doctor said no exercise, which I think would include the fifteen-minute walk home."

"I've...I've..." stuttered Arryn. "I've never ridden on a dragon."

"Well, then," said Fern, "you're in for the time of your life."

Amy laughed and rubbed Fern's wing with her good arm. "You're incorrigible," she affectionately told her dragon.

"I take after my rider," said Fern.

"I believe we're supposed to be getting these two home," said Jupiter.

"Right," said Todd. He offered Amy an arm, and Arryn realized it couldn't be easy to get onto a dragon with a broken arm.

"If she'd let me," said Todd, "I'd just lift her up, but she's a stubborn one."

"Just like her husband," said Jupiter, with obvious affection in his rich, deep, musical baritone.

Once Amy was settled, Todd turned to Arryn and said, "I hope you'll be OK with my lifting you up behind Amy. Once you're better we'll teach you how to get up by yourself, but for now, may I?"

Arryn nodded, and Todd lifted her very gently around her waist and told her where to grab and when to sling a leg over. Amy said, "Just put your arms around my waist. Fern would never drop a passenger, but I suspect you'll feel safer if you hold on to me." Arryn grabbed Amy tightly around the waist. "Hey, you don't need to hold on that tightly," Amy said with a laugh.

As Arryn loosened her grip just a bit, Todd vaulted onto Jupiter, carrying Arryn's bag as well as Carnation.

Jupiter and Fern took off but didn't go very high. Arryn looked around and was amazed that she could see all of Havenshold. It felt weird to be in the air, but she also felt surprisingly safe, knowing somehow that Fern would never let her fall. In a matter of a few minutes, they were circling a large sandpit in the back of a sprawling home. Once the dragons had landed, Todd jumped down and helped first Arryn then Amy to the ground.

Amy muttered, "This blasted arm," but then she regrouped and said, "Right then, let me show you to your room first, Arryn, and then I think breakfast is at the top of our list."

"I'll make the breakfast," Todd said. "You show Arryn her room and whatever else she needs right now, and then I want the two of you on the couches in the family room. Breakfast will be served shortly."

Amy smiled, gave Todd a kiss, and told Arryn, "You know, he's enjoying this."

Todd handed Arryn her bag as well as Carnation, and Amy showed her into the kitchen through the back door, saying, "We almost never use the front door. Now your room is this way. We thought you'd like Emily's old room. That's what Lucy used until Harriet chose her. It's also where Chloe stayed for six years. They found it very comfortable, and I'm sure you will too."

Arryn followed Amy down a twisting hall, with rooms taking off at odd angles. As they walked, Amy said, "It's easy to get lost at first. That's what happens when a house is built randomly, but you'll get the hang of it in no time." She stopped in front of an open door that led into a purple room. "This will be your room."

Arryn looked around in wonder. There was a bed with a lovely purple quilt and a few stuffed animals. A dresser and shelves stood along two of the walls, with the shelves containing an assortment of books and more stuffed animals. She saw two doors on a third wall, and Amy opened one to show her the closet and another that led into a beautiful bathroom with purple fixtures.

"Wow," said Arryn.

"Thanks. We like it. Now why don't you put your bag down? And bring Carnation if you wish. We'd better find our way back to the family room before Todd starts hunting for us. He's going to be a bit overprotective for a few days, but I think we both really scared him. He'll grow out of it, but just bear with him until he does."

Arryn nodded, grabbed Carnation, and followed Amy to the room across from the kitchen. "As with almost everything here," Amy said, "this room also grew randomly. The couches are old but comfy. There are also a couple beanbag chairs, but personally I've never figured out a graceful way to get out of them. And there are some overstuffed chairs as well. Go ahead and pick a couch, and I'll grab us some comforters. Todd will have a fire going in the fireplace shortly, I'm sure."

"Did I hear you take my name in vain?" Todd said, as he entered the room carrying several comforters. "Here you go. I've got the fire already laid. I'll just put a match to it before I bring in breakfast."

Soon the three of them were settled very comfortably, enjoying omelets and hot tea.

"Everything to your liking?" asked Todd.

"Just perfect," said Amy, giving him a big smile.

"Delicious," said Arryn. "And thanks so much, both of you."

"Our pleasure," Amy said as Todd nodded.

It was three days before Dr. Brian was sure that Lena would live. Emily visited briefly every day, and once Lena was conscious and Dr. Brian agreed, Emily came and sat with her to discuss her future.

"I'm glad to see you're making progress," began Emily. "Dr. Brian says you'll heal, but it'll take a long time, especially your leg."

"Yeah, he told me the same thing," said Lena, sounding dejected. The had a large bandage covering the right side of her face where she'd been slashed and extending down her neck. Her right leg was encased in a blue plaster cast from her hip down to her ankle and it was elevated using ropes from a long bar above her bed.

"I'm afraid I have more bad news for you," Emily said.

"That's all I get," said Lena, sighing heavily. "All I've ever gotten."

"Your shop is gone," said Emily.

"Gone! Where?" shouted Lena, who tried to sit up but couldn't because of the angle of her leg.

"The volcano shook several times, and one of the quakes caused the shop to collapse right into the tunnel then into the cavern. Everything was destroyed."

"All my pots? Even the rainbow pot?" moaned Lena.

"I'm sorry, but yes, everything," said Emily. After a few moments, she went on. "Unfortunately that isn't all of it. Damian and Frank torched your home before they set out for the kidnapping."

"They did what?" said Lena, staring at Emily in disbelief.

"They burned your house to the ground. Nothing could be saved."

"But they lived there too. I gave them a home. I tried to help. How could they?"

"They were wanted criminals from Forbury. They robbed a number of mines there."

"I didn't know that," said Lena, shaking her head in denial. "They just said they'd lost their jobs and had nowhere to go. And I needed their help. I thought it would work out, but it never does, not for me."

"Lena, they were really evil. They weren't just petty crooks."

"Did they get away?"

"No, they were killed in a tunnel collapse," said Emily. "The volcano was very angry."

"Volcanoes can't be angry," Lena said, looking puzzled.

"This one can. We're learning a lot about her, thanks to a young girl named Rya."

"*Her*?"

"Yes. Her name is Jaluhz. She was very upset by all the anger and hatred that was going on inside her, with you and Damian and Frank. That's why she shook. She was trying to get rid of the evil."

Lena shook her head. "So why am I even alive? You're making this up."

"No, I'm not. We're still working on figuring all this out, but my guess is that Jaluhz knew just how bad Damian and Frank were. So she killed them. But she kept a pocket open for Arryn and you. Again I'm guessing. I haven't had enough time to talk with Rya, and I'm guessing Rya hasn't gotten a clear picture yet either, but I think Jaluhz tried to save Arryn, and since Arryn tried to help you, Jaluhz saved you as well."

"Poppycock," said Lena.

"Think what you like, but believe me, most of the tunnels in that area were completely filled. You and Arryn were in a very small pocket, the only surviving pocket after Jaluhz's tremors— tremors that were very specific in their impact."

"What about—"

"About this?" said Emily, as she held a large green emerald in her hand.

"That's mine," said Lena, as she tried to move to grab it.

"Lena, you know what you were doing was illegal. This isn't yours."

"But it's my retirement, and Damian and Frank stole it from me. It's mine."

"No," said Emily with sadness in her voice. "If you want to apply that reasoning, it should be Arryn's, as she got it out of that tunnel you forced her into, but it isn't hers either."

"She tried to save me," said Lena slowly. "Even after all I did to her. Damian killed her, didn't he?"

"Thankfully, no. He knocked her unconscious, but she's fine now, and she's in a lovely foster home with Amy and Todd. She's going to get schooling and a new start on life. Which brings me to you."

"I've lost everything," Lena sobbed.

"So now you have no choice. Dr. Brian will be keeping you here until he's sure you're stable. He's checking out your heart as well as your injuries. Once he releases you, I've reserved a ground-floor apartment for you at the Havenshold Boardinghouse."

"I can't pay for that. I don't have a cent to my name."

Emily tossed the emerald into the air then pocketed it before saying, "So now you have no choice but to be sensible. I've been trying for years to work with you, and you've always been too proud and too stubborn to accept help. This emerald is going into Havenshold's benevolence fund, and your rent and whatever else you need will be paid from that."

"Have it all figured out, have you?" said Lena. "Poor stupid Lena can't take care of herself."

Emily shook her head. "That's not what I think. You want to know what I think? I think you're a remarkable woman who's struggled for way too long. You've suffered so much, yet you still keep fighting. I admire your spirit. But honestly, Lena, you've also got a lot of problems because of your early abuse. You don't feel you deserve to be loved or helped. You push people away whenever they try to get close to you. Well, fate's handed you an opportunity."

"An opportunity?" snapped Lena, waving a hand at her leg.

"Yes, an opportunity. Sometimes people have to reach the very bottom, losing everything that matters, before they can change. You've hit that spot. I'm offering you a helping hand, as will others. What you do with this chance to turn things around is up to you. If you can put your anger and defensiveness aside, I think you'll find the world can be pretty wonderful."

"Yeah, right," said Lena.

Nurse Beatrice walked in then. "That's enough for today, Emily," she said. "Lena needs a lot of rest."

Emily nodded. "Just think about it, Lena. Please. For your sake. I'll be back. That you can count on."

Lena turned her head away, and Nurse Beatrice walked out with Emily.

"She's a tough cookie," said Nurse Beatrice. "I hope you don't mind, but I eavesdropped on your conversation. Thought it might help me help her."

"I think your brand of tough love will work on Lena, if anything can," said Emily. "Keep me posted, and I'll stop by at least once a day while she's here."

"Dr. Brian has arranged for a therapist from Alfredsville to come next week and start seeing her. She needs all the help we can give her. Her body will mend, but she needs a new way to see the world."

— 11 —

THE NEW YEAR

After Emily left the hospital, she headed to the library to talk with Chloe. Once she was seated across from Chloe's desk and Chloe had handed her a mug of her favorite ginger tea, Emily said, "I just talked with Lena. Dr. Brian says that if there aren't any complications, she'll make a pretty good recovery. She'll probably always have a limp because of the severity of the break, and she'll also have a scar across her cheek and down her neck, but she's lucky to be alive."

"I'm glad," said Chloe.

"I told her about her home and her shop. She took it really hard of course. I think that shop was her life."

"You know," said Chloe as she lifted her tea mug for another sip, "I get why the shop is gone. The volcano—I mean Jaluhz— had every right to protect herself. But why did Damian and Frank feel they had to burn down Lena's home? That was just real spite."

"I agree," said Emily, using her tea mug to warm her hands. "Maybe they were trying to remove evidence, but I suspect they were getting back at Lena. She isn't the easiest person to be around. And obviously they were using her to hide out. They were scamming her, and the final insult was to burn her home.

It wasn't even much of a house. It was rat infested and filthy. I was in there once. But it was all she had—that and the shop."

"So she'll have to accept some help now," said Chloe.

"Yep," said Emily, looking down at her mug. "I got her an apartment at the boardinghouse. Dr. Brian's arranging for physical and mental therapy. We'll see. But as I was talking to Lena, trying to make her see this as an opportunity, I told her about Jaluhz. I also showed her the emerald and said it would go in the benevolence fund."

"Bet she didn't like that," said Chloe with a chuckle.

"No, she shouted that it was hers. I told her the volcano saved her life—she'd better not get greedy and try to go back there. But then I got to thinking. I told Lena that to try to help her change. But did Jaluhz save Arryn and hence Lena? Have you talked with Rya? What does she think?" asked Emily as she drank her tea.

"I haven't yet, but Harmony and Rya asked to see me, and they'll be here shortly. I've tried to give Rya some space to recover and settle in. If you could've seen her clinging to Harmony when the baron, Oswald, and Harmony arrived at the hospital the other night, well, you'd see she's really been shaken."

"I hadn't thought about that," said Emily, frowning slightly, "but suddenly she's got people relying on her ability to read a volcano."

"And she was trying to rescue a friend from an underground prison. That's way too close to what Rya herself went through just a few weeks ago."

"That's right," said Emily, crossing her legs the other way. "I hadn't picked up on the parallel. Poor kid."

"And Rya and Arryn really did seem to click right from the beginning. Arryn likes Aster also, and I think the three will be good friends, but there's something special about the bond between Rya and Arryn. Anyway, I just figured Rya could use some space."

Emily nodded. "I guess there's no immediate urgency, but I'd sure like to know what's happening."

Chloe shook her head. "No, when Bertha popped in briefly the other night, she said nothing would happen until fall. So I figured if Bertha could hibernate, then Rya could have a few days off."

"Definitely," said Emily. "But really, what do you think? A sentient volcano named Jaluhz?"

"I know," said Chloe, with a wry smile. "It's a lot to take in. We do know our planet is sentient, though, so it makes sense."

"Yeah," said Emily. "The planet brought King Alfred back in time. But that was over five hundred years ago. Five hundred and nearly forty-one, to be precise. I wasn't living then. But now I had to orchestrate a rescue with Esmeralda, getting advice long distance from Oswald, while a young girl tells me a volcano is sad. Somehow it's different when it's right in my backyard."

Chloe laughed. "Yes, it is." She stood up and got more tea for them both.

"But what to you think about what I told Lena? Do you think Jaluhz really did save Arryn?" said Emily as she held her mug for a refill.

"Well, we all saw that tiny space where Arryn and Lena were trapped. And both Oswald, seeing it through Esmeralda's eyes, and Gregory said the space shouldn't have been there. It should have been part of the collapse. So I'd say you're right. Want to stay and ask Rya? They should be on their way."

"Well, just for a few moments," said Emily. "I don't want to take away from their time with you, but I'm so curious. While we wait, tell me...how are your preparations coming for the start of school? Have all the out-of-town students arrived?"

"Yes, and we have six from outside Havenshold this year, along with two from Havenshold. I've found lodging for all six of them, and most of them still have their parents here with them through New Year's," Chloe said as she looked at some papers on her desk.

"I'm sure it's gratifying to find parents supporting their students," said Emily.

Chloe nodded and set one file aside. "I only have one student whose parents stormed in here, dropped their son off, and said they had to get back to manage their farm that their son thought he was too good for."

"Oh, that's sad," said Emily, frowning.

"Very sad. But I have Ernest staying with a lovely family with a son the same age, and I think Joan, the mom, fully grasps the situation and will be a big supporter of Ernest. It should all work out."

"Well, let me know if I can help in any way. You do such a fantastic job with these young people."

"Thanks. I really appreciate your support, Emily."

Just then Harmony tapped on Chloe's open office door, and Chloe waved them in. "Great to see you all," said Chloe, as Harmony, Rya, and Artemis found seats.

"Hi," said Emily. "I'm not going to stay, but Rya, I wanted to ask you something."

Rya sat on the couch with Harmony on one side and Artemis on the other. "Sure," she answered with only a slight bit of hesitation.

"Well, it's about Jaluhz. I was talking with Lena, and I made something up, or I thought I did, about Jaluhz saving Arryn and Lena, but then I got to thinking. We all saw the space they were in, a space that really shouldn't have been open. What do you think?"

Rya was quiet for a few moments before she said, "I think Jaluhz didn't want Arryn to get hurt. I don't get any idea that

Jaluhz cares about Lena especially, but she doesn't feel about Lena the way she did about Damian and Frank. Lena was so close to Arryn when they were trapped—if Arryn was going to be safe, then so was Lena. At least that's what I think."

Satisfied with the explanation, Emily nodded. As she stood she asked, "Why do you think Jaluhz cared about Arryn? Does she care about us? As people I mean?"

Rya cheeks turned pink, and she finally said, "I think Jaluhz saved Arryn because of me, because Arryn is my friend, and I care about her."

"Ah," said Emily nodding at Chloe. "That makes sense."

Rya rubbed Artemis's fur before going on, "But I also think that overall, as long as people don't harm her—as long as she doesn't have to feel anger and hatred inside her the way she did with Damian and Frank—well, I think she doesn't want to hurt any part of this planet."

"Nice to know," said Emily, "*very* nice to know actually. Well, thanks, Rya. And nice to see you, Harmony. I'm so glad the baron and Oswald could bring you along for a visit."

"So am I," said Harmony, patting Rya's hand. "It's good to have a few days with family. Clyde and Aster are busy cooking, and it's fun having us all together."

Emily laughed. "That's so true. Gregory and I always eat well when the baron comes to town. And we're spending more time with Lance as well, catching up and relaxing. Who couldn't enjoy time with Oswald? He keeps us all amused and happy. I assume we'll be seeing you all at the New Year's festivities tomorrow?"

"Definitely," said Harmony, smiling warmly. "See you then."

After Emily left, Chloe moved over to one of the chairs next to the couch and asked, "Can I get anyone anything?"

Harmony and Rya shook their heads, while Artemis merely tipped hers questioningly. Chloe laughed and reached for the biscuit tin she always kept on hand for visiting dogs, cats, and now a fox. "Would you like a bit of something, Artemis?" she asked.

"Please," Artemis answered, "and thank you."

Chloe took a biscuit out of the tin and handed it to Artemis, who took it in her teeth and hopped off the couch. She sat on the floor at Rya's feet and crunched it happily.

"So, Harmony," said Chloe, "you said you wanted to see me about something. How can I help?"

Harmony nodded and said, "I want to understand Rya's gift so I can help her more. She said she talked with Bertha, but she was pretty uncertain what it all meant."

Chloe looked over at Rya with a grin. "Truth be known, Bertha has that effect on all of us."

"Really?" said Rya, sounding relieved.

Nodding, Chloe said, "Yes, really and truly. I was your age when I first met her. I ran away after the dragon hatching when I wasn't chosen. My mother was yelling and screaming at me, saying that I'd ruined my sister's chances to be a dragon rider and that I'd ruined the family and finally, that she was disowning me, and well, it was pretty horrible. I was sure everyone was laughing at me and that I was the biggest failure ever."

"You?" asked Rya.

"Yes, me. And the egg hatchings always take place during the winter solstice, so it wasn't exactly warm out. I ran and ran until I couldn't run anymore. Then, as I was reading a heart-felt letter my father had managed to slip into my candidate robes before I took off, I heard a shot then saw a mother bear with her two cubs running toward me. A hunter was taking aim, and without even thinking, I yelled, 'Stop.' He fired his gun again, but to my total amazement, the bullet hit an invisible shield and bounced off. That's how I met Bertha, and that's how I learned I'm a mage. I had no idea where my power came from. I don't even know why I yelled at the man—except everyone knows that bears are a protected species—but I did, and that was the start of my true path."

"That's amazing," said Rya, with wonder in her voice. She sat up a bit straighter, and her forehead wrinkled in concentration. "It's kinda like when I saved my school from the mudslide. I didn't really know what I was doing, and I'd been wrong before about what was going to happen. I had no idea how I knew the mudslide was coming."

"Exactly," said Chloe, as she put her right foot on her left knee. "Our experiences aren't that different. You're just beginning to grow into your true self and have a lot left to learn. Bertha is actually a terrific teacher, but as you said earlier, sometimes she can leave you more confused than when you started."

"No kidding," said Rya, with a chuckle. "All her talk about seers and so on."

"Yes, that was a bit convoluted," said Chloe, reaching for her tea mug that she'd put on the corner of her desk. "If I understood her correctly, she was saying that while your gift is very different from hers, you still can predict natural things like the weather. This isn't the same as knowing that our planet will be in danger six years in the future, but in a way, I see some similarities. You can tell when things are going to happen for instance."

Rya shrugged. "I guess."

"What's this about her training with Bertha in the summer?" asked Harmony. "Rya mentioned that to me."

"Bertha suggested that, and I think it would be a good plan. By then Rya will have had time to settle in, start her apprenticeship, and feel comfortable. If anyone can help Rya expand her gift, it would be Bertha."

"Well, I really like Bertha, and I have the greatest respect for her," Harmony said. "I just don't want Rya to undergo too many changes right now. She's still reeling from what happened in the fall."

"I'm OK, Grandma," said Rya, turning a bit pink with embarrassment.

"Yes, you are," said Harmony, patting Rya's knee, "but all this has been a lot to take in."

"For sure," said Chloe, in agreement. "Why don't we just wait and see what things look like come summer?"

"Sounds good," said Harmony. "By the way, I'm planning to move back to Havenshold."

"You are?" said Chloe, her eyes widening in surprise. "That would be great!"

"Yes, now that I'm back with my family, I want to be around for them. Clyde seems pleased about it, as long as I'm not living with him. The baron showed me a small parcel of land on his estate that isn't being used. He said I was welcome to move my animal sanctuary there. It's several miles outside Havenshold, so I won't be on top of Clyde, but I'll be close by for Rya and Aster, when she's not out on a mission."

"That sounds perfect," said Chloe. "But what about your island? And the home Clyde just finished up for you?"

"It'll all still be there, and maybe I'll summer there. I just don't know. But there's a cottage on the parcel that the baron would allocate to me, enough for me to live in. It used to be the home for a retired farmhand who passed away several years ago. Lance has offered to lend a hand with fencing off some areas for my rescued animals, so I think it'll all work out."

"It'll be wonderful, Grandma," said Rya, with genuine warmth in her voice.

"I hope so, and I always can return to Sanctuary if this doesn't work out."

"So when will you move?" asked Chloe. "Is there anything I can help with?"

"I hope to be back within the month," Harmony told her. "I'll leave the day after tomorrow, just as Rya starts her apprenticeship. The baron and Oswald have offered their assistance in ferrying my animals over to the baron's place in Forbury, and then I'll arrange transport to bring them here."

"Well, keep me posted, and know that we'll all be looking out for Rya," said Chloe, uncrossing her legs.

"And she and I have been practicing her telepathy so she knows she can reach me whenever she needs or wants to," Harmony said as she stood.

Chloe and Rya stood also. "Thanks, Chloe," Rya said.

"Enjoy the rest of the holiday. I'm sure I'll see you both at the festivities," said Chloe.

"Yes, and Arryn is going to be able to come. Isn't that fantastic?" said Rya.

"It certainly is," said Chloe.

The next morning, New Year's Day, dawned bright, clear, and cold. It was a perfect day for skating on a pond at the edge of town. All kinds of food and craft booths were set up in the courtyard in front of the library, so Chloe didn't have to go far to enjoy the goings on. The courtyard was crammed with people from Havenshold and surrounding villages. She ran into friends, new students, and parents until she was exhausted. Everyone was nice, and they all wanted to share their latest news, but after a bit, Chloe decided to take a walk.

She strolled past the marketplace, where everything was closed up for the holiday. If any of the merchants wanted to sell their wares during a festival such as this, they always set up a booth with the others. As a result Chloe had a peaceful walk past the shops with no crowds. She stopped when she came to the hole that had been Lena's shop. No one had had time to do anything about it except rope it off.

This looks horrible as well as dangerous, thought Chloe. She closed her eyes and envisioned an open space with a few benches in the spot where Lena's shop had been, a space between the two adjoining shops. She then envisioned the walls to the adjoining shops as they should be, whole and painted, solid and safe. She felt the magic flowing around her as the area transformed to match her vision. When she was done, she opened her eyes and saw everything was as she'd wanted. She was tired, so she sat on one of the benches she'd created.

Emily walked past and noticed Chloe. "Just couldn't wait, could you?" she said with a laugh. "I was going to get a crew working on this tomorrow."

Chloe smiled. "I hated to see it. I don't know if anyone will want to build another shop here, but I thought this would keep things nice and safe until something is decided."

"You're right of course," Emily said as she sat beside Chloe. "I'm glad you did this. Somehow a mage working to repair the damage from a hurt volcano seems very fitting."

Chloe laughed and said, "I suppose so. Sometimes I want to do more than I really should. I mean, I could have just rebuilt Lena's store, but really, it's not my place to do that or to decide what she might do at this point."

"I get it," said Emily, patting Chloe's arm. "Magic isn't supposed to be a substitute for what we can do ourselves. And Lena will not be up to running a store for a long time, maybe never. She's close to retirement age anyway, and her health is far from good. I think your solution is excellent."

They talked for a bit, and Chloe mentioned that Harmony was moving back to the area. "Yes, I know," Emily said. "The baron won't stop talking about it. Those two are becoming really good friends, and I suspect we'll be seeing more of the baron and Oswald as well."

"Well, they both deserve the best," said Chloe. "Where's Gregory?"

"He's with the baron, Oswald, and Lance, and the plan is for all of us to meet up with Clyde and his family for dinner. I just needed a break from the crowds."

"That was my plan too. If one more person invites me for dinner before the fireworks, I'll scream."

Emily chuckled. "So many people think that being alone means being lonely. Anyway, I won't invite you, although I hope you know you'd be most welcome."

"Thanks, Emily. I think I'll just head home and spend the rest of the afternoon with Calliope. I'll be at the fireworks display tonight, and I love the fact that it gets dark so early. The summer fireworks are always so late, and I have the opening day of Pathfinder tomorrow."

— 12 —
FIRST DAY

As the new-student orientation began, Chloe looked around the table that she'd set up in the main area of the library, where the nine new students sat. Each of them had a notebook and pen provided for them in case they wanted to jot something down. There were five young women, including Arryn, and four young men, including Ernest. Most of them were just sitting nervously, looking around the library, not chatting, which wasn't surprising since most of them didn't know each other yet. The two students from Havenshold sat together occasionally whispering quietly, but even they looked nervous. Chloe wasn't surprised that the students were on edge since Pathfinder Academy was a small school, relatively new, that took a very different approach to helping teens find their path. These students were the ones who didn't take a traditional approach of following in the footsteps of their parents or other family members. Thankfully all but Ernest and Arryn were coming from supportive environments, which made Chloe's job much easier. She noticed that Ernest was sketching on a piece of paper and from what Chloe could see, the drawing looked really advanced. Chloe would wait until their individual meetings to find out more about them, but she was pleased by the way the students were quiet and attentive. She thought that boded well for their commitment to the school.

Chloe stood to welcome them all and once again, as she'd done in her previous orientations, after a few comments regarding how Pathfinder Academy worked, she spent most of the time sharing how she, Lucy, and Gretchen had found their paths. She was so grateful that each year Lucy and Gretchen were willing to take part in the orientation. Certainly they each had a unique story to share, and she hoped their stories would help these students—all of whom were uncertain about what they wanted to do or even who they were—realize that everyone has a story to tell, and sometimes it takes time to figure out what you want to do in life.

Chloe had just finished sharing her story and was introducing Lucy when the front library doors flung open, and Emily and Clyde, a tall man with broad shoulders, brown hair that, like Aster's, stuck up in the back and brown eyes, rushed in. Arryn looked at them in alarm as they went over to Chloe. Emily whispered in Chloe's ear, "Something's wrong with Rya. We need you to come with us to the hospital."

Chloe nodded and stood, turning to Lucy and Gretchen. "Could you two finish this orientation then talk with the students over snacks? You know the drill."

Lucy said, "Don't worry, Chloe. We'll take care of everything."

Chloe turned to the students. "I'm sorry. Something's come up, and I have to leave, but Lucy and Gretchen will finish the meeting, and there's plenty of food to eat afterward. Please stop by the library again later this afternoon, and check the message board outside my office. I'll have posted the times for our individual meetings, which will take place tomorrow. Thank you."

Arryn, who was sitting closest to Chloe and had overheard just a bit of Emily's remarks asked, "Is Rya OK?"

"I'm going to check on her," Chloe said. "The best thing for you to do is listen to Lucy and Gretchen. As soon as I know anything, I'll let you know."

Chloe snatched her coat from her office and hurried out of the library with Clyde and Emily.

"What's happened?" she asked as they rushed toward the hospital.

"We don't know," said Emily.

As soon as they reached the hospital, Nurse Beatrice directed them to one of the examination rooms. Dr. Brian was in there with Rya, who was moving restlessly on the table. Artemis was next to her on the table with her front paws on Rya's chest, saying, "It's OK, Rya."

Dr. Brian looked up. "I had to give her a mild sedative," he said. "I couldn't get her to calm down any other way. And as you can see, she's still restless. Clyde, could you explain again what happened? I was too busy trying to stop her thrashing to hear what you said."

Clyde nodded. "Well, we officially started her apprenticeship this morning, and Rya seemed excited about it. I showed her everything in my workshop, and then we started her first project. She was leaning toward artistic woodworking, as she had done such a great job carving a fox before her graduation."

Artemis chimed in. "She was fine—she really was—and it was fun for us both. But then it went all wrong."

"All of a sudden, she sat down on a bench, holding her head and crying that it hurt so badly. Then she started thrashing, and she kept repeating 'Jaluhz, Jaluhz' over and over. I couldn't get her to stop thrashing, so finally I grabbed her up, holding her as tightly as I could, and ran over here with her."

Dr. Brian said, "Yes, Nurse Beatrice said you came panting through the door, and Rya was still thrashing and trying to get out of your arms. I've never seen anything like it."

"Artemis," Emily said, "you have the strongest telepathic bond with Rya. Can you tell us what she's thinking or seeing or anything?"

"I can't reach her the way I usually can. I'm frightened, so frightened. I can't find her. All I see is flames and lava everywhere, pouring out of Jaluhz."

Chloe placed a hand on Artemis's back and said, "We'll figure this out, but you must stay calm for Rya. Keep sending her your love and calming thoughts."

"I'll try," replied Artemis, keeping her paws on Rya.

Chloe turned to the others. "Obviously this has something to do with Jaluhz, but what?"

"Didn't Bertha assure us everything would fine until maybe fall?" asked Emily.

"What's wrong with my niece?" said Clyde, his large hands clenching and unclenching. "I don't understand."

"None of us does really," said Chloe. "But Rya's gift as an empath to the natural world apparently has connected her to the volcano."

"Yes, I know that, but why this? This is more than a connection."

"That's the understatement of the year," Dr. Brian said. "And I'm helpless to do anything. From what Artemis said, it seems as if the volcano is trying to communicate with us, and in the process she's taken over Rya's thoughts."

Suddenly the entire hospital shook, as a few bottles fell onto the floor next to Emily. They could hear shouts from the front of the hospital and a several crashes as things in other rooms fell. "A tremor," said Emily as she stooped to pick up the bottles, "and a big one. We need Gregory. Maybe he knows what's going on with Jaluhz."

Dr. Brian nodded. "I'm going to get Rya into a bed. We'll keep a close watch on her. That's about all we can do. And then I need to check on the rest of the hospital."

"I'm staying with her," Artemis said, nestling up to Rya on the table. "I won't leave her."

Clyde said, placing a hand on Artemis's back, "No one will argue with that, and I'll stay with you both. There's nothing else I can do. I don't know a thing about magic or volcanoes, but I love Rya, and maybe my presence can help her."

"I'm sure it will," said Chloe. "Emily, can we meet in your office? The orientation is still going on in the library, and I'd like to avoid a panic. Arryn already has picked up on some of this, but the other students seemed unaware of what was happening."

"That works," said Emily. "And I'll have Lucy and Gretchen meet us there as soon as they can."

"And could you please contact your mother and ask her to head over to Pathfinder to meet Arryn after the orientation? She and Rya are already really close, and I don't want Arryn under more stress."

"Excellent idea," said Emily, as she turned to leave the examining room.

"Hang in there, Rya," said Chloe, patting her shoulder. "We'll be back shortly."

As Dr. Brian and Nurse Beatrice wheeled the table Rya and Artemis were on out of the examining room, with Clyde opening doors along the way, Chloe and Emily left the hospital and headed to Emily's office. As soon as they arrived, Emily called out to Rupert, saying, "Can you find Gregory and bring him here? We have an emergency."

"Anything to do with that last tremor? We're getting reports of damage but so far nothing major."

"Most probably," said Emily, "and thanks for the report. Now get Gregory. We need him here now."

"Right," said Rupert, as he raced out of her office.

Gregory arrived a few minutes later. "I really need to be monitoring the volcanic activity right now," he said. "Can't this wait?"

"Not really," said Emily. Then she quickly updated him on what happened with Rya, concluding, "We're sure Rya's condition has something to do with what's going on with Jaluhz."

"Sounds like it, but I don't know what I can do to help. I can tell you that the seismic activity is much higher and that the pressure within Jaluhz is rising. I also can tell you that neither of these things bodes well for keeping the volcano calm."

Just then Esmeralda squeezed into the office, saying, "Something really bizarre just happened. I now have a new memory, but it's of something that happened soon after King Alfred arrived."

"What?" said Emily.

"How can that be?" said Chloe.

"I don't know," said Esmeralda. "I'm as bewildered as you. But suddenly I received a new memory from Sophia's time, something that she was a part of. She was talking to a girl who was only a shimmer, but in that shimmer, she looked a lot like Rya."

"Oh, no," said Chloe.

"I've contacted Matilda, and she also has this new memory. By the way, she and Queen Clotilda are on their way here now."

Gregory shook his head. "So you have a new memory of something old, and somehow Rya is involved."

"Sorry, Gregory," said Esmeralda. "It's making my head spin as well, but that's what I have. And I think this new memory must be related to whatever is happening with Jaluhz."

Just then Lucy and Gretchen arrived and were brought up to speed. Clotilda and Matilda arrived a few minutes later, with Rupert following them, trying to announce them. Clotilda, a tall handsome woman in her late seventies, with short grey hair and wire framed glasses, swept into the room followed closely by Matilda, a gorgeous purple dragon, deeper in color than Esmeralda and a bit larger as well.

"That's OK, Rupert," Emily said. "But please grab some paper and a pen and take notes for me."

Nodding, Rupert nod quickly took a seat between Emily and Esmeralda.

Matilda confirmed she had the same new yet old memory from a supposed interview between Sophia and a girl who looked like Rya.

Just as the time paradox was giving them all a headache, Rya walked into Emily's office with Artemis and Clyde.

"Rya," said Chloe. "How are you?"

"I'm fine now," said Rya, with a grin on her face. "After Artemis helped me convince Dr. Brian that I'm back in my own body, he let me go. I had to get over here and tell you what happened. It was all so weird."

Emily looked around her now very crowded office and said, "Everyone, try to find a place to sit and make yourself comfortable, and let's hear what Rya has to say. By the way, Rya and Artemis, I don't believe you've met Queen Clotilda and Matilda."

"Your Majesty," Rya said hastily, as Artemis bowed.

"No ceremony now," said Clotilda, waving one hand at her. "Just call me Clotilda. Now have a seat, young lady, and tell us your story."

Rya sat in a chair with Artemis in her lap; Clyde sat right next to her. Once everyone was settled, she took a deep breath and began. "Well, the day started out fine. I was with Uncle Clyde, choosing wood for a new carving project when I suddenly felt a sharp, searing pain in my head. I don't remember a lot after that, but I think I was shouting for Jaluhz."

"You were," said Clyde, worry etched across his face even now, "and you were thrashing around. You really had us scared."

"Sorry," said Rya. "Then I had this weird dream, although it wasn't like any dream I've ever had. I was standing in a courtyard in front of a building that looked something like the library, and a tall man was there as well, but mostly I noticed this lovely purple dragon. She didn't look like either of you, Esmeralda and Matilda. She was a bit different. Then I started asking her questions I didn't even know I had. I asked her about the world they came from and what the land looked like. She showed me images—terrible, frightening images I can't even describe."

"Don't try," Esmeralda said, moving her tail to a more comfortable position. "Some of us in this room have seen them. We know what horrors you witnessed. What happened next?"

"Well, I asked if the dragon knew anything about the volcano, and she said it was dead in the other world—dead after a horrible and violent eruption before the dragons came to that world. She didn't have any more information, but even that much seemed to scare me...or whoever was in my head with me. After that I seemed to fade away, and the next thing I knew, Artemis was licking my face, and I woke up in the hospital ward."

"Can you add anything to that, Artemis?" Chloe asked.

"A bit, I think. I was so scared after Rya collapsed because I couldn't sense her...you know, in her head."

Everyone except Clyde and Gregory nodded at that, since the rest of them were all bonded and telepathic. Clotilda looked at Artemis and said, "That must have been terrifying. I can't even imagine that."

Artemis, curling more tightly in Rya's lap, agreed. "Yes, it was. Clyde and I took Rya to the hospital, but they couldn't do anything. So I just sat on top of her in the bed. She was still restless, although the sedative had stopped the thrashing. Then suddenly I felt Rya back in her head where she belongs. That's when I started licking her. But I'm telling you, for a while she wasn't in her body at all."

"Gads," said Gregory, running a hand through his light brown hair. "And I thought my head was spinning before."

Chloe said, "Aster's going to have a fit that she's not here with us for this. But she and Jasmine left yesterday, didn't they?"

Emily nodded. "Yes, I sent them back out to the border, once their vacation was over. But if you need them, I can bring them back."

"Maybe," said Chloe, looking thoughtful, "but even though she'd be really interested, I don't think she knows any more about this than we do. You know, I've always wondered whether the planet knows about its alternate future."

"What do you mean?" asked Clotilda in a puzzled voice.

"Well, the planet protected itself by sending King Alfred and his companions back in time. We know that now. We also know the female purple dragons keep the memories for all dragons, and they've known about time travel, well, ever since Sophia's been around, I guess."

"That's correct," said Matilda, "but only the female purple dragons know—not all dragons—and we've guarded those memories."

"Quite so," said Chloe. "But why do you dragons hold the memories? Why doesn't the planet keep its own memories?"

"How do you know it doesn't?" asked Emily.

"Well, if it did, wouldn't the volcano already know all this? And if so, why did Jaluhz need to send Rya back in time?"

"Jaluhz remembers only one eruption," said Rya slowly. "At least that's what I'm feeling from her, and it was an eruption long before there was real life on this planet."

"That must have been the eruption," began Gregory, "that made Draconia the rocky land it is and created the outlying islands."

Rya nodded, her hands massaging Artemis's back. "Yes, that's the only one Jaluhz seems to find real. But now, with all that's happened to her with Damian and Frank and Lena, she's worried. She doesn't *feel* right, for lack of a better term. And she's heard about the riders traveling in time and wonders if there's something else from the past, something to do with her. It's all pretty vague, but I think that's why she needed to ask Sophia questions."

"Are you having any more luck communicating with her?" asked Chloe.

"Not a lot," admitted Rya, shaking her head, "although I do think she knows we're trying to help her."

"I'm wondering if Lena knows any more than she's told us," said Emily, and she looked over at Rupert to be sure he was keeping up with his notes. "I'm beginning to wonder if Damian and Frank did a lot more mining than we know."

"Do you think Libby might know anything more now?" asked Chloe. "Rya, you said you were outside a building that looked like the library."

Before Rya could answer, Clotilda said, "Matilda and I have to return to the capital shortly, but may I make some suggestions first?"

"Of course," said Emily, turning to Clotilda.

"Obviously I haven't been involved in this as much as you have, but it's clear that things have changed as far as Jaluhz is concerned. It's possible that she was due for another eruption. From what you've been able to figure out from the timeline, I think this may be about the time she erupted in the alternate world, right?"

Emily nodded. "That's what Aster's calculations estimate, and Bertha apparently thinks that as well, but with an eruption in the fall."

"So something has happened to speed things up, and the only thing we know that has changed is Lena's mining operations. My suggestion would be to interview Lena further, search for any other possible mining sites, and finally pick Libby's brain. I'd be really interested to hear if she also has a new memory from the past. It really makes my head hurt to say that, but you know what I mean," Clotilda concluded, massaging her temples.

"I agree," said Emily. "We have three different avenues to pursue, and we need to pursue them all."

"Great. Well, keep me posted," said Clotilda. She and Matilda stood and carefully made their way to the door, stepping over Esmeralda's tail and squeezing past the couch as everyone in the room said good-bye. "And if we can help at all, please let us know."

"I've never felt anything so strange before," said Matilda, "as I felt with a new memory sliding into my head. I didn't know that was even possible."

"I agree," said Esmeralda, "and if it never happens again, it'll be too soon."

"One thing that hasn't been mentioned is the mole network," Lucy said, once Clotilda and Matilda had left. "I'm going to try to find out if they can help, either to let us know where other digging sites might be or where the pressure is building... maybe even both."

"I'll help you with that," said Gretchen, as she and Lucy stood. "I may not be able to speak 'mole,' but I can chart whatever you find out."

"And I'm going to get back to my seismic records," said Gregory, squeezing past the couch.

As Lucy, Gretchen, and Gregory filed out of the office, Chloe and Emily looked at Rya with concern. "How are you feeling?" Emily asked her.

"I'm OK. I mean, it really was strange, and the headache at the beginning wasn't nice at all, but I think Jaluhz realized she was forcing her way into my head and that it was too much. I really like her, you know. She's...I don't know...different. I can't explain it, but I want to help her so much."

"Well, you can't help her if you don't get some rest," said Clyde, standing and offering her a hand up.

"You've got that right," said Artemis, as she jumped off Rya's lap. "We need to get you home. You've had quite a day."

Chloe nodded. "Quite a day indeed. Traveling more than five hundred years back in time and talking to King Alfred's dragon Sophia."

"I envy you, Rya," Esmeralda said, as she shifted herself into a more open space now that Matilda had left. "Maybe some-time we could talk, and you could tell me what she was like."

"Certainly," said Rya. a note of wonder in her voice. "I'd like that."

"But first you're going to go home and rest," said Clyde, with a determined voice.

"Yes, Uncle Clyde, I promise, but first I have to let Arryn know I'm OK."

"How about I ask my mom to bring Arryn over to see you for a bit?" Emily suggested. "That way you can head home now. I think Clyde and Artemis are right—you need food and rest."

"OK, if that's all right with your mom and Uncle Clyde."

Clyde said, "Of course," and the three of them headed for the door, with Artemis leading the way. As they reached it, Clyde turned to Emily and Chloe. "Thank you," he told them, "both of you. I feel so helpless when magic is involved. I really do appre-ciate the way you watch over both Rya and Aster. Thanks."

"Our pleasure," said Emily, with a warm smile and a twinkle in her brown eyes.

Once everyone but Chloe had left, Emily turned to Rupert. "Were you able to get everything down in your notes?"

"Yes, although I suspect no one else would be able to read my abbreviations. I'll work my notes up into a complete read-able copy by the end of today."

"Thanks, Rupert. You're a lifesaver." Emily looked at Chloe. "Yikes. I don't think either of us ever stopped for lunch."

"I know I didn't, and now it's nearly four in the afternoon," said Chloe.

"How about we go out for something to tide us over?" Emily suggested.

"Nice idea," said Chloe. "We sure deserve it."

— 13 —

MENACE

After their quick late lunch at the tea shop next to the ice cream parlor, Chloe thanked Emily and said good-bye. Then she headed back to the library, realizing she still had to create the schedule for tomorrow's individual student conferences. *Heavens, did this day start with orientation? What a day.*

She settled in at her desk as Calliope landed on top of her papers. *Where have you been all day?* she said with a hint of irritation. *I had to run the library all by myself.*

"I'm sorry. I'll fill you in this evening. But I'm sure you ran things admirably as always."

Of course, said Calliope smugly, as she settled on top of Chloe's papers and groomed herself.

Chloe smiled as she pulled out the school roster, which was all she needed for the moment, and began to draft the schedule for tomorrow's meetings with the nine new students. The meetings would last forty-five minutes each, with a fifteen-minute break between. That way if any meeting ran long, it wouldn't throw the entire schedule off.

A few students stopped by, looking for the schedule, and Chloe waved them into her office to give them their time slots.

"I'm sorry I had to leave orientation this morning. Do you have any immediate questions?"

They assured her that they were fine and that Lucy and Gretchen had covered the basics. Then they made note of their conference times and left. Chloe made sure she gave the first appointments of the day to those she had talked to personally since she was posting the list a lot later than she'd anticipated. *I don't like it when things aren't just the way I planned them. I hope the orientation really did go all right for the students.*

You worry too much, said Calliope.

"I know. Well, I've done all I have to do," Chloe said, as she posted the list on the board outside her office, turned out the lights, and shut the door.

As she and Calliope walked to the back of the library to the door to their apartment, Chloe noticed that Gregory was still in his office working. She stopped in to say good night.

"Are you about done for the night?" asked Chloe.

Gregory looked up from his calculations and shook his head. "Hi, Chloe. I really should go home. I keep thinking that if I look at the numbers one more time, they'll suddenly make sense."

"I'm afraid none of this makes any sense. But maybe a good dinner and a peaceful night's sleep will help. That's what I'm hoping anyway. I've arranged for a breakfast meeting with Libby. If I discover anything, I'll let you know."

"Thanks," said Gregory, standing up and reaching for his coat. "I think this whole time-travel thing has messed with my mind. Rya is one strong young lady, isn't she?"

"Yes, she is, and I'm so glad Harmony will be moving here. Do you know what your father has in mind as far as a time schedule?"

"Emily contacted Harmony today after what happened to Rya, and Harmony and my dad are working on moving the time frame up. The details aren't all set yet, but Emily told me Dad will help Harmony pack then leave several of his men to arrange for the transport of the three goats, numerous chickens, several sheep, and lots of dogs and cats. I'm not sure of the exact count, but the plan seems to be to get Harmony settled in over the next week or so, rather than having her wait for her animals to arrive."

"Oh, that's good news," said Chloe, relief evident in her voice. "I really felt for Clyde today. He obviously cares about Rya, but once again he's smack in the middle of all this magic stuff, as he calls it, and he seems totally confused. Well, we're all confused, but he's the only one involved in this situation who isn't telepathic at all and has no magical abilities."

"I can't imagine how tough that has to be. I don't know for sure," Gregory said, "but I suspect Emily will try to get Aster and Jasmine home to help support both Rya and Clyde if this situation escalates. They do a marvelous job of touring the small villages, making folks aware of what dragons and dragon riders do, taking care of those in need, and they may have to spread the word about the volcano if we think an eruption is imminent. But if not, I think Emily will reassign them to Havenshold for the duration of this crisis."

"We'd both better call it a night," said Chloe, turning to leave the office.

Nodding in agreement, Gregory said, "For sure, and thanks for letting me rattle on. I'm really worried. If we have a volcanic eruption, well, it will destroy not only Havenshold but in all probability, all of Draconia."

Gregory left the library, and Chloe and Calliope settled on the couch in their apartment for dinner and snuggles before heading off to bed.

The next morning Chloe showered and dressed quickly before she and Calliope went into Libby's apartment for an early breakfast. Libby was knitting away in her chair, and the breakfast was all laid out for Chloe and Calliope. Once they were settled, Chloe asked, "So do you have a new memory like Esmeralda and Matilda do?"

"Yes," said Libby. "I'll tell you about it if you keep eating. You have a long day ahead of you with nine students to see, and I didn't notice a lunch break anywhere on your eight-to-six schedule."

Chloe waved her hand offhandedly. "Oh, I'll grab a bite during one of my fifteen-minute breaks." However, she did settle in to a mushroom and cheese omelet with toast, followed by a large blueberry pancake. Calliope had her own bowl with her favorite kibble, so they were both most content.

"Right then," began Libby, her knitting needles clacking away. "Where to begin? First off I was as surprised as Esmeralda and Matilda. I'd never received new memories about the past before. I honestly don't even know how that happens, and for me to admit that is saying a lot.

"I don't know a great deal about the sentient nature of our planet. How sentient is she? Does she keep up with day-to-day doings or just the general big picture? Is she the way I was before Gregory opened Pathfinder Academy inside me? I had become really sleepy. Oh, I was alert enough in King Alfred's day, but as the years went by and people rarely came inside, I sort of fell asleep. But now I have an entirely new life, thanks in large measure to you. I'm very alert, and I can even reach outside my actual walls and take in what's going on in the outside world."

Libby looked at Chloe over the top of her glasses and smiled before continuing. "So is the planet like that? Does she fall asleep, so to speak, when things are going as they should, and then wake when she's in trouble? I don't know. Does she remember the alternate world, where she was being killed?"

"We've wondered about that," said Chloe, as she finished her omelet and started on her pancake.

"I simply don't know. We do know that each time the planet was in danger she took action. First she brought dragons into existence and made them so they'd bond with humans in a magical and mystical way. Then she brought them back in time—not once but several times—each time going farther back in her history. The last of these time travels was the one we're familiar with, when King Alfred arrived and he and the dragons took over the land of Draconia, giving us four nations, each protected by magically bonded creatures."

Libby pushed her glasses up higher on her nose and paused to count her stitches before continuing. "But does Jaluhz remember what she escaped from? The evidence we're getting from her would suggest that she doesn't. Rya feels—and I think she's right—that Jaluhz only remembers one very ancient eruption. We do know volcanoes have cycles, and I'm becoming more and more certain that we're approaching a time when Jaluhz will need to erupt again.

"However, her actions yesterday in taking Rya back in time to talk with Sophia are indicative, I believe, of a growing awareness in Jaluhz. Just the way I slowly woke from my slumber, I think Jaluhz is doing the same. The planet instilled a greater and greater sense of service into the dragons and their riders with each trip back in time. So that means, it seems to me, that the planet wants humans to live here too. Given that supposition, I can see how Jaluhz would be worried about how her natural cycle will affect the planet as a whole—all the life that's now on it, life that wasn't there when she had what she believes to be her last eruption."

Chloe reached for her mug of tea. "So you think Jaluhz is becoming more sentient, more aware of what's going on around her?" Chloe asked.

"Yes, and that's why she wanted more information. I believe the time-travel episodes were powered by the planet using the volcano's energy. So then Jaluhz would have residual memories of her power bringing the riders here to our time. She just traced the trail back, so to speak, using Rya. But she wasn't aware of all the details, which is why a shimmering image of Rya was there, rather than her entire body."

Chloe sighed deeply. "Well, I hope Jaluhz learned what she wanted to know and doesn't try that again. Between her power and lack of technique, she really took a chance with Rya's safety."

"I agree," said Libby, putting her knitting down. "In a way, though, it was good that she didn't do a complete transport, because King Alfred was totally unaware of Rya's shimmer, and Sophia didn't share the conversation she had with Jaluhz through Rya. That keeps our timeline in tact, so as hard as it was on Rya, in the end it was the best possible way it could have happened."

Chloe finished the last bites of her pancake and put her dishes on the table next to her. "Well, if Jaluhz were able to communicate more fully with us," she said, "Esmeralda could have shared those images without Jaluhz needing to take Rya back in time."

"True," said Libby. "But think of Jaluhz as one of your students, awakening to a new potential but uncertain about how to use it, or what to do."

Chloe nodded. "I get it. That helps. And I hope that Rya and Jaluhz will develop a stronger bond, that Jaluhz will trust Rya, and most important, that Jaluhz is a quick learner so she can develop stronger communication skills now that we really need them. We all know Jaluhz is in trouble, but we have no idea how to help her."

Libby picked up her yarn again and examined the multicolored scarf she was knitting then said, "I'm betting she and Rya will work it out. Now you'd better get out of here. Your first student arrives in ten minutes."

Chloe stood and Calliope jumped off the couch. "Thanks, Libby. And thanks so much for breakfast. Everything was delicious."

Yes, thanks, Libby, said Calliope. *It was tasty as always.*

Chloe and Calliope headed out to the library and Chloe's office. When she arrived, her first student was waiting for her in the hallway. *As Libby said, it's going to be a long day,* she thought, *but an exciting and productive day as I get to know my new students.*

Emily was determined to have a chat with Lena, so while Chloe was busy interviewing students, Emily headed to the hospital. Seeing Nurse Beatrice at the front desk, she stopped to get an update on Lena.

"How's she doing?" she asked.

"She's improving physically," said Nurse Beatrice, her forehead wrinkled in concentration. "Her blood pressure has stabilized and the scars are healing. We've started having her try to move around on crutches, just short distances, and all that is going as well as can be expected. The big problem now is that she's so depressed. Dr. Brian is hoping to transfer her to her new apartment at the boardinghouse in the next day or so. He thinks she'll do better in a different environment, one where other people are around."

"Will she be able to manage on her own?" asked Emily, concern in her voice.

"Thankfully we have one of Chloe's students, Georgette, who started at Pathfinder last year and who wants to be a nurse. She's been training with me for most of the past year, and she's agreed to stay with Lena until she's better."

"I hope Georgette knows what she's getting herself in for," said Emily, with a sad shake of her head. "As you know, Lena isn't the easiest person to get along with."

"That's the understatement of the year," said Nurse Beatrice, "but Georgette has been working with Lena here, so she knows what she's like. Also, Martha, who runs the boardinghouse, has been brought on board as far as what Lena's been through and what her needs are, so Georgette will have some support there as well."

"And Dr. Brian still has the therapist coming as well, right?" said Emily.

"Right. He's arranging for physical and mental therapy for her."

"Well, it sounds like you've covered all the bases, and the rest will be up to Lena. Is it OK if I go in and see her?"

"Yes," said Nurse Beatrice. "I doubt she'll ever let on, but she looks forward to your visits. You and Georgette are about all she has now."

Emily headed into the ward, where Lena was the only patient. Lena, wearing pink hospital pajamas and a robe, was sitting up in bed with her leg, still in its cast, elevated on pillows. Her long grey and brown hair was tied back in a ponytail. She looked up as Emily approached. "Oh, you again," she said. "Can't stay away, huh?"

Emily smiled. "And miss your cheery disposition? Never."

Emily sat in the chair next to Lena's bed. "I hear you're going to be getting out of here and into your new apartment soon. That'll be nice."

"I guess," said Lena. "Doesn't much matter where I am now. Lost everything."

"Time to make a new start. But today I have to ask you some questions."

"What about? I don't know anything." Lena tried to twist away, but was unable to move much.

"About Damian and Frank and the mining you did on the volcano," said Emily.

"I told you all about that," Lena said defensively.

"Did you feel yesterday's earthquake?" Emily asked, trying to approach things from a different angle.

"Nearly knocked me out of bed," Lena huffed.

"Pressure is building inside the volcano, and we think it's a result of the mining. But we've checked the area where we found you and Arryn, and it looks OK. So we're wondering if Damian and Frank did more mining in other areas."

"Don't know. They worked for me eight hours a day, five days a week, but I don't know what they did on their days off."

"Did they make any friends?"

"How would I know?" Lena reached for a long thin stick which she then tried to stick down her cast to scratch an itch.

"Well, did anyone come around your place asking for them? After all, they did live with you, so wouldn't you have seen if anyone visited them?"

"Maybe," said Lena.

Emily gave her a little time to think. Finally she said, "So do you remember any of them?"

"I'm thinking," complained Lena, squirming to get more comfortable. "About a week or so before the accident, two guys did come to the house, now that you mention it."

"Did you know them?"

"Never saw them before," said Lena.

"Did you hear anything they said?"

"Just Damian yelling that he'd told them never to come there. Then he and Frank took off with them. That's the only time I saw anyone."

"What did they look like?"

"I don't know," snapped Lena. "I wasn't paying that much attention. They were just regular guys in work pants and shirts, nothin' special."

"Thanks, Lena. At least we know there were two other guys, and if Damian didn't want you to see them, well, they probably weren't just casual friends."

"What's the difference?" asked Lena.

"Well, it means there are probably other mining sites, and we have to find them before the volcano erupts."

"I don't know nothin' about that," said Lena, reaching for a glass of water on her bedside table.

"But at least we now can be pretty sure there are at least two more guys and that they were doing something that Damian didn't want you to know about."

"If I'd known, I would've demanded a cut. After all, I was giving them a home, and they were working for me."

"Exactly," said Emily, as she stood. "We've got to find those guys. I appreciate your help."

Lena shrugged. "Whatever."

Emily shook her head and turned to leave. "Things will get better, Lena, if you let them."

"Yeah, right," said Lena with heavy sarcasm.

After she left the hospital, Emily headed back to her office, where she met with Rupert. "We have to find a way to track those other two guys," she said after she'd updated him. "Any ideas?"

Rupert's deep blue eyes lit up in excitement. "Seems to me that Damian and Frank would've had a place to stash whatever gems he and Frank got from the volcano. There are a number of small caves on that side of the mountain, near where we rescued Arryn and Lena."

"I remember that now," said Emily, making some notes in her notebook. "They're too small to be of much use as dragon homes, so we've just left them alone."

"But what if Damian and Frank were using one of those caves to hide their loot? I don't know if these other two guys would know about it. If they do, then they've probably already taken whatever was there. But if Damian and Frank kept it secret, well, those two guys might be looking for it. If so, we might be able to find them."

"Good thinking," said Emily, smiling at Rupert's enthusiasm. "And we had the dragons flying over that area before the rescue, so that would have kept them from searching for any possible stash then. Do you think you and some of the others could set up a watch without tipping these two guys off?"

Rupert considered this for a few moments then said, "I can think of a couple spots where we could observe much of that side of the mountain without being seen."

"All right then," said Emily. "You and Whipper can be in charge of this. I'm guessing you'll want Hannah and Firebird to help."

"Just keeping it in the family," said Rupert with a coy smile.

"And your wife always has liked playing detective, even when she was small," Emily said. "As the youngest in our family, Hannah was always trying to find out what the rest of us were doing. OK, go for it, but don't tackle these men on your own. If you discover anything, let me know."

Rupert stood. "I promise," he said, clearly eager about this new assignment.

Once he'd left, Emily reviewed his notes from yesterday's meeting to see what else she could do before she headed to Gregory's office to check on his progress.

Gregory, Lucy, and Gretchen were hard at work in Gregory's office when Chloe walked by to meet with her first student. Gregory waved at her then turned back to his charts.

"So, Lucy, what do you have on the mole front?" he asked.

"We've gotten a hold of a few moles. Gretchen, do you have our map?"

"Right here," said Gretchen, as she pulled out a fresh map.

"Thanks," Lucy told her. "OK, here's what we've gotten since the meeting, and I'll start by saying it isn't much."

"I was afraid of that," Gregory said.

"But it's a start, and Gretchen and I are going back out as soon as we show you this," said Lucy, pointing at their new map. "We've been concentrating on the area of the mountain near the rescue site, working outward from it in a circular pattern. So far we've contacted five different moles, but their tales are all the same. Each of them has been disturbed by humans, with encounters similar to what Arryn felt when she was reaching for the emerald and came across a mole scurrying past her."

"Can you tell how recent these encounters are?" asked Gregory.

"That's the problem. Moles aren't good with time. They just give vague references to things like 'the other day,' so I'm not sure."

"What's your best guess? Do you think any of these encounters happened after the rescue?"

Lucy shrugged. "Maybe."

"Remember the mole you found last night?" said Gretchen, looking at the map on the table. "You seemed to think he had new information. He was right here," she concluded, pointing to a spot in the volcano that was the farthest from the rescue site.

"Oh, yeah. Thanks, hon," said Lucy. "Yes, as I said, we're moving outward, and this last mole did seem to think her encounter was yesterday. Again moles don't do time well, but she seemed pretty certain that it was a recent encounter. Since it's been nearly a week since the rescue, that might mean someone else has been in there."

"Excellent," said Gregory, after he'd made his own notes. "We really need to know that someone else is still involved or else we have no explanation for why the volcano remains so unhappy, no explanation for the increased pressure and seismic activity. I really want those things to be caused my humans, because we stand a chance of fixing human messes more than we do of stopping natural activities."

"And Jaluhz wouldn't be unhappy if an impending eruption were part of her regular cycle, would she?" asked Gretchen.

"I guess, but she might be if she were worried about what might happen to life on this planet," Gregory said. "But more than that, I'm putting my stock in Bertha, who said we had until fall to figure this out. The fact that things are heating up so soon—"

"Hey, nice pun," interrupted Gretchen, a big grin on her face.

"Unintentional, I assure you," said Gregory with a slight smile. "Anyway, the fact that we have a crisis now, months before we should have, leads me to believe that humans have interfered with the volcano."

"So we just have to find those humans and put right whatever they've done," said Lucy, as she and Gretchen stood. "We'd better get back out into the field and try to find more moles then."

"Thanks so much, you two," said Gregory, "and be careful."

Gregory went back to his charts after Lucy and Gretchen left. He'd been at it for several hours when Emily poked her head in to see how he was doing. He told her about Lucy's mole report and what Lucy and Gretchen were now doing.

"Sounds like you're making progress," Emily said. "Well, let me update you on what I learned from Lena."

When she was done, Gregory said, "So we're now fairly confident there are at least two more men involved in the illegal mining. I'm glad Rupert and Hannah are watching the mountain, but Lucy and Gretchen are working in that area to find moles. Could you warn them to be really careful now that we know these two guys may be there? If Lucy and Gretchen stumble across the hiding spot, they could be in real danger."

Emily was quiet for a few minutes, her eyes closed in concentration, and Gregory knew that meant she was communicating telepathically. He'd gotten quite used to that in their two years of marriage. He was able to communicate with Emily and Esmeralda, primarily if they initiated contact, but that was the extent of his telepathic abilities. He certainly valued that quick form of communication, though, as he'd seen time and again what a difference it made.

Emily opened her eyes, smiled, and said, "I've updated Lucy and Gretchen, and they've got Sage with them as well. Lucy said moles aren't real fans of dragons, so they didn't bring Harriet and Ruby, but they did promise they'd let Harriet and Ruby know, and maybe they can find a spot close to Lucy and Gretchen that won't spook the moles but will protect Lucy and Gretchen."

"Thanks, hon. That's about all we can do, I guess," said Gregory, putting his notes away and standing up. "We have to hope something will turn up soon, because I don't like the readings I'm getting from Jaluhz."

"People are beginning to worry about the increase in tremors, and the last tremor damaged some property, so that adds to the stress," Emily added, as she too stood and they prepared to leave.

"I know," said Gregory. "I hate waiting."

— 14 —

EXPLOSION

That day Chloe met with student after student. She was thrilled that each one was able to develop a first course of study to investigate a field they were interested in. She maintained a list of people throughout Havenshold who were willing to share their expertise, allowing a student to observe or even work beside them for a few months. This allowed students to explore various options to find a path that truly suited them.

As she'd suspected from the orientation meeting, when she saw him drawing as he waited, Ernest, a quiet young man with auburn hair, slim build, and blue eyes, wanted to be an artist. His parents saw absolutely no future in that field, which was a shame. Havenshold had many fine artists, and indeed the arts were an important part of life not only in Draconia but in all four of the world's nations. She would arrange for him to spend a day or two in a couple different studios so that he and the willing artists could decide where he'd fit best.

Then there was Anita, a bubbly young woman from Alfredsville with long dark brown hair which she wore in braided pigtails, average height and just a bit stocky, with hazel eyes that seemed always to be twinkling. She wanted to be a baker and had been baking for her family for a number of years. Any one of Havenshold's bakers would be lucky to have her for an apprentice, and again, Chloe would make sure that Anita was able to work with those who were willing before she had to make a final commitment about an apprenticship.

Most of the remaining students were undecided, but they all had been able to pick a starting point and now Chloe was filling out the paperwork necessary to get them visits with those in fields of interest to the students.

The day was long but rewarding, and Chloe was amused and grateful that a cheese and tomato sandwich appeared on her desk midday just after she'd finished with one student, allowing her time for a quick lunch before the next arrived. Libby was so thoughtful.

Chloe's last meeting of the day was with Arryn. She'd deliberately scheduled her for last because she felt that meeting might take longer. When Arryn walked in promptly at five, Chloe asked her if she wanted a cup of tea. Arryn sat down across from Chloe's desk and shook her head.

"How's Rya doing?" Chloe asked.

"She seems OK now. Amy took me over to Rya's home last night, but we didn't stay long."

"And how do you like it at Amy and Todd's?"

"They're so caring and nice, and they seem to like me living there," answered Arryn, as she stared into her lap, twisting her hands.

"That's good," said Chloe, watching her for a minute then continuing. "Is something bothering you, Arryn? You don't seem very happy."

"At the orientation yesterday...well, I met the other students, and they've all graduated and seem eager to try a career path, even if they don't know what that path is. I don't fit in with them. I dropped out of school."

"Ah," said Chloe, as she opened Arryn's file. "And you're worried because you dropped out of school quite some time before you ran away to Havenshold."

Arryn looked up in surprise. "You knew?"

"Once I got your records from your last school, yes. Miss Bronson, your previous teacher, sent everything to me, and she has lovely things to say about you."

"Yeah, she tried, but Steve—that's my sister's husband—kept telling her there was no point in my going to school because I had to look after my mom. So I haven't been in school since my dad died. I'm four years behind. By the time I make all that up, I'll be twenty years old."

Chloe smiled at the way Arryn emphasized "twenty" as if that would make her an old lady. "Miss Bronson says she always made sure you had the textbooks for both of the years when you were at home," she told her. "She also says she wanted to administer the end-of-year exams to you because you said you'd studied all the books."

"But Steve said no," said Arryn.

"Miss Bronson wanted to get help for you so you could still attend school. She wanted to find someone who could look after your mom during all or part of the school day."

"Yes, she did try really hard. She even found someone who wouldn't charge much, but Steve got mad and said we weren't taking charity and could look after ourselves. I know my sister felt horrible about it, but with her kids—and she always seemed to have another on the way—she couldn't help me. So I gave up."

"Did you?" asked Chloe. "You kept reading the textbooks."

Arryn looked at Chloe, and her brown eyes lit up. "Oh, I love to read. I'll read anything. It's a way to find a better place, to forget my life."

"Books also can lead you to a different life. Miss Bronson was really upset when you ran away after your mother died. She was hoping that maybe you could return to school."

"Steve said that if they had to take me in, I'd be their maid and nanny in order to earn my keep, so school never would have happened."

"I can understand why you ran away," said Chloe. "That certainly wasn't much to look forward to. And when Lena refused to let you go to school, what did you think?"

"She said she'd teach me all I needed to know, and honestly I was already two years behind and didn't want to be in a class with younger kids, so I agreed."

"Makes perfect sense," said Chloe. "Did Lena teach you anything?"

"Her idea of teaching was to yell at me to do something, but she never told me how to do it. But I eventually figured things out on my own. And her shop was such a mess. I couldn't stand it. I organized all her paperwork, and soon I was doing the billing as well. She had this crazy system where she wouldn't bill people, letting their tabs get really big, waiting until she needed money to pay her rent or whatever. Then she'd go pounding on doors, handing out bills and demanding that the customers pay right then and there."

"What?" said Chloe, frowning at this information. "That's not good business."

"I know, and the customers weren't very happy, many of them, because they wanted to pay as they bought their merchandise. They didn't always have large sums on hand to pay when she just randomly showed up. But she thought she was pretty smart because she knew then that her bills would be covered." Arryn took a deep breath and continued. "Lena's lousy at managing money. So if she has some, she spends it on things she doesn't really need, and then when her bills come around, she can't pay them. I set up a true accounting system and made sure her customers had their bills right away. And since some of the pots were large and had to be delivered, I set up a delivery-rate plan. Lena always said it was too hard to calculate the bill at the time, because of the different delivery charges, depending on whether the customer lived in town or the outlying areas. I made a map with zones and set fees for delivery. That way everything could be calculated right at the time of the sale."

Chloe gave Arryn a wide smile. "Wow, that's impressive."

"Yeah, well, Lena didn't think so. She was furious because then she didn't have money for the rent one month. She'd let it dwindle away on more new pots or whatever. So I showed her how to budget her money, which she hated. She hated any-thing that smacked of organization."

"Thanks for giving me all that information," Chloe said. "Now let's get back to the matter of your education. From what you've told me, it's clear you've learned a lot in the last four years."

"I guess," Arryn said with a shrug. "Oh, and I've kept read-ing. Some of Lena's customers would sneak books to me when she wasn't looking. Lena didn't want me getting ideas, she said. Anyway, I've been able to keep reading. That's probably the only thing that kept me going. I took a light from the shop and hid it in the storage room. I kept my books there also, so Lena wouldn't know."

"The real question here," said Chloe, "is what you want. Even if it would take four years, which I'm pretty darned certain it won't, the main thing is what *you* want. What are you willing to do? Because help is available, but the driving force has to be you."

"But I'm still not like the others," Arryn said, a hint of sad-ness in her voice.

"The others aren't like the others," said Chloe with a chuckle. "We're all different. And you've had a much harder road than many people. You mentioned escaping into your books, but did you ever think about changing your reality?"

"Changing reality? That's not possible," said Arryn.

Chloe raised her eyebrows. "Really? The only reality is that what we believe—our basic belief system—determines our reality."

"I don't get it," said Arryn.

"Well, look at Lena as an example. She's a very sad case of someone who had a horrible childhood and as a result came to believe she doesn't deserve anything. She doesn't feel entitled to even the basics in life: a home, financial security, friends, and so forth. She fiercely believes that she's unworthy, and so her very life determines that this reality remains. She doesn't have anything, doesn't bring order into her life. She's always on the edge of disaster, even though plenty of help is available. But she won't see that because of her beliefs, her firm conviction that she doesn't deserve anything. Do you see how her beliefs determine her reality?"

Arryn's face lit up with understanding. "So when I showed her how things could be different, how she could make the most of what she had and move forward, she rejected everything I did."

"Precisely," said Chloe. "You can keep looking at all the hardships you've suffered, and you can do just what Lena did. Or you can realize that things don't have to stay the same. That you can develop new beliefs in a better life for yourself. That you can realize you deserve love and friendships. I know how hard it is to change your belief system, because I had to do that. And I've shared my story with you, how the changes I made then helped my entire family to change. Our beliefs are very powerful, and yes, they determine our reality."

"That's a lot to take in," said Arryn.

"It is, and it'll take time. But the first step is one you can make here today. Are you ready to move forward? Do you want an education?"

Arryn stared at her hands for a few moments then looked up and said, "Yes, Yes, I do. No matter how long it takes."

"Excellent," said Chloe, smiling brightly. "Now for the good news. Miss Bronson sent me the end-of-year exams for the two years you were at home. I then spoke with Miss Crimson at Havenshold School and showed her your records as well as Miss Bronson's comments. She's given me the exams for the two years you've been here, as well as the final graduation exams. And she's authorized me to administer them whenever I think you're ready.

"My suggestion is that we start the testing tomorrow," Chloe continued. "I need to know where you are at this moment. Miss Bronson was pretty confident that you would have passed her two exams, and I'm sure she's right. Then we'll see how much more you've learned on your own. I have to tell you, at first I thought you'd be behind in math and science, since I figured you'd been reading history and literature. But now, hearing how way you devised an entire accounting system—billing and budgets—for Lena's business, I've revised my guess. You're a natural student. I'm suspecting you might just be lacking some science credits. The tests will let us know that for sure, but you could be a lot closer to graduating than you think."

"Really?" said Arryn, who was starting to look excited.

"And I'm very sure Amy and Todd would be happy to help you, as will I. Todd loves to invent things, so his science skills are excellent."

"Wow, I had no idea that I could test out. Maybe this'll work after all," Arryn said, smiling.

Chloe grinned as well. "It will work, one way or another, if you want it to. Unfortunately Lena never saw a way to get out of her trap, but you have a chance to start on a very different path, and that path can be anything you want it to be."

Arryn took a deep breath and said, "I'd like that."

"Terrific!" said Chloe. "Then I'd like you here tomorrow morning at eight sharp, and we'll start on the testing."

Arryn stood and came around the desk to hug Chloe. "Thank you so much," she told her.

"Hey, you're the one who has to do all the work," Chloe said with a laugh, as she returned Arryn's hug. "Now get out of here, and get a good night's sleep. And please ask Amy to pack you a lunch for tomorrow. She always did that for me, and I know she'd be happy to do the same for you. You'll probably be here all day."

"Got it," said Arryn, as she left the office looking much happier than when she'd arrived.

Chloe gathered her papers and set her desk in order. Then she and Calliope headed off for a quiet evening. "It's a lovely start to the school year, Calliope, and we have some amazing students."

Seems so, but I'm hungry, whined Calliope.

Chloe laughed and turned out the light.

The next morning Arryn arrived a few minutes early, carrying a lunch sack Amy had packed for her. Chloe took her into the lab next to her office where she'd set up the first exam for Arryn. "I thought you'd be more comfortable in here," she said. "I use this lab when I'm teaching a science class, but I don't have anything going on at the moment. It'll be quiet, and no one will disturb you. If you have any questions, I'm right next door."

"OK," said Arryn a bit nervously.

"Don't worry. Just do your best. Any gaps in your education can be remedied, but we want to give you credit for everything you already know. Here's your first exam." Chloe pointed at the packet on the table. "Now give it your best shot, and when you're done, please bring it in to me."

Chloe went back to her office to do paperwork. Gregory had updated her on the investigations surrounding the volcanic activity, but so far they hadn't learned anything new. There was nothing to do but wait, so she figured she might as well knock out more of the inevitable school paperwork.

After an hour and a half, Arryn walked into her office with her test and a smile. "This was really easy," she said.

"I was hoping that would be the case," said Chloe. "Why don't you take a break, and then you can start the next one? While you're doing the second test, I'll grade this one."

"I'm good," said Arryn. "I really want to take the next test."

"OK," said Chloe with a broad smile. "Here it is, and good luck."

Arryn left the office with a skip in her step, which made Chloe happy.

Chloe opened Arryn's completed test and started grading it. "Calliope, there's something to be said for waiting to take tests. Arryn's answers are much more complete than a twelve-year-old's would be."

She definitely is smart...nearly as smart as I am.

"No one's that smart," Chloe said with a wink.

So glad you realize that, answered Calliope.

Chloe finished grading Arryn's first test and wrote up her report for the records. Arryn came in shortly afterward with her second test. "How did that one go?" asked Chloe.

"These are really easy. I sure wish Steve had let me take them before. I just figured I was too far behind to catch up."

"Well, you got top marks on this first test, and I'm betting the same will be true with this one. But I do think it would be a good idea to take a lunch break before doing any more. OK?"

"Sure," said Arryn, as she reached for her lunch bag, which she'd left on a table next to the couch. She looked up as she pulled a sandwich out of her bag, just in time to see a sandwich appear on Chloe's desk.

"Hey, how'd that get there?" asked Arryn, as she took a seat on the sofa.

"Oh, the library looks after me," said Chloe nonchalantly. "Would you like some tea to go with that?"

"Sure," Arryn said, looking very puzzled.

Chloe made them each a mug of tea then said, "So Rya seemed better last evening?"

"Yeah," said Arryn between mouthfuls. "She said she was fine, and Clyde actually stopped hovering over her, so I'm guessing it was actually true. She also said her grandmother was on her way."

"Yes, Harmony's moving back here, at least for the winter. The baron is helping with the logistics."

"Rya told me about that. She and Clyde seem very happy about it. I think they need her. Rya has a lot of responsibility now—with the volcano and all—and I really feel for Clyde. He's like me. Neither of us has any magical abilities, so all this stuff seems strange. He said he feels so helpless when Rya's dealing with the magic stuff."

Chloe nodded. "Yes, I understand. And Clyde used to fear magic, even Aster's when she first discovered hers, so he's come a long way, but Harmony will be able to help both of them and ground them through all of this."

"I like Rya a lot," Arryn said, blushing slightly. "I hope this stuff gets figured out soon so we can just have fun together."

"We all hope that," said Chloe, smiling at her.

Arryn finished her cookie and said, "I'm ready for another test."

"If you're sure," said Chloe.

"I want to finish as many as I can so we'll know where I am."

Chloe handed the third test to Arryn. "Sounds like a plan. Here you go."

Chloe graded the second test then had time to do some more paperwork before Arryn returned. "How'd that one go?" she asked.

"It was a bit harder, but I think I did OK."

"Well, you got almost every question right on your second test, so everything you might have done before you came to Havenshold has been signed off on. What do you think about taking another test? You have one more regular end-of-year test and then the final graduation exam."

"I want to take the fourth one now. And if I don't pass part of it, can I just retake that part once I study whatever I missed?"

"Definitely. As you know, these tests are divided by subject, so you'll only have to retake the subjects you didn't pass."

"Then I definitely want to give it a try," Arryn said with a smile.

"Here you go," said Chloe, "and good luck again."

Chloe graded the third exam and noticed that the literature and history scores were nearly perfect, as was the math. Arryn passed the science section comfortably, although her marks were a little lower than her other scores.

"It's as I thought, Calliope," said Chloe. "She's having no trouble with the things she would have read in the books people loaned her, and her math, well, she's figured all that out because of her efforts with Lena. But her science is a bit weaker. She may need help there."

Still, it's pretty amazing to have tested out of at least three years of school, said Calliope. *I like her. She's really smart and nice as well.*

Chloe ruffled Calliope's fur. "Yes, she is, and you're right about it being amazing. Our students continue to surprise me with their drive and determination. Arryn was overwhelmed when she first came in today, letting herself be intimidated by what others her age have done, but she's actually done more than most of them. She's self-taught, and it wouldn't have worked if she weren't so determined, so curious, and yes, so smart."

Chloe worked on the last of her paperwork as the clock ticked away. The last test was talking Arryn longer, but that didn't matter, as there was no time limit. Finally, at five in the afternoon, Arryn returned. "Not sure about this one," she said, handing the test to Chloe. "Parts of it were easy, but the science...I don't know."

"Well, have a seat. I won't keep you in suspense for long. You passed the third exam, by the way, with top marks in everything but science, but your science score was still above average."

Arryn said, "Is it OK I find a book in the library while you grade that? It'll make me more nervous to watch."

"Certainly," said Chloe, smiling.

As Arryn left the office to browse the stacks, Chloe got to work marking the fourth test. Again Arryn had the highest possible scores in literature, history, and math. She managed to squeak a pass in science, but it was a real squeak, just two points higher than what was necessary. Chloe signed off on the required paperwork and slipped all four tests into an envelope to send to Miss Crimson at Havenshold School. Then she and Calliope headed out into the stacks to find Arryn.

When Arryn saw them, she said, "You won't believe this. When I started walking through the stacks, books seemed to move so they were sticking out for me."

Chloe smiled. "Actually I would believe it. Try talking to Aster about it sometime. Did you find something you'd like to check out?"

"Yes, I found a botany book that looks pretty cool. Can I take it home?"

"Certainly," said Chloe, "and here's how you check out any book you want to borrow." Once she had explained the check-out system, she said, "You passed your fourth exam as well, Arryn. Congratulations!"

"I did? Really?" Arryn smiled widely. "I thought the science was hard, and I wasn't at all sure about it."

"Well, that was your lowest mark. You got top scores in everything else, but your science score was just barely passing."

"So what do I do now?"

"I think the library already has answered part of that. I'd like you to bone up on your science before you take the graduation exam. Your marks on that final exam will be all that shows on your permanent record, so I don't want to rush you through this. I know if you study, your science marks can be right up there with the others. You just haven't had any science classes for several years. It's actually pretty amazing that you squeaked a pass."

"Well, I like science, but I wasn't been able to borrow as many science books 'cause I guess most people don't read them."

"That's probably true," Chloe said. "So here's what I'd like to propose. We'll discuss possible career paths, and you can sign up to try out whatever interests you, just the way the other new students are doing."

Arryn raised an eyebrow. "Really? But I haven't graduated yet."

"But you're really close, so in addition to whichever path you'd like to sample, I'll have you study science with Todd. Since you're living at their home, I don't think it'll be hard for you and Todd to get together during the evenings and weekends or whatever fits around whatever else you want to try out."

"That sounds great! I'll be a real Pathfinder student."

"Silly, you always were. Every student takes a different path."

"I know," said Arryn, hugging the botany book to her chest, "but it just feels more real now. I felt so stupid when I knew I hadn't finished the last four years of school, even though part of me knew I was smart. Does that make any sense?"

"Perfect sense," said Chloe. "Now why don't you head home and share your fantastic news with Amy and Todd? Then think about the path you might like to investing—" Chloe stopped midword as a giant explosion shook the very foundation of the library, knocking over several table lamps and even one small table. Both Chloe and Arryn staggered to keep their balance and Chloe was glad that except for Gregory, no one else was in the building.

"Oh, my gosh. What was that?" asked Arryn.

"I don't know," Chloe said, as Gregory rushed out of his office and through the library.

"That can't be good," he said, racing for the front doors.

Chloe turned to Arryn. "Can you get home now? I should follow Gregory."

"Sure," said Arryn. "I know the way even in the dark, but do you need help?"

"If I do, I'll let Amy and Todd know, and they'll tell you, but for now I don't want to have to worry about your safety. I've already alerted Todd telepathically that you're on your way, so you'll probably meet him partway. Meanwhile, unless I contact you otherwise, plan to be back tomorrow, right after lunch, with ideas about which path you might like to explore. I hate to shove you out the door, but I really need to find out what just happened."

"Sure, and thanks, Chloe, for everything. I hope everything's OK."

Once Arryn had left, Chloe closed her eyes, focused on the surrounding activity, then teleported herself to the back side of the volcano. As she rematerialized, she gasped. The explosion was caused by a dynamite blast that had cut away half of the mountain near the bottom. Hot lava was oozing out of an enormous hole. Then she saw Dr. Brian and Nurse Beatrice hurrying over to two forms that lay near the hole. It was dark, so Chloe set up a magical flare to light the area then walked over.

Gregory was standing by what turned out to be Lucy and Gretchen on the ground. Dr. Brian was working feverishly to stop the bleeding in Lucy's midsection, while Nurse Beatrice was bandaging Gretchen's head. Gretchen had been knocked out, but she woke up as Nurse Beatrice was checking her for more injuries.

"Lucy...where's Lucy?" shouted Gretchen.

"She's right here," said Nurse Beatrice. "Dr. Brian is working on her."

"Is she OK?"

"We don't yet know how bad her injuries are."

"I have to see her. She'll need me," Gretchen said.

"You will, I promise," said Nurse Beatrice, "but first you have to let Dr. Brian work."

Gregory came over and knelt next to Gretchen, who was now sitting. "Gretchen, can you tell me anything about what happened?" He noticed that her left hand was heavily bandaged and there was another bandage on her left cheek. She was covered in dust and dirt and there was a bump on the back of her head.

"Not really," she said. "You know we were out here so Lucy could contact more moles. She was talking to one of them, and then the mole suddenly said, 'Run!' before taking off. Lucy stood, and I moved back a few steps. Then there was a massive explosion, and part of the mountain was blown away."

Gregory nodded. "Thanks, Gretchen, and for what it's worth, I think that mole saved both of your lives."

Just then Dr. Brian called to Chloe. "Can you transport Lucy and me directly to surgery? I have her stabilized, but I need to operate right away."

"Lucy," wailed Gretchen, "I love you. Be strong."

Once Chloe had teleported them, she turned to Nurse Beatrice and Gretchen. "You two are next. Surgery also?"

"Might as well," said Nurse Beatrice. "I'm needed there, and I know Gretchen wants to be with Lucy."

"Right," said Chloe, "and Harriet and Ruby are probably there already."

"I know," said Nurse Beatrice in what sounded like a resigned voice, except to those who knew her better. She really did understand the nature of dragon-rider bonds, and for all her bluster, she loved them both.

Once Chloe had teleported Gretchen and Nurse Beatrice, she turned to Gregory. "Any ideas?"

"No," he said, "except this wasn't natural. Emily already has the dragons and riders looking for evidence, but that's hard to do in the dark. I wouldn't have had Lucy and Gretchen out here if I'd known something like this might happen."

"It's not your fault, Gregory, and you know you couldn't have stopped them. Lucy loves her moles and Gretchen loves Lucy."

"I know," said Gregory miserably. "I just hope they'll be OK. I don't know what I'd do if Lucy doesn't pull through. I feel responsible for her being here and she's such a wonderful person."

— 15 —
VIGIL

Chloe suspected no one in the dragon-rider complex slept that night. She knew she certainly didn't. She remained at the hospital awaiting word on Lucy. Gretchen's injuries were much less severe, as she had been farther away from the blast. Dr. Brian was working feverishly to stop Lucy's bleeding. Both Harriet and Ruby, as well as Sage, were in the operating room with Gretchen, staying out of the way, but sending all the telepathic healing energy they could.

Chloe sat in the waiting room along with others who came and went. The courtyard outside the hospital was a waiting area also, and dragons and riders stopped by when they weren't out on patrol. Emily switched the search teams frequently to keep their eyes fresh and to give them some relief from the dark and the cold.

Gregory entered the waiting room just before dawn. He'd been back and forth all night, unable to decide whether he could do more for Lucy by waiting or by pacing back and forth in his office, reviewing the latest data from the volcano.

"Any word?" he asked, as he slumped down into the chair next to Chloe.

"No, nothing," she replied.

"Shouldn't we have heard something by now?"

Chloe shrugged. "I don't know. Obviously we'd have gotten bad news by now, so I'm hoping the lack of news is good, if that logic makes any sense."

"It's really eerie in the courtyard. The dragons and riders aren't talking. They're holding a silent vigil for Lucy."

"She's one of their own," said Chloe.

"Remember when Harriet chose her? She wasn't even a candidate. She hadn't been picked because she was missing a hand. Then, when Harriet refused to hatch and called to Lucy, who was in the stands—well, it was amazing."

"I was too young to be there," said Chloe, "but I've heard the story many times."

"What strikes me now is that people tried to stop that bonding. They said Lucy wasn't capable of being a real rider because of her disability. My dad was there, and he supported Emily's brother, Hans, who was leading the dragon riders then. He said that if Oswald could choose him, then Harriet had every right to choose Lucy."

"He was right."

"Even at their graduation nine years later," Gregory continued, "there were still some skeptics, so she and Harriet put on one of the most amazing aerial graduation dances ever. Now, all these years later, it gives me goose bumps to see and feel the solidarity for her. They want to be there in the courtyard. Emily is still sending a few pairs out to search for the two guys and to keep an eye on the lava, and of course they all take their turns, but keeping vigil seems to be the most important thing for all of them."

"I suspect you and I never will know what that kind of bond feels like, not only between a dragon and his or her rider but also between all the riders and dragons. I noticed that Amy and Todd are out there with Fern and Jupiter, and I've heard that Aster and Jasmine are flying all night to get here."

"Emily said that Hans and Firebird have cut short a diplomatic mission in Sanwight and are heading here. Jake and Harmony are coming as well, along with William and Thunder. Lucy fostered with Emily's family, so they're really hurting. She's just got to make it," said Gregory, bowing his head.

"She certainly has a lot of healing energy aimed at her. It's so thick in the air that it's almost palpable."

"You know," said Gregory, "I don't even notice anymore that Lucy's missing an arm. I don't know if you know this, but she lost the rest of her bad arm when she and Sage were hunting for survivors in the collapse at one of my dad's mines. If she hadn't been traveling back and forth then, her father never would have gotten a second crack at shooting her. She just does so much for everyone. She has to make it."

Chloe placed a hand on Gregory's shoulder. "Dr. Brian and Nurse Beatrice are the best, and they got to her right away. We can't lose hope now."

Gregory nodded. "You're right. We'll fight with her."

Chloe looked down at the floor under her chair and noticed a small brown mole, nearly hidden in the shadows. "Look, Gregory. Have you ever seen a mole inside a building?"

Gregory looked as well and said, "Never. That has to be one of Lucy's moles. I wish I could talk to him or her."

"I do too, but I suspect this little one is part of a larger network of moles also on vigil for Lucy."

"Well, thank you, mole," said Gregory.

Gregory and Chloe were amazed to see the mole bow his or her head in acknowledgment before curling up in a tight ball.

The sun was rising over the courtyard when Dr. Brian finally came into the waiting room looking exhausted, dark circles under his eyes, his hair all rumpled. Chloe and Gregory looked up, and Dr. Brian nodded. Then looking through the large window by the glass doors and seeing the crowd outside in the courtyard, he said, "Come on. I'll tell everyone at once."

As they went through the doors, Chloe noticed that the mole followed as well. All heads turned to Dr. Brian, who said, "Lucy has lost a lot of blood, but I've managed to stop the bleeding and close up her abdomen. She's still quite ill, and she'll have to be monitored closely, but I'm confident that, barring any complications, she'll recover."

The shouts, roars, cheers, and applause were deafening. Dr. Brian held up his hands. "I do want to say I've never experienced what I did tonight. Well, last night I guess," he corrected as he looked up at the bright, sunny sky. "I thought I was losing her a number of times. Then I'd feel a presence guiding me to another spot that was bleeding, another injury. My hands might have done the actual work, but it was your presence, your healing energy waves that really saved Lucy. So thank you. I'm humbled by your support. And I would ask that you keep sending Lucy healing thoughts and energy as her body works to rebuild her system."

"Can we see her?" someone shouted.

Dr. Brian laughed softly. "No visitors for a bit...until I'm sure she's truly stable."

"You mean no visitors except Gretchen, Harriet, Ruby, and Sage" said someone else with a chuckle.

"Yes, you have that right. They won't leave her side, but your energies are also very important. So do what you need to do, but as you go through your days, keep holding Lucy in your hearts. She needs you, and I really mean it when I say *you* saved her."

"Thanks, Doc," another rider shouted, and the group began to disband.

Chloe looked down then tapped Gregory on the shoulder. "Look," she said. "I think that mole is a messenger."

They watched as the mole scurried into the bushes. "I guess Dr. Brian had more help than even he knows about. I can't wait to tell Lucy about her moles."

Emily and Esmeralda walked over to Chloe and Gregory. "Isn't that absolutely the best news about Lucy?" Esmeralda said.

"Sure is," said Emily, with tears of joy in her eyes.

"Lucy always has been a fighter," said Gregory.

Chloe nodded. "Emily, have you found out anything?"

Shaking her head, Emily said, "Not really. It'll be easier now that it's light out, but the perpetrators of this explosion seem to have gotten away. And we don't know if they found Damian and Frank's stash. We don't even know who they are. We're running out of clues."

"Well, as much as I'd like to wring their necks," said Gregory, "I think the bigger problem is the volcano."

"Yes, of course," said Emily. "Lava is still pouring out of the hole, with no end in sight. At least it's moving slowly. But as it exits the volcano, it spreads out, and it's already moved close to the town edge on one side and a similar distance on the other. It's making a larger and larger triangular wedge as more lava flows out."

Chloe turned to Gregory. "Have your dad and Harmony arrived yet?"

Gregory frowned with a puzzled expression at the apparent non sequitur but answered, "They're due in this morning. Why?"

"Well, we need to know how Jaluhz is handling all this, which means checking in with Rya. Do you remember when Aster and Jasmine were nearly killed by the black magician while they were doing their bonding dance?"

Now both Emily and Gregory looked confused. "Yeah, but what's that got to do with anything?" asked Emily.

"That was when we first became aware of Harmony. She was still on her island, on Sanctuary, but she was able to send some kind of energy that strengthened Aster and Jasmine so they could break off the contact with the black magician."

"So you're thinking," said Emily, beginning to catch on, "that Harmony could help strengthen Rya's contact with Jaluhz."

Chloe nodded. "We know Harmony is telepathic, but she also has an energy that I've never been able to put my finger on. It's a very positive, harmonizing energy..." She smiled. "Pun intended. And Rya needs all the support she can get. The volcano is erupting. Thankfully the spread of lava is slow, but it's no less damaging. Communicating with Jaluhz is a vital part of our approach now, and that's a lot of responsibility to put on Rya."

"Aster did it when she was Rya's age," said Emily.

"Yes, for sure. But I'm noticing," said Chloe, "that Rya has a much more sensitive nature, a vulnerability. I think that's why she can communicate with or feel the natural world. She needs that sensitivity to be an empath, but at the same time, it makes her more vulnerable to the stress. She knows what we're expecting. She knows what's at stake. And she really wants to help both Jaluhz and Draconia. That's a lot of pressure on one set of young shoulders."

"I get it," said Emily. "So you think Harmony can strengthen her communication with Jaluhz while also supporting Rya."

"That's my hope," said Chloe. "And thank heavens for Rya's bond with Artemis. I suspect that fox has been holding her together just as dragons do with their riders."

Esmeralda let out a low chuckle. "That fox is an amazing little thing, and you're quite correct, Chloe, about the nature of their bond and the strength Artemis has to watch over and calm Rya."

"And the reverse is true as well," said Chloe.

"As soon as Harmony arrives, I'll bring her, Rya, and Artemis with us to your office," said Emily.

"Actually," said Gregory, "let's meet in my office so we can take a look at my seismic and pressure gauges. I don't know if they'll be of any help, but maybe Jaluhz's reactions will register on them."

"Sounds reasonable," said Chloe.

"We need some breakfast," said Emily. "It looks as if we're going to need all our resources, and none of us has slept. So why don't we say we'll meet in an hour in Gregory's office?"

"Will Harmony be here by then?" asked Chloe.

"I just heard from the baron, and they're at Clyde's right now," said Emily. "He spoke to me telepathically as soon as they arrived. I'm going to have him and Oswald come as well. Their knowledge of mines may help."

"See you all in an hour then," said Chloe, as she headed toward the library.

When she walked into the library courtyard, she noticed a small group of people standing in front of the library steps. As she approached, one of the men said, "So are you going to fix this volcano for us?"

"I'm working on it," said Chloe, as she continued toward the front doors.

"That's why we have a mage, right?" the man went on.

Chloe just waved a hand, acknowledging the comment, and headed into the library as quickly as she could. *This could get ugly*, she thought, as she walked to the rear of the library. *I need to talk with Libby.* She knocked on Libby's door and entered when Libby called out to her.

"I figured you'd be here soon," said Libby, sitting in her chair and looking up from the book she had been reading.

Chloe flopped onto the couch then noticed Libby had placed a plate of scrambled eggs and toast along with a mug of strong black tea on the table next to her.

"Thanks so much, Libby. This is just what I need. That and some advice," she said, as she took a sip of the tea and picked up her plate. "The good news is that Lucy should recover completely. Dr. Brian is...I believe the correct term is 'cautiously optimistic.'"

"That's very good news. She's such a lovely young lady."

"A crowd is starting to gather on the library steps, and they've made it clear that they expect me to zap the volcano or some such thing," said Chloe between mouthfuls.

"I guess they think that's reasonable. After all, you did move an asteroid."

"But that was different," Chloe said with a shrug. "The asteroid wasn't a part of this planet, and I just sent it on a different course. But now..."

"Yes?" asked Libby with encouragement.

"Well, that guy outside...he thinks I'm a mage for the people on this planet and probably thinks I'm Draconia's mage, here to make his world function the way he wants. But I'm the mage for the entire planet, not just humans. I'm here to help ensure the health of the planet as a whole, but right now I'm not sure just what that means." Chloe put down her now-empty plate and took another sip of tea. "It seems to me," she continued, "that Jaluhz should have some say in all this. Isn't it the height of arrogance for humans to say that everyone else and everything else is of less importance?"

"I've always thought so," said Libby.

"And what about this eruption? It wasn't a natural occurrence. Whoever is responsible managed to set off their dynamite in a spot that resulted in the current situation, something I'm sure wasn't intentional. But might it not be a blessing in disguise?"

"How so?" asked Libby, smiling and putting her book on the table next to her.

"Well, Bertha said Jaluhz would be erupting in the fall, as part of her natural cycle. We have no idea what that eruption would have looked like. Maybe Jaluhz would have had a truly violent eruption—not that any eruption doesn't come with a certain amount of violence, but you know what I mean. One where the top blows off and lava and ash rain down everywhere.

"As far as eruptions go, this one has some real advantages. The lava is moving at a slow enough pace that people can get out of the way. I suspect Gregory will tell us that, left unchecked, the lava will spread over most of Draconia, which poses a problem for not just us but all life in Draconia. Jaluhz, however, apparently needs to erupt every few million years, and right now is her natural time." Chloe let out a deep sigh. "If I just plug the hole, her pressure will build again, and who knows what will happen?"

"And the other thing," she said, racing on, "Jaluhz has done a lot not only for Draconia but also the entire planet. Much of our energy comes from her. I'm not just talking about hot springs for the dragons and riders but also the planet's largest source of energy. We've been doing all the taking. Isn't it time we did some giving?"

Libby looked carefully at Chloe and said, "I agree with you, but you'll have a tough time trying to sell 'volcano rights' to those who are in danger of losing their homes, their land, everything but their lives."

"I know," said Chloe, looking very discouraged. "Say, do you know who Gregory and I saw inside the hospital waiting room? One of Lucy's moles. Can you believe it? I can't imagine what it must have taken for that mole to leave his or her underground tunnel and come into a stone-and-brick building then stay there all night, waiting for word on Lucy. Then, once Dr. Brian told us Lucy was holding her own, the mole ran off. He or she was obviously a messenger for the mole community."

Libby smiled broadly. "Lucy always has shown respect and love for the moles—well, all life actually, but she has a special relationship with the moles. And they were trying to give back to her. I have no doubt that among the healing energy that Dr. Brian felt, there was mole energy, along with human and dragon energy."

"I'm sure of it. There as a united front pulling for Lucy, not just one species. I guess I'm saying there has to be a balance. We have to respect the rest of the planet. There has to be a way to look after Jaluhz yet not lose all of Draconia."

"And I'm sure you'll find that way. Understanding others is one of your greatest strengths," Libby said with a warm smile. "Don't start doubting yourself now."

Chloe nodded. "Thanks, Libby. Still I'm not going to be railroaded into action. I definitely need more data. And I sure hope Rya can, with Harmony's help, discover what Jaluhz wants and needs. Rya felt Jaluhz was sad, which might mean she doesn't want to destroy Draconia. If I can find a way to allow her eruption to proceed as it needs to for her sake, but not lose all of Draconia in the process—well, if I can do that, I'll be content."

"That's a tall order," said Libby, "but I'm sure you can do it. Just be aware that it'll be tough to convince people that this is a good plan."

"Where's that bear? Why's Bertha hibernating when we need her?"

"I suspect," said Libby, smoothing her skirt, "she doesn't believe she's needed. She has confidence in you, Chloe. However, if things get to be too much, more than you can handle, I have no doubt she'll wake up. I'd be very surprised if she weren't aware on some level of everything that's going on now."

Chloe shrugged. "I suppose. Nice that one of us can sleep."

Libby chuckled as she said, "You need to head to your meeting now. I suspect you'll have quite a handful of folks there. Just remember to keep your focus. You're quite right that you're the planet's mage, responsible for the well-being of all. Gather the data you need, and I think you'll find help in some unlikely spots. You may feel all alone at times, but remember you can always call on me. I can find you even when you're not inside me, so to speak. And you'll have supporters. I'm also sure of that."

"Thanks, Libby," Chloe said, giving her a hug. "You really are the best, and I've at least clarified my thinking. Now I need to find out what Jaluhz is thinking."

"Good luck," said Libby, picking up her book again.

— 16 —

RIOTING

As Chloe walked into Gregory's office, she noticed that Libby was right. There were even more folks here for the meeting than she'd expected. Yes, Emily, Esmeralda, and Gregory were there, along with Rya, Artemis, and Harmony. But added to the numbers were Aster, Sasha, and Jasmine, all of whom looked tired from flying through night to get to Havenshold. The baron and Oswald were also present. Most surprisingly Clyde was there. When Chloe's eyes met his, he came over and said, "I don't know that I can help, but I needed to be here to learn. Is that OK?"

"Of course, Clyde," she said. "You're always welcome."

"Thanks," he said, as he rejoined his family.

It's a good thing I made Gregory's office so large, Chloe thought. *Yet the absence of Lucy and Gretchen is enormous. Everyone's so quiet. They're feeling it too.*

"Let's get started then," Gregory said. "That crowd out in the courtyard is growing, and they seem to want us to make this all go away."

"I have Hannah and Rupert keeping an eye on them," said Emily, taking a seat at the large round table. The two dragons and Oswald sat off to one side and Artemis, Calliope, and

Sasha joined them. Chloe sat down next to Emily as the baron, Rya, Harmony, Aster, and Clyde found seats.

"Great. So let's start with what we know," said Gregory, standing by his wall of hanging maps. "I'll begin with the volcano information as I have it, if that's OK." As the others nodded, he began. "First Jaluhz has a large rupture on one side that's allowing lava to pour out. The plus to this—and trust me, it's a very large plus—is that her pressure levels have dropped significantly. This means she won't have a full-scale, blowing-her-top-off, destroying-all-of-us-in-an-instant eruption.

"This slower—dare I say gentler—eruption means we should have no loss of life, either human or livestock. We will, however, continue to lose trees and any crops as the lava burns through them. Similarly houses and buildings in the path will be incinerated. And various gases, primarily sulfur dioxide, are present, which will make our air quality far less than optimal."

"How far will this spread?" asked Emily, looking up from the notes she was taking.

"Potentially it could cover much of Draconia."

Aster said, "I have some information about that, if I could share it."

"Of course," said Gregory with a smile, as he took a seat next to Emily.

Aster stood and addressed the group. "I have one of the history books from King Alfred's time, and it discusses how this eruption took place in his alternate world, long before his time of course. That eruption was the full-blown one Gregory just mentioned, but I thought the map of what the eruption covered might be relevant."

Aster opened a large book, placed it in the center of the table, and showed everyone the map. Then she sat back down in her chair next to her father. As they all got a chance to see it,

Emily said, "All of Draconia and a bit of Forbury are depicted as being covered in lava. Is that possible, Gregory?"

"I'm afraid so," he answered. "I don't know that it'll be the same in this case, but I do know that this eruption, even though it's much slower than the previous one, could go on for years."

"Years?" said the baron, raising his eyebrows.

Gregory nodded at his father's exclamation. "The advantage the slower flow gives us is offset by the time factor. This lava could flow for...I don't know...ten, fifteen, even twenty years."

Everyone was silent at this prospect. In the distance they all heard raised voices and an occasional banging on the front doors.

Esmeralda said, "That crowd certainly isn't going to like that news."

"Rya," Gregory said, "can you tell us anything about Jaluhz's current status?"

Harmony put an arm around her granddaughter's shoulders and nodded to her. "I'm getting a bit more information," Rya said, "but again it's mostly images. When the explosion went off, I knew it immediately. Jaluhz cried out in pain and anger. Then, as the lava began to seep out of her, I felt a sense of relief. She had been...well, uncomfortable, I guess you could say. And now I get feelings of both relief and sadness. She really doesn't want to destroy anything. I mean, look at how she saved Arryn. Sure, she was fine with bringing the tunnel down on Damian and Frank, but honestly they deserved it. But Jaluhz saved Arryn and even Lena."

Chloe spoke then. "Rya, do you think Jaluhz is open to a solution that might allow her to have her natural cycle but without destroying Draconia?"

"I think so," said Rya, chewing on her bottom lip. "She certainly has conflicting feelings now. I'm very sure about that."

Harmony nodded. "As you know, I've been linking with Rya on this to support her and help strengthen the images. I can't reach Jaluhz directly, but I can see what Rya sees, and I agree with Rya's assessment."

"What do you have in mind, Chloe?" asked Emily.

Chloe shook her head. "I don't know." She paused for a long time then finally said, "I can tell you what *won't* happen. I'm not going to do as one man in the courtyard asked and stop up the hole. I need to be really clear here about my role as mage."

Chloe looked around the room and found all eyes intently focused on her. "I'm the mage for the entire planet, not just for the humans alone, as those people in the courtyard seem to think. I'm here for all life on this planet, for the overall health of the planet. And Jaluhz is part of that. We know she's sentient, as is the entire planet. We know she has needs, and her needs are just as valid as ours or anyone else's."

The room was silent. Chloe stared down at the table as she went on. "The asteroid wasn't part of our world, and I was able to push it off course. But this is different. I can't just get rid of Jaluhz. She's part of our world. And how can we forget all the good she's brought us? All the energy? All the warmth? And no, I don't mean just hot springs for the dragons and their riders."

Emily spoke up, kindness and support evident in her voice. "Chloe, we're with you on this. We know what you mean."

Chloe looked up in surprise to see smiles and nods. Jasmine said, "Do you think those of us who are bonded and who are in service to this planet wouldn't get what you're saying?"

Chloe gave a tentative smile. "I'm sorry for doubting you all, but this isn't going to be popular. I do think we can find a solution that'll work for both Jaluhz and Draconia, but it'll take some time."

Clyde said, "May I speak?"

"Of course," said Gregory.

"Well, I just thought...I mean, when I came to this meeting, I didn't think I'd have anything to offer, but I really wanted to learn more about what Rya and my mom are doing. Nearly my whole family is here, after all. But suddenly I realized I have a perspective that's very different from anyone else's in this room. I'd like to share that if I may." He stopped and looked around the table, his large hands twisting in his lap and he brown eyes focused in concentration.

The others nodded, and Clyde went on. "I'll try to keep this brief—many of you know my story anyway. But here goes. Aster was all the family I had for fifteen years, after my wife died giving birth to her. We were close, and it was a good life, but I kept a major secret from her. I didn't tell her that her grandmother was still alive. This was a dreadful betrayal of our relationship, and Aster was deeply hurt. She needed space, so she and Sasha took off for a camping weekend in February. They were caught in a sudden blizzard and found refuge in a cave. As a result they met Jasmine. By the time Aster returned, she'd discovered her dragon magic.

Clyde stood up and walked around the table to the map wall, the only wall where he could pace a bit without stepping on dragons or Oswald. He ran his hands through his hair, making the cowlick in the back stick up even more, before he went on.

"Suddenly I was afraid of my own daughter, the girl I'd raised from birth. She said she wasn't any different. She said we all have magic, and that mine is with wood. Still her magic was different. She and Sasha could carry on conversations I couldn't even hear. And Jasmine—well, she was so big, and even though I've lived all my life in Havenshold, I really haven't been around dragons that much, not up close like this." He looked over at Jasmine and smiled.

"But I had an enormous incentive to come to terms with this," Clyde continued. "Aster is just too important to me. So we talked and worked through our difficulties, and finally I welcomed Jasmine by rebuilding the front entrance of our home so she could come inside, instead of just sticking her head through a window."

That brought a round of chuckles, and when the room was quiet again, Clyde went on. "I'm the only one in my family who doesn't have dragon magic of some kind. My mom, my reclusive artistic sister—whom I really hope I'll get to see again—my daughter, and now my niece. That's a lot of incentive to come to understand dragon magic, what it is, and what it can offer.

"But most of the people in Havenshold, and indeed all of Draconia, don't have that incentive. Many of them fear magic, as I did. I know Queen Clotilda and Matilda have made Aster, Sasha, and Jasmine roving ambassadors in order to keep magic and dragons close to as many as possible in an effort to break down fear and barriers, and I know Aster and Jasmine do a lot of good.

"That crowd out there now...they're scared. What they're seeing is the loss of everything: their homes, their lands, their very livelihoods. And they know dragons and their riders fix things. They know Chloe saved the planet. They honestly don't care, at the moment, about any 'us.' Right now they only care about 'me and mine.'

Clyde resumed his limited pacing, gathering his thoughts before he continued.

"Everyone in this room—and in fact all those with magical bonds everywhere—well, you maybe don't realize how exceptional you are. I've watched Aster, Sasha, and Jasmine and now Rya and Artemis. You all have a very high level of empathy for others, other people, other species, everything, which I believe stems from your bonds and your commitment to service.

"And several of you didn't know you had magic until, like Aster, you were hit over the head with it, so to speak. But once you discovered your gifts, well, that's just how you see them:

gifts. And that goes for all of you, from Sasha and Calliope all the way to the largest dragon.

"You don't have to worry about whether you'll have food on the table or a roof to sleep under. And Baron, you've suffered greatly, I know, with the loss of the only love in your life. But you've never had to worry about your very survival. And then you and Oswald found each other, and there are few stories more wonderful than yours. How have you shown the change in your life? By becoming the biggest philanthropist on the planet."

Clyde finally went back to his chair and sat down, staring at his hands for a few minutes before looking around the table again.

"But the people out there—they don't understand magic. And they're very scared. The only point many of them see to having magic in our world is to fix things when they get bad. Oh, most people are a lot like what I've heard about Lena. They don't ask for help. They do their best to figure things out on their own, to survive however they can, some barely, and some comfortably. But when they come across something they have no control over, they expect the dragons and their riders to fix it. And if it's really big, then they expect 'their' mage to make it all right again.

"I'm really afraid the volcano—sorry, I mean Jaluhz—isn't our biggest problem. I'm afraid we could be facing a major split between those with magic and the majority of the population. This could turn very ugly indeed." Clyde sighed and said, "Well, that's just what I see."

The room was absolutely silent; no one said anything for the longest time. Finally Emily looked directly at Clyde and said, "Clyde, thank you. You arrived saying you didn't think you had anything to offer, but in fact you've offered us the most important perspective yet."

The baron also looked at Clyde. "You're right," he said. "Jaluhz could be the catalyst that breaks open the divide that's always been there, just below the surface of our society."

Oswald spoke up for the first time. "I've always known what it's like to be different. I mean, I was born without one wing and had to have the other amputated. A wingless gryphon. That's pretty ridiculous."

The baron started to interrupt, but Oswald placed a big front paw on his lap and said, "No, Baron, it's true. But I found you—a middle-aged, lonely soul—and together we've made a darned good team for more than twenty years. We both know what it's like to be different, and yes, your wealth does isolate you. Now I'm seeing we aren't alone in this. As Clyde said so well, all of us with magic are different, and we're the minority. Aster, do you think this kind of situation is what caused the loss of magic in the alternate world?"

Aster was quiet for a few moments, thinking, then said, "Yes, Oswald, I do. When I first suspected the time travel, I looked carefully at our planet's history. Magic had been eradicated, along with the gryphons and unicorns, because it was deemed evil and unnatural. The dolphins escaped only because they headed out to deeper waters. Then, when our planet brought in the dragons, they soon were subjected to the same slaughter and were nearly extinct when King Alfred arrived here. There were only thirty or so dragons and riders at that time.

"But I always thought it would be someone like the black magician who would bring that about. I honestly hadn't seen the potential in a situation like this. But I guess anything can be used as a wedge to drive us apart—if, as Dad said, the divide already exists."

Gregory cleared his throat and said, "So what do we do to prevent this from happening?"

"I don't know," Emily said, shaking her head. "Chloe?"

"I'm not sure," said Chloe solemnly. "I won't hurt Jaluhz; that isn't the answer. We need her, and I hope she needs us."

"Agreed," said Esmeralda. "We support you on that."

Oswald said, "Isn't the lava the real problem? I suspect no one would care what Jaluhz did if there weren't a blanket of moving lava out there. Can we do something with the lava itself?"

"You're right, Oswald," said Gregory, with a bit of excitement in his voice. "But what can we do with that much lava? We can't put it back where it came from, but where else could it go?"

Chloe said, with a wry smile, "And if anyone thinks I can just move it, even with all the help I had when I moved the asteroid—well, that was a matter of hours, but Gregory says this lava will keep flowing for years. There's no way, even with all the help in the world, that I could maintain anything for ten or more years."

"Obviously," said Oswald, also smiling, "no one could do that, no matter how powerful."

"What happened to the lava in the eruption that Jaluhz does remember? The one from before our planet was fully formed?" asked Jasmine.

Gregory stood and went over to his hanging maps. He pulled down a map of the entire world. "Well," he said, "Draconia received the brunt of it, as we know, which is why even today our soil isn't worth much, and then we think the outer seven islands were formed, first Harmony's Sanctuary and the small island off the coast of Forbury, and then the five islands in the Sprite Sea."

"OK," continued Oswald. "We're certain that covering Draconia with lava again isn't a good option, but what about another island or two? Is there a way to channel the lava so it goes out to sea? Would that harm anything?"

Chloe said, "The seas have absorbed lava before, but I don't know at what price.

Aster frowned and then smiled saying, "That's how the other islands were formed, so it should be OK. And as the lava pours into the sea, it will cool instantly. If we can get it to the sea, it should gradually form an island right off the coast of Forbury."

Gregory examined his maps, and the baron stood and went over to get a better look as well. "Dad," Gregory said, "with all your mining experience you know more about what's underground than anyone. Lucy and Gretchen have mapped as many fault lines as they could find. Any ideas?"

Looking thoughtful the baron ran his finger along some of the lines. Oswald came over, and the two were silent, but the others in the room could almost hear the thoughts sliding between them.

Finally the baron said, "We may have the beginnings of an idea."

Gregory nodded. "Go for it."

"The shortest path from where the lava is now flowing out of Jaluhz to the sea runs along this major fault line," the baron explained.

"That's where we had the major earthquake in 531 AA, the one that destroyed Cliffside," said Emily.

"Yes," Gregory said, "the town where both Lucy and Gretchen came from. They were heavily involved in relocating everyone in town to Chauncey's Creek."

"I don't know if it's possible," the baron continued, "but we already have a major slice into the crust of the planet there along the fault line. If it could be deepened and widened, well, maybe..."

"But Dad, that fault line pretty much ends in Forbury, near one of your copper mines," Gregory said.

"I know, but it's also pretty close to the sea. We might be able to extend the line, and I do own all that property, so if some of it gets covered with lava, well, I'm OK with that."

Emily looked over Gregory's shoulder. "How deep and how wide would we need to make the line?" she asked.

"It'll take me a few days of measuring the flow to know exactly, but it'll need to be a major trench for sure."

Aster spoke up. "People have started moving back into that area. Jasmine and I have warned them about the danger, but they don't seem to care. They're sure we won't have another big quake."

"And the fault line also runs through a number pieces of property belonging to ranchers," said Emily. "We'd have to evacuate the area around the old Cliffside, but we'd also need to cut a swath through a number of ranches before we reach Forbury."

"Another problem," said Gregory, "is that the lava is fanning out. It obviously won't just flow in a stream without some help. And while the fault line is close to where the explosion happened, it isn't that close. I'd say it's a good half mile away."

"For sure it won't be easy," said Oswald, "but I don't see a better option."

"Neither do I," said Gregory.

"I'll need to bring Clotilda and Matilda in on this," said Emily, "as we aren't talking about just Havenshold. I don't have the authority to confiscate property outside of Havenshold, and I'm afraid there'll be some pretty unhappy ranchers along that route."

"There's a shorter distance north across part of Granvale," said the baron, moving his fingers along the map to show where he meant, "but that's a bad idea in my opinion. First the natural flow of the land is southwest. We'd have to dig a much deeper trench to make the lava flow north, so the shorter distance would be outweighed by the need to dig a lot deeper. And Granvale never has suffered from a volcanic eruption, which is why its land grows most of our world's food. It certainly wouldn't help to mess with that to appease some ranchers."

"I agree," said Emily, scribbling notes as quickly as she could.

"In addition the fault line," said Gregory, pointing at the map again, "has done a lot of our work for us."

Emily turned to Chloe. "What do you think?" she said. "You've been very quiet."

"I'm sorry," said Chloe, and then she turned to Rya. "Can you check with Jaluhz and see if this'll work for her? I can't think why she'd care what happens to her lava once she expels it, but I'd just like to check. It seems to me that we'd be showing her we care about her, and I'd be willing to bet that everyone would be in favor of keeping Jaluhz happy."

Rya nodded. "I'll try, but like you, I don't think she'd care. She just seems so relieved to be getting rid of it. And if I can let her know that the amount of destruction will be a lot less, well, I think that would make her happier."

"I agree," said Chloe. "So yes, let's start on the baron and Oswald's plan. And obviously we want to start doing something here so people realize we aren't just sitting around."

Gregory nodded. "I'll start on the numbers right away, but we do need to start channeling the lava flow toward the fault line. We can't worry about the far edges of the apron as much as the center. If we can get the center moving toward the fault line, I believe the edges will then pull toward the lower center. I think some of that land will be lost, but that was always inevitable."

"Right then," said Emily. "I'll start lining up dragon crews to begin digging a trench. Baron, can you and Oswald help me map that out?"

"Of course," said the baron.

"And we need to dig a reasonable distance in front of the flow," suggested Oswald. "We can't get too close, or we'll be overwhelmed by the heat and gases."

Chloe said, "Once you have the path marked out, and a trench going to the fault, I'll be able to cut the last part magically. But I'll need somewhere for the lava to go once I've cut that half mile or so."

"And meanwhile the lava continues to flow," said Artemis, who had been very quiet up until then.

"I know, Artemis," said Harmony, "but we can't act any faster."

"I know that," said Artemis. "I just hope that crowd does too."

"I'm going to ask Clotilda and Matilda to come here today, and then they can address the crowds and let people know what we're trying to do," said Emily.

"Excellent," said the baron. "This lava is leaving Havenshold, and Clotilda and Matilda rule us as well as the rest of Draconia, so their words should carry more weight than ours."

Everyone stood and began to leave. Gregory already was gathering his notes and instruments so he could take on-site measurements. Chloe asked, "Where can I be of the most help?"

Emily said, "If you could say something to reassure that crowd as I ask them to disperse—well, face it, they want their mage."

Chloe groaned and said, "Sure."

"It's probably best if you don't mention Jaluhz's rights," said Harmony with a smile.

"Yeah, I got that," said Chloe.

The group opened the library doors and began to exit. Several people in the crowd, which contained about seventy-five people, started to shout, and Emily held up her hands for quiet. Then she began, "I know this situation is very upsetting, but we need to be sure we have all the information before we act."

"What do you need to know?" a man called out in a very angry voice. "Just blow that volcano out into space. You can do that, mage, right?"

"No," said Chloe somberly and deliberately, "I can't. And have you all forgotten how much we've relied on the volcano?"

"Doesn't matter now," yelled another. "She's out of control and needs to be stopped. Just plug up that hole."

Emily fielded that remark. "First, if you really want to help, we need information about who set off that explosion. More importantly, however, you need to understand that if we do as you say and plug up the hole, the pressure inside the volcano will build to the point where she'll blow her top in a gigantic explosion, and then we'll all be killed instantly. Right now no lives are in danger."

"But we're going to lose our homes, our lands, our shops," shouted a woman near the back of the crowd.

"As I said, we're looking at the options to minimize that," Emily replied. "But you need to give us time, and yes, there will be—and in fact already has been—some property damage. You've all felt the increase in earthquakes over the last few weeks." She was glad to notice a number of nods and a quieting of the crowd. "A volcano is a natural wonder and has its own cycle. Earthquakes and eruptions are a part of that. We're very lucky that our volcano—and by the way, her name is Jaluhz—has such a lengthy eruption cycle. She's only erupted once before in our history, and that was back when the planet was forming. That's why Draconia has the terrain it does, and that's where the islands came from."

"You named the volcano," said the first man in disbelief.

"Yes," said Chloe, deciding it wouldn't do any good to say that Jaluhz had told Rya her name. "But the point is that we can't take from her all the energy we like and then try to destroy her when she does what's natural for a volcano."

"Why not?" asked the man. "She's trying to destroy us."

"Enough," Emily said. "I'm here to assure you that we're dealing with the situation in a way that ultimately will cause the least amount of harm to everyone. Queen Clotilda and Matilda will be here this afternoon, and at that time, we'll have more information to give you. Until then please return to your homes and shops."

"Yeah, right," said the man, who was both tall and muscular, with dark brown hair and eyes.. "They're just trying to protect their sacred volcano for their dragons. I say we capture the mage and force her to do what we want. Who's with me?" And with that, the man as well as about twenty others pushed towards the library steps, rushing for Chloe.

"Sir," said Emily, holding up her hands, "would you like to be arrested for intent to start a riot? If not, I suggest you let us get on with dealing with this situation. We're looking out for everyone's best interests. Havenshold depends on all of us, and you should know that."

"Just words," snarled the man again, who had slowed but not stopped. "You riders all stick together. I saw you all in the hospital courtyard last night, just because someone got hurt."

Then he burst into a sprint and reached for Chloe, grabbing the sleeve of her coat. Chloe took a step back, but did not engage with him as she figured that would truly start a riot.

Emily sent out a telepathic call to Hannah and Rupert, and she included Chloe in the conversation. *You need to take this man into custody. I think he knows a lot more than he's saying.*

Hannah and Rupert moved quietly and swiftly, until they were standing on each side of the man, as Emily said, "What do you know about that, sir?"

"Oh, no, you're not getting me." he turned to run, but Hannah and Rupert each grabbed an arm, and as Hannah turned him around so that his arms went behind him, Rupert tied them together with a strong rope. They had him in custody before he could take a single step.

"See what they do?" shouted the man. "If anyone disagrees with them, they arrest them."

Emily called out to the crowd, "Can anyone tell me about this man? His name? Anything?"

There was silence until finally a woman said, "That's Zeke, and he's been bragging about how rich he's going to be. That's all I know."

Emily nodded to Hannah and Rupert. "Well, Zeke," she said, "we have some questions for you."

"Won't tell you nothin'," said Zeke, as he tried to pull his arms out of the ropes.

"That's your right," said Emily, "but you're coming along with us. Meanwhile I would ask the rest of you again to please disperse. If anyone knows anything pertinent to yesterday's explosion, please come to either me or Chloe."

— 17 —

TAMING LAVA

Chloe stared out over the expanse of lava, mesmerized at the gash in the side of the mountain from where the molten lava continued to escape. The sheer power of the endless flow held her riveted. It was bright red-orange with bits of yellow in the center, turning to crusted black around the edges. The heat was intense, even where she was, which was a good hundred yards from the lava, on a cliff overhanging the flow. Aster and Jasmine stood with her, with Sasha sitting on Jasmine's back, also staring.

Finally Jasmine said, "So this is the source of the heat we've enjoyed for centuries."

"Yes," said Chloe. "Jaluhz provides almost all the energy that powers not only Draconia but also the other nations."

"She's truly amazing," said Aster. "I sure hope we can find a way to regain her trust. If I were her, I wouldn't want to deal with people ever again. Look at the horrible gash that was blown into her side."

"I know," Chloe said sadly. "You know, Aster, your dad is a wise man. It took courage for him to speak up in front of us all, and he's right. He's right that those of us with magic, especially those with bonds to others, have greater empathy for those around us, but at the same time, we don't get just how many people resent or fear us—maybe not openly, maybe not all the time—but when something like this happens...well, you heard the crowd outside the library. Are we only seen as a way to fix things, and otherwise we just have it easy?"

"I don't know," said Aster, her voice streaked with sadness as well.

"There's a lot of truth in Clyde's words," said Jasmine, "and maybe that explains why we rally around our own. Has anyone heard how Lucy's doing?"

Chloe nodded. "Gretchen sends me updates. Lucy's still unconscious, but she's holding her own."

The three of them watched as Gregory, Oswald, and the baron hiked around the lava flow making sure that they stayed at least fifty yards away from it and made various calculations. Emily had Esmeralda fly over the flow as Gregory asked about depths and rates.

Finally Aster said, "I really thought we were helping people see that we're all different but that we have so much in common. I thought Jasmine and I were putting a face on the magic, which would make a difference."

Chloe turned to her and said, "And you are. You three have made a real difference. Clyde is proof of that. I've shared the reports I've received from the small villages you visit, and they prove you're making a difference. Not only have you helped a lot of people in need, but you've also just visited so that villagers could get to know you and pet Jasmine, and feel more comfortable around magic."

Aster shook her head. "I know we help, and we make things easier. But do they only care because of what we do? Do they ever really see us?"

"That's a tough question," Jasmine said, "and you could ask that about anyone really. Do any of us ever really see others?

I'd like to think that some of us do. And change happens slowly, even more slowly than the rate of this lava flow."

"Maybe our work is like this flow," said Chloe. "We're trying to change so much, to help people see the world from a different perspective so we can all work together. But that would be a huge change. People, even riders, do tend to think first of themselves, but eventually we'll come together."

Just then Emily and Esmeralda joined them on the overhang. "This is an awe-inspiring sight, isn't it? I suspect Oswald, Gregory, and the baron are going to be here making measurements and calculations for a while, but I have to deal with Zeke. Chloe, would you help me listen to his case?"

"I'd be happy to," said Chloe.

Emily said, "Thanks, and Aster, could you, Sasha, and Jasmine take our place in helping Gregory, Oswald, and the baron?"

"Sure, Emily," said Aster.

I can see a lot from my perch on Jasmine's back, said Sasha.

"I'm sure you can," said Emily with a laugh.

As Emily, Esmeralda, and Chloe walked to the rider complex and Emily's office, Emily asked, "Did I overreact when I arrested Zeke?"

"I don't think so," Chloe replied. "His hatred is driven by something. Maybe he even feels guilty if he's the one who set off the explosion, and he's hiding that guilt in his anger. Anyway, if he doesn't know anything and if you can reason with him, you can always let him go."

"Thanks, Chloe. That's why I want you with me. You always seem to have an accurate perspective on things."

Emily, Esmeralda, and Chloe walked into Emily's office and sat down. Rupert stuck his head in and said, "Do you want to see Zeke now?"

Emily sighed. "Yes, let's get this over with."

Rupert left and returned a few minutes later with Hannah and Zeke, who still had his hands tied behind his back. Rupert untied the rope and motioned him to a straight back chair in front of Emily's desk. Hannah stood behind the chair and Rupert moved to his usual spot on Emily's left side, between her and Esmeralda. With Chloe sitting to the right of Emily they made a formidable grouping.

Zeke slouched in the chair, shoving his long brown hair out of his eyes, his stained shirt untucked, and looked at Emily saying, "So what are you going to do with me. Get the mage to erase me?"

Emily refused to rise to the taunt. "We'd like to know what you know about the explosion."

"Yeah, I'm sure you would, but I ain't talking."

"We know Damian and Frank had two men helping them mine the volcano. Lena saw them, and I'm sure she'd be able to identify you."

"That old bitch," Zeke scoffed. "She don't know anything. Damian had her hoodwinked. She even let them live in her home."

"Ah, so you do know them," said Chloe.

"Yeah, so?" snarled Zeke. "I know lots of folks. That don't prove nothin'."

"Who worked with you?" asked Emily.

Zeke shrugged. "No one."

"Lena saw two men with Damian and Frank. Who was the other one?"

"Maybe she just imagined it."

Emily looked over at Rupert. "Did you run a check on Zeke's family and friends? I know you haven't had a lot of time."

"All we've found out so far is that he has a brother named Norman," said Rupert.

"You leave him out of this," said Zeke.

"Oh, so he knows something, does he?" said Emily. "Rupert, maybe we should bring him in. Do you know where he lives?"

Rupert nodded as he opened his notebook. "Norman lives with Zeke on the outskirts of Havenshold. Should I try to bring Norman in?"

"No," shouted Zeke, rising from the chair and moving toward Emily. "Don't you touch my brother."

"We just want to ask him some questions," said Emily, as Hannah grabbed the back of Zeke's shirt and forced him to sit.

Zeke shook his head. "No, I won't have it."

Chloe turned to Emily. "Can I ask Zeke about Norman?"

"Certainly," said Emily.

Chloe turned to Zeke. "You're very protective of your brother. You look after him, don't you?"

"Sure," said Zeke. "That's what brothers do."

"So don't you think Norman would want to help you?"

"He can't," said Zeke.

"Why not?" continued Chloe, in a soft and sympathetic voice.

"He's not smart like me. He's never been quite right. I have to take care of him, and I don't want him upset."

"That's admirable," said Chloe, "but if we can't sort this out, you won't be around to help Norman. What will happen to him then?"

Zeke's jaw dropped open. He scratched his head and finally said, "You keep twisting things around. You can't keep me here."

Emily took over again. "I'm afraid we can, Zeke. You tried to start a riot, and you're a known associate of Damian and Frank. That's enough for us to keep you for a day or so while we search for more information, and we'll start that search with Norman." She turned to Rupert and said, "Go find—"

"No!" Zeke yelled, once again trying to stand but Hannah pushed him back down into the chair. "Wait. Don't get him. He don't know nothin'. He just does what I tell him."

"And what did you tell him?" asked Emily.

"Well, Damian told me there are riches inside the volcano, and you dragons and riders hoard them, and that's why you don't have to work much. He said, 'Why should they have them all?' We was deserving of them. So we were going to rob the volcano—that's what Damian said. It was our right. We should get some riches too."

Esmeralda turned her body so that she was closer to Zeke and then let out a low growl.

"So that was the plan, was it?" said Emily, looking at Rupert to be sure he was getting this all down. "But then Damian and Frank were killed."

Zeke nodded and twisted in his chair. "Yeah, so then it was up to me. I figured I'd just get even more. Damian was so cautious. And he had to make that woman happy. She wanted a cut too."

"You mean Lena, don't you?"

"Yeah, her shop was in the perfect spot. We could go through the tunnel in the back of it and get right inside the volcano. Then we found another way in that the old woman didn't know about, so me and Norman could help ourselves without her knowing."

"Ah," said Emily, "so Norman was the other man Lena saw."

"Yeah," said Zeke reluctantly, "but as I said, he don't know anything. He can't think like we do. He just does what I tell him."

"So after Damian and Frank died, what then?"

Zeke squirmed, trying to avoid Emily's piercing stare. "Well, like I said, I figured it was up to me. The plan was a good one, but Damian had taken too long, being too careful, and look, it didn't get him anywhere. So I figured I'd just blow up the damn volcano, and the riches would come pouring out."

"You were right about that, just not about what the riches were," Emily said. "But didn't you see Lucy and Gretchen on the mountain when you set off your explosives?"

Zeke nodded. "They were crawling all over the place. I couldn't wait. They were never going to leave, and I had to work in the dark, see, so no one would see me. I wasn't sharing all that wealth with anyone."

"So you didn't care if they got hurt?" interrupted Chloe, a harshness in her voice.

"Nah," said Zeke, shrugging. "The world would be better without you riders and dragons anyway."

Esmeralda let out a louder growl. Zeke turned toward her but said nothing.

"So you went ahead with your plan anyway," said Emily, keeping her eyes fixed on Zeke.

"Yeah, only I hadn't figured on the lava," said Zeke.

"We'll get to that in a moment," said Emily, in a very tight voice, "but again what about Lucy and Gretchen?"

"I didn't care. The one's a cripple anyway. I remember all the talk when she became a rider. Plenty of people said she'd cheated and shouldn't be a rider 'cause she was crippled. And then the other one...well, it ain't natural, two women together, is it? So the world would be better without them. So what? No biggie." Zeke stretched out is legs in front of him and leaned back in his chair.

Esmeralda stood, which caused Zeke's chair to tip even further backwards, stopping only when it bumped into Hannah. "You're a miserable excuse for a person," Esmeralda snapped. "You aren't worth even the tiniest bit of Lucy or Gretchen."

Zeke looked at Chloe, his eyes pleading for help. "I know my rights," he said. "You have to protect me. You're the mage for all people."

Chloe turned to Zeke and said in a very calm, quiet voice, "I'm the mage for everything and everyone on this planet, which includes dragons and the volcano. If I were you, I wouldn't push your case that way."

"You, you...you people, you're all the same," snarled Zeke. "You keep all the riches to yourselves so you don't have to work hard like regular folks. Then you use your magic to make us behave."

Emily smiled. "That didn't work too well with you. We certainly didn't make you behave."

"You're right," said Zeke. "I know your number. You can't control me like you do the rest of Havenshold."

Chloe spoke then. "You seem to have everything figured out, and you found the volcano's riches. Well done."

"What...what do you mean?" stammered Zeke, with a puzzled expression. "I only found that damned lava."

Chloe nodded. "That's what I mean. You seem to have a very strange idea about the economics of this planet."

"The eco...what?"

"You think the riders have it easy, don't you?" she replied. "That they're living off jewels."

"Yeah," said Zeke, nodding eagerly. "That's what Damian said."

"Well, Damian was wrong," continued Chloe, leaning forward a bit. "The dragons and riders have herds of cattle and sheep, which they raise to feed themselves and trade for supplies. In addition they're in charge of the volcano."

"That's what I said, didn't I?" yelled Zeke.

Chloe held up her hand and continued. "Yes, you did, but what you don't get is what the riches are. The riches are all the energy and heat stored within the volcano—energy and heat that's then siphoned off to power not only Draconia but also the other three nations. That power is Draconia's greatest export, and it allows us to then import all the things Draconia can't make on its own. That's the real truth."

Emily went on, saying, "So when Chloe said you uncovered the volcano's riches, she meant that hot molten lava. But you've now ruptured the side of the volcano so that her riches, instead of staying inside where they could be harvested as energy, are now spilling out all over the land, destroying everything in their path."

"But you can stop that," said Zeke, looking at Chloe, his eyes pleading that she'd agree. "You're a mage after all. You stopped the asteroid, so this should be easy."

"No," Chloe said, shaking her head, "it isn't either easy or simple. The damage you've done will be hard to stop. That lava will keep pouring out for years and years."

Emily added, "And let me tell you something else. If Lucy dies, you'll be charged with murder."

Zeke shook his head, panic beginning to rise in his voice. "No, that's not right. She's...she's not all there. That doesn't count. She doesn't even have two arms. No, I can't be charged with that."

Esmeralda let out a roar that shook the walls. "You scum," she growled, "she's worth a thousand of you. And we don't measure people by how many arms they have. You'd better hope she recovers, because if she doesn't, well, have you ever seen an angry dragon?"

Zeke fell to his knees and cried, "You can't do that."

Esmeralda said, "Just watch me."

Emily held up a hand. "Esmeralda, please sit down."

As Esmeralda sat back on her haunches, her eyes boring into Zeke, Emily said, "And Zeke, no, she not only can't, but more importantly, she wouldn't. Unlike you, she doesn't think it's right to blow things up just because she wants to. This has gone on long enough. You've admitted to setting off the explosion that caused severe injury to the volcano and two of our riders, one of whom is fighting for her life. You'll be sent to Alfredsville, to the palace, where Queen Clotilda and Matilda will decide what to do with you."

"You can't do this!" shouted Zeke, again trying to stand. Hannah shoved him down hard into his chair, nearly tipping it over.

"Rupert, Hannah, take Zeke back to the holding room and arrange to have him sent under guard to Alfredsville. He can wait there until Clotilda and Matilda return to the palace." Emily turned back to Zeke. "Clotilda and Matilda will be arriving here shortly to assess the damages and help us develop a plan for dealing with the lava flow you've unleashed. I think it would be better for you if she didn't deal with you here. If you think Esmeralda is scary, wait until you meet them. Now get him out of my sight before I do something I'll regret," she told Hannah and Rupert.

As they reached for Zeke, he said, "But what about my brother? He can't manage on his own. He needs me."

"You should have thought of that before you blew up the volcano," said Emily, a steely coldness in her voice.

Chloe looked at Zeke with pity in her eyes and said, "You think we're selfish monsters, but we'll make sure Norman is properly taken care of, and we won't use him to commit crimes. Your concern for him is touching, but it would have been more touching if you'd reached out to the community to get him the help he needs and deserves."

As Hannah and Rupert marched Zeke out of the room, Emily said, "Once you have him secured, please find Norman and assess the situation. If it's as Zeke has stated, I know you'll treat him gently and kindly. Maybe take him to Dr. Brian for assessment, if you think that's appropriate."

Rupert nodded as they left.

"Whew," said Emily, reaching for her mug of tea. "That was beyond horrible."

Chloe nodded. "I'm honestly not sure Zeke has ever thought for himself. He seems to have believed everything Damian told him. Still he admits to knowing that Lucy and Gretchen were there and setting off the explosives anyway, so there's not much doubt of his guilt."

"I agree," Emily said, "and if the residents of Havenshold realize Zeke caused the lava flow, well, his life here won't be worth much. That's the main reason I'm sending him to Alfredsville. We need to keep the townsfolk from doing something they'll ultimately regret."

Esmeralda said, "But what he said about Lucy...that was monstrous. I know there were grumblings at Harriet's hatching about her choosing of Lucy instead of one of the candidates, but that was years ago."

"Zeke's comments aren't the general consensus," said Chloe. "I think he was grabbing at anything to defend himself, and he might have heard some of those grumblings years ago and just brought them back up. Most of Havenshold thinks very highly of Lucy. Gretchen is updating me, as I'm sure she's doing with you, and she says that the outpouring of cards and gifts from the townsfolk is quickly filling the main hospital lounge. Nurse Beatrice is scrambling to find places for everything. That's indicative of Havenshold's true feelings."

"You're right of course," said Esmeralda, with a nod and a smile. "And Clotilda and Matilda have just landed. They're on their way to speak with us."

Emily's office door opened, and Queen Clotilda entered with Matilda right behind her. "Where's Rupert?" Clotilda asked. "We didn't even get a chance to speed past him before he could announce us."

Emily laughed. "You do enjoy that, don't you? Hannah and Rupert are looking into something for me. Let's bring you up to date."

As Clotilda sat in a comfortable chair across from Emily's desk and Matilda sat on the floor next to her, Emily and Chloe recounted recent events.

After Emily and Chloe had shared everything that had transpired, Clotilda said, "Wow. You do have a lot going on, don't you?"

"We flew over the lava flow to check it out before we landed," said Matilda. "That's a lot of lava. It just keeps pouring out, spreading across the landscape. It may not be moving quickly, but it is moving inextricably."

Chloe nodded. "And it'll only get worse."

"I get that," said Clotilda, "and I also gather you aren't in favor of stopping the flow."

Chloe looked at the queen and started to say, "I really don't think—"

Clotilda smiled. "Relax, Chloe. I get it, and I'm on your side. We can't change natural events, and even if this one was man-made, Jaluhz needs to have her eruption. Given that fact, this actually may be a blessing. However, it in no way excuses what Zeke did. What a loathsome man. We'll deal with him once we're back at the palace. You did right to send him there, Emily."

"Thanks," said Emily. "I'm afraid Clyde hit on the real problem. If we don't handle this lava disaster properly, we could see a real social upheaval."

"I agree," said Clotilda. Then she turned to Chloe, "So what can you do, wondrous mage?"

Chloe looked up from her lap, then saw an enormous smile on Clotilda's face, and knew she was teasing. Chloe relaxed and said, "Well, if Oswald, Gregory, and the baron can propose a way to channel the lava and get it to flow toward the Ercesa Ocean, my thought was to have them work on that channel ahead of the actual lava. Gregory has made it clear that it isn't healthy to be too close to the front of the flow. Once they've dug the channel far enough that they'll be able to stay well away from the flow, I'll bring the lava to the channel. We need to continue digging the channel, but the lava flow is slow enough that once we have a large section of channel made, the rest can be dug even after the lava begins to fill it at this end."

"Can you do that alone?" asked Clotilda.

"No, I certainly don't have that much power. I think we'll need to set up a bit of the power grid we used when I moved the asteroid. I don't think we need to involve the bonded pairs from the other nations. If I can draw on the strength of Draconia's pairs, I'll probably have enough power to bend the flow into the channel."

"Well, it sounds like a viable solution, provided Gregory, Oswald, and the baron can work out the actual engineering of it all," said Clotilda, rapidly jotting down some notes as she spoke.

Emily went over to the map of Draconia that was hanging on her wall and pointed along it from Havenshold to the border with Forbury. "The problem we really need your help with is getting permission to take over this swath of land along the fault line."

"I see," Clotilda said, nodding. "And I understand people have moved back into the area that was Cliffside, so there also will be some relocation involved. Let me think about this. Obviously I'll do it since it's in the best interest of all of Draconia, but given the discord that has arisen in Havenshold—which surprises me since I've always thought we had a good relationship with the townsfolk—I'll need to do it as gently and tactfully as possible."

"I really believe," Chloe said, "that once the townspeople settle down and begin to think, rather than just react in fear, they'll come around. And once we have the facts and figures to present a real course of action, it'll make a big difference."

"I know you're right," said Clotilda. "Let's just hope Oswald's plan is actually something we can do."

"That gryphon has always been pretty darned sharp," Emily said with a laugh. "I'd bet on him any day of the week." There was a knock on the door, and she called out, "Come in."

Oswald and the baron entered, greeting Clotilda and Matilda as well as Chloe, Emily, and Esmeralda. Once they'd gotten comfortable,, the baron in a chair next to Clotilda and Oswald on the floor next to him, the baron said, "Gregory is brilliant."

Clotilda smiled. "And he comes by it honestly, I'd say, Baron. You're no slouch, you know."

The baron blushed slightly. "Maybe. Anyway, he's gone back to his office to crunch more numbers, but he asked us to come here and give a preliminary report."

"So will Oswald's plan work?" asked Clotilda, cutting to the chase.

"Of course," said Oswald, with a smile that showed off a couple dimples in his cheeks. "Did you have any doubts?"

Everyone laughed at that as Esmeralda said, "You two are a matched set."

"Again of course," said Oswald.

"Enough," said Chloe, once she could stop laughing. "Could we have some actual details?"

"Certainly," said the baron. "Gregory's making estimates regarding the rate and amount of flow, but the plan Oswald proposed this morning is sound. We'll need to create a trench that's probably a half mile wide and about the same depth."

"That's a very big trench," said Matilda.

"Yes, well, there's a lot of lava," said Oswald.

"And you'll follow the fault line," said Clotilda.

"Yes, and that's where we're hoping Jaluhz might be able to help. If she can open her fault line either wider or deeper, well, that would help a great deal. The fault line peters out as it reaches Forbury, so if it's at all possible for her to extend the line, it would really make a huge difference."

"Rya and Harmony are doing all they can to improve communications with Jaluhz," Chloe said. "Clyde has put Rya's apprenticeship on hold while we figure this out, although I think

Rya is doing a carving as a way to help her to focus. I'll pass this request on to them, and they can see if Jaluhz understands and is willing."

Matilda asked, "Am I right in assuming that if Jaluhz can do this, it'll mean more earthquakes?"

The baron nodded. "According to Gregory, yes. The only way Jaluhz could widen, deepen, or extend the fault line is with earthquakes. So if she's willing, we think it would be better to have more smaller quakes rather than fewer large quakes."

Emily frowned and said, "I'd sure think so."

"But there'll still be a lot of digging involved," Clotilda said, looking at the notes she'd already made. "And the dirt that's dug out has to go somewhere. The area of land that'll actually be involved will be closer to a mile wide, don't you think, Oswald?"

"Yes, that's my thought as well," he replied, waving his left front paw. "We can pile the dirt up, but even so it'll take up about a quarter mile on each side of the trench. I haven't figured out the angle of slide, but as you know, any piles have to be wider at the bottom than the top."

"So I need to begin negotiations with those owning land along the trench and for a half mile each side of it," said Clotilda, standing up so she could pace a bit.

The baron nodded. "That's the bottom line."

"I'm sure glad you own the land we have to cross in Forbury, Baron," said Clotilda, looking at the baron as she sat down again. "And many thanks for your generosity in making it available. Buying out the rest of the land is going to put quite a dent in Draconia's treasury."

"Once Gregory has the figures," Oswald said looking at Chloe, "especially those regarding the rate of flow, we'll figure out where to start digging. We'll try to make the distance you have to move the lava as short as we can."

"Thanks," said Chloe with a wry smile. "I'd appreciate that, but remember, the safety of those doing the digging is more important. This all sounds possible, which is a relief. I'm going to meet with Rya and Harmony just to clear it with Jaluhz and keep her in the loop."

"And then, Chloe," began Clotilda, "you'll need to don your mage robes and make a public announcement." Chloe groaned as Clotilda continued. "You know that's needed. By the end of the day, you should have enough information, including where the digging will start. And hopefully we'll have even better news about Lucy, which you can include. Emily, you need to send out the information now that there will be a public announcement on the situation later this afternoon. Hopefully that'll help calm people and let them know that we'll be acting."

Nodding, Emily teased, "And it's always so nice to see Chloe in formal garb."

Chloe rolled her eyes as Clotilda and Matilda stood. "We'll get a hold of the land records and begin contacting the owners," Clotilda said. "I'll also send someone to the folks residing along the fault line. Hmm, I think Aster, Sasha, and Jasmine should do that, don't you, Emily?"

"They'd be perfect. They know nearly all the small communities scattered within Draconia, and they probably have ideas for locations where these folks could move. I'm assuming we'll offer help with their moves and their transitions to new locations."

"Of course," said Clotilda, moving to the door. "I'll assign them to the task as my roving ambassadors, which will give them my authority to act."

After Clotilda and Matilda left, the baron said, "Oswald and I need to help Gregory. We'll keep you posted."

"Thanks, baron, and thanks, Oswald," said Emily.

They each gave a wave as they headed out of the office.

"I'm going to find out what Hannah and Rupert discovered about Norman then start spreading the word about your public announcement," Emily told Chloe. "Do you have a preference as to the time?"

"Never," said Chloe with a hopeful tone. "No, seriously, how about four? It's still light out until nearly five, and I sure don't want to add darkness to the mix, but I do want to make it late enough so we've got some really definite information about the plan."

"You've got it. Four this afternoon in the library courtyard."

"Well, I'd better go talk with Rya and Harmony," said Chloe as she left the office.

She heard Emily call out, "Good luck with Jaluhz" as she headed down the hall.

— 18 —

PROCLAMATION

Chloe walked through town, past the library, and on to Clyde's house, a lovely two story home with fir paneling and a round attic window. It was a twenty-minute walk and gave her a chance to organize her thoughts. She arrived as Aster, Sasha, and Jasmine were saying good-bye to everyone.

Aster had just lifted Sasha onto Jasmine's back when Chloe approached. "So you're off again?"

"Yeah. Clotilda wants us to start relocating people who are living along the fault line."

We're going to find them much better places to live, said Sasha. *We know all the best spots.*

"I'm sure you do," Chloe said with a warm smile.

"We'll keep in touch," said Aster, "and let you know when we have everyone out of danger."

Aster ran and gave hugs to Clyde, Harmony, Rya, and Artemis before vaulting onto Jasmine. "Bye, everyone," she shouted, as Jasmine leapt into the air.

The rest of them waved until the three were out of sight. Then Clyde said, "Would you like to come inside, Chloe?" He motioned toward the lovely and usual front door, one with double doors which were now opened wide, allowing space for a dragon to enter. The door had a number of intricate carvings, telling the story of Aster and Jasmine's bonding.

"Yes. Thank you."

Clyde led the way, heading for the large family room right off of the kitchen near the rear of the home. The walls were also fir paneled, giving a lovely warm and yet bright look to the room. There were several old but comfortable couches as well as a couple of overstuffed chairs.

Once they were settled in the family room, Artemis said, "Betcha want to know what we know."

Rya ruffled Artemis's fur and smiled as she said, "Now don't tease."

Chloe chuckled. "You two certainly are looking much less stressed. I take it things are going more smoothly."

"Yes, Grandma has been a huge help," Rya said, with a big grin on her face. "Well, in lots of ways, but I guess you want to know about Jaluhz."

"You're right," said Chloe, nodding, "but I also care about you for more than just your ability to reach Jaluhz, so again I'm very glad to see you're looking better. And Clyde, you seem calmer as well."

Clyde simply nodded. Chloe turned back to Rya and Artemis and said, "So what have you two found out?"

"Well, it was all Rya actually," said Artemis. "Harmony and I just supported her. Is that the right way to say it, Harmony?"

"Yes, it is," Harmony said with a warm smile.

"Anyway," said Rya, "I'm getting much clearer images from Jaluhz. You know, she's really quite magnificent and very smart. I think she's been the biggest help—as she learns more about us, she's figured out better ways to communicate. It's absolutely amazing. She's not entirely happy about the gash in her side, however, as she thinks it looks ugly."

Chloe really laughed at this. "So she's a bit vain, is she? Well, maybe once all this settles down, we can make her look a bit nicer. What else?"

"Even if she doesn't like how it looks," went on Rya, "she admits to feeling a lot better. The pressure inside her has lessened already. I think she's beginning to realize the explosion actually was a good thing, even though she really doesn't like the guy who did it. But she let me know that now she won't have to blow everything out of the top in a giant eruption. I actually got the idea that she likes this slower, long-term solution because it'll provide her with a constant balance. And she seems to think it'll be easier for us to deal with as well."

"So she's fine with whatever we do with the lava? We'll try to make it attractive for her," Chloe joked.

"Yes, she's fine with that."

"Do you think she'd help us with it?" asked Chloe. "We want to make use of the existing major fault line, as we figured that would be the easiest place to make the channel, but first we want to make sure she's OK with that, and second, we'd like to know if she could help with a series of smaller earthquakes aimed at widening and deepening the fault. That way the dragons and riders wouldn't have to do so much digging."

Harmony placed a hand on Rya's shoulder, and Artemis scooted onto Rya's lap as Clyde said, "They're going to chat with Jaluhz now. Do you want to come into the kitchen for some tea? Their conversation may take a few minutes."

"Sure," said Chloe. "Thanks."

Clyde and Chloe sat at the large butcher block kitchen table after Clyde had poured the tea. "So, Clyde, how are things going now that your mom is back?"

"Actually," he said, looking over at Chloe, "surprisingly well. She's really changed, which I discovered while working on her home in Sanctuary, but I was worried that being back in Havenshold...well, she might change back, so to speak."

Chloe smiled. "She's always been a very good person, Clyde. You've told me that. She just needed to learn to give you space and not be so overprotective. And you've said you've had a real incentive to learn about magic, so that probably has concerned her." Clyde nodded, and Chloe went on. "I've learned that nothing is more important to Harmony than her family, so her incentive to get along with you has been every bit as great as yours."

Clyde said, "I know. And she's really good with the girls. Right now I'm so glad she's here for Rya."

"So has she moved into the cottage on the baron's estate?"

"Yes, he helped her with the move, and he's arranged for some of his miners to bring the animals and the rest of her things. They should be arriving in another day or so."

"But you just finished expanding her home on Sanctuary. What's going to happen with that?"

Clyde shrugged. "I don't think my mom has decided. I think she's going to try this out for the winter. Our winters may not be the mildest, but they're much better than Sanctuary's. And here she's not alone. Honestly I think we all worried about her being so isolated. And the baron seems really concerned about that as well. I think the two of them are beginning to like each other," he said with a sly grin.

"They've both been alone for so long that it would be nice if they found comfort in at least a friendship, if not more," said Chloe.

"I agree, and the baron said something about using Sanctuary to help young people who are struggling. I don't know that anyone has thought further than that, but there's no rush. And I really do like having her here—she's close but not too close. I've missed her as well."

Chloe said, "Well, it'll all work out."

"Chloe," Rya called out, "we've got some answers."

As Chloe and Clyde entered the family room, Rya said, "Jaluhz...oh, I do love her! She caught on right away about what we were asking. And she thinks the plan is a good one. She's definitely willing to help, but—and here's the really neat part—she wants to be sure there's nothing along the fault line that could be injured or killed when she makes an earthquake. Isn't that something? A volcano caring about us?"

Chloe smiled. "Yes, it's definitely something. And I can see you're in love with our volcano."

Rya's face lit up. "She's fabulous. I'm going to stay in touch with her even after we have all this sorted out. I'm her friend now, and that's what friends do."

"For sure," said Chloe, looking over the top of Rya's head at Harmony to see love and pride for her granddaughter beaming from her eyes.

"I need to make sure we evacuate the area around the fault line," said Chloe.

"Yeah, and Jaluhz said she can't exactly predict the effect of the earthquakes. She said it isn't an exact science. She showed me images of plates sliding deep underground then showed me how they sometimes snag."

"Let her know we've asked for help in clearing the areas along the fault line, and we do understand that she can't precisely regulate earthquakes. I'll talk with Gregory to see if he can help me decide just how far we need to evacuate folks. And I'll let you know, either through Harmony or by coming to you myself, when we're ready."

"That would be fine," said Harmony. "You and I can keep in touch telepathically, since Rya can communicate telepathically only with members of our family."

"Great then," said Chloe as she stood. "And Rya, please convey our heartfelt thanks to Jaluhz for everything."

"Jaluhz also wants to know about Lucy," said Rya. "She seems really concerned about Lucy and Gretchen's injuries."

"We'll keep you posted there as well. For now let Jaluhz know Gretchen is healing quickly and doing fine, and Lucy is still unconscious but definitely holding her own."

"Oh, that's good news," Harmony said with a sigh. "I know I'm not alone in holding that young woman in my thoughts."

Chloe nodded. "Yes, a lot of people are, as well as Lucy's moles. That's just got to make a difference." After a brief pause, she went on. "Well, I've got to get back to the library and decide what I'm going to say later this afternoon in the proclamation I have to make, complete with robes and everything."

"We'll be there for sure," said Clyde, with a twinkle in his eyes. "Can't miss an official mage function."

Chloe groaned before giving everyone hugs and heading out.

As she walked back to the library, she thought, *I really need to talk to Libby about this. How much do I disclose to the people of Havenshold, and how much is too much?*

First she checked the message board outside her office. After all, even with everything that was going on, she still had a school to run. Thankfully there were only a few notes, and the questions were easy to answer, so she jotted down the answers, folded the papers back up so the students' names were showing, and retacked them to the board.

Calliope strolled by. *So are you back now for a while?* she asked. *I've had to manage everything alone.*

"Yes, I'm back for a bit, but I have a proclamation to write, and I want to talk with Libby about it. Are you coming?"

To Libby's? Wouldn't miss it. She has the best treats.

Chloe laughed, picked up Calliope, and hugged her. "You're the very best. Do you know that? And I know you want to hear the latest news. It's not just the treats that are calling to you."

Calliope shrugged. *Of course I know I'm the best, and how can I help you or run the library if I don't know what's going on?*

"Good point," said Chloe, as she knocked on Libby's magical door, a door only she and Calliope could see. They entered when they heard Libby's cheery hello.

Libby motioned her to the couch as she said, "I thought I'd be seeing you about now."

"Yeah, well, I have to make this proclamation, but I don't yet have all the information I need," Chloe said, taking a seat. "I'm going to check in with Gregory to get more details, but my greatest dilemma at the moment is how much to share. Do I tell the townsfolk that Jaluhz is sentient and cooperating? When we let her name slip out the last time...well, let's just say it wasn't well received.

"Yet I think Aster is right that part of the reason we've had problems with magic and started to lose our magic was because we were trying to hide it, minimize it, so we wouldn't alarm people. That strategy didn't work well. So should I just be up front about the nature of Jaluhz? Should I use this as a teaching moment to help broaden horizons? Will they even care? Or are they just too concerned with the effect the eruption will have on their lives? Will I make things worse if I try to show our understanding of the volcano when they're in danger of losing their homes, shops, and so on?"

Libby was quiet for a few moments, and Chloe picked up the mug of tea that had materialized on the table next to her, as Calliope crunched the treats Libby had conjured up for her. Finally Libby said, "You've noted many times that you're the mage for our world. That means you're Jaluhz's mage as well as Havenshold's or Draconia's or whatever. Furthermore Jaluhz is helping—cooperating in every way she can—to minimize the impact her eruption will have. That, in itself, is pretty darned remarkable, and she deserves the credit."

Libby paused and pushed her glasses back up her nose. Then she continued. "Even beyond that, our horizons tend to get narrowed if we don't work at expanding them. I think Aster's right. We saw how the riders began to lose their telepathic abilities, for instance, when they narrowed them down to just their own dragon. We've learned so much about magic, particularly telepathy, since William, Lucy, and others started expanding our knowledge and abilities in that field. If you don't use something, you'll lose that ability."

Libby looked over at Chloe, a smile making her eyes crinkle a bit. "Don't sell our citizens short, Chloe. I know there was a lot of dissent in that crowd outside the library, but that seems to have been spearheaded by Zeke. I suspect there are more people who will respond positively—who'll be glad to know Jaluhz is trying to help—than those who'll scoff and ridicule the idea of a sentient volcano. So I say, tell it all."

"Thanks, Libby. I don't know about everyone else, but I'm always happier when I know the full extent of a problem. I don't want information kept from me. We can only hope that those who gather to hear the proclamation this afternoon feel the same way."

Chloe finished her tea and then said, "Well I'd better get cracking on this. I definitely need to know what Gregory has figured out. There will be a lot of questions about logistics and so forth. Thanks again."

"Any time. One thing you can guarantee: I'll always be here. And I'm always ready to listen."

Chloe and Calliope headed into the library and stopped at Gregory's door. "Have you figured anything out yet? I'll need all the information you can give me. My proclamation needs all the facts I can muster."

"Come on in, Chloe," said Gregory, motioning to a chair next to the baron's. Oswald was standing next to the table. "You too, Calliope," he added.

Calliope jumped up on the table as Chloe sat. Once they were settled, Gregory continued. "I've done a lot of calculations," he said, "and I'll need more information about how long it'll take to relocate people before I can give a final answer about where we'll start digging, but my guess is that it'll be a mile or two outside of Havenshold, right about here," he concluded, pointing at the map.

"I see," said Chloe. She was quiet for a few moments before asking, "How big of an apron of lava do you anticipate will have formed by then?"

"It'll have covered the far outskirts of Havenshold, possibly even the far end of the market area. We'll probably lose three homes and several shops," Gregory said sadly. "The lava will reach them in the next day or so, but we can't have people moved by then, much less dig a trench."

"I know," said Chloe, sadness in her voice. "Time isn't our friend, but we still need it. Rya communicated with Jaluhz, who's willing to try to help by creating some small earthquakes designed to widen and deepen the trench. But she also was honest about how unpredictable that process is."

"She's right there," said Gregory. "We all know how far away even a small earthquake can be felt."

The baron spoke up. "So you're thinking about more evacuations?"

"I'm guessing so," said Chloe, "even if they're temporary. What do you guys think?"

"People won't be happy about leaving their homes," said Oswald. "Some may refuse."

"I don't envy Clotilda and Matilda," said Chloe. "They're the ones who have to enforce the evacuations."

"Most of the people who live anywhere near the fault line are pretty earthquake savvy," said Gregory. "If we explain what's going to happen, do you think they might just go somewhere safe during the actual quakes then return to their homes? I gather that Jaluhz is willing to schedule these, so to speak."

"There usually are aftershocks," said the baron, "sometimes for days."

"Not only that, but most people fear earthquakes and might be happier if the trench was just dug," said Oswald.

"Remember what we said about time," said Gregory. "Even if we can bring in some gryphons to help the dragons, it would take too long to do this entirely by hand. My best guess is that if we have to do it manually, we won't be ready for the lava for at best several weeks. By then the lava apron will be a lot bigger."

"I can help some, with my magic," said Chloe, "but even so, it's going to take too much time. I think we need Jaluhz to open up a large piece of the fault. We might be able to do the digging without Jaluhz's help once we get a long enough piece of trench dug so that our digging speed exceeds or at least stays ahead of the lava flow, once we get the lava starting to flow into the trench, but that needs to happen sooner than later."

"I agree," said the baron. "Gregory, your estimate on rate of flow...Does that change if the lava is confined in the trench? Will it flow faster?"

"It might," said Gregory reluctantly. "We won't really know until we see the lava in the trench, but it might be like confining a river."

"I agree," said Oswald, "and right now we estimate the flow at nine hundred sixty feet each day. That means it'll cover a mile in five and a half days. So we should really plan for a mile every five days to allow for a slight increase in the speed. I'm not sure how fast the dragons and riders can make the trench, but I'd think it would take them at least that long to make a mile of trench. So they need to have probably ten miles of trench opened before the lava gets funneled in."

The baron nodded. "Then we definitely need Jaluhz's help. Without that we can't possibly get far enough ahead of the flow without abandoning a lot more ground, a lot more homes, and a lot more property."

Chloe said, "For sure, which means I have to write a really persuasive speech so people can see this and realize the earthquakes will help in the long run."

Oswald smiled. "I sure don't envy you that task, especially after I heard about the crowd's mood earlier today."

"Yeah, I know," said Chloe. "Well, I'd better get writing. If you figure out anything else, please come tell me."

"We will, and we'll be out there with you in case people have questions you can't answer. At least we'll be supporting you," said the baron.

Chloe nodded and she and Calliope headed to her office to compose her thoughts. Calliope sat on her desk, saying, *I thought I'd read as you write, and then I can make better suggestions.*

"Thanks, Calliope, but I think I'd do better if you just listened to it once I've finished it.

If you insist, said Calliope, as she jumped over to the couch.

Chloe worked—writing, and rewriting—trying to put her thoughts in order. She really didn't want to just read something aloud. She wanted to speak from her heart, shifting things as she took the pulse of the crowd. As she grew more and more frustrated, she finally decided to make a general outline of all the points she needed to cover and then wing it.

That's pretty chancy, said Calliope.

Chloe shrugged. "Maybe so, but I speak better that way, and I want this to be a heartfelt speech, acknowledging what has happened, what will happen, and how it'll all be solved."

Just then Emily walked in. "I wanted you to know that Lucy is awake now and is responding to questions. She's regained a lot of her color, and Gretchen is actually starting to relax a bit."

"That's marvelous news. I'm so relieved. I'll be sure to stop by soon and say hi, but I imagine she's going to be inundated with visitors pretty quickly."

"She already is, and Nurse Beatrice has had to set up a schedule where people can sign up for a visiting slot," said Emily.

"Well, I think I'll begin my speech with that good news. Hopefully it'll set the tone for the entire proclamation."

"How's it coming along?" asked Emily.

She's going to wing it, said Calliope.

Emily raised an eyebrow. "What?"

"I don't want to read a prepared speech," said Chloe, "so I've made notes so I don't forget to cover everything, but I'm just going to speak from my heart."

"If you're sure," said Emily, with noticeable hesitation in her voice.

"Yes, I am. After all, we're going to be asking people to prepare for earthquakes, to accept the loss of several homes and shops, to vacate property, and so on. I have to make them believe that I'm aware of the sacrifices and that the sacrifices are necessary to keep the losses at a minimum."

"OK," said Emily, shaking her head. "And I'll have riders spaced out within the crowd just in case there's any trouble."

"Thanks," said Chloe. "Gads, is it three thirty already? I'd better go find my mage robes. You wanted a show after all."

Emily laughed. "It's all for a good cause. I'll get out of here and let you get ready."

"Thanks, Emily, and thanks for having some sympathetic listeners for me there."

Chloe chose her favorite purple velvet robes, made sure she had her note cards and a handkerchief in her pocket, and prepared to head out. Gregory, the baron, and Oswald joined her as she walked out through the front doors of the library and stood on the top step. She was amazed to see the size of the crowd. There must have been nearly two thousand people, nearly four times as many as this morning. The courtyard was packed. As the tower chimed four, Chloe stepped a bit ahead of the baron, Gregory, and Oswald, and held up her hands for silence. Once she had everyone's attention, she began.

"The last few days have been very difficult for us all. I want to begin by saying that we have some very good news. Lucy, the rider who was severely injured, is now awake and responsive."

Heartened to hear loud cheers, Chloe went on. "I'd like to begin by clarifying my role as mage. The last time I was out here, there were a lot of accusations made, people assuming they knew what my job is. There also was disbelief about the nature of the volcano—that she is a she and that she has a name, Jaluhz."

"Do we care?" asked a voice from the back.

Chloe noticed Rupert moving toward the voice, and she continued. "Yes, actually, you do. My job is to be the mage for the entire planet, and that includes Jaluhz. In addition," Chloe went on quickly, "you should know that we're able to communicate with her, and she's going to help us."

"Hasn't she already helped? Didn't she save Arryn and Lena?" asked Mary, the owner of Sweaters and Yarns.

"Yes, thank you for the reminder. She did, in fact, save them both, and she isn't the one who blew a hole in her side, causing the current lava flow. And that flow is what we now need to deal with. The flow will continue for a good many years, with estimates currently being anywhere from ten to twenty years. This being the case, we need to find a solution for all that lava."

"Can't you just stop up the hole?" someone shouted.

"Possibly," said Chloe. "But would you like the entire top of the volcano to blow off at once? The same amount of lava would spill out. The difference would be that it would spill all at once, killing most of the life in Draconia."

There was absolute quiet after that. "Jaluhz didn't start this," Chloe continued, "but she and I agree that the current situation is a lot better than the alternative, and volcanoes do have a cycle of their own, meaning they have to erupt from time to time. Thankfully for us, the length of time between Jaluhz's eruptions is in the area of a million years or so.

"Back to the lava. The most viable option is to dig a trench so the lava can flow out to the ocean, possibly making another island." Chloe went on to explain all the logistics, including which homes and shops would be lost, when the lava might begin to flow into the trench, and finally the need to accept Jaluhz's help with planned and hopefully minor earthquakes. After giving an overview, she went through every single detail, as far as they'd been worked out. She explained her own role in helping with the trench and, most important, in managing the lava apron, moving it so that the lava would flow into the channel.

The crowd was silent. Shocked expressions appeared as people tried to absorb the magnitude of the situation. It took Chloe a good half hour to explain everything. When she was done, she asked if there were any questions.

People asked about the earthquakes the most. Gregory and the baron stepped up to explain the rate of flow versus the rate of digging and how much more property would be lost if they didn't have Jaluhz's help. Several people questioned the numbers, but once they were convinced of the accuracy of the figures, their acceptance for the plan began to grow.

Mary asked, "How can we help? What can we do? This seems to be falling entirely on you and the dragons and riders. Can't we do something?"

"Thanks, Mary," Chloe said. "Yes, you can. Those of you who might have extra space in your home, please let Emily know.

We'll have to evacuate people from the immediate area of the fault so they won't be hurt during the earthquakes, so it would be nice if we had temporary homes for them. I'm not sure how long the earthquake phase will go on, but knowing we had some shelter for those in need would help. Those currently living in the actual fault zone, the area where the trench will go, are being relocated as I speak. But we'll need temporary housing for them, I'm sure."

Chloe looked over at Emily who said, "I'll have a sign-up sheet posted by the archway into the riders' courtyard where those who have extra space can sign up."

Chloe nodded, and continued. "Please keep away from the lava flow, no matter how tempting it is to watch, as harmful gases are escaping. I know the lava is fascinating, but it's also very dangerous. In addition, the lava sets trees and brush on fire. If you notice a fire that's spreading, be sure to notify the dragons and their riders.

"Other than that, try to have patience and understanding, especially for those we know will lose their homes and shops. We're working on plans to rebuild those in another area of Havenshold, but again it will take time."

"What about the guy who did this? What's going to happen to him?" someone called out.

"That'll be up to Queen Clotilda and Matilda. Thank heavens Lucy is recovering, because otherwise he'd be facing murder charges."

"Do you really think this plan will work?" asked a woman in the front.

"We have every confidence in it," said Chloe. "Not only do we have our own experts here—Gregory, Oswald, and the baron, all of whom are well versed in volcanoes and mines—but Jaluhz herself believes it will work. As she said, that's how the other islands were formed. We've chosen the most obvious path, where there's already a deep fault, and it's also the shortest path. No one can guarantee the plan, but it seems viable."

Emily came forward and said, "Thank you, Chloe, for your very detailed, complete explanation. Everyone here now knows exactly what's going on and what to expect. If there are any further questions, please come to my office, but it's getting dark and colder now. I'm sure, after you've all slept on this, more questions will arise, but please know that we're trying to do our best to make this as easy as possible."

There was a shout from the back. "Thanks to our mage!"

This was followed by lots of cheers as the crowd began to disperse. Mary stepped forward to speak with Chloe. "I'm so glad you shared everything with us. That took courage. We live on Jaluhz's energy, and it's so nice to know she cares about us. I think I'll design a new sweater with her and the lava flow on it."

"That's an excellent idea, and yes, Mary, she does care. It may take a while for folks to wrap their heads around the idea of sentient volcano, but I really felt they deserved to know that information."

"Thanks again, Chloe. I'll show you my design as soon as I complete it."

As Mary left, Emily chuckled. "I can see it now," she said. "Jaluhz is going to find her picture on everything: sweaters, pot holders, blankets, you name it."

"Hey," said Gregory, "Havenshold could use a mascot. Who could be better than Jaluhz?"

Oswald said, "If people rally around her, they won't rally against her, and face it, this lava is going to become a major part of all our lives—from Havenshold, across Draconia and Forbury, and all the way to the sea. We can have contests to name the lava river. The possibilities are endless."

"Well, you can run the contest," Gregory said. "You'll have to think of some cool prizes."

"Soon we'll have songs and dances and everything, all centered around Jaluhz," said Oswald. "She'll have a whole new image."

The baron laughed and ruffled Oswald's fur as he affectionately said, "You're incorrigible!"

Oswald shrugged. "Well, we'll need something to make things a bit happier and lighter. There's a lot of work ahead for us all."

"You're right, Oswald," said Chloe, "and I for one will appreciate all your efforts."

"People did seem a lot calmer tonight," said Emily.

Rupert walked over to join them and said to Emily, "I talked to that guy in the back who was mouthing off. Turns out his home is one of the ones that will be destroyed. But when he found out we would build him a new home in a safer location, he sure changed his tune. He couldn't say enough good things about us."

"Clyde and all the other carpenters are going to be very busy. We need to find locations for those new homes," said Emily.

"There are so many little details in all this," Chloe added.

"I'm going to need to start delegating fast," said Emily, "and Rupert, my boy, you and Hannah are going to be at the top of my list for those I can delegate things to."

Rupert actually looked very pleased, as if he'd received the prize of the century. "Really? I'm happy to do whatever you want. I'd like more responsibility actually. I know my dragon Whipper is a male purple, not a female purple, but since you don't have a female purple at the moment, well, we'd be happy to try to fill that gap."

"I'm sure you would," said Emily. "But don't figure on taking over anytime soon. Esmeralda and I are here for the long haul."

"Oh, I know," said Rupert, "and we're sure glad about that. It's just that I'm your second-in-command, but I don't have that much to do. I'd love to have more. That's all."

"You got yourself out of that hole very nicely, Rupert," the baron said as Rupert blushed.

"OK," said Emily, "let's not tease him anymore. Chloe is right. There are myriad details involved in all this, and we need to start assigning specific areas to specific people. Gregory, Oswald, Baron, you have all you can handle engineering the channel for the lava flow. The rest of us will have to look into housing, relocation, and all the other details. But for tonight we've all had enough, and Chloe, you can tell Calliope from me that you 'winged it' beautifully."

— 19 —

BRACING FOR EARTHQUAKES

Aster, Sasha, and Jasmine headed first for the former village of Cliffside, where they found that twenty-two families had returned to live in the nine years since the major earthquake had destroyed the town. Aster called the families together in the center of their small settlement which had been set up with boulders arranged in a circle for people to sit on and explained what had happened. As she talked about the eruption and the need to open the fault line to allow the lava to travel to the sea, she saw the worry in the townsfolk growing.

Finally she said, "There are a lot more details if you want them, but the main point is that we need to relocate you to a safer place."

"Where?" asked one woman as she stood up and started to pace.

"We have nowhere else to go," said another.

Jasmine spoke then. "We have some ideas, but we want to hear from you first. We need to know what you're looking for. Do you want to stay isolated, as you are now, or would you consider moving to an existing small village, one that would welcome the growth?"

"We came here because we wanted to stay together," said the first woman, taking a seat again. "I'm Marigold, and we've enjoyed our isolation, as you called it. However, as our children grow, we realize our community is too small to be viable." Marigold looked at her fellow villagers then said, "I think we'd like to move to somewhere with others—a small place like this one but just a bit bigger."

There were nods all around, and Marigold continued, "This isn't the easiest spot to try to make a living anyway, and we worry every time there are tremors, but the land was available, so we've stayed."

"Have you heard of Chauncey's Creek?" Aster asked, looking around at the small group of about thirty people. "That's where the other villagers who used to live here moved nine years ago."

"How far away is it?" asked Marigold, who was obviously the spokesperson for the village.

"Not far," said Aster. "You could easily walk there in about five or six hours. It's roughly fifteen miles away. And many of those living in Cliffside relocated from here, so you'd find sympathetic folks. I'd need to check with the mayor, but if you're interested, Jasmine, Sasha, and I will fly there now and get their reaction."

"Yes, please," said Marigold after she held a quick conference with the other parents.

"Great," said Aster, as she, Jasmine, and Sasha stood. "While we're doing that, everyone needs to pack up their things. We'll carry the bulk of your belongings so you won't have to lug them. We also can arrange for transport if needed. We should be back in an hour or two with more information."

As the villagers absorbed the impact of such a sudden move, Aster, Sasha, and Jasmine flew to Chauncey's Creek, where they met with the mayor and explained the situation.

"You mean there are people still trying to live in that devastated area?" Arnold, the mayor said, once he'd heard the request. He was a heavy set man, with a kind face and twinkling blue eyes. "Let me call the town leaders together, and we'll make a decision. We do have some land just outside of town that might work for them."

Aster said, "Excellent, Mayor. I think they'd like a place where they could stay together then gradually become a part of the village. This move must be rather overwhelming for them. Thankfully they'd apparently already figured out that they're too small a community to last. Nevertheless we need to move them today or tomorrow, which is a sudden change."

"Just give me an hour to talk with the others on the council," the mayor said. "Feel free to stop in at Nancy's Café. I know Nancy would appreciate a firsthand account of how Gretchen and Lucy are doing. She's been quite worried about them. It's hard to be a parent when your kid leaves home, and Nancy loves not only her daughter, Gretchen, but Lucy as well."

"We're definitely going to stop in there," said Aster. "That was on our list as well. So once you come to a decision, you'll find us there."

Aster, Sasha, and Jasmine had no trouble finding Nancy's Café, as it was on one of the main corners in the town. As they walked in, a plump middle-aged woman with red hair and blue eyes came hurrying over with a worried expression. "Gretchen and Lucy are OK, aren't they?"

Aster smiled. "Yes, Nancy, they're doing well. Gretchen is pretty well healed, and now she's even willing to sleep at night since Lucy is out of danger."

"Oh, thank heavens. I was afraid when you walked in that it was bad news," said Nancy.

"No, we're here on a different matter entirely, but we knew Gretchen and Lucy would want us to update you."

"And Lucy will recover? Gretchen would be devastated if she lost her. Well, we all would," said Nancy.

"Dr. Brian is a lot more confident now, and he expects her to make a complete recovery."

Nancy smiled widely. "Well, then, please have a seat. Anything you want is on the house."

"Thanks so much, Nancy. We'll have whatever your lunch special is, if that's OK," said Aster as she and Sasha slid into one of the booths and Jasmine sat next to the table, pulling her tail around so that it fit underneath.

"We have vegetarian chili today and there's plenty to go around. Jasmine, do you need extra?" asked Nancy.

Jasmine smiled. "No, a regular plate is fine, but if you added some extra greens, well, I wouldn't say no."

"You've got it. And I have something special for you, Sasha, as well. Be right back."

She's a lot like Gretchen, said Sasha.

Aster and Jasmine chuckled, and Jasmine said, "You've got that right."

Nancy brought out their chili and cornbread, as well as some turkey for Sasha, and then sat down with them to chat. She wanted all the news about the volcano. Aster also shared the story about how the moles had saved Lucy and Gretchen's lives and how one of the moles had held vigil for Lucy. That story was going to be handed down through the ages. It was already growing to the point where Jasmine had heard someone say the moles actually had dragged Lucy and Gretchen out of harm's way.

Nancy laughed at this, saying, "Rather like a fish story, huh? Still it's amazing the moles knew what was coming, which allowed Lucy to get up from the ground and stand before the explosion. If she'd still been lying on the ground listening, I'm sure she would have been killed. And the volcano has a name and cares about us. This is a wonderful world, isn't it?"

As Aster, Jasmine, and Sasha were finishing their meal, the mayor walked in along with a few councilpersons. He came over to the table and said, "We'll be happy to welcome those villagers. We've decided on an area, the one I told you about, which will have enough space for them and also be close enough to the town center that they can come enjoy Nancy's fine food and get to know us."

"Thank you so much," said Aster.

"Do you know when they'll arrive, and will they need housing? We still have a lot of winter left," said the mayor.

"Yes, they'll need housing, although the riders will bring temporary shelters for them, sturdy enough that they should see them through the winter, but any help you can offer would be most appreciated."

"Hi. I'm Dr. Penelope," said a gray-haired woman. "We all know what it's like to have to relocate suddenly. Nancy and I led the original Cliffside refugees, and we've made a good home here, wouldn't you say, Nancy?"

"Definitely," said Nancy, "and we'll do for these folks as was done for us. You can trust us to look after them."

"And the temporary housing would be much appreciated," said the mayor. "That way we can help them make a fresh start by spring."

Aster, Sasha, and Jasmine stood, and Aster said, "Thank you all so much. I suspect they'll wait now until morning to set out, but I'm going to have dragon riders arriving with the housing this afternoon, if you can just show me where you want to locate them."

The mayor opened a map, showed them the area he and his council had marked off, then handed the map to Aster.

After Nancy gave Aster a hug with instructions to pass it along to Gretchen and Lucy, the meeting broke up. Aster, Sasha, and Jasmine flew back to the old Cliffside to report to Marigold and the others.

"You'll be most welcome there," said Aster. "They have a parcel of land on the outskirts of town that will accommodate all of you. I'm going to have some dragon riders deliver some temporary shelters for you. Each shelter can easily house four adults and several children. They aren't fancy, but they'll protect you through the winter. Now if you can just give me a head count and how many shelters you'll need, I'll start that in motion."

Marigold looked around at the small group and counted, asking folks to separate into groups that would be manageable. Finally she said, "It looks as if we could use ten or eleven, if that's not too much trouble. We can share with a couple families in each. And thank you so much!"

"Great. How about a few wagons for your belongings? I could have four wagons or so here first thing tomorrow. Then we'll need to have you moving out. I'm not sure how soon the digging will start, but the scheduled earthquakes will be occurring shortly, so we'll need you out of the area first thing tomorrow."

Marigold looked at her group and then said in a firm voice, "We'll be ready."

Aster, Sasha, and Jasmine took off to find their own shelter for the night, and then Aster sent her reports to Clotilda and Emily.

So can we have ten or eleven shelters set up by the time the villagers arrive? If I were Chloe, I could just conjure them, but honestly, I think it's better not to use that much magic anyway, quite aside from the fact that my only magical gift is telepathy, Aster asked Emily.

I agree, and the riders are happy to do this. I'll put Rupert on that right now. And you'll have your wagons as well. Nice work, Aster.

Thanks. We're going to spend the rest of the day flying along the fault line to see if there are any other people living too close.

Excellent, Emily said. *I look forward to your next report.*

Chloe sat at her desk, and for the first time in a day or so, she had a moment to catch up on school matters. Several students had asked to see her, so she met with each of them. Then she noticed Arryn walking past her office door with a stack of books in her arms, so she called out to her.

"Hey, Arryn. How's it going?"

Arryn turned and came into the office. "Great! Todd's set up a science program for me so I can learn a bit about a lot of different sciences, and he's designing experiments and everything."

Chloe laughed. "Just be sure the two of you don't blow something up. Todd can get carried away."

"He's fun," said Arryn, "and Amy's great too. I love living there."

"That's what I like to hear," said Chloe. "So are you back for more books?"

"Yes," said Arryn. "This library is absolutely amazing. I'm finding so many fascinating books, books on history and science, as well as some mysteries. I hope that's all right."

"Of course. Read as many as you want," said Chloe.

"Thanks. Well, I'd better return these and find a few more. I have to be back soon for another science session with Todd."

"Have fun," said Chloe, as Arryn went skipping out of the office, nearly running into Emily.

"Oops, sorry," said Arryn.

"No worries," said Emily.

After Arryn had headed into the stacks, Emily came into Chloe's office and said, "It's so gratifying to see her so happy. And my folks are thrilled. My dad is designing all sorts of experiments."

"So I heard, and I agree," said Chloe. "How can I help you?"

"I just needed to get out of the office. And I received a report from Aster. Should we see if Gregory is free, and I can update you both?"

Chloe stood and said, "Let's just head on down to his office."

Gregory looked up as the two of them walked in. Chloe thought he looked exhausted and haggard, but then a lot of responsibility was resting on his shoulders. "Hey, there," she said, as she and Emily walked in. "Emily wants to share an update with us."

"Great," said Gregory. "Have a seat."

Emily shared Aster's report with them then concluded with, "It looks as if Jaluhz can start the gentle earthquakes—if there is such a thing—tomorrow. I know you're eager to see if they'll work without too much destruction."

"Yes," said Gregory, "and that's good news, as the one certainty in all this is that the lava will keep right on flowing. Dad and Oswald will be here shortly, and we'll try to figure out where we want Jaluhz to focus. Maybe Rya will be able to ask Jaluhz for suggestions."

"That's a great idea," said Chloe. "When you guys are ready, let me know, and I'll see if Rya wants to come in here for the consultation with Jaluhz."

"I'll let you know," said Gregory, as he turned back to his desk, which was covered with papers and notes.

Emily and Chloe left, and Emily said, "He's been practically living here since the explosion. I sure hope we get this plan underway soon. It's driving him crazy not knowing if it'll work."

"Tell me about it," Chloe said with a sigh. "I need to contact my mother to see if she'll be on the food brigade again when I have to draw on the bonded pairs for energy for my part of this show. I have no idea how long it'll take to move the lava, redirect the lava, or whatever the heck it is I'm going to be doing. And speaking of that, I'd like to have as many dragons and riders as possible here in Havenshold. I'm sure you remember the drill from the so-called War of the Asteroid. Can you arrange that?"

"Sounds like the perfect task for Hannah. I'll get her on it and have her start contacting riders and dragons. Thankfully I believe William still has all the charts from then, so we'll know which pairs work best together and so forth. I'll have Hannah work with him. He and Jake returned when Lucy was injured, so he should be in his office shortly."

"Thanks, Emily," said Chloe.

By afternoon Gregory said he was ready to discuss the scheduled earthquakes with Rya and Jaluhz, so Chloe contacted Harmony to ask them to come over.

We'll be right there, answered Harmony.

About fifteen minutes later, Rya, Harmony, and Artemis walked into the library, and Chloe took them to Gregory's office, where Gregory, Oswald, and the baron were waiting. Once everyone was comfortable, Gregory began.

"Here are the maps of the fault line," he said. "We'd really like to know what Jaluhz thinks, but our plan was to split the fault wider and deeper, beginning about here." He pointed to a spot a mile or so outside Havenshold's town limits. "We'd then want that widening and deepening to continue for as long and far as we can. Would you ask Jaluhz for her thoughts, Rya?"

Rya nodded. "I'll try."

Harmony placed an arm on Rya's shoulder, and Artemis jumped into Rya's lap. Everyone was very quiet as Rya concentrated. Finally she opened her eyes and said, "Jaluhz agrees with your plan. She does seem concerned about the area surrounding where Cliffside was. That's where the largest rupture in the fault line is, and I get the idea that she thinks that even a minor earthquake there could have wide-reaching effects. But she suggests we start where you indicated and see how things go."

"Excellent," said Gregory. "And thanks."

"When do you want to start?" asked Rya.

Gregory looked over at Chloe, who said, "Well, if these are truly going to be minor quakes, and you're starting just outside Havenshold, you could start now. The only people near the fault zone are in the Cliffside area, according to Aster and Jasmine, and they'll be moving out tomorrow morning."

Gregory nodded. "Then let's get it started."

"The sooner we start, the sooner we'll know what we're dealing with," Oswald said.

"I agree," said the baron.

"I think you're right," said Chloe, "so Rya, please let Jaluhz know that whenever she's ready, we'd like to start."

Rya closed her eyes again and, after a few moments, said, "She agrees."

They all waited in suspense. When they didn't feel any tremors, Chloe said, "Well, I for one would like to take a look at the lava flow, and maybe we can see what's happening from there."

Oswald held up a paw. "You don't want to get too close. I'd recommend having a dragon fly over the area."

Chloe nodded. "You're right. I'll ask Emily to send someone."

Just then they all felt a small tremor.

"OK, we know Jaluhz has done something," said Artemis, "and at least here, it was pretty gentle."

Emily walked in and said, "So it's begun then."

"Seems so," said Gregory.

"We were wondering if you could ask a dragon to fly over the lava flow and give us a report," said Chloe.

"Of course," said Emily. "In fact, Gregory, why don't you come with me, and we'll fly over the area with Esmeralda? Then I'll send reports back to you, Chloe, which will allow Rya to let Jaluhz know what has happened on our end."

"Excellent plan," said Gregory, as he prepared to leave with Emily.

After they left, Oswald said, "It's times like this I wish I could fly."

"Hey, buddy," said the baron, "you're perfect just the way you are."

"I don't think flying's such a good thing, even if I'm only a passenger" said Artemis. "I really don't like it."

They made small talk for a while, and finally Chloe said, "I have the first report from Emily and Gregory. Nothing much happened. The crack might possibly be a tiny bit wider but not enough to make any difference. They want to know if you can ask Jaluhz to do the same thing again, but this time maybe do it three or four times in a row. They'll keep watching from the air while that happens."

Rya nodded and again contacted Jaluhz. Soon after that there were indeed a series of tremors, which Chloe had to admit were a bit alarming, but they all were developing real trust in Jaluhz.

After a few minutes, Chloe announced, "That's better. Emily says the crack is beginning to widen, but it's going to take more force to get it anywhere near what they want. She'd like you, Rya, to check with Jaluhz about the best way to do that. Should she continue with the series of smaller shocks, or should we try one slightly larger shock?"

Rya said, "I'll check."

After a few minutes, she said, "Jaluhz is going to try one stronger shock. I get the idea that she wants to find out what the largest shock would be that wouldn't cause a lot of damage. She did warn me that it might take a while to judge just how large a shock can be without destroying things."

Chloe consulted with Emily then told Rya to ask Jaluhz for a bigger tremor. Rya nodded, and sure enough, a few minutes later, they all felt a significantly stronger tremor. This time a few books fell off one of Gregory's bookcases.

As the group waited for a report, Oswald said, "I don't think we're going to want to go any harder than that. If we're seeing books fall here, the other side of Havenshold is going to find at least minor damage."

"I agree," said the baron.

And they waited. Finally, Chloe said, "Good news. That last tremor definitely widened the fault line. There's still a long way to go, but Emily thinks we should stop for now to give folks a chance to catch their breath. Gregory is on his way back now while Emily deals with the minor damage and shattered nerves of some of the townsfolk."

A few minutes later, Gregory walked in, saying, "This is going to be harder than I thought. My best guess is that we'll need at least six more quakes like the last one to make enough of a difference so we can then finish the channel manually. And the split only widened for about half a mile. This is going to take a lot of earthquakes at this rate, which won't do much for any of our nerves."

Rya was very quiet then finally said, "Jaluhz agrees. But she also says she can do more once we're farther away from town. She'd like to start at the spot that's the widest, once everyone is evacuated, at the old Cliffside location. She thinks that if she can do a bigger quake there, it'll rip up and down the fault line. Right now she's working in an area where the fault line is little more than a crack."

Oswald nodded. "That makes a lot of sense."

Gregory looked over at his father who said, "What about an alternating scheme? I suspect the residents of Havenshold would like a bit of a break. Maybe we should work from both ends?"

Gregory nodded and said, "And we can have digging going on here while Jaluhz is widening farther down and vice versa. I'd really hoped to get the trench going here, far enough to stay ahead of the lava flow, and just keep going, but I can see we can't do that. I suppose it doesn't really matter, as the trench has to be opened all the way to the sea. I just wanted to get the flow entering the trench as soon as possible. It would make things easier for you, Chloe. The longer we wait, the wider the apron that you'll have to corral will be."

"Believe me, I know," said Chloe. "I'm going to meet with William tomorrow to set up the bonded-pair energy grid again. But I'll just have to work with whatever there is once you're ready."

"Unfortunately," Gregory said, "that seems to be the case. Rya, can you let Jaluhz know she can give a strong quake to the Cliffside area late tomorrow afternoon? That'll give people plenty of time to evacuate. Meanwhile if she finds any advantages to doing quakes anywhere else, let us know."

Rya conveyed that information to Jaluhz then said, "I think she might want to keep...well, the image she gave me was of jiggling, but I don't know if that's the precise term. She wants to keep moving things around the opening we've got now until she can do a big shake in Cliffside. From what I could gather, she doesn't want this to settle. She thinks once she has the— what do you call it?—rip, opening, she'd rather not let it close. So I think we're in for a shaky night, but I believe it won't be anything more than really minor ones."

"Rya, you're amazing," Harmony told her granddaughter. "Your communication with Jaluhz is getting so much stronger. I'm so proud of you."

"Thanks, Grandma," said Rya, blushing.

"I'm barely helping anymore," said Artemis with a sigh, "but I sure love listening in and seeing the images Jaluhz shows you."

Rya ruffled Artemis's fur and said, "Hey, I couldn't do it without you. We're a team."

Gregory said, "I hope you know, Rya, that without you and your ability to reach out to Jaluhz, we wouldn't have a chance."

Rya blushed even more and said, "Thanks, guys."

They all felt a slight tremor, and Chloe said, "Yep, a shaky evening."

"For sure," said Oswald, "but I think Jaluhz is right. You know how things seem to settle down after a quake. We don't want that right now."

"Let's call it a day," said the baron. "I don't think there's any more we can do until we hear that the area around Cliffside is clear."

"Emily will let us know as soon as Aster and Jasmine give us the green light," said Gregory.

— 20 —

THE LAVA CHANNEL

First thing the next morning, Chloe met with William to set up the activation of the energy net. As she sat in his office, she said, "We should only need the bonded pairs from Draconia, or at least I hope so."

"Do you have any idea how much energy it will take to move that much lava?" asked William, a tall, willowy man with brown hair and eyes which sparkled when he talked about his work.

"No, honestly I don't."

"Well, I was thinking maybe we should try some smaller experiments. Remember what you did when you prepared for the asteroid? You moved smaller rocks, then moved up to bigger boulders, then moved them from farther away. Each time you were able to strengthen your technique as well as discover which bonded pairs worked best together in supplying you with their energies."

"Yes," said Chloe, conjuring up mugs of tea for both of them as they sat at the small round conference table. "But you made the charts showing how we grouped the dragon-rider pairs, so we know have all that information now, don't we?"

"We do, although we have new dragons and riders so we can add to that. But the lava is a very different commodity. I think it would be good for you to practice beforehand to see whether you can shift the direction of part of the flow by just a bit and how much energy it takes. I'm sure we can get volunteers to work with you," said William, his voice rising in excitement.

Chloe nodded and chuckled. "You're right and you do love experiments"

William took a sip of tea and then stood and started pacing. "Another thing...the dragons and riders will soon be digging as much as they can each day. They're going to be tired. That will certainly affect how much energy they'll have to give to you. With the asteroid, we set up the grid with Bertha monitoring it so the energy fed through her, and she kept track of which ones of us were tiring, giving us a break, without you losing any energy. I realize the asteroid was bigger, but there's a lot of lava out there. Who's going to monitor the grid so you receive a constant level of energy but none of us gets depleted too much?"

"I have some ideas about that," said Chloe, jotting down some notes for herself. "I'll take care of that end of things. You're right, though, about the need to have alert and rested riders and dragons. I'll talk to Gregory and see if he can make allowances regarding just where the channel needs to be so we can give everyone a day of nondigging before I move the lava."

"Excellent," said William, sitting down again and making his own notes. "Jake said he and Harmony would be happy to help us with preliminary experiments, as will Thunder and I. We're one of your more powerful foursomes, so that should give us some indication at to how many pairs you'll need."

"I'm sure Amy and Todd, as well as Fern and Jupiter, also will be happy to help us. So let's start those experiments today, if that works for you."

Both of them were making notes when they heard a knock on William's door. They looked up, and Chloe said, "Mom, what are you doing here?"

Hazel, a tall, thin woman in her early sixties with short red hair which had turned mostly grey, blue eyes, and a fair complexion like her daughter's, put a hand on the doorjamb as another tremor hit. Once it was over, she walked into the office and said, "Well, I figured you'd want me to organize the support for the energy grid again—you know, the food and beverages for the bonded pairs."

"Please have a seat, Hazel," said William, motioning to a chair next to Chloe's.

"Yes, Mom," said Chloe, with a warm smile, "we certainly do want you to set that up. It'll only be dragons and riders this time. You won't have to enlist your helpers from the other nations. We really appreciate your help."

"I remember just how much food those dragons and riders consumed before, so I wanted to start organizing things. And do you know," said Hazel, her blue eyes getting bigger, "how folks are starting to rally around this? Mary's organizing contests to design a volcano logo for Havenshold. I'm getting orders for clothes that have Jaluhz on them in various different designs. One lady wants sequins and beads to depict the lava. It's quite amazing."

William nodded. "I have to admit, when I heard you explaining the idea of a sentient volcano, I thought the townspeople would scoff and turn on those of us with magical abilities. I really thought you'd opened a can of worms. But the opposite is true."

Hazel said, "People are taking pride in *their* volcano, *their* Jaluhz."

"But how are they handling the tremors?" asked Chloe, with a hint of worry in her voice.

"Oh, that's really remarkable," said Hazel with genuine enthusiasm. "I don't know who started it, but Mary and Oswald are leading the contests. We now have contests to guess how many tremors there will be in a given hour, how far the lava will move in a given time period, how wide the trench will get after the next tremor, and so on."

As another tremor shook the office, William said, "It's fantastic. There are small prizes for each mini contest. I'm not sure of the complete details, but I'm starting to hear about a major festival once the lava river is established, complete with a queen and king of the festival."

Chloe shook her head in wonder. "Who knew?"

"It makes sense," said Hazel. "Of course all of us are used to a tremor or two now and again. You can't live on a volcano without that. But now the tremors are coming quite frequently. I think turning folks' minds to contests—counting the tremors to see if their guesses were right—well, it keeps them from panicking or worrying so much."

"I'm going to have to thank Mary and Oswald, and you too, Mom, for all this support. You're right...It's just the way to handle things."

Hazel stood, saying, "Well, I only wanted you to know I'm activating the support group. When you have a better idea of just when you're going to be doing your lava-moving act, let me know. By the way, there are guesses about that as well."

Chloe laughed. "I'll let you know, and thanks, Mom."

"Well, I have to make sure your grandmother knows where that lady wants her lava beads, so I'm going to take off for now."

After she'd left, William said, "Your mother is quite incredible, a real dynamo of energy and organization."

"Yes, she is," said Chloe. "I never thought she'd change so much. She'd spent her whole life trying to get a dragon rider in the family, feeling bitter that she'd failed as had my grandmother by not being chosen. And she disowned me when I wasn't chosen, saying that I'd ruined the family and stolen my sister Zelda's chance at being a dragon rider. When I became a mage, well, Amy especially helped her to see the world differently, so that she was proud of having a mage in the family. She also started supporting my sister as a dress designer and work with her, coming up with great designs for bead work and other trims, and now she thrives on the excitement and the adventure. Her dress designs are so popular, with their detailed beadwork, but she's also careful not to take over my sister's shop. Zelda's designs are very different, with a different market, and they're working so well together. Anyway, back to our trials. Should we start after lunch? I think by then Jaluhz will be concentrating her efforts in the Cliffside area."

"Sounds good," said William, rubbing his hands together in excitement.

That afternoon Chloe and William walked through the marketplace toward the edge of town. They noticed all sorts of different Jaluhz merchandise and signs springing up everywhere. Outside Mary's sweater shop a large board stood that listed the current contests as well as the winners from earlier ones. William and Chloe stopped to talk with Mary.

"This is a magnificent thing you're doing," said Chloe.

"Well, I figured things are going to be rather difficult for a while," said Mary, "and distractions are always good. A number of the local merchants have offered prizes, including baked goods from our bakery, ice cream sundaes from the ice cream parlor, and even full course dinners at the riders' cafeteria. Now I have people wishing for another tremor because their guess was higher than the current count. It's really funny how perspectives can change."

"So true, and you're doing something really helpful," said William.

"And that Oswald," said Mary. "He's a real character, isn't he? He keeps stopping by with more contest ideas. I love working with him."

Chloe laughed. "Yes, he's quite a character. He's also very smart and savvy. Well, we're meeting up with Thunder, Jake, and Harmony to see how hard it is to move lava, so we'll leave you, but thanks for everything!"

"Hey, we could have contests about that! How far can the mage move lava on her first try?" said Mary, smiling.

"Please," said Chloe, "No. I couldn't take the pressure."

"Just kidding," Mary said, smiling. "But beware, eventually there'll be contests around this."

After they said good-bye to Mary, William and Chloe walked out of the town limits and stared at the lava flow. It looked thick, red, and angry, and even though they were on the cliff some fifty yards above it, it was a daunting sight. Thunder, a light brown dragon, Jake, and Harmony, a lovely deep brown dragon, quickly joined them.

"I haven't been out here for a day or two," said Chloe. "It just keeps right on moving, doesn't it?"

"'Morning, Chloe," Jake said, a tall man in his late forties with a stocky build, like his father, Todd. "Good to see you. And yes, it does. From what I hear, it'll continue moving for years."

Chloe nodded. "Yes, that's what Gregory said."

"When it's all flowing into the channel, we'll probably need to build bridges so people can cross the flow safely," said Jake, his brown eyes twinkling with humor.

"I'm sure you're right," said Chloe, "but could we cross one bridge at a time?"

Chloe smiled as William and Jake groaned. "That was a really bad pun," Harmony said.

"Say, Harmony," said Chloe, "have you met the other Harmony in Havenshold?"

"No," the brown dragon answered, "but I'm sure I will. Think of all the confusion two Harmonies could cause."

"What do you want to try to do with the lava?" asked William.

Chloe looked at the flow. She saw where the three houses and probably one shop had been. Now the lava was flowing down the mountainside, and thankfully there were no more houses in its way.

"Hmm," she said. "Well, see over there on the very edge?" She pointed to the far edge of the apron. "Maybe I could make it turn in on itself just slightly."

"Moving the lava back onto itself would be the hardest part of the entire operation," Thunder said. "You'd really be fighting its natural motion."

"Of course," said Chloe. "You're right."

"So instead," Thunder suggested, "why don't you try to shift the front center part, the leading edge? We know that eventually you'll want that leading edge to head farther to the left, toward the fault line, so why not see if you can get a small bit to move that way?"

"Great idea," said Chloe. "Now remember, you four, you can't let me drain you, so if you start feeling tired, just break off our link."

"We remember the drill," said Jake, reaching for William's hand. "Ready when you are."

Chloe focused her attention on one small part of the very front of the flow then gathered up the extra energy from William, Thunder, Jake, and Harmony and pushed at the piece she'd selected, trying to make it go left. She put all she had into it, but she couldn't detect any shift at all. Finally she felt the other four pull out of the link, and she dropped to the ground, exhausted.

As they all looked at the front of the apron, Chloe said, "I didn't shift a thing, did I?"

"I can't see any change," said Jake, running his hand through his short brown hair.

"Wait," said Harmony. "There in the center. I may be imagining it, but I think the center line is just a tiny bit farther to the left."

They all stared and watched. Finally William said, "It's possible. But it sure is a very small shift, if it is even a shift. And who knows if it was our doing or not. Maybe the ground was lower there."

Chloe, this is Harmony. Are you there?

At first Chloe looked at the brown dragon standing next to her, and then she shook herself. This was the other Harmony. *Yes, I am, and I'm standing next to another Harmony, whom you have to meet, a gorgeous brown dragon. Do you have news?*

I'd heard there's a dragon with my name, Harmony said. *Yes, I wanted to let you know that Jaluhz showed Rya an image of someone shifting her flow. It was a very, very small shift, but she wanted you to know she felt it.*

Thanks, Harmony. I needed to hear that. Please thank Jaluhz and Rya as well.

Chloe looked at the others and said, "Guess what? We weren't imagining it. Jaluhz just let Rya know she felt a very small shift in the direction of her flow.

"Excellent," said William. "So you did make a change."

"Yes," said Chloe. "That's the good news. The bad news is that it's going to take a lot of energy to make any real difference."

Jake nodded and said, "I have an idea. You know when we were wondering if the shift had actually happened, and William said the ground might have been a bit lower there? Well, would there be a way to sculpt the ground so the lava would be more inclined to flow toward the trench?"

Chloe thought for a few moments then said, "We can't have anyone that close to the flow, but maybe I could use my magic to change the terrain itself."

"Hey, you moved walls in the library to make our offices. I bet you could," said William.

"I'd need to have the support of at least part of the energy net," Chloe said. "And I'll talk with Gregory to see what the most effective change would be. We could start that part of the operation just about any time, perhaps tomorrow after I have the information. The sooner I can start turning the flow, the shorter the distance will be to move it into the trench."

Jake gave William and hug before he vaulted onto Harmony and said, "I'll help whenever I can. Right now we're supposed to be part of the digging crew. Good luck."

"Thanks, Jake," said Chloe.

William and Thunder walked with Chloe back to the library so they could consult with Gregory as well. As they walked into Gregory's office, they heard Oswald give a loud cheer.

"What's the good news?" asked Chloe.

"Emily and Esmeralda are flying over the Cliffside area," Oswald said, "Jaluhz just did a major earthquake, and the area split open beautifully into a wide, deep trench."

Gregory added, "According to the information we got from the first flyover, the trench won't need any more digging for about a one-mile stretch. We're going to see if Jaluhz can capitalize on that major opening to split things on each end of it, but this is major progress."

"Emily and Esmeralda are heading back here now," the baron said. "They also have some news from Clotilda they want to share."

While they were waiting, William and Chloe told the others about this morning's experiment and their ideas about sculpting the terrain.

Gregory, the baron, and Oswald pored over the maps and drawings, checking various elevations, curves of the land, and so forth. Finally Gregory said, "You know, if we could have a gentle subsidence running from in front of the flow toward the fault, well, it couldn't hurt. Of course it'll fill right up with lava, and I don't know that it'll change the main direction, as the lava has a flow pattern that starts inside the hole in the side of the volcano, but it might make a difference."

"The thing is, Chloe," said the baron, "you don't want to put too much effort into that and not have the energy when we really need it."

"True," said Chloe. "But if I worked on it now, I'd be able to rest before the main event, I guess you'd call it. How long before you'll be ready for that?"

Gregory said, "I'm not sure. Rya's warned us, thanks to her empathic weather abilities, that a big snowstorm is headed our way, which isn't exactly unexpected at this time of year, but it'll slow down the work. Jaluhz can still send tremors, of course, but the digging won't progress well in a blizzard. We can't have dragons or riders out in something like that. So factoring in weather delays, I'm guessing this may take close to a month. I really had hoped for faster progress, but there it is."

"Meanwhile the lava keeps flowing," said William. "Will the increase in time caused by the blizzard affect where you start your channel?"

"Possibly," said Oswald, "but if we can get things opened up where Gregory wanted, then even if the lava apron isn't in exactly the right spot, some of it should fall into the channel. It won't be the river we need until we can make the channel longer, but we have to keep digging at it however we can."

"I agree," said Gregory. "So back to the subsidence plan, Chloe. If the ground is solid rock in that area, as I suspect, you aren't going to be able to make it sink. I have no idea what your powers are capable of, but you'd have to move some serious rock to make a dip."

"Hmm," said Chloe. "I was afraid of that. Well, back to the drawing board."

Emily and Esmeralda came in just then. "I may have information that will require more changes," Emily said.

"What's up?" said Gregory.

"First off, the split at Cliffside is truly amazing. Jaluhz did a fantastic job, and a deep canyon is now running through that area. But there are two large ranches just northeast of there—ranches with the fault line running through them—and the owners are refusing to allow any digging on their property."

"What?" said Gregory, his eyebrows raised in astonishment.

"Yes, I'm afraid so," Emily said. "Clotilda and Matilda can confiscate the property, but before they take that step, they wanted to know if we have any other options."

Everyone stared at the area on the map where the ranches were located. The baron said, "I know those ranchers, and they've always been selfish and out for power, just the way I used to be. My guess is they're trying to get more power, more land, something out of the queen."

"I'm afraid you're right," said Emily. "Clotilda is offering very fair compensation to all the landowners along the fault line. Most of them have been cooperative. As one of them apparently said, they've all known about the earthquake fault so it isn't as if they can build on the land anyway. But these two ranchers seem to think they have the power to do whatever they want, and they're making outrageous demands. They want Clotilda to give them prime land somewhere else, in exchange for their less than desirable land on the earthquake fault, even if she has to displace someone else to get the new land for them."

The room was quiet for a moment, and then Oswald burst out laughing. He couldn't stop laughing, and the others looked at him as if he'd lost his mind. Then he pointed to the map and laughed even harder. Soon Gregory and the baron joined him, laughing uncontrollably.

When the three of them finally had pulled themselves together, Emily said, "Can you please share the joke?"

Gregory and the baron nodded to Oswald, as Gregory said, "You do the honors, as you spotted it first."

"Sure," said Oswald. "Emily, tell Clotilda to call their bluff. Tell her to let them know that since they turned down her generous offer, we've made other arrangements."

"But what—" began Emily.

"See here," said Oswald, pointing at the topographic map. "These two ranches are hemmed in on both sides by steep mountains. In effect they're already in a canyon. If they had let us dig along the fault line, most of their ranches would have been spared. But since they don't want that, we'll just respect their wishes and let the lava flow. The minute the lava reaches the end of the channel that we're able to dig, it'll spill out all over their lands. The mountains will prevent the lava from going any farther, either to the north or south, and the lava will therefore keep moving, in a much wider stream of course, toward the sea."

"We'll have to modify," said Gregory, "what happens when the lava flow leaves the second ranch, and that will require us to build a large funnel-shaped channel at that end, but I don't think it'll require significantly more time or energy than if we'd channeled all the way through their lands."

Emily's mouth hung open for a minute until she realized it. "So you're saying we'll just tell them fine, we won't build a channel across their lands?"

"Yes," said Oswald. "That's it. Just call their bluff. Also, if they haven't had a change of heart by the time our channel reaches their border, well, it'll be too late for us to protect their remaining lands. These channels are taking longer to dig than we anticipated, so they'd better make up their minds sooner than later, or the lava will make the decision for them."

"Clotilda is *so* going to love this," said Emily.

"I really, really can't stand bullies," Oswald said, "and these two are trying to make money from our current difficulties. If I were Clotilda, I'd give them one more chance to accept her offer then just walk away. Let them figure out what's happening as the lava approaches."

"Yes," said Emily, "I agree, and that's just what we'll recommend. Of course we'll have to evacuate them as well as all their livestock when the lava gets close, if they haven't already figured it out, but by then they'll have lost everything. Their land, houses, outbuildings will all be covered in a large molten river of lava that will no longer support their livestock. People can be such fools."

"I'm sorry to say," the baron began, "that I've worked with these two, and while I might have been greedy in the past, and even tried to take the throne, this is unspeakable. They've never really liked their family lands, because of the fault, and while I understand that, trying to hold Clotilda hostage to the current situation is heinous."

"Agreed," said Gregory.

"Thank heavens they're the minority," said William. "And we can balance them with people like Mary and Hazel. Speaking of which, Oswald, thanks so much for helping with all those contests."

The baron ruffled Oswald's fur. "Oh, he's a kid at heart, and he's in his element, trying to figure out more things that people can guess."

"I never thought," said William, "that I'd get so used to tremors. Jaluhz has them so often now that I really wonder when there aren't any. Like this afternoon, when she was working in Cliffside...it was so quiet here I couldn't figure out what was wrong."

"Amazing how quickly we can adapt," said Emily. "Have any of you won one of the contests? I heard Mary is keeping track of the winners, and eventually the people who've won the most guesses will be crowned Queen and King of the Lava."

"Wow, this has really taken off," Gregory said with a smile. "Life will be pretty dull around here once the lava stream is contained and running on its own."

"Never," said Chloe. "Jake's already talking about the need for bridges over the lava stream to provide easier access. This whole eruption thing has changed the face of Draconia permanently."

"And don't forget," said the baron, "that you still have to get the lava across Forbury. I'm thinking that could be a bigger challenge because the fault line runs out at my copper mine. Although, as smart as Jaluhz is, maybe she'll be able to extend it for us."

"Regardless," said Emily, "life is never dull around here. I need to head back to the office and give Clotilda this exciting update. She'll be overjoyed to be able to tell those nasty ranchers to go take a hike."

Emily and Esmeralda left, and William and Chloe decided to take another look at the energy grid before calling it a day.

"Thanks for everything," Chloe told Gregory, Oswald, and the baron. "And I sure enjoyed hearing you laugh so hard."

"Let us know if you need more information about shifting the lava flow," said Gregory.

"You know, the one I think I really need to talk to..." said Chloe, who quickly added, "not that you haven't been helpful. But after what you said about the direction of the flow coming from inside the explosion—well, I think I need to check in with Jaluhz. Maybe she can shift something internally, or maybe she could give me an image and allow me to shift it. Worth asking anyway."

The baron looked at Chloe and said, "You amaze me. You come up with such imaginative solutions."

"Thanks. Comes from teaching, I think. Especially teaching those who are taking different paths. I have to come up with innovative solutions all the time."

"Don't sell yourself short," said the baron. "You're really bright and quick, and I know you and Jaluhz will think of something. Good luck."

— 21 —
A CHANGE IN PLANS

Chloe arranged to meet with Rya first thing the next morning so she could have some questions answered. Rya and Artemis arrived at Chloe's office right after breakfast. Chloe looked up from her mound of papers as they came in.

"'Morning," said Chloe. "Thanks for coming in. How are you, and how's everything going?"

"Really well," said Rya, as she took a seat.

"She can talk to Jaluhz easily now," said Artemis, hopping onto Rya's lap. "Well, it isn't talking exactly, but you know what I mean."

"That's terrific," said Chloe.

"Yeah, Grandma has been a lot of help, showing me how to focus my power, and Jaluhz has learned a lot about how people work and what our bodies can handle and so on."

"That's incredible," said Chloe. "And now I'd like to draw on those talents, if I may."

Chloe explained yesterday's attempt to move the lava and the ideas she'd had after that. "I guess I thought that because the lava is moving already it would be relatively easy to turn it. Yesterday, however, I learned that the lava definitely has a momentum, not to mention a mind of its own. And Gregory says the ground underneath the lava apron is solid rock, with no tunnels, so my idea of making the land dip wasn't practical either. So now I'd like to find out if Jaluhz thinks we could change the direction of the flow from where it begins, at the explosion site."

"Let me see if I have this right," said Rya. "It's as if a hose were shooting out water, and you want to shift the direction of the hose."

"Something like that. Face it, if Zeke had planted his explosives a bit farther over, the lava would be flowing toward the fault line. I just don't know if Jaluhz can shift it or if she can help me know where to shift it, so that I'd be turning the lava flow more from the source, in a gentler curve."

"OK, give me a moment," said Rya as she stroked Artemis's fur.

Chloe was quiet and still as Rya closed her eyes, concentrating. After a few minutes, Rya said, "Thanks," then turned to Chloe. "Jaluhz understands what you'd like. She says you've learned a lot about lava flow and the physics behind it. You're right that the most effective way to accomplish what we all want is to change things at the source, so to speak.

"However, Jaluhz doesn't have the power to do that by herself. She gave me an image of someone trying to operate on his or her own body. It wouldn't work well. She can guide you, and she can provide the power you'll need to change her internal configuration, I guess you could say. The vent inside her that's been ruptured needs to be sealed then opened farther inside her in order to give us the right angle. The gash in the mountainside also needs to be filled on one side and opened on the other, but she thinks much of that will happen when the lava builds up pressure from the new rupture."

"OK," said Chloe. "I understand all that, but how do I do it?"

"That's the tricky part," said Rya. "You'll have to work from inside Jaluhz."

"What?" Chloe's eyes opened wide and her jaw dropped in shock and surprise.

"Yeah, you'll need to teleport into the spot Jaluhz gives us and work from the inside. But obviously the heat inside a volcano is too great for any person. So Jaluhz says you'll need to place an energy shield around yourself to protect you while you're inside. She can't do that because she's the heat in the first place."

Chloe took a very deep breath then said, "So instead of moving lava, I'll be doing surgery on a volcano, from inside the volcano."

"Yep," said Rya, with a big grin. "You've got it."

"Wow," said Chloe. Then she thought long and hard as Rya and Artemis waited. Finally she said, "So I need my energy network to help support a shield around me to protect me from the heat of the volcano while Jaluhz guides me to seal one rupture and open another."

"Exactly," said Rya.

"Easy, right?" said Artemis.

Chloe said with heavy sarcasm, "Yeah, really easy."

"Oh, one more thing," said Rya.

"What?" said Chloe, with suspicion in her voice.

"It'll be tricky to time it. You have to seal the current rupture so nothing more comes out it, but you'll have to open the new rupture nearly instantaneously, or the pressure will cause an eruption out of the top, something none of us wants."

"And Jaluhz knows where the new rupture should be?"

"Yeah," said Rya. Then she closed her eyes for a few moments before continuing. "Jaluhz has decided it would be best if the outside hole were prepared in advance. She thinks we should be able to line up the trajectory from the volcano to the fault line so it meets in a smooth path. I guess that'll make sense to Gregory, Oswald, and the baron. She thinks the new opening will be far enough from the current one so that if they don't work for long periods at a time, they'll be able to do it safely."

"Yikes, this is all a bit overwhelming," said Chloe, running her hands through her hair.

"You can do it," said Artemis with absolute confidence.

"If you have any more questions, let me know," said Rya. "Uncle Clyde and I are building like mad now, with other carpenters and volunteers, on the three new homes for those who lost theirs, but he said that whenever I need to help you, I can."

"That raises another question," Chloe said. "I'll be inside Jaluhz. She'll be guiding me. But Jaluhz and I can't communicate directly. How will that work?"

"Grandma and I have gotten really good with communicating with each other, so I can transfer Jaluhz's images nearly instantly to her, and then she can send them to you."

"OK," said Chloe. Then realizing she sounded a bit ungrateful, she went on, "Thank you, Rya, and please thank Jaluhz as well. This offer of hers is fantastic, and it's a very good plan. I just need to work out how I'm going to be protected in that kind of heat."

"You will," said Rya, as she and Artemis stood. "I think you'll have nearly a month because weather delays will slow the channel cutting. That's why we have to get back to work. The first big snowstorm will hit at the end of the week, and we need to have the homes framed and closed in by then. Gotta run. See you."

Rya and Artemis went racing out of the library. Chloe sat at her desk, totally stunned. Gregory, Oswald, and the baron walked by, and when they noticed her staring into space, they came into her office.

"Is everything all right?" asked Gregory.

"Yes, and no," said Chloe. She updated them on the change in the plan. She saved the bit about her having to do the work from inside the volcano until the very end.

"What?" said Gregory.

"You're going into the volcano?" said the baron.

"Cool," said Oswald, "I mean, that should be an awesome experience."

"If she lives to enjoy it," said Gregory, raising his eyebrows.

"Well, according to Rya and her weather forecasts, the channel won't be ready for nearly a month," Chloe said. "So I'm supposed to use that time to figure out how to create an energy heat shield. You'll have to find the spot on the mountain that you think is right for the new location of the lava flow, and then you'll have to open it up."

Gregory looked at his father and Oswald, and when they nodded, he said, "We can do that. We've already got some ideas on that. If the explosion had taken place about fifty yards to the left and a bit farther down, it would have shot the lava right into the fault."

"Yes," confirmed Oswald. "Our part in this is fairly straightforward."

"And as Jaluhz mentioned," said the baron, "we'll restrict the time that the dragons and riders dig so that it's done in small bits. We also won't use explosives, as we certainly don't want to repeat Zeke's mess."

"Great," said Chloe. "I'll leave that you to. Oh, Rya said that the first snowstorm will hit by the end of the week."

"Thanks," said Gregory. "We'll have the channel digging go into overtime until then. The dragons and riders will be fine with that, knowing they'll get time off during the storm."

The three of them stood, and as they left the office, the baron, shaking his head, said, "Good luck with your part."

"Thanks," said Chloe.

Chloe looked across the office and saw that William was in, so she headed over to update him. Once she'd brought him up to speed, she said, "So I need a way to figure out this heat-shield thing."

"No kidding," said William. They both thought for a moment or two, and then William said, "How about we start by having you put a shield around something else, and then we ask for some dragons to try to get through it with their fires? I'd like to start with a test that isn't likely to fry you."

"Me too," said Chloe, with heartfelt agreement.

"What if we had a pan of water for you to shield, instead of shielding yourself? I bet Harriet and Ruby would be willing to help. They don't want to leave the rider complex, as they want to stay close to Lucy. Although she's improving rapidly, she's still in the hospital. So if we went to the courtyard outside the hospital, I bet they'd try to break your shield. Thunder could join us there, and you'd be able to test your shield against three dragons."

"Let's start with one at a time and build up, but yes, that's a great idea," said Chloe.

After closing his eyes for a few moments, William said, "OK, I've called Thunder, and he'll get Harriet and Ruby and meet us there. Should we stop by the cafeteria for a pan?"

Chloe said, "No, I'll provide the pan of water. I'm betting we'll have an audience soon enough as it is, without alerting the cafeteria crowd by asking for a pan of water."

William laughed. "You're right there."

They walked to the rider compound, where the dragons already were waiting. As they approached, Harriet said, "Lucy wants to know what you're up to now."

Chloe groaned. "We're trying to see if I can create a heat shield. I'll explain everything later. Let's just try it out." She conjured a large pot of water then said, "I'm going to create a shield around this pot. Then I want one of you to try to heat the water. OK?"

The three dragons argued about who should get to try first, but by the time Chloe was ready, Harriet had gotten the nod to try first. The blue dragon was small—the smallest dragon actually—but she proved she had a mighty fire in her belly. She blew flames at the pot, and the shield held for a minute or two, but then it collapsed and the water boiled.

"Wow," said William. "Uh, that didn't last long, did it?"

"No," said Chloe, as she sat down on the ground in defeat. "I had no idea how much energy it takes to shield against heat. I made a shield years ago, before I even knew I was a mage, and it stopped a bullet from hitting Bertha. So why is this so hard?"

William thought for a moment then said, "Well, the bullet hit in an instant, and then it was gone. It didn't keep pummeling the shield the way Harriet did. By the way, Harriet, awesome flame."

"Why, thank you," said Harriet shyly.

Emily and Rupert walked into the courtyard just then. "What's going on?" asked Emily.

Chloe explained their experiment and also the sad results. Rupert said, "Is it possible that the shield requires the same amount of energy as what's in whatever is being deflected? So you'd need as much energy as Harriet had in her flames. By the way, Harriet, truly magnificent flames."

Harriet turned a bit pink as she said, "Thanks."

"So I need my energy net just to save a pot of water?" said Chloe, sighing. "I guess you're right, Rupert. I need to have as much energy for the shield as Harriet has in her flames, even if it's only to keep a pot of water from boiling."

"Well, let's try it," said William. "Refill the pot with cold water then draw on Thunder and me, and this time Ruby can make the fire."

"OK," said Chloe.

The second try was more successful, but after ten minutes or so, the shield collapsed.

"Well, we know the secret of creating a strong heat shield," said Emily. "Now do I dare ask why you need a heat shield?"

Chloe shared the current plan, after which Rupert, with awe in his voice, said, "You're heading into the volcano, into the part where there's lava? That's something."

"Sure is," said Chloe in a resigned voice. "I'm just not sure what."

"This is going to take a lot of energy," Emily said. "Do we have any idea about the relative temperatures of the molten lava and the dragon flames?"

"I don't, but I'm betting Gregory does or soon will," said Chloe.

"Let's add Esmeralda and me, and Rupert and Whipper, along with William and Thunder," suggested Emily, "and let's have both Harriet and Ruby try to flame the shield."

"Great idea," said William. "Then we'll have data for Chloe on her own, Chloe with one bonded pair against one dragon, and Chloe with three bonded pairs against two dragons. Hopefully, with that and a bunch more data, we'll be able to extrapolate to see how big an energy shield we need."

"And this is just for a pot of water," said Rupert. "Wonder what it'd be like if Chloe had the shield around herself?"

"Let's just wait to test that, shall we?" said Chloe.

"Right," said Emily. "Step by step. OK, let's try this. Ready Chloe?"

Chloe refilled her pot with cold water, made her shield, linked telepathically with the three bonded pairs, and nodded. Harriet and Ruby smiled then blew their flames right at the shield. Chloe put everything she had into it, but within fifteen minutes, the shield was down.

"That's OK," said William. "Your shield lasted half again as long even though there was twice the heat."

"I'm sure glad we have a month to work on this," said Chloe with a sigh.

"A month?" asked Emily.

"Yes. Rya says we're going to get socked with a few major snowstorms—the first at the end of this week—so she and Gregory think that it'll be about a month before the trench is completed far enough for us to start the lava flowing into it."

As yet another tremor shook the area, Emily said, "So another month of these frequent tremors, I'm guessing."

"Afraid so," said Chloe, "but right now I'm grateful for additional time."

"I'll set up a trials sheet the way we did when you were dealing with the asteroid," William said. "We'll run experiments and figure out the number of pairs you need to hold the shield for... what? Twenty minutes? Do we even know how long it'll take you to repair a rupture and create another one?"

Chloe shrugged. "I have no idea, but I'd like to know that my shield will hold for longer than I need it to. I don't want to cut it too close. Maybe Rya can get an idea from Jaluhz."

"I think this has been enough for this morning," said Emily. "Chloe, you look exhausted. You need some lunch and time to rest. William, once you have a proposed schedule, please let me see it. I'll work at coordinating it with the digging. I suspect Gregory will want round-the-clock digging before the snowstorm."

Chloe nodded. "Yes, I think he did say that. I was so worried about heat shields that I didn't remember that."

"Well, let's face it," said Emily. "We need both to make this work. We have to have a trench, but without your efforts to move the rupture, the trench will be worthless. And without the trench, you'll just be shooting lava out over another area of land. We'll coordinate this—trust me. And yes, even if I have to live with these tremors for a longer period of time, I'm grateful for the additional month."

"Hey," said Rupert, "once the snow starts, why don't we hold the tests out at the trench where the snow is? Then, when the shield gives way, the dragons will be melting the snow and unfreezing the ground. We can help both causes."

Emily smiled. "That's a great idea. OK, Chloe, eat and rest. William, please get me a schedule of the testing you want to do. And thanks, both of you."

William offered Chloe a lift on Thunder, and while it wasn't that far, she was grateful for the offer. *How long has it been since I really had to use my powers?* she wondered. *I'm out of shape, and I'd better get back in shape fast.*

When they reached the library, Chloe thanked William and Thunder then headed to Libby's apartment, where she knew she'd find food and comfort. She knocked on the door and entered, nearly collapsing on Libby's couch. "What a morning," she groaned.

"So I gather," Libby answered, as a large bowl of hearty vegetable and barley stew materialized on the table next to Chloe. "Now eat first, and then tell me what's concerning you."

Chloe hadn't realized how hungry she was until she took the first bite. As she was eating, Calliope walked in, jumped up next to her, and said, *Are you really going to go inside Jaluhz?*

"That seems to be the only way," said Chloe, as she put down her empty bowl.

"What's worrying you about all this?" asked Libby. "After all, you did move an asteroid."

Chloe was quiet for a few moments, thinking. Finally she said, "You know, in everything I've done, I've never personally been in danger. Oh, sure, if I'd bobbled the asteroid, we all would have been killed, but I wasn't in danger while I was working. This seems different. I'll not only be repairing one rupture and making another, but while doing that—with perfect timing, I might add, or else the top of Jaluhz will be blown off—I'll also have to protect myself. I mean, at least long enough to accomplish the task. And I realized I also haven't been using much magic lately—not anything that would test me—and frankly I'm out of shape."

"Well, you have a month to get in shape," Libby reminded her, "and don't forget, Jaluhz is providing the energy to support your magic for the repair. She just can't provide it for your heat shield."

"Yes, I know. And if Jaluhz has enough power to have powered King Alfred's time travel, well, then she has a lot. Sure hope she hasn't gotten rusty in more than five hundred years."

I don't like the sound of this one bit, said Calliope.

"I can't say I'm overly fond of doing this either," said Chloe, "but no one else can do it, and it's the plan with the best chance of success. Don't forget, this lava is going to be flowing for a lot of years. We need to be sure it's flowing where we want it to go. I'm glad I have Gregory, Oswald, and the baron figuring out the exact locations for me. This definitely is going to be a team effort."

"So you're running tests using dragon flames and your shield around something else. Eventually you'll have to run a test with the shield around you," said Libby.

"I know," said Chloe, "but not until I can keep a pot of water from boiling. Gives new meaning to the saying, 'Can't even boil water,' doesn't it?"

"You're tired now," Libby said, "and as you say, you need to get back in shape. I'll tell you what. You work with William over the next week or two. See how things are shaping up and how much of an energy net you really need. I'll add myself into the net, but only as an extra, to give you a safety cushion. I'd like you to be confident about the net with the bonded pairs, sure that you can succeed with that. I'll be your backup."

"And after a couple of weeks?" asked Chloe.

"Well, if you're finding you're way short of the mark, I'll wake up that hibernating bear and get her down here. She has more energy than even I do, and that's saying something. She probably has as much as Jaluhz, or close to it anyway. And I won't hesitate to wake her. She'd want to be here. But you know, if we can pull this off without her, we'll have teasing rights for years."

Chloe grinned at that, and Libby said, "I knew I could get you to smile. But truthfully you'll have whatever resources you need. And while Jaluhz is located in Draconia, and we're the ones who'll suffer from the lava if it isn't contained, the other three nations do need us, and they wouldn't want a bunch of refugees if Draconia becomes uninhabitable, so I'm sure they'd step in as they did with the asteroid, if needed."

"You're right," said Chloe, "and thanks. It's just a lot to take in all at once."

"Of course," said Libby. "I have faith in you and so do many others. Now how about having some faith in yourself?"

Chloe stood then hugged Libby. "I know, but that's harder. Now I'd better find out what William has in store for this afternoon's trials. Thanks, Libby, so much."

Calliope jumped down and followed Chloe out, saying, *I have faith in you too, but don't forget that I depend on you for regular meals. So don't go getting yourself fried in any volcano.*

"I'll sure try," said Chloe with a smile.

Calliope headed into Chloe's office as Chloe walked into William's. He looked up when she came in and said, "You're looking much better. That's good, because I have a plan for this afternoon."

"Somehow I thought you would," said Chloe. "And I'm glad you do, William. I'll need all the help I can get to prepare for this."

"No worries," said William. "Now Harriet and Ruby have agreed to be flame throwers for now. That way we'll always have the same amount of heat for each trial, and besides, they're not on digging detail as long as Lucy is in the hospital."

"Sounds like a plan. What about the energy from the bonded pairs?" asked Chloe.

"At least for this afternoon, Amy, Fern, Todd, and Jupiter have agreed to come and help. Hannah and Firebird are free for this afternoon as well, and of course Thunder and I are here. Emily said Rupert and Whipper might be able to join us later on, but right now we have at least four bonded pairs, and remember, the grouping of Amy, Fern, Todd, and Jupiter is far stronger than just two bonded pairs."

"I do remember since Amy and Todd are so close, and each of them has a partial bond with their opposite's dragon. So we do have a lot of energy for me to draw from. Let's try it out."

Chloe, William, and Thunder headed back to the hospital courtyard. As they passed Mary's shop, she came out and said, "See our new contest? We're guessing how long you can hold a shield. It's just for this afternoon, so William, be sure to stop by and give me her longest time. Then we can have a benchmark, and the next contest will be for how long it'll take you to break that benchmark. Isn't this fun?"

Chloe groaned. "This will be the ruin of me."

William smiled. "I'll be sure you have your numbers, Mary."

When they entered the courtyard, the others were already there. After William and Chloe thanked them all, the afternoon trials began. Chloe held up better this time and was remembering how to pace herself, when to draw on the energy from others and how to shift the balance so she wouldn't drain everyone all at once.

"You're definitely improving," said Amy, after one trial during which Chloe's shield had held for nearly thirty minutes.

"How are you two holding out?" Jupiter asked Harriet and Ruby. "You've been throwing a lot of fire."

"I think we'll sleep really well tonight," Harriet said.

"Let's give Chloe another challenge then call it quits," said Jupiter. "I'll switch to flame throwing along with Harriet and Ruby."

"What?" said Chloe. "I need you as part of the energy net."

"Not really," said Jupiter. "Todd can work with both Amy and Fern, so you'll only lose my energy. And I guarantee that whatever figures Gregory and the others come up with, Jaluhz is going to be at least as hot as three dragons."

Chloe said, "You're right, Jupiter. And thanks...I think."

William got ready to time this trial, and everyone settled into his or her respective roles. Chloe put up the shield all around the pot. As she nodded, three sets of flames shot toward the shield. Chloe started to waver, but then she remembered Libby's words of encouragement and pulled herself together, taking energy as she needed it, trying to feel the shield, where it was strong and where it might be weakening. When the shield finally collapsed, Chloe heard cheers all around.

"What? How'd I do?" she asked.

William said, "You managed to hold that for thirty-one minutes, even with three dragons and even with a slightly smaller energy net."

Todd came over and shook her hand, saying, "You rock!"

Chloe smiled and thanked them all. "I still have a long way to go," she said.

"But look at how much you've improved in just this afternoon," said Amy. "You'll do it. We know you will. And whenever you need us for more tests, let us know, OK?"

"OK," said Chloe, grinning as she finally realized what she'd accomplished.

On their way back to the library, William and Chloe stopped at Mary's shop, as they had promised. "Thirty-one minutes, with three dragons shooting flames," William told Mary.

"Wow," she said. "The highest guess we had was twenty-three minutes. That person will be the winner, but he sure was way low. Nice job, Chloe. And be sure to let me know when you're doing this again."

Chloe smiled. "You can pretty well figure we'll be testing every day until the actual time for the real test arrives."

"Great," said Mary. "Have a nice evening."

"You, too," said Chloe, as she and William headed back to the library.

Once they arrived, William said, "I want to write out my notes. And I'll have to confirm it with Emily, but I'm thinking we'll do tests each afternoon. That'll give you the morning to keep up with your students, and more people seem to be free in the afternoons. Does that sound all right?"

Chloe nodded. "Sounds fine, and again thanks so much for organizing this."

— 22 —

FLAMING THE MAGE

The next two weeks went by in a blur as Chloe did test after test on her abilities to create a strong heat shield. She placed shields around larger and larger objects, moving to rocks and boulders just to be sure she could make a shield large enough to cover her and allow her room to move and work.

She spent her mornings meeting with students as they checked in with her regarding their progress with their studies or apprenticeships. She worried that she wasn't able to focus on them as she usually did, but they seemed to be doing well, and they also seemed very interested in what she was attempting. Several mentioned they had won one of Mary's contests.

As the second week was coming to an end, Todd stopped by to say he felt Arryn was ready to take her graduation exams.

"Really? That's very exciting. Thanks so much for working with her."

Todd smiled. "I can't take much of the credit. I did help her set up the experiments for the lab portion of her science exam, but that girl is a voracious reader. She devours books, and she's gotten where she is all on her own. She's smart, determined, eager, and very sweet. I really enjoy working with her."

"Excellent. Well, as you know, my afternoons are rather busy, but if Arryn could come in early tomorrow, say around seven, she'd have plenty of time to take her exams. There's no time limit, but the notes Miss Murphy from Havenshold School gave me indicate that most students complete the exams in four to five hours."

"She'll be here, ready to go. She's really excited."

The next morning Arryn was standing outside the main entrance of the library a bit before seven, waiting for Chloe to open the doors.

"Good morning," said Chloe, smiling.

"Hi," said Arryn, walking in with a stack of books. "I'll just return these and be right there."

"We should set you up with a reading spot in the library. Then you wouldn't have to lug so many books home."

"Oh, could you?" said Arryn, her face lighting up in excitement. "I love this library."

Chloe nodded. "Let's get these graduation exams knocked out first, and then we can decide where your path will lead you next."

Once again Chloe set Arryn to work in the lab area of the office. "Here's your first exam, literature, and when you complete it, I'll give you the next one. There are four in all. After literature, you'll have history, math, and finally science. Good luck!"

"Thanks, Chloe," said Arryn, as she opened her first exam.

Chloe returned to her office and said to Calliope, "Arryn sure has blossomed in the short time she's been with Amy and Todd. She just needed the right environment, but then that's true for all of us, isn't it?"

Sure is, said Calliope. *And I love how she's taken to the library. I've probably seen more of her than I have of any other student. She's in and out of here all the time.*

"Well, start thinking about which reading nook you think she'd like best, because I think she's going to be spending a lot more time here."

Excellent, Calliope said with a grin. *I know the perfect spot.*

Chloe filled out progress reports on her students while she waited for Arryn. In a little less than an hour, Arryn walked in holding out her first completed exam. "Ready for history," she said.

"Here you go," said Chloe, as she took the completed exam and handed Arryn the next one.

Chloe graded Arryn's literature exam while Arryn took the history one. When she was finished, she rubbed the top of Calliope's head and said, "This is excellent work. Arryn certainly has earned top marks on this exam. Her answers go well beyond the requirement, and she shows a remarkable depth of understanding."

I'm guessing her life experiences, as tough as they were, have given her a deeper insight into life, and that's helping her now.

"I agree," Chloe said, as she wrote up her formal comments on Arryn's literature exam. She planned to send all her comments to Miss Murphy, who would then send them to the education board so they would become part of Arryn's permanent record.

"I'm ready for math," said Arryn about forty-five minutes later.

"You're speeding through these," said Chloe.

"I write fast," said Arryn with a smile, as she took the math exam.

Chloe graded the history exam while Arryn was taking the math test. "This exam is just as excellent as the last one, Calliope. I think Arryn has read more history books from the library, as she's included a wealth of information that isn't in the standard curriculum."

She's always got a pile of books, said Calliope. *I'd say she not only writes fast but also reads fast.*

Arryn took a full hour on the math test, and when she came in with the completed exam, she said, "I went through this one twice, just to be sure I didn't make any careless errors."

"Checking your work is always a smart idea," Chloe said with a smile. "Now here's your final exam, the science one. Good luck."

After Chloe corrected the math exam, she exclaimed, "She didn't miss a single answer!"

Calliope purred very loudly.

The clock struck eleven as Arryn walked in with the last of her exams. "Here you go," she said.

Chloe nodded as she took it. "If this one is as well done as the other three, you won't only have passed—you'll have passed with top marks. I'm assuming you'd like me to grade this now."

Arryn nodded eagerly and, with a wide smile, said, "Please!"

"Why don't you go out into the library with Calliope, and she can show you a spot she thinks you'd like, a reading nook you can have as your own?"

"Cool," said Arryn.

Calliope jumped down off Chloe's desk and led the way out of the office.

Chloe got to work grading Arryn's science exam, and when she finished, she thought, *Todd was right. She was more than ready. She's a natural-born student.*

With those thoughts Chloe completed her comments on the science exam then filled out the required paperwork—including her overall evaluation of Arryn—slipped everything into a large envelope, sealed it, and addressed it to Miss Murphy. Then she went in search of Arryn and Calliope.

When she found them, she said, "You know, this was always my favorite nook when I was a Pathfinder student."

"Really?" said Arryn. "Calliope showed me this one first, and then a few of the others, but this one just felt right, and look, not only is there a comfy pink chair, but the table next to it already has a book on it, one that looks really interesting. It's about philosophy, and I haven't read much of that. I've been concentrating on the exam subjects."

"That's wonderful," said Chloe, as she sent out a thought to Libby. *You really have her hooked, you know.*

I know, came Libby's reply.

"You've passed your graduation exams with the very highest marks," Chloe told Arryn. "Congratulations! I'm sure Amy and Todd will want to have a celebration for you. My guess is they're already working on that, and Amy probably has a cake baked and decorated. Todd was very confident that you'd breeze through, and he was right."

"I love living there," said Arryn. "They're so kind and thoughtful, and their house always has something going on."

"I remember," said Chloe. "Now do you have any thoughts about what your next step might be?"

"I'm not sure," Arryn said with a shrug. "I know want to keep reading lots of different things, like this philosophy book. I figure if I read enough, I'll find the subject I'm most interested in, but right now, well, I haven't explored enough. Is it OK just to keep reading what I find interesting?"

"Definitely," said Chloe, smiling. "Our world has a lot more to offer than most of us ever realize. How about you check in with me each week and share what you've been reading and what your thoughts are?"

"Oh, that would be terrific," said Arryn.

"But I want you to promise to do other things besides read. You're friends with Rya, right?" Arryn nodded. "Well, hang out with her when you're both free, as well as Aster, when she's in town and free. And what about other nonreading activities? Is there anything you might like to try, perhaps in the arts?"

"I've been stopping in at Mary's," Arryn said. "Well, everyone has, as we're all making guesses for the contests, and she has new contests several times a day."

"I know," said Chloe, sighing, "and lately many people have been trying to guess how well my shield will hold up, but you were saying?"

"Yeah, well, the contests are helping to lighten the mood about the tremors, but even more, I started talking with Mary. She's passionate about making sweaters, and she said she'd teach me to knit. I thought that might be kinda cool."

Chloe smiled. "Yes, I think that would be excellent. Why don't you set up something with Mary? Is Rya interested in learning to knit as well?"

"Nah," said Arryn. "If wood isn't involved...well, she's just not into knitting. But she did say that if I made something, she'd wear it. So that's something."

"Yes, it is. Well, once again, many congratulations on your exam results. You'll receive a proper certificate from Miss Murphy, and once this lava situation has been sorted out, we'll have a ceremony to present it to you, but as of this moment, you're an official graduate, and as you said at the start of this year, a proper Pathfinder student."

Arryn gave Chloe a big hug and said, "Thank you. For everything. I can't wait to tell Amy and Todd."

She grabbed up the philosophy book and her coat and raced out of the library, calling, "I'll be back, Calliope."

Chloe laughed as she picked up Calliope. "Maybe you two can't talk, since Arryn isn't telepathic, but I'd say you have a real admirer nonetheless."

Hey, talking isn't everything, Calliope said with a shrug. *She really belongs here. She loves books.*

They returned to Chloe's office, where Chloe found her lunch, a bowl of hearty vegetable and barley soup and some fresh bread, waiting for her. She put Calliope on the desk and said, "You know, Calliope, I'm really lucky to have so many people looking out for me. And thanks, Libby, for the lunch."

Calliope purred as Chloe ate, preparing for another afternoon of heat-shield tests.

William walked into her office as she was finishing her lunch. "I wanted to talk to you about the testing," he said.

"Have a seat," said Chloe, wiping a crumb from her lips. "What wondrous torture have you devised for me now?"

"Well, you're really getting strong, and you can keep a much larger shield in place for a half hour, even with five dragons shooting flames at it. I wouldn't think you'd need a lot longer than that to do what you need to do inside the volcano. And Gregory's readings indicate the heat generated by five dragons is probably comparable to what you'll be exposed to inside Jaluhz."

Chloe let out a small sigh. "It's the 'probably' and the 'wouldn't think' that have me nervous, but go ahead."

"I think we need to move to the next phase. We need to have you shield yourself."

Chloe's mouth dropped open, but she quickly shut it before saying, "I knew this day had to come, but it has me worried."

"I know," said William, "and I remember what you've said about never being in real danger before. This is certainly dangerous. But I talked with Emily and Esmeralda, and we're sure we can do this safely."

"Let's hear your plan," said Chloe.

"We want to start small and easy, just the way we did with the pot of water. We thought Esmeralda could be the flame thrower."

"What?" said Chloe, clearly surprised. "She has the hottest flames of any of the dragons. This is your idea of slow and easy?"

William held up a hand. "Wait. Hear me out. We picked Esmeralda because you already have a very strong telepathic bond with her. You're familiar with her, and you've worked with her for years. She also has the best control over her flames. She can stop them faster than any of the other dragons. I know because the dragons have had their own contests over this—testing their heat and also testing how quickly they can start and—more important for you—stop their flames. Esmeralda has won all those contests, hands down."

"So you're saying that if my shield fails, Esmeralda will know that as quickly as I do and then be able to stop her flame before I'm reduced to cinders?" said Chloe.

"Yep, you've got it," said William, who was nearly bouncing in his chair with enthusiasm.

"You're really enjoying this," said Chloe.

"Well," William said, looking a bit sheepish, "it's what I do, studying telepathy and telepathic powers and so on. Experimenting with the use of the energy net. I know folks think I'm a bit weird, but I love it. So yes, I'm really excited about this, and to be a part of something so new and different—well, it's amazing. But don't think I'd ever take any chances with you. I wouldn't."

"I know that, William, and trust me, I do appreciate the fact that you love this. We never would have been able to set up the energy net using pairs from all four nations to stop the asteroid if it hadn't been for you. And believe me, I'm really relying on you now, not only so I can fix Jaluhz and the lava flow, but this time, quite literally, to save my life."

William turned bright red with embarrassment. He said, "Well, thanks."

"So where are we going to try this test? And who will be my bonded pairs?"

"We'll be in the hospital courtyard again," said William.

"Great," said Chloe with heavy sarcasm. "You know we draw more and more people each time, all of whom have a guess in at Mary's shop about how long I'll hold out or how many dragons I can shield against."

"Yep," said William with a smile. "You'll have an audience for sure. But look at it this way. Your tests are really boosting the townspeople's morale. I honestly don't know how any of us would have dealt with the nearly constant tremors if it weren't for Mary and Oswald's contests, and your testing, which have provided us not only with things to guess about but also first-rate entertainment."

"Gee, thanks," said Chloe.

"Really," said William, as he warmed to his topic. "You know people—regular people, not riders—well, they've always been leery of dragons, and before all this, they certainly would have run from a dragon that was shooting fire. But now, well, they crowd closer each time, safely out of the way of the flames, of course, but near enough to feel the heat and enjoy the spectacle. And honestly the dragons are reveling in the new attention. Several of them, like Harriet and Ruby, now have admirers who want to meet them and touch them. It's incredible."

"Just as long as I don't get fried," said Chloe. "Now who did you say would be in my energy net for this experiment?"

"Amy, Fern, Todd, and Jupiter volunteered several days ago, when they realized this would have to be the next step. And Thunder and I will be there as well, since even though we aren't necessarily the strongest bond, we're the ones you've worked with the most."

"OK," said Chloe. "No time like the present. We'd better get over there and try this out."

As Chloe and William approached the rider complex, Chloe realized the crowds were far larger than ever before. William patted her shoulder and said, "Oh, yes, the other plus to the crowd is that it'll make you nervous."

"And that's a plus?"

William nodded. "Definitely. After all, don't you think you'll be really nervous when you teleport inside Jaluhz? I want you to be used to making the very best shield in the most nerve-wracking scenarios we can possible devise."

"I guess," said Chloe, as Mary came over to say, "Good luck. We've had more guesses for this trial than any of the others."

Once Chloe and William entered the courtyard, the crowds squeezed in behind them. Arryn raced over from where she'd been standing with Amy, Fern, Todd, and Jupiter. "I know you'll ace your exams too," she told Chloe. "Good luck!"

"Thanks, Arryn," said Chloe, who then went over to stand about six feet in front of Emily and Esmeralda.

"Don't worry, Chloe," said Esmeralda. "I won't hurt you. I promise."

"And I'll be in the link as well," said Emily.

"Thanks," said Chloe, her voice showing a bit of a tremor.

"OK," said William. "Whenever you're ready, Chloe."

Trying to ignore what was about to happen, Chloe gathered her focus. She'd gotten used to seeing lots of dragons shooting fire, but she wasn't sure what it would be like to have it all aimed at her. She formed her shield, completely surrounding herself, and drew some energy from Amy, Fern, Todd, Jupiter, William, and Thunder; she hoped it would be enough to make a solid shield. Her plan was to continue to draw on their power to maintain the shield for as long as she could. Finally she nodded to Esmeralda.

Esmeralda started with smaller flames, which Chloe's shield easily deflected, and then she opened up with full flames. The crowds gasped as the flames seemed to envelope Chloe. When Chloe saw all that fire coming at her, she suddenly panicked. Her shield collapsed immediately, but thankfully so did Esmeralda's flames. Chloe's hair was slightly singed, but otherwise she was fine, although very embarrassed.

To her surprise, the crowd cheered and applauded. William came over and said, "That was a first-rate try."

"Really? I don't think my shield lasted even a minute," said Chloe.

"None of us would've been able to do anything like that," said William. "And actually, if we count the time from when Esmeralda first started her flame, you held your shield for three minutes."

Amy placed a gentle hand on Chloe's shoulder. "And you didn't draw on any of our power. I felt your panic—really we all did. But you didn't open yourself to our power or our confidence in you. You have to remember that you aren't alone in this." She smiled warmly at Chloe. "Yes, you'll be the one who actually teleports inside Jaluhz. But you'll be taking us with you, in the form of our energy. And you'll also be taking all our love and belief in you. You have to remember that. It'll strengthen you more than you can know right now."

Todd put an arm around Amy's shoulders. "Listen to her, Chloe. She's right. We believe in you. Now you need to believe in yourself and in us."

Tears ran down Chloe's face, and she hugged Amy and Todd. "Thank you. Thank you so much." Then she turned to William and said, "Well, shall we give this another try?"

"Definitely," said William, who turned to the crowd and called out, "Let's hear it for our mage. She's going to do it again."

Thunderous applause erupted from the crowd along with lots of cheers and shouts of "You can do it!" Wiping her tears away, Chloe smiled and went back to her spot. A hush fell over the crowd as she again concentrated on building her shield. This time she took more energy from her energy net, making a much stronger shield, and then she nodded.

Again Esmeralda started slowly, but she ramped up to full firepower much more quickly. Chloe heard Amy in her head saying, *Trust us,* which allowed Chloe to focus on her shield and not on the fact that tons of dragon fire was being shot at her. She could almost feel the spots that were weakening, but she wasn't yet strong enough to stop them. However, the shield collapse happened in a more controlled way, and this time Esmeralda was able to stop her flames before the shield was completely down.

The courtyard was awash in cheers and applause. Chloe wondered whether any of them even felt the tremor that shook the ground. William shouted until the crowd quieted enough to hear him. "That was ten minutes and not a single singed hair this time!"

Chloe said, "Really? I held out that long?"

"Yes, you did," said Esmeralda, "and I didn't go easy on you. I gave you my full heat, and my flames are the hottest of any other dragon."

"Wow," said Chloe. "I really did that? Well, only because of my wonderful energy net. Thank you guys."

"It's still your power, Chloe," said Amy. "We're just giving you the food you need, so to speak. What you do with it is totally up to you and your mage power."

"Want to try it again?" asked William eagerly.

"Why not?" Chloe relied. "I think the worst of it is seeing the flames coming at me. But if I can gain confidence in the protection of my shield, I think I can get past that."

"And face it," said Emily, "none of us knows what the inside of Jaluhz looks like. It won't be dragon flames shooting at you, but you might find yourself surrounded by hot lava. So, as William said, we want to prepare you for anything."

Chloe nodded. "OK, let's try again, and Esmeralda, let me have it right away. Although I will say I'm very glad your first tests started out gently."

Chloe put her shield around her. This time she closed her eyes and focused all her energy and attention onto the shield. She nodded to Esmeralda but kept her eyes closed. When she was sure Esmeralda's flames were coming at her, she opened her eyes, then just felt the shield. She drew on more power when a spot started to weaken. She also shifted the energy around the shield so the shield was evenly protective. When she felt her own energy and that of her net weakening, she sent a thought to Esmeralda, *Enough*, and the flames stopped while her shield was still intact.

The crowd, roaring and hollering in delight, was loving this. William announced the time, and Chloe was stunned to find out she'd held her shield against the full heat of Esmeralda's flames for twenty minutes.

Mary announced the winning guesses for Chloe's three trials today then added, "The winner for that last trial didn't come close. The highest guess anyone made was fifteen minutes. Great job, Chloe."

"Thanks," said Chloe.

William held up his hands. "Thank you everyone, for your support," he called out. "I know it's really helping Chloe. We're done for today, but we'll be back tomorrow afternoon for more trials, and we'll have Chloe shielding against two dragons. So don't miss it!"

As the crowd dispersed, several people came over to thank Chloe and let her know they appreciated what she was doing. Chloe was grateful for their kind, heartfelt words.

Finally she went over to Esmeralda and Emily. She hugged each of them and said, "Thank you for helping me, and thank you for not frying me, Esmeralda. Amy said I had to trust all of you, and she was right. I knew in my heart that you wouldn't let your flames burn me, but my head had to learn that too. Thanks!"

"Well," said Esmeralda, "none of us could do what you're doing. And as wonderful as people think Jaluhz is—and she is—she's still a volcano, and she doesn't have to do anything she doesn't want to do. She has her own cycle, which is much stronger than any of us. The fact that you've made a sort of bond with her, through Rya, so she's at least amenable to helping us out...well, that's huge."

"Thanks, Esmeralda, and you're right. Rya says she's had to learn how to even see Jaluhz's images, how to try to interpret what Jaluhz is communicating. Rya's tried to explain it to me, but it's so different from our communication methods that it's difficult to explain. Ranks right up there with knowing we have a sentient planet but that we have no way to know what she's thinking either. So the fact that we've managed to get this much communication and work done together at this level... well, that's the real miracle here."

Emily nodded. "You're right about that. Now you'd better get some rest since tomorrow you'll have two dragons shooting fire at you!"

Chloe chuckled. "I've got my support in my energy net. I'll be ready."

— 23 —

A HITCH IN THE PLANS

The next afternoon found Chloe again in the hospital courtyard. She was glad the courtyard was expansive because there was more of everyone: more dragons, more riders, and definitely a larger cheering crowd. As Chloe looked around, she saw not only Harriet and Ruby but also Lucy and Gretchen. Chloe ran over to them and hugged both Lucy and Gretchen before saying, "It's so great to see you here. I knew you'd been released from the hospital, Lucy, but thought you were supposed to stay home. You're looking really good, with your color back and a bounce in your step."

Lucy laughed. "Well, I'm still not on the duty roster, and I'm supposed to be resting, but Dr. Brian says I'm nearly at a hundred percent, and well, Gretchen and I really wanted to help. I can't lift anything and certainly can't vault onto Harriet until the incisions in my belly heal, but I don't have more than occasional twinges of pain, for which I'm most grateful."

Emily and Esmeralda came over and joined them. "I've agreed to let them be part of your energy net," Emily said, "but I've also got my mother monitoring Lucy, so if she starts to lose too much energy, Mom will shove her out of the net."

"Yeah, foster moms can be a bit overprotective," Lucy said with a smile, "but I've promised to behave."

Chloe chuckled. "I know, but most of the time, that's a good thing. So what's up for today?" she asked, turning to Emily and Esmeralda.

"As promised," said Esmeralda, "you'll face two dragons. I've chosen Jupiter to join me. After me, he has the hottest flames and, even more important from your point of view, I'm sure, the best control."

"So he won't be in my energy net then," said Chloe.

Emily said, "I've added Hannah and Firebird to the net. So altogether you'll have Amy, Fern, Todd, Lucy, Harriet, Gretchen, Ruby, Rupert, Whipper, Hannah, and Firebird."

As she was speaking, a large orange dragon and a rider landed in the courtyard. Emily looked up and said, "Hans, I didn't expect you."

"Neither did I, Sis, but Clotilda needed me to update you on the situation with those ranchers, and Fire Dancer and I heard about the trials, so we couldn't miss the fun."

Chloe groaned. Hans turned and looked at her, saying, "Hey, Chloe, you know we've always taken good care of you. Didn't we help when you had to do your first mage tour of the other nations?"

Chloe ran over and hugged him as she thought, *Where would I be without Amy and Todd and their supportive family?* "I'm really glad to see you both," she said. "You spend so much time in the other nations as the queen's ambassadors that we never see enough of you."

"Well, this is where the action is now, and Aster and Jasmine are returning as well," said Hans. "Now how can we help?"

"For the first trial," Emily said, "let's add you two to the energy net. Then if this goes the way I think it will, I have another idea."

Chloe thought there was something devious in Emily's tone, but she just nodded.

Again the crowd quieted as Chloe focused. When she nodded, Esmeralda and Jupiter shot their flames at full strength right at her. Chloe kept her eyes open this time but stayed fully focused on the heat shield. As various spots in the shield weakened, she drew on her energy net and was pleased to note that she was able to strengthen them, maintaining the shield's integrity. Finally she said to Esmeralda, *Enough*, and the flames stopped instantly, replaced with thunderous applause, cheers, and shouts.

Chloe looked over at William, who said, "You made the half-hour mark! That's incredible."

"Well, I did have a much larger energy net this time," Chloe said, smiling.

"And a lot more fire," noted Jupiter. "Fantastic job!"

"I knew you could do it," Emily said, "so that's why I want to try a third dragon, and I want them to shoot flames from all around you."

Chloe nodded. "That makes sense. After all, we do have to get up to five dragons, and I have to be able to hold the shield for half an hour, but I know I can't do that yet."

"No," said Emily, "and we'll need a larger energy net for that as well. But let's just try the three dragons, realizing you probably won't be able to maintain that for as long. I just want you to get used to being surrounded by heat."

"So who are you adding to breathe fire at me?"

"Fire Dancer," said Emily.

"Keeping it all in the family," teased Chloe. "Your dragon, your dad's, and now your oldest brother's."

Emily laughed. "There's a real advantage to coming from a large family with so many riders. But the reality is that the family bond is nearly as strong as the direct bond. And that's why I put Hannah and Rupert in your net. Even the spouses of family members have a strong connection."

"Thanks for that backhanded vote of confidence, sister-in-law," said Rupert, with a big smile on his face. "Shall we go on strike, William?"

"Nah," said William. "She means well."

"OK," said Emily sheepishly. "Sorry. But shall we try it?"

"Yes," said Chloe. "And I do appreciate the way you've chosen the flame throwers—trust me."

The crowd hushed as Jupiter, Esmeralda, and Fire Dancer took up positions around Chloe. Suddenly she realized she wouldn't be able to see all of them at once. *Wonder if that'll be an advantage*, she thought. *I really don't like seeing the flames, so maybe.*

When Chloe was ready, she nodded, and in perfect unison, the three dragons shot their flames right at the heat shield. Chloe grabbed power from her energy net and quickly realized she was snatching energy from the net in panic. Taking a deep breath, she steadied the flow and focused on the shield. She discovered she had to be much more aware of it all around the full sphere. Previous trials always had shown weak spots in the front, where the flames were concentrated, but now she had to keep track of the entire sphere, watching more spots, strengthening in more places. She maintained control until she thought she couldn't hold out any longer, and then she mentally called out, *Stop.*

She staggered when the flames stopped and her shield dropped. William reached out to catch her before she fell. The crowd waited, and Chloe waved. "Just tired," she said.

William announced, "Fifteen minutes against three dragons," and the crowd cheered once again.

"That's definitely enough for today," Emily told the crowd.

"But do stop by tomorrow," added William. "We'll have more excitement for you then."

As if to emphasize his statement, another tremor shook the ground. Chloe heard many shouts of "Thanks, Chloe" as the crowd dispersed.

Hans walked over to Emily. "I need to talk with you and Chloe," he said. "We have a situation. And William, this could affect Chloe's trials, so you might want to sit in on this also."

Once they were all gathered in Emily's office, Emily asked Rupert to find a snack for Chloe and tea for them all. After Rupert returned, everyone sat down. Emily turned to Rupert to make sure he was ready to take notes, then said, "This sounds serious, Hans. What's up?"

"Well, you know those two ranchers who refused to let us make the channel across their property?" Emily nodded and Hans went on. "Clotilda did exactly what Gregory, Oswald, and the baron recommended. She called their bluff. They still didn't budge—that is, until yesterday. Apparently they decided to go see the lava flow for themselves, and what they saw scared them. They barged into the palace yesterday, demanding an audience. When Clotilda and Matilda met with them, they said they were entitled to protection and wanted the channel dug there after all."

"But isn't it too late?" asked Emily.

"That's why I'm here," said Hans. "To find out if anything can be done. Clotilda has told them they won't receive any of the compensation funds, and in fact, if they want this, they'll have to donate heavily to the Draconia relief fund, which helps those in need. They've agreed to that, so Clotilda told them she would find out, but she did warn them it already may be too late. If, in fact, it is too late, she'll let them know so they can evacuate their lands."

Emily thought for a moment then said, "Rupert, can you find Gregory, Oswald, and the baron and ask them to come here right away?"

"Sure," said Rupert, as he stood and headed to the door. "I'm pretty certain they're out at the lava flow. I'll be right back."

Chloe ate the sandwich Rupert had brought as they all made small talk while they waited.

Rupert came running back to say, "They're on their way," and then he bent over to catch his breath.

A few minutes later, Gregory, Oswald, and the baron walked in. Once they were seated, Emily explained the situation.

The baron chuckled. "So now those two ranchers want help, do they? I figured that would happen."

Hans nodded. "Clotilda would like to know if there's any way we could do this. She doesn't want the entire plan jeopardized, but at the same time, getting them to fork over a sizable contribution to the relief fund would be nice."

"True," said the baron.

Gregory said, "We're on a very tight schedule, as you know, and the latest snowstorm hasn't helped. We're almost ready with the first section of the trench. With the dragons working nearly round the clock in shifts, even through the night, we'll finish about a day ahead of our target date, which is a little less than two weeks away."

"And we've also got the second section well underway," said Oswald, "but we need to have at least those two sections completed before Chloe does her thing. We need a reasonable safety margin in case of further weather delays. It's only early February, so more snowstorms are the norm, not the exception. One thing we can count on is that the lava won't stop."

"In fact," said Gregory, "there's a possibility that the flow rate may even increase when it comes from the new location. We won't know until Chloe makes that rupture, but it is a bit lower, and the pressure may be greater. That's another reason we need to make sure we have as long a completed trench as possible."

"And," said the baron, "we're also working on creating the outside hole where the rupture will occur. That's what we've started today. Granted, that won't take long, but it's just one more consideration."

Hans nodded at all this and said, "So is there any chance? After all, you'll have to do something in that area. As I understood it from Clotilda, if you don't make a channel across their lands, you'll have to make a large funnel at the other end to get the lava contained again and heading into the trench at Cliffside, a trench that'll have to be extended to the sea."

"That's true," said Gregory, "but we'd have more time, the time it takes for the lava to cross their rather extensive lands."

"I understand," said Hans.

"There might be a way," said Gregory, who turned to Chloe. "What do you think? Would Jaluhz be willing to do another big earthquake, and do it along the ranchers' lands?"

"So they'd have to deal with the consequences of a major quake, but even if they lost more lands, they wouldn't lose everything?" said Chloe.

"That's what I'm thinking," Gregory replied. "We might need to refine the gash she'd make, but that wouldn't take nearly as long."

William spoke up. "And don't forget, please, that every resource we send to rescue these jerks means fewer dragon-rider pairs for Chloe in her testing. She's doing really well, but she needs the full two weeks of training."

All eyes turned to Chloe as Emily asked, "How are you feeling about your shield?"

"I discovered today how much harder it is to maintain the shield when I have heat surrounding me. I'm also worried because I'm using all my concentration, all my focus on monitoring my shield. But when I'm inside Jaluhz, I'll need to be concentrating on repairing the rupture then making another one. That means I need to get to the point where I can maintain the shield almost without thought."

"Exactly," said William, "which means you'll need to practice every afternoon, and you'll need more and more pairs in your energy net as we add two more dragons to the fire brigade."

"Nice term," said Emily, smiling at him. "I get your point. Rupert, you're in charge of the schedule. Are we maxed out?"

"Nearly, although I've gone ahead and started bringing in any dragons and riders who aren't currently in Havenshold. Aster and Jasmine, for instance, will be arriving this evening."

"How did the relocation to Chauncey's Creek go?" asked Chloe.

"Really well," said Emily. "I think it's a good fit for the newcomers and the existing residents. The temporary shelters are complete, so the riders who were doing that can return as well."

Rupert looked through his notes. "I can make sure there are enough pairs each afternoon for Chloe's practice sessions," he said. "I think we'd all agree that those sessions have to be our first priority. If Chloe isn't prepared, well, nothing else much matters, does it?"

With that sobering thought, the room fell silent. Finally Emily said, "Hans, let me check with Rya. It would appear that the only possibility is if we get a major quake to split the trench across their lands. The fault is already there, and Jaluhz has done some minor quakes in the area, but when those guys said, 'No trench,' I think we all just stopped everything on their land."

"How likely is Jaluhz to help?" asked Hans.

"That's anyone's guess," said Chloe. "Rya's made it pretty clear that Jaluhz is very different. She is, after all, a force of nature. She doesn't need us at all. I haven't exactly figured out what she thinks of us, if indeed she does think about us at all. My best guess is that since she was the power that allowed King Alfred and his company to be brought back in time, and since the planet wanted that to happen—for the good of the entire planet—at some level she does want this to work. More than that, I can't say, but I'll ask Rya to try to convey our concerns."

"Can't ask for more than that," Hans agreed. "And Rupert, you can add Fire Dancer and me to your roster. Clotilda has assigned us to Havenshold for the next two weeks, until the big day."

"Oh," said Oswald, "we should have a better name than that! Let's have a contest to name the day when Chloe enters the volcano. I'll confer with Mary."

Everyone laughed at this, and then Emily said, "Oswald, you're the best. Even though we tease you about all your contests, you and Mary have kept everyone's spirits high through all these tremors."

"The good news," said Gregory, "is that we won't be needing any more tremors close to Havenshold. The trench at this end is nearly complete."

"That's fantastic," Emily said with a sigh of relief.

"Well, I'd better go see Rya," said Chloe as she stood. "I'll let you know as soon as I have any information. Gregory, could you loan me a map with the area marked so I'll know just what we're talking about?"

Gregory reached into his back pocket and pulled out a dirty, stained but still legible map. "Here, take this. I've got plenty. And I'll mark the part of the fault line that goes through those ranches. Rupert, a pen?"

Rupert handed him a pen, and Gregory marked the map before giving it to Chloe. "Here you go, and I've actually thought about this. A major quake in this spot could really help us in the second section as well. It would speed things up a lot."

"But we aren't going to change the date of the big day, or whatever you're calling it?" said Chloe, a bit of apprehension in her voice.

"No," said Gregory. "We'll stick to a week from Friday so you'll have ten days until then. If we get our first two sections finished earlier, we'll just move to the next one. After all, we still have a very long way to go. The farther ahead we get, the less pressure there will be to rush."

"Thanks," said Chloe. "I'll let you know soon."

"We need to get back out to the spot we're preparing for that moment," said Oswald. "I'll stop by Mary's shop on the way and let her know about the naming contest."

After the meeting broke up, William walked with Chloe to the library. "Was it a lot harder to keep the shield when it was being fired from all sides?" he asked.

"Yes," said Chloe. "I need to do this often enough that it becomes absolutely automatic, like breathing."

William nodded. "Well, if there's anything you can think of that I can arrange as a test, just let me know."

"Thanks. I think it's just a matter of practice, practice, practice."

"Maybe we should have a morning session as well then," William suggested.

"Sounds good."

"Great. I'll check with Rupert and get that on his schedule. He's right. You're our number-one priority now."

Chloe nodded. When they reached the library steps, she said, "I need to find Rya now. Thanks, William and yes, let's have a morning session and then a long lunch break before the afternoon session, starting tomorrow."

Chloe went into her office and sent out a call to Harmony. *I need to see Rya as soon as possible. Can you tell me where she is?*

She and Clyde are working at one of the new homes. I'll send her over to you in a few minutes.

Thanks, Harmony, said Chloe.

Chloe grabbed some chocolate chip cookies and a mug of tea and put out some treats for Calliope as she waited.

You doing OK? asked Calliope.

"Yes," said Chloe. "It just hit me this morning how much I still have to do and how little time is left."

Glad you didn't forget my afternoon treats, said Calliope as she rubbed up against Chloe's arm.

Chloe chuckled. "Never."

A few minutes later, Rya and Artemis walked in. "Hi, Chloe," said Rya. "You needed me?"

Chloe nodded. "Hi, Rya. Hi, Artemis. Yes. We've got a situation." After they were seated, she went on to explain about the ranchers.

"So they were jerks, and now they want help?" asked Rya.

"That's about the size of it," said Chloe. "And we don't have the resources now to do it in time. They waited too long. That's been an area where Jaluhz hasn't been doing the tremors to help us, because they refused."

"So now what?"

"Well, the only thing we could think of was a major quake along that part of the fault line. If Jaluhz were willing to do that, she could make the quake just as large as she wants. That would open up the trench across their lands, and it wouldn't require resources we don't have. At the same time, this isn't Jaluhz's problem, so we don't expect her to rescue these guys. We're only wondering if maybe she might enjoy a big quake. That would help us make the trench faster, so ultimately it would be helping the project and not just the stupid ranchers."

"Got it," said Rya. "And again my communication with Jaluhz isn't like anything I've even heard about. I don't get what you'd think of as real images. It's more like impressions and feelings. But I'll try."

Chloe opened Gregory's map on her desk and pointed. "Gregory has marked the section of the fault line so you can see where we're talking about."

Rya looked at the map and again said, "I'll try." Artemis jumped into her lap, and Chloe sat quietly at her desk and waited. Rya seemed to take longer this time, but finally she said, "I think Jaluhz finds this funny. I'm not sure, but that's the feeling I got. Even so, the idea of a major quake seems to appeal to her. I think all these small controlled quakes have been hard on her. I'm not sure, but I think she'd like to just shake without any worries. She's going to do it tomorrow, just after sunrise. I'm feeling she has a lot of pent-up energies she wants to let go of, so you should make sure that a large area around the fault line is cleared. Who knows what she'll let loose?"

"Thanks so much, Rya," said Chloe, "and I'm glad this is something Jaluhz finds to be fun, if that's the right word."

Rya and Artemis stood as Rya said, "Well, we'd better get back to Uncle Clyde. We're working really long days now, even with the bad weather. Sure glad the houses are all enclosed."

"Give him my best," said Chloe. "And thanks again."

Once Rya left, Chloe decided to walk over to Emily's office. "I think the exercise will help clear my mind," she said to Calliope.

I think a nap will clear mine, said Calliope as she curled up on the couch.

As Chloe passed Mary's shop, she saw that indeed another contest had been posted: the naming contest. She also noticed Arryn was inside, listening as Mary showed her something with her knitting. Chloe kept on going but thought, *I'll stop in if they're still there after I report to Emily and Hans. It would be nice to have a distraction.*

Chloe knocked on Emily's office door and entered when Emily called out. Rupert and Hans also were there, and Chloe said, "Well, I have your answer. Those ranchers may not like what they get, but they asked for it. Jaluhz apparently finds the situation to her liking. She's been working so hard at controlling her tremors that she's built up a lot of stress. The thought of just being able to have a really good shake seems appealing to her, and she's agreed. She'll give you the major quake tomorrow, just after dawn."

"Great," said Hans.

"Rya did suggest," said Chloe, "that Jaluhz seems really pleased at the prospect, so you'd better clear a large area around that fault line. There's no predicting how large a quake Jaluhz will produce or what the effect will be."

Hans laughed. "It would serve those ranchers right if they lost most of their land, but I'll contact Clotilda immediately, and she can evacuate the area."

"And I'll let the town know," Emily said. "We're far enough away that we shouldn't feel anything major, but it doesn't hurt to be careful when dealing with a volcano."

"For sure," said Chloe. "Did you hear from William?"

Rupert waved his papers and said, "Yep, already working on it. You'll have a session at nine, then a break from eleven to two, and then a session from two until you're finished for the day."

"And Esmeralda and I will be at all your sessions," Emily said, "as will Fern, Jupiter, and my folks. We want you to have some consistency in your energy net."

"Thanks," said Chloe as she stood. "Now I'm going to stop in at Mary's shop and just relax."

"You've earned that," said Hans, "and again thanks."

Chloe left them and headed to Mary's shop. When she walked in, Mary and Arryn smiled. As she held up two knitting needles with bright-pink yarn attached, Arryn said, "See? I'm starting."

"Very nice," said Chloe.

"We're starting with a scarf and just the basic knitting stitch with nothing fancy. But it'll be colorful and warm," said Mary.

Chloe sat with them, watching and just relaxing. She could see why people knitted. It did seem to be calming—well, until something went awry, she realized, as Arryn exclaimed in dismay, "I only have forty-nine stitches, not fifty."

Mary took Arryn's needles. "Here's your dropped stitch," she said, pointing. "I'll bring it back up where it belongs. There's nothing that can't be fixed."

"Thanks, Mary," said Arryn.

Chloe wondered, *I hope that's true. I hope I can fix Jaluhz.* She watched for a bit longer then said, "Well, thanks for letting me sit here. I'd better get back to the library now."

Mary stood and gave Chloe a hug. "Any time."

"Oh, there may be a large tremor tomorrow after dawn," said Chloe. "Emily will be sending out a message, but after that, I don't think Havenshold will have any more. The nearest section of the trench is just about complete now."

"Excellent," said Mary, "although it'll be harder for us to come up with contests. Oswald had a great idea about naming next Friday, and thank heavens you'll now have two practice sessions a day."

"How did you know?" said Chloe. "That was just decided."

"Oh, I know," said Mary with a wink. "I have my sources."

Chloe laughed. "Well, I appreciate all the support. Have a great evening. And good luck with your scarf, Arryn. I look forward to seeing it when it's done."

— 24 —

THE DEFINING MOMENT

Chloe was awakened the next morning when Calliope suddenly dived under the covers, racing down to huddle at Chloe's feet. Then the bed shook and the room along with it. The earthquake seemed to last for forever, but later Chloe found out it was only twenty-seven seconds long. She heard several crashes and once the shaking ended, she got up to check out the damage as Calliope decided to stay under the covers. Fortunately, nothing broke. A few of the wall hangings had fallen, but they were woven pieces and couldn't break. And a small bookcase fell over, scattering books, but nothing major.

Once Chloe was dressed, she headed into the library and went directly to Gregory's office. She was pleased to see not only Gregory, Oswald, and the baron but also Lucy and Gretchen.

"'Morning," she said. "Glad to see you two especially," she continued, nodding at Lucy and Gretchen.

"Dr. Brian said I could come back to work for four hours a day," Lucy said.

"And I'm here to make sure she doesn't overdo it," said Gretchen.

"That was some quake this morning," said Chloe. "I thought it was going to happen only near the two ranches."

Gregory chuckled. "I don't know that we'll ever understand Jaluhz. And realistically we probably can't."

"I'm sure nothing in nature views things the way we do," said Oswald. "And we have a hard enough time understanding ourselves."

"True," said Gregory, "but right now I'm wondering if Jaluhz has a sense of humor. That quake ran the full length of the fault line, although it definitely was centered around the two ranches."

"And the moles let me know," said Lucy, "that they'd been told to evacuate all their tunnels along the fault line. They spent the entire night moving. They somehow were kept safe."

"I could study Jaluhz for the rest of my life and never figure her out," said Gregory with true awe in his voice.

Emily walked into the office. "You'll never guess what happened," she said, frustration in her voice. "Those two ranchers are complaining again. They told Clotilda and Matilda that the earthquake made and I quote, 'a horrific, ugly scar' across their lands, wider and deeper than the rest of the trench."

"Wow," said Gregory. "No wonder we felt the quake in Havenshold."

"Yeah, well, Clotilda laughed in their faces, and Matilda said that if they chose to try to hold the nation ransom, they should be grateful they have any land left at all."

"Good for her," said the baron with a smirk.

"Esmeralda and I have flown over the fault line from Havenshold to Cliffside, and it looks as if Jaluhz has finished the work. I've sent Aster and Jasmine to check things out even further along the line toward Forbury, but from what we could see, Jaluhz has created a lot more of a trench there also."

"Amazing," said Oswald.

"If we can confirm what you saw," said Gregory, "it means our trench is ready to go more than a week early."

William walked in then and said, "I do hope you aren't thinking Chloe should act sooner now."

"Uh, no, of course not," said Gregory, the look on his face making it perfectly clear that he'd thought just that.

Chloe laughed. "Nice try, Gregory, but I'm not going to be ready any sooner because of this. As it is, I'm not sure I'll be ready in time."

"Sorry," said Gregory. "I just got excited."

"What it does mean," said William, "or I hope it does, is that since we won't need dragons and riders to be frantically digging, we can have them available to train with Chloe. That should make the training easier and more effective."

Emily nodded. "That was my thought as well. I've just sent out orders that all bonded pairs are to be available during the training times."

"That's going to make for a very full courtyard," said Chloe. "I can draw on their power from a distance, so if you want some of them to be in the fields, that would certainly work."

"Great. Just the way you drew on power from the other three nations for the asteroid, which means more townspeople can watch. Excellent," William concluded, rubbing his hands together.

"We need to verify the trench," said Gregory.

"And I need to get a decent breakfast," said Chloe.

"Meet you in the courtyard at nine," said Emily, and the meeting broke up.

The next ten days settled into a predictable routine. Gregory was able to verify that the trench was complete all the way to Cliffside, and in fact it was nearly complete from there westward, into Forbury. "It's as if Jaluhz decided to open herself up for this," he said one morning, as he and Chloe enjoyed their mugs of tea. "We'll have to finish the trench to reach the Ercesa Ocean, but we'll have plenty of time to do that. And we'll also have gryphons to help with the digging. I think it'll take until summer before the lava fills what Jaluhz has opened for us."

"That's wonderful," said Chloe. "Well, off to training."

Chloe was finding it easier each day to maintain her shield. By the end of a week, she could hold it for the required thirty minutes against the combined flames of five dragons. But she still wasn't certain that she'd reached the point where the shield maintenance was automatic.

Four days before she was scheduled to teleport into Jaluhz, William decided to test her concentration by having the crowd help. Once Chloe had her shield established, and she was under fire, he had the crowd make great deal of noise. Then he had them shout questions at her. They tried all sorts of things, even sirens and bells, to distract her.

The first time they did this, Chloe nearly lost her shield, and she was glad the flame-throwing dragons sensed this and turned off their flames. William walked over and gently said, "You do realize that while the dragons will cut their flames, Jaluhz won't cut her heat."

Chloe said, "I know. Sorry. Let's do this again."

Two days before what she was beginning to think of as her defining moment, the moment she'd been preparing for most of her life—or so she saw it now—William announced to the crowd that the naming contest was over. Oswald and Mary walked to the center of the courtyard.

"There were many creative names submitted," said Mary.

"Some of them were rather long," said Oswald, "like 'The Day the Mage Adjusted the Lava Flow.'"

This brought a chuckle from the crowd. Mary went on. "We're thinking February is usually a pretty dull month, and we need a regular festival about now anyway, so we wanted a name that would be easy, one we can use year after year to commemorate this moment. And so the winner is 'Emergence Day,' submitted by Clyde Perkins, and his prize is a month of breakfasts at the bakery."

The crowd cheered as Mary and Oswald motioned for Clyde to come forward. Then Oswald said, "Clyde, can you share with us why you chose this name?"

Clyde looked around at the assembled group, took a deep breath, then said, "Yes, I can. I picked it because Chloe will be making a new opening for the lava, which will emerge from the side of the mountain and flow into the channel, giving us a new river of lava to add to our landscape."

The crowd cheered, and after a minute or so, Clyde held up his hands, and they quieted. He went on, "But I also chose the name as a reminder for all of us. Do you remember how angry many of us were when the lava first started to flow? Do you remember how many people grumbled because Chloe wouldn't just make the volcano go away? Those of us without magic...well, we've had a way of looking at the riders as if they were freaks somehow, but if we had to have them, they'd better fix things for us when we needed them to."

The crowd was silent now, but Chloe noticed that many were nodding. Clyde continued, "We have a lot to thank Jaluhz for. The last month has been incredible. Oh, don't get me wrong—it's been really hard for those who lost their homes. And the daily tremors were nerve-wracking, to say the least. But look at us now. We're all working together. We're really helping and not just standing back, waiting for others to fix things for us."

He paused and stared at the crowd before resuming. "I look around, and I'm so happy to see that those of us without dragon magic are laughing and sharing with those that do. We have a common bond now, a unity we've never really had before. So that was my real meaning behind Emergence Day. We've all emerged from our narrow, blind perspectives, and I'm thrilled that this will become an annual festival, to remind us, once the crisis has past, that we have so much in common. My daughter, Aster, says I do have magic, that what I do with my wood is just as much magic as what she does. It's taken me a while to believe that. But you all have magic, in the way you go about your daily lives. So let's celebrate our bonds."

Clyde looked down at his feet then finally said, "Well, I guess that's about it."

The cheers were loud and supportive, and there were even chants of "Clyde! Clyde! Clyde!" which made him turn bright red.

Mary and Oswald came to his rescue. Mary said, "Thank you so much, Clyde. We need to get that speech down in writing and read it each and every year."

Rupert stepped forward with his notebook, saying, "I've got it, and we'll have it printed by the day's end."

"Thanks," said Mary. "So Emergence Day it is...the day after tomorrow. And we'll all be here to support Chloe as she undertakes this momentous task for all of Draconia."

"Don't forget," William told the crowd, which was breaking up. "We still have a day and a half of training for you all to watch."

Chloe found Rya in the crowd and said, "Can you come talk with me over lunch? I have some questions about the teleporting."

"Sure," said Rya, and she and Artemis walked with Chloe to the library.

Once they were settled in Chloe's office, Artemis said, "I like being in your energy net. Thanks for having us."

"Hey, you're a bonded pair, and we need everyone," said Chloe. "Thank *you*."

"So what were you wondering?" asked Rya.

"Well, do you know where I should teleport? Do you have a map from Jaluhz? I'm guessing things will look very different once I'm inside. Are there passageways? Tunnels? How will I know where to make the new rupture? I'm figuring the current rupture will be rather obvious, the place where all the lava is pouring from, but I'll have to create a place for a new one really quickly. I'll have to open the new one nearly as soon as I close the current one, or the pressure will cause an eruption out of the top. How will I know where to make a hole for that new eruption?"

Rya smiled. "Those are all really good questions, but honestly I have no answers for any of them."

"What?" exclaimed Chloe, wide-eyed.

Rya went on, "What I get from Jaluhz...well, I've called it images. I've called it feelings, but really there aren't words to describe her communication. I just get a feeling of what she might want. It's pretty nebulous."

"Nebulous?" said Chloe. "How can I teleport into *nebulous*?"

"You can't," said Rya.

"You mean this has all been a big hoax?"

"No," said Rya. "What I should say is that you can't, but Jaluhz can. I think you're supposed to start the teleportation into the current opening. My best guess is that Jaluhz will take over, bringing you to the first spot, guiding you as you close it, moving you faster than you could possibly ever do on your own to the second spot, and guiding you again to make the rupture. Once that's done, you'll be able to do your own teleporting out of there."

"You think? Your best guess?" said Chloe with panic rising.

"I'm sorry, Chloe. I wish I had more for you. I'm still convinced that if you can shield yourself, Jaluhz will guide you through the rest of it."

Chloe sighed. "Well, that's disquieting. But if you think that's what will happen, I'll just have to go forth with that."

"I'm sorry, Chloe. I can't give you a map or anything like that, but truly I do believe it'll work," Rya said.

"Thanks, Rya. Sorry I'm so rattled. It's just a lot to take in."

"Believe me, I know. Well, we'll let you eat your lunch. See you at the afternoon trials," as she and Artemis stood.

"Yes, and thanks," said Chloe as they left.

She sat at her desk, stunned by this latest twist. Calliope jumped onto the desk and said, *So you'll just have to trust, huh?*

"I guess," said Chloe, biting into her sandwich.

That afternoon William devised yet another test for Chloe. "I want you to move your shield around. Unfortunately we can't practice having you teleport with the shield under flames, but I want you to walk and move inside the shield. The dragons will keep their flames on you at all times."

"Got it," said Chloe.

Although the afternoon training went well, Chloe was very distracted. She guessed that if she could maintain the shield while worrying about Rya's latest information, she was doing well.

When they quit for the day, Amy came over to speak with her. "You were somewhere else this afternoon, worrying—and I felt it—but you still kept your shield up. I think you're ready, and I think you have enough support with the size of this energy net. You'll do great," she concluded, as she hugged Chloe.

"Thanks, Amy," said Chloe. "I certainly couldn't have done any of this even a month ago, so I hope I'm ready."

William joined them. "Yes, you are ready," he said, "and I think you need a day of rest before Emergence Day."

Chloe looked surprised. "Are you sure I'm ready? I don't feel ready."

"We're sure," said Amy. "Now you need to sort out your worries and put them aside. You can't take them into Jaluhz. So get some rest, talk with Libby, and just relax."

Chloe nodded at them both as William said, "We've set the time for nine in the morning. That way it'll match your training times. OK?"

"OK," said Chloe as she started to walk to the library. She turned and said, "And thanks. However this turns out, thanks."

Chloe had a restless evening and didn't sleep well that night. Calliope finally said, *I'm going to find another spot if you don't stop twisting and turning.*

"I'm sorry," said Chloe.

You'd better have breakfast with Libby in the morning. You're turning into a basket case.

"I will, I promise, and I'll try to lie still. Please stay," said Chloe.

Calliope snuggled up against Chloe's back and said, *Of course I'll stay.*

In the morning Chloe entered Libby's apartment and exclaimed, "Bertha! You're here!"

Racing over to hug the big bear, Chloe burst into tears. Bertha patted her on the back. "Now, now, child," she said." You know I wouldn't miss your big day."

Libby smiled. "Forgive us for not letting you in on our plans, Chloe. Bertha needed as much of her hibernation as possible, but we've still been in touch occasionally."

Chloe finally let go of Bertha and sat on the couch. She reached for the plate of pancakes which Libby had placed on the table next to her, and took a bite before saying, "Do you know what Rya told me? About teleporting into some nebulous location?" Bertha and Libby nodded. "You always taught me,

Bertha, that to teleport I have to have a firm picture of my destination in my mind. How am I going to do this?"

Bertha looked at Chloe with a twinkle in her eyes and said, "You aren't going to teleport." When Chloe started to sputter again, Bertha held up a paw and said, "Listen to me. You're a strong person, and you like—or I should say *need*—to be in control. You run the show. But guess what? This time you won't. This time you're going to need to trust—and trust in something that none of us truly understands: the power of nature."

"You told me before that you're afraid because for the first time in your life, you'll actually be in danger when you work," Libby said. "This entire plan depends on you, or so you think, yet you can't control it. You've done all the training, and I must say, you've done it beyond our wildest dreams. I really thought you would have needed to add me to your energy net by now, but you've grown, and so has your power."

"But how can I just teleport to a general location?" asked Chloe.

"What do you think others feel when you teleport them? They have no clue really about where they're going or what's happening to them," said Bertha.

"But I do," said Chloe.

Bertha chuckled. "Well, this time, you'll be the passenger, and Jaluhz will know."

"Didn't Rya tell you that all you had to do—and believe me I know it's a big 'all'—is protect yourself?" asked Libby.

"Well, yes," said Chloe, taking a drink from her mug of tea.

"And didn't Jaluhz teleport King Alfred and all thirty of his companions with their dragons back in time, many hundreds of centuries back in time?" Libby asked.

"Well, yes, I suppose," said Chloe.

Both Libby and Bertha laughed now. Finally Bertha said in a very kind voice, "This job is going to stretch you in very uncomfortable ways, and I don't mean the heat. It isn't the danger either. It's the fact that you won't be in charge, and for you that'll be the real test."

"But..." stammered Chloe.

"But nothing," said Libby. "You're going to have to trust, and I don't mean trusting your energy net, which you've learned to do. I mean trusting yourself, letting your control go, and turning yourself over to Jaluhz. That's what you'll have to do to succeed."

Chloe sat very quietly on the couch, deep in thought. She finished her pancakes and put her plate down. Finally she said, "I guess I'm more like my mom and my grandmother than I knew."

"Oh, yes," said Libby with a warm smile, "but that's a good thing. In fact let's look at how your mom has changed. Hazel is a strong woman, and in her element, she's in charge and runs the show. She now runs it with a great deal more tact and kindness, but she runs it. But she's also learned when to hand the reins over to you or your energy net. Well, now it's your turn. You're going to have to hand your reins over to Jaluhz. Can you do that?"

"I sure hope so," said Chloe.

"And by the way," said Bertha, "I'll be in your energy net too, monitoring it and shifting the energy drains around, just as I did for the asteroid. Libby will be there also. You won't need us, provided everything goes according to plan, but my experience has been that things don't always go according to plan. Libby and I will just be monitoring, but we'll be your backup. If your shield needs more energy, or if the job takes longer than expected, we've got you covered."

"Thanks, you two, and Bertha, sorry about shortening your nap, but I'm sure glad you're here."

"Me too, sweetie."

They spent the rest of the day talking. Bertha shared some of Boris and Berla's exploits from last fall. Libby shared her hopes for Arryn.

"I'd really like to see her become a librarian," Libby said. "She has a love of books and a real gift for fixing them, as well as for inspiring a love of reading in others. She could repair the older volumes that are in need of help. She could bring more readers into the library. It would be lovely."

Chloe smiled. "I think you've already hooked her, but I'll certainly mention it as a possibility. We definitely could use a librarian, and that isn't a profession that she'd even have heard of before she came here."

Chloe slept much better that night, and after having breakfast with Bertha and Libby on Emergence Day, Chloe and Bertha headed to the rider-complex courtyard. Libby said as they left, "I'll be with you the whole way. Good luck, and remember to trust!"

When they arrived in the courtyard, Emily, Amy, Todd, and William all came over to greet Bertha. Amy said, "I'm sure glad you're here, Bertha."

"Couldn't miss this," answered Bertha, "not even for my winter nap."

"Ready, Chloe?" asked Todd.

"Hope so," said Chloe.

This time the crowd was hushed and silent, and all the dragons were with their riders. Rya and Artemis stood at the front of the bonded pairs, and Bertha went over to stand next to them, bending down to ruffle Artemis's fur and saying, "Kinda small, aren't you."

Artemis looked up at the bear and said, "Kinda big, aren't you?"

Bertha chuckled. "You'll do," she said. "Glad you're both here."

Chloe stood alone in the center of the courtyard, focusing and breathing deeply, before she made her shield. Then she thought, *Jaluhz, I'm yours now. Show me what you want me to do.* She started a teleporting sequence with the vague general direction of the explosion area from which the lava was currently flowing. As soon as she started the teleportation, she felt a loss of control. She began to panic, but then heard Bertha's voice. *Trust, Chloe. Trust and relax.*

Chloe then concentrated only on her shield as she felt herself move heaven knows where. She opened her eyes when she felt the motion stop, and she was amazed. She was deep inside Jaluhz, with molten rock surrounding her. She saw the gash in the side of a lava vent. As soon as she began to wonder how she would repair it, she felt a new power surge through her, and her hands began to work magic. She was being guided by a power beyond her understanding. She just worked, following the path of the gash, not really understanding what she was doing, but doing what needed to be done. Inside Jaluhz she lost all sense of time and place. There was nothing except her, the lava, and the gash.

Slowly the gash began to close. Chloe worked faster, her motions becoming surer and more confident. She didn't think; she just trusted and worked. As she sealed the last of the gash, she suddenly was whipped to another part of the volcano. Chloe had absolutely no idea where she was, but Jaluhz did, and she figured that was more than enough. *Now how do I create a gash and where and how big?* Just as Chloe's thoughts began to run to worry, a calming presence enveloped her, and again she felt a surge of energy. She was guided toward the right spot, and she saw a glowing circle. She cut along the edge of the circle, making sure she kept as far back from it as possible, periodically checking her shield to be sure it was intact.

Chloe had no idea how long she stood there cutting the new opening. She was cutting through a much deeper vein right now. She felt her shield start to bobble, but then she felt Libby and Bertha shoring it up. *We've got you, kid,* she heard Bertha say, and she returned to the job at hand.

Finally she saw a trickle of lava, and then she was flung backward just before the lava exploded out of the gash she'd made. She watched in total amazement as the lava broke through the side of the mountain, easily opening the last bit of rock where Gregory had made the hole on the outside.

And then Chloe was gently lifted and teleported back to the courtyard, where the crowd erupted in cheers and applause. A feeling of thankfulness swept through her as she landed. *Thank you, Jaluhz,* she said.

— 25 —

EMERGENCE DAY FESTIVAL

Once Chloe announced she was fine, her mother handed her a very large sandwich.

"What took you so long?" Emily asked Chloe.

"What?" she said through a mouthful of sandwich. "How long was I in there?"

"Nearly two hours," said Esmeralda. "We were concerned."

Chloe's eyes widened. "Two hours? Are you kidding me?"

Bertha shook her head. "No, they aren't. That's why you felt Libby and me stepping into the net. Despite your mother's delicious chocolate bars, which she gave to the riders in nearly a constant rotation, they couldn't hold up much longer without our help."

Amy and Todd joined them. "Bertha's right," Amy said. "Without their help, well, I don't even want to think about it. It took you nearly an hour and forty-five minutes to seal the first rupture. Thankfully cutting the new rupture didn't take nearly as long."

"I can't believe I was in there so long. I had absolutely no concept of time."

"Figures," said Bertha. "I don't think Jaluhz does either. Anyway, Libby and I stepped in so the bonded pairs could get some rest, and Hazel plied them with a thick stew as they rotated in and out of the energy net. And it was a good thing, because at the end, for the time you were cutting the new rupture, we felt another drain on the net."

"Really?" said Chloe.

"Trust me," said Amy, "it was real and more than a little scary."

"My best guess," said Bertha, "is that Jaluhz used some of our power as well."

"But why?" said Chloe. "She has a ton of her own."

"We may never know," said Bertha, "but I think the reason it took you so long to seal the rupture is because Jaluhz was being extremely careful about how much of her power she gave you. She saw what happened to Rya when she first contacted her. But then, as you and Gregory figured, the opening of the second rupture had to happen much more quickly. She couldn't afford the luxury of allowing you to take your time. She literally would have blown her stack if the new rupture hadn't happened quickly enough. I could tell she fed you a lot more power for that, but I'm guessing she was afraid to feed you too much, so she decided to augment her power with some of ours to give you more of the kind you were used to handling."

"Makes sense," said Chloe, as she finished her sandwich.

"Hey, doesn't anyone want to see if it worked?" asked Gregory.

The baron put a hand on his son's shoulder. "Of course it did," he said. "You made the calculations."

Just then Clotilda and Matilda landed in the courtyard. As Clotilda jumped down, she said, "It's looking good out there. Great job, Chloe."

"Is the lava heading for the trench?" asked Gregory.

"Let's go see," said Chloe. "I'd like to see what it looks like from the outside."

The entire crowd headed to the edge of the lava apron and stared at the hillside, where sure enough the lava was flowing from a new spot. There was absolute silence as they all watched the slow-moving lava flow. Chloe was very glad the major earthquake the week before had split the trench so that it was a lot closer to the flow. Originally they'd had to dig it quite a ways in front of the flow because of safety concerns, but now the lava was within a few feet of the trench.

As they watched, the crowd began a countdown. Finally, after about fifteen minutes, the lava met the front of the trench and rather gracefully, Chloe thought, slid over the lip and into the trench, ready to begin its journey to the sea.

The cheers and shouts were deafening. The baron and Oswald thumped Gregory on the back, shouting, "We knew you'd do it!" Chloe looked around and realized Clyde was right. It had taken them all, and they had worked together for more than a month, never giving up, and now Jaluhz and Draconia had been saved.

Finally Clotilda said, "Didn't I hear there was a festival celebration to be had? An Emergence Day celebration?"

"Just give us a few minutes," Hazel said. "We're nearly set up. Please wait until you hear the sound of the horn."

Hazel and her crew quickly headed back to the rider courtyard. The crowd waited in companionable conversation, each with something to share or a question to ask. Chloe made her way over to Rya and said, "You were right. There's no way to describe Jaluhz or her communication methods."

Rya smiled. "Once I realized that and began to relax with her, I did much better."

"And you were right that I could trust her," Chloe said. "I have absolutely no idea how I knew what to do. My hands just seemed to move, but I was controlling them. It was my magic, but I honestly have no idea how I knew what to do. There was no voice, like telepathy. There were no images showing me a finished product or whatever. I just knew without knowing how." Chloe shook her head. "Oh, I'm not making any sense."

Rya said, "Maybe not, but I get it. That's exactly how it is. You know without realizing that you've learned. It's truly different, really powerful, and totally inexplicable."

"Well, I'm certainly in awe of Jaluhz and not a little humbled that she allowed me to help her. Being surrounded by all that molten lava, well, I thought I'd be terrified, but it was so beautiful that I was just...I don't know. I can't explain, but it was lovely and so powerful. I felt so small and insignificant in its presence."

"I would have liked to have seen that," said Rya.

Chloe smiled. "Well, after I've rested, maybe I could form an image of it to show you."

"I'd like that. After what you did, Jaluhz isn't sad anymore. She seems to be...I guess *content* is the best word. She's content and relaxed. I think she's going to take a very long nap."

"My thoughts as well," said Chloe.

Just then the horn sounded, and Clotilda and Matilda called to Chloe to lead the way to the festival. As Chloe entered the courtyard with Clotilda and Matilda, she was blown away by all the decorations and the booths that had been set up, each with different foods and crafts. Hazel and her crew had hidden everything in a large cave right off the courtyard and so only had to pull it all out. There were balloons and ribbons, signs showing where all the food was, and it looked a lot like the New Year's celebration. There was a small stage in the center that Clotilda and Matilda led Chloe to.

Once they were standing in front of the crowd, Clotilda said, "We have a lot to celebrate here today. Each of you has contributed to the success of our adventure with Jaluhz, each in your own way. I'd like to call several people up here for special recognition. Mary and Oswald, please accept these tokens of thanks." Once they were on the stage, Clotilda hung small gold medallions with a dragon embossed on them around their necks. "You two have kept the sanity of Havenshold intact for the past month, kept everyone's spirits high, and kept us focused on the task at hand, and for that we all thank you."

Once the cheers died down and Mary and Oswald left the platform, Clotilda said, Hazel, Clyde, will you please step up here?" As they stood in front of Clotilda, she said, "Hazel, you organized the support group for our energy net. If that weren't enough, you also orchestrated this incredible festival. Clyde, you've worked tirelessly behind the scenes, bringing many people to help, and you've raised three new homes, despite the snowstorms, so those who lost their homes now have housing—and beautiful housing at that. Thank you both."

Hazel and Clyde accepted their medallions and left the platform. Clotilda said, "There are many, many more of you to thank, but it would take all day to do that. But there are some we can't forget. Gregory, Oswald, Baron, William, Rya, and Artemis, please come up here. You six have worked many, many hours, figuring out the nature of the volcano, supervising the placement of the trench, and monitoring the training of our mage. You've kept us in touch with Jaluhz and helped us communicate. All of you led the way for today's victory. Thank you."

"And last, but certainly far from least, we have our mage," Clotilda continued.

As soon as the words were out of her mouth, the crowd erupted in applause, cheers, and shouts of "Chloe, Chloe, Chloe," and Chloe herself turned bright red.

Clotilda held up her hands for silence then continued. "Chloe, you've gone where none of us ever could or in truth would want to. You went into the heart of Jaluhz, at great peril to yourself.

Why? Well, certainly to help us, but you've made it very clear that you're the mage for the entire planet, so I suspect you went as much for Jaluhz as for us. Some people wanted you to take a different path. They wanted you to 'tame' Jaluhz or get rid of her. I'm sure many of us doubted you when you said Jaluhz is sentient and also has a right to be heard. We live on this planet, but all too often, we forget the power of nature herself. We forget until a blizzard hits that the weather can be cruel and that we have no control over it. Nor should we, I think. We need something greater than ourselves, lest we become arrogant and thoughtless.

"You found a way, a way to help Jaluhz fulfill her natural cycle but fulfill it in a way that allowed us mere mortals to survive as well. It was a tough path to take, but then you've never taken the easy way out. We're very proud to call you our mage, and we realize you have a much larger role in this world, a role that requires you to care for everything and everyone, from the smallest and weakest to the all-powerful Jaluhz.

"So please accept our sincerest thanks. I have no fancy gifts or titles to offer, as I know those don't interest you. I thought about a new home for you, until I realized how happy you are right where you are. I understand now what I've wondered about for years: why you aren't part of a bonded pair. It's because, I think, that you're bonded to our entire planet. All that being said, I found this fellow." Clotilda turned to Emily, who was holding a small, tan, wiggling puppy with a curly tail that was nearly larger than he was. "This little guy got pushed out of his pack because he wouldn't stop talking. If you think Calliope would stand for it, I'd like to present you with Shosty, whom I understand is going to grow to be about eighteen pounds."

Clotilda handed Shosty to Chloe, and the crowd laughed as Shosty licked Chloe's face then said, in a surprisingly loud voice, "You taste good."

The crowd roared with laughter, and Chloe hugged Shosty. Then she turned to Clotilda and said, "Thank you...thank you for standing with me, even when I didn't know what I was doing. Thank you for Shosty too. I can see the library is going to get a bit more lively."

Chloe turned to the crowd. "And thank you, one and all," she said. "You believed in me even when I didn't believe in myself. You trusted me, supported me, and helped me through every part of my training. Once I've had a chance to recover, I'd like to try to share my experience inside Jaluhz. It was incredible. And now we can say we're the only nation with a river of lava. I suspect there'll be another naming contest for that as well."

Clotilda spoke again once the laughter died down. "Now I'm turning this festival over to Mary and Oswald, who are ready to announce the winners of the various contests."

Clotilda, Matilda, Chloe, and Shosty left the platform. Chloe and Shosty went to stand next to Bertha. She looked Shosty straight in the eyes, and he didn't flinch. "You're all right," said Bertha.

"So are you," answered Shosty.

"Oh, you've got a good one here, Chloe," said Bertha.

They were quiet as Mary and Oswald started. Mary said, "Many thanks to all of you for entering our month of contests. Each individual contest already has been announced and the prizes awarded. Thanks to all the merchants who offered prizes. This really has been a lot of fun. We have three overall winners to announce today. First there's the winner of the best design for our new Havenshold logo, featuring Jaluhz."

Oswald said, "And that winner is non other than Arryn, a new arrival to our beautiful town, and I'm sure we'll be seeing much more from her! Come on up here, Arryn."

Once Arryn had accepted her award, a trophy and a generous gift certificate to Mary's yarn shop and her drawing, which showed an idealized volcano, orange and yellow, on a purple background with a large dragon in front of it, had been uncovered for all to see, Mary continued. "And now we want to announce the festival king and queen. As we stated at the beginning of the contests, the king and queen will be the man and woman who made the most right guess and who won the most individual contests."

Oswald said, "The king is Ron, Havenshold's excellent vegetable vendor."

As Ron went up to the platform, the crowd cheered him on.

Then Oswald said, "And the queen of the festival is Hazel Winsong."

The crowd obviously was very pleased at this announcement, and Chloe beamed with pride. She saw her father, Henry, and her sister, Zelda, in the audience, cheering loudly, which warmed her as well. Although her parents were divorced, they were still a family and still cared about each other.

Once the king and queen had been crowned, Mary said, "Let the festival begin! Celebrate and enjoy!"

Chloe watched as people moved toward food booths or danced on the improvised platform to the sound of the band, with flutes, trumpets, and drums. Many stopped by to congratulate her. Then Chloe noticed Emily and Arryn approaching; Arryn was pushing a wheelchair. As soon as they got closer, Chloe realized it was Lena in the chair. She went over and said, "How good to see you, Lena. How are you doing?"

"OK, I guess," said Lena. "These two insisted I come. That Emily...she thinks she knows it all. She wouldn't rest until I said I'd see Arryn. Guess it's OK."

Chloe smiled. "Yes, it is, and I'm glad to see you. Do you like the boardinghouse?"

Lena shrugged. "I guess. Getting used to it anyway. That Georgette...she's always bustling around, trying to get me to smile. But she's a good kid."

"Yes, she is," said Chloe.

"Well," said Emily, "let's get you back to her. Dr. Brian told us not to tire you out."

"Yeah, he's another busybody," said Lena. "Guess he means well, though."

Chloe laughed. "Good to see you Lena, and keep smiling."

After they left, Chloe said to Bertha, "Do you think I could sneak out of here? Crowds really aren't my thing, and I'm exhausted."

"I'd say you have every right to do whatever you want," said Bertha. "And you can always use this new pup as an excuse."

"Hey, I'm not an excuse," said Shosty. "I'm a reason."

"Did I hear we have a talking dog now?" said Artemis, as she and Rya came over to speak with Chloe.

"Why not?" said Shosty. "We have a talking fox, don't we?"

"Well, are you telepathic also?" asked Artemis.

"No need," said Shosty. "Talking in your head is pointless. I want to be heard."

Artemis said smugly, "Some of us can be heard in more ways than one."

"Now be nice, Artemis," said Rya. "He's only a pup. Who knows what talents he might grow into? Chloe, have you seen Arryn? We were going to hang out."

"She'll be right back. She and Emily just left to take Lena home."

Rya smiled. "You know that Lena. She acts tough, but she was so happy to see Arryn the first time Arryn visited her. I think underneath she's kind. She just doesn't know how to show it."

"You're right," said Bertha. "Now if you two will excuse us, Chloe needs to take Shosty home so he can meet Calliope, a meeting I for one don't want to miss."

Rya laughed. "Let me know how it goes."

Artemis looked Shosty over then said, "A word to the wise, kid: that Calliope is full of herself. She takes her responsibility as library cat very seriously. So if you want to keep your new home, I suggest you let her think she rules. That way you'll get a great place to live, and Calliope will be kept happy—something that, believe me, we all want."

"Oh, Artemis," said Chloe, "Calliope is very sweet."

"Maybe," said Artemis, "as long as she isn't challenged."

Chloe, Shosty, and Bertha worked their way out of the crowd, which took a lot longer, as everyone wanted to congratulate and thank Chloe, but eventually they made it back to the library. As they headed through the front doors, they heard a hiss.

Chloe called out, "Calliope, now stop that. Come on out here and meet Shosty. Clotilda and Matilda gave him to us for the library."

Calliope came around the corner from Chloe's office and said, *So a dog, huh?*

Shosty was about to shoot his mouth off when Chloe whispered in his ear, "Remember Artemis's advice," as she gently placed him on the library floor.

Shosty stood there for a moment then said, "May I come in, Calliope?"

Calliope gave him the once-over, walking all around him, sniffing, and finally said, *I guess.*

Chloe said, "She says you can stay."

"Thanks," said Shosty, as he took off at a run, racing through the stacks.

Chloe then heard Libby. *Congratulations, dear. I can see I'm going to become a much livelier place indeed.*